Finding James

Finding James

Cover and Interior Design by Lance Buckley

www.lancebuckley.com

ISBN: 978-1-0909-7183-8

FINDING JAMES

a novel

NANCY BLAHA

For Jeff Blaha

My husband and best friend.
Thank you for never giving up.

ACKNOWLEDGEMENTS

IT TAKES A VILLAGE TO WRITE A BOOK—AT LEAST IT did for me. And I'd like to thank my precious village.

A huge thank you to my writing coach Lisa Kron, (www.wiredforstory.com) for her endless encouragement, insight and motivation. (Onward!)

And a thank you to my editor Annie J, (www.just-copyeditors.com) who made my words flow.

And to Lance Buckley, (www.lancebuckley.com) who designed my amazing cover.

And to the friends who took the time to read and critique my manuscript, I thank you for your time, support, honesty and friendship.

And to my husband Jeff Blaha, who left me alone night after night as I struggled to try and put this story together. (Except when he'd periodically come into my office and remind me to "get up and stretch.") Thank you for your bottomless love and support. I love you!

And a special thanks to Ron and Tina Konkin, at Relationship Lifeline (relationshiplifeline.org) for teaching me the true meaning of forgiveness.

And to my sponsors and friends - both in and out of recovery, and to my parents, brothers, sisters and the rest of my family, I'm grateful for you all.

And most of all to God who was, is and always will be there for me. I wouldn't be here without You, let alone be able to write this book that will hopefully inspire others.

—Nancy Blaha

CHAPTER 1

LA TRAFFIC. I'D BEEN SURE I'D TAKEN OFF EARLY enough to beat the rush, but already, I was stuck in gridlock. Frustrated, I watched as the car in front of me started to edge forward, and no sooner did I lift my foot off the brake than someone behind me laid on the horn.

I glanced into my rearview mirror. In the car behind me, a man waved his fist in anger as he shouted something I couldn't hear anyway. Apparently, he didn't seem to approve of the three-foot gap between my bumper and the car in front. That unused space ahead was too much for him, I guess.

I glared back at him in the mirror, deciding to move up just slightly to accommodate him anyway—only to be forced to hit my brakes again within seconds. I squeezed the steering wheel tight, my knuckles whitening. How I hated LA traffic.

Sometimes, I wished I'd picked somewhere else to move to, but after my brother had died, all I'd wanted to do was to get as far away from South Carolina as possible. And Southern California had seemed the best place to head to and start a new life. At least, it had appeared to be at first.

A white Lexus caught my attention as it pulled up even with my car and I glanced over at the woman at the wheel. There was something quite peculiar about her, the way she sat there with her shoulders hunched up so high that they almost touched her ears.

She must have felt me watching her because she quickly turned in my direction. As I stared back, I was shocked to see streaking lines of mascara streaming down her face. My heart ached.

"What's wrong?" I asked out loud though I knew she couldn't hear me. "Are you miserable like me, trapped in an unhappy marriage?" At least that had been the case up until a few weeks ago. Up until then, if she'd glanced over at me, she'd have seen me sitting in my car looking the exact same way she looked now. And all because I dreaded what I was going home to.

Would Dan be in a bad mood again because no jobs had called in that day? And when I tried to cheer him up like I usually did, were we only going to end up arguing again, like we did most every night?

Gone was the easygoing guy I'd fallen in love with—the guy who hated to argue. That guy had disappeared right around the time the recession had hit last year. And since then, all we seemed to do was fight over money. Same old thing, over and over.

And while it was true that his contracting business had slowed down quite a bit and things had gotten a bit tight, I still had my teaching job at the school, so it wasn't like we couldn't pay our bills. But still, not working as much as he wanted to, had been stressing him out, especially since his dream was to start a family soon. Though as far as I was concerned, that wasn't going to happen anytime soon. In fact, it wasn't going to happen at all.

With all the fighting we'd been doing, the timing was terrible, not to mention what a big financial strain having children would put on us. But the truth was, it wasn't about the money. It wasn't about the timing. It was about me, about how I wasn't sure if I was even cut out to be a mother after all. Not today, not any day.

What if I had a child who turned out like my brother James? Between being born with one leg twisted and two inches shorter than the other, and tiny weak lungs that had left him struggling with permanent asthma, that poor guy had had it rough from the moment he'd appeared into the world.

"Lame James!"

My eyes teared at the heartbreaking memory of how the kids used to call James either that or *The Breather.* Then they'd find out he was my twin, and stare at me, incredulous. "But you look so normal. What happened to him, then?" they'd ask, not holding back the first thing to blurt from their ignorant mouths. And I never did try to answer; James was my brother, and I looked out for him, and it was none of anyone's business but ours.

Sometimes, they'd ask me their crude questions right in front of James and I always wondered which was worse; was it worse to be him, or to be me—the *normal, healthy one* left to live a life of guilt for being born this way, with functioning limbs and lungs.

I knew one thing for sure. It would surely break my heart if I had to watch my own child suffering like my brother had done. I couldn't handle it, and my own mother sure hadn't been able to, either. She'd constantly fussed over James. "Are you warm enough? Did you take your pills today? Don't stay up too late."

At least she appeared to care when she hadn't been hiding herself away in her room with a bottle in which to immerse her sorrows. No, there was no way I'd chance ending up like her. That thought terrified me almost as much as the thought of having children.

But sadly, I couldn't tell Dan any of that since he didn't even know I had a brother to begin with, let alone about how James had tragically died. And I wouldn't dare tell him about my mother or anything else about my past, either. I'd decided a long time ago to keep all that to myself, and I intended to keep it that way—at least for now.

Not that he hadn't been curious at times, especially when we'd first started dating. Back then, he'd wanted to know everything about me, every tiny thing there was to find out. But as soon as he'd seen how his questions would upset me, he'd back right off and we'd fall into an uneasy silence, neither of us sure what to say anymore. The past was a place I wouldn't go back to.

"Everyone has skeletons in their closet," he'd said. "And when the time's right, I know you'll tell me everything."

Well, he was wrong. I'd always known that the time would probably never be right to chance cracking open that door, and the longer I kept things from him, the harder I knew it would be. Though, maybe it was just as well. Who knew what might happen if he uncovered the truth?

The woman in the Lexus wiped her cheeks on her palms and turned back to face the sea of cars. I wanted to hear her story; was she in the same sort of predicament as I'd been with Dan? Unknowingly, she had brought everything back—the pain, the guilt, and the tears.

Maybe it would have been better if Dan had pushed me more to talk about my past. Maybe then, I might have opened up and he'd have understood why I was the way I was, and why I kept things so close to my chest and was afraid to have children of my own.

But then again, the thought of talking about any of my history—even with my own husband—was too risky, especially after what had happened with me and Joey. I felt that old familiar ache in my chest again as I thought about my first real love.

I'd thought for sure Joey and I would always be together, that nothing could separate us. But, of course, that sadly didn't prove true and we broke up before I left South Carolina, and I hadn't talked to him since.

I'd always wondered if it wasn't because he'd known too much about me and had seen the writing on the wall, just like everyone else seemed to have done back in Easley.

Maybe he'd seen that with a mother and brother like I had, the chances were pretty good that there was something quite wrong with me too, something he didn't yet know about, and he wasn't about to risk finding out.

That was the one thing I could never have said about Dan at least; no matter how bad things would have turned out between us, I knew he would never leave me and that if anything, I'd have to be the one to throw in the towel first. And I had almost done that very thing on several occasions this past year, having promised myself way back that I'd never end up stuck in a marriage like my parents had suffered.

Yet sadly enough, our own marriage was beginning to look just like theirs, sounding like it too, what with all the bickering we'd been doing lately.

In fact, I'd been ready to leave after our last big blowout, all over something I'd done in signing Dan up at our local gym.

When I'd told him, it was like I'd committed a crime or something; instead of being happy about it, he'd just got annoyed and upset. So much for my gift, then. Well, of course, I had to have some hidden motive, didn't I?

"What are you implying, then?" he'd asked me, more than a little upset. "Are you saying I've gotten out of shape since I haven't been working out like I used to? Are you ashamed of me? Is that it?"

Of course not, I tried to tell him, and it was the truth. I'd never stopped finding him attractive, not even for a moment. I'd just thought that if he got out more and got some exercise, he might start to feel better about himself again, less downbeat.

But I'd got it wrong again, like always. So, I would cancel the membership, then; what else could I do? And just as I was about to do that, I was wrong once more. Now, he wanted to keep it, so he said.

He even apologized, telling me that if it meant that much to me for him to go, he'd give working out a try, after all. Yes, he'd keep it. He was grateful for my gift. Well, why, then, did I feel so utterly miserable?

My head spun, and I didn't know which way was up. But he did do it. He did give the gym a try, and what a dramatic difference it made in him right from the start. His attitude was better. He said he felt better, and the old Dan was gradually coming back; he seemed way more upbeat—just how he used to be.

He started doing things around the house, like the other day when I came home to find that not only had he washed all the laundry, but he'd gone grocery shopping too. And the next night, dinner had been waiting when I'd got home from work, a dinner that he had shopped for, and prepared, and cooked himself. I was so relieved that he seemed to be getting back to his old self, to the Dan I had loved, and the one who'd helped me forget Joey.

And unlike in the past when I'd call him during the day and hear the TV blasting in the background, when I called now, it went straight to voicemail. That meant he was either working, running errands, or down at the gym. To tell the truth, I didn't much care where he was and what he was doing, as long as he wasn't moping around the house anymore.

Then there'd been yesterday, and the huge bouquet of flowers. Flowers! He hadn't given me any in such a long time, and what made it even more special was that he'd obviously taken the time to hand-pick the arrangement himself. It had smelled so good with all my favorites in it, with tulips, roses...even some daffodils, so hard to find around here—especially at this time of year.

If I'd known working out would have made that much of a difference in him, I'd have suggested it a long time ago, and at least the house would have been a lot cleaner if I had. A small smile crossed my lips at the thought.

And though things weren't totally back to where they used to be, I was beginning to have hope again that we were going to make it after all.

I turned back to the car in front of me to find it had moved up a few feet. I followed suit now, hoping there was a sliver of a chance that I'd still make it home early enough to surprise Dan, just as I'd planned.

I smiled again, now overcome by the sudden, strange thought that came back to me; maybe I was the one who was going to be surprised, because of the way he'd kept asking me this morning what time I was going to be home? Did he have something special up his sleeve, something he'd planned again for later tonight? I felt lucky, excited too.

I looked over at the time on the dash. Maybe the right thing to do would be to give him a little heads-up that I was on my way, just so that whatever he was planning, the surprise wouldn't be ruined by me showing up too early. It set my mind off, thinking back again.

Joey was like that, too. Joey used to love to plan surprises like that, back when we were dating. One time, he'd picked me up from school and on the way home stopped at the park, where he had a picnic all set up for us to celebrate our second year together. So romantic...

I was still reminiscing about that day as I pushed speed dial to call Dan's cell, but as it started to ring, I guiltily pushed the memory of Joey away. I'd been thinking about those times with my old boyfriend a bit too much lately, although it must only have been because of the distance, the growing divide between me and Dan over this past year. At least I wasn't obsessed about Joey anymore, not like when I'd first left South Carolina and moved to California.

Back then, no matter how hard I'd tried not to think of him, it had seemed to be all I did. I'd driven myself crazy in those days, checking my cell phone every few minutes with the hope that he'd called or texted since the last time I'd looked, sometimes checking over and over until the red light finally began blinking and the phone battery faded away. And then, frantic, I'd find myself digging for the charger, panic-stricken that I might miss his call or his text in the few seconds of downtime. But of course, the call and the text never did come, even when I plugged the wretched thing in again. So, I'd just sit staring at it, hoping, craving.

In those days, I must have looked at his Facebook page over twenty times a day, too, unable to help myself. It all seemed so pathetic now, with hindsight.

Dan's voicemail came on. I hung up and tried the home phone. He was busy. Busy preparing another surprise for me.

I remembered how it was such a relief when I fell for Dan and was able to get Joey off my mind, at least for the most part. But there were still days when I'd hear a song on the radio or see someone who reminded me of him, and there I was, plunged right back down that cavernous black hole, missing him again, longing.

Facebook. That was my downfall. I should have never started checking out his page again like I'd begun to do a few weeks ago, that had only succeeded in stirring up old feelings. Seeing Joey's face had just made me miss him again, as if nothing had changed, and time had stood still. Seeing Joey's face made Dan's own pale in my mind once more. But I did it anyway, the furtive looking, the checking, the scrolling and all the clicking to see who Joey's friends were now, where he was going, and with whom.

And there he was, staring back at me from his profile photo, looking just as handsome as I remembered, with his strong chin and intense dark eyes. And then—I reeled for a moment, suddenly shocked to see him in a police uniform in the next photo that came up on the page.

Never in a million years did I think Joey would ever be a cop, not after what had happened to his father! Joey's dad had been tragically shot and killed during a routine traffic stop, and anytime we'd be out, and a police car would go by, Joey would go into how, "I, for one, will never have a job where I can be taken from my family in an instant like my dad was." And he'd immediately remind me of how hard it had been on his family, and how he still couldn't understand what his father had been thinking to take that kind of risk.

Yet, there Joey was in that uniform. Apparently, he had changed his mind over the years, though for the life of me, I couldn't imagine for one minute what that reason could have been.

And still I kept scrolling, hungry to fill in all the gaps of Joey's life since we'd last met.

It was the next photo that really ripped my heart out. There was my Joey, standing next to a young boy who was the spitting image of him, the same chin and dark eyes, no mistaking him as Joey's boy. He even had his hair parted on one side just like Joey did. I couldn't believe my eyes.

Joey was a father? Really?

And what made it even worse was that the boy didn't appear much more than seven or eight years old at the very most, and since I'd only been gone from Easley a little over eight years, that meant either Joey had been seeing someone while we were together, or he'd started dating pretty much as soon as I was out of his life.

My spirits sank, my heart now in a spasm of sudden palpitations. Was that why he had been willing to let me go so easily, because he'd been interested in someone else? Though I found that hard to believe, what else could it be?

The truth hurt, but at least if that was the case, all the more reason I was thrilled that Dan and I were getting along again. The heck with Joey! I had someone else too, someone who loved me more than Joey had ever done. I must have been stupid to even think of looking at that man's profile again and I pushed the invasive thoughts away.

"Hello, you've reached Dan's Contracting Service and the home of Karen and Dan." I jumped, startled as Dan's deep voice filled the car. "Please leave a message. We'll get right back to you. And make it a great day!" *Beep.*

"Hi, Honey," I said, once again pushing Joey from my mind. "I'm stuck here on the 91 but wanted to let you know that I took off a little early and I'll hopefully be home soon. Looking forward to spending a nice evening with you." I started to hit *end*, then added, "I love you," and hung up.

The car in front of me came to a sudden stop. I hit my brakes as once again, I was reminded of how bad the Los Angeles traffic had gotten over the years. Every freeway from the 5 to the 405 to the 91 could be jammed at most any hour of the day. They'd even given the congested areas names like *the Orange Crush* and *Corona Crawl.*

I really missed the open roads back in Easley; they were nothing at all like this. Back there, you could go for miles, sometimes never seeing another car for a long time. I remembered how Joey would pick me up and we'd just go out for a drive. Sometimes, his sister Beth—my best friend at the time—would come with us too. He'd play chauffeur while Beth and I would gossip and laugh and laugh. Those were great times and the memories made me warm inside.

Sometimes, we'd stop at the Dairy Queen on the way home to get hot fudge sundaes or banana splits, racing to eat them before they'd start to melt and drip sticky ice cream down our hands and arms.

I found myself smiling again, the smile growing wider as I noticed the traffic on the 91 starting to move again. But within seconds, it faded back to a grim expression of frustration as the line of moving vehicles slowly ground to a stop once more. I rubbed my neck as it began to knot up. I guessed I wouldn't be getting home early after all. Maybe I should just get off the road somewhere, call it a day and find an alternative route? I scanned the side of the freeway, searching for a sign.

Imperial Street exit lay two miles ahead. That was what I'd do; I'd get off there, then. Anything was better than sitting here for the next hour, so I turned my signal on. Though I didn't know where Imperial could possibly take me, I figured I'd take it anyway.

As I tried to merge over, my frustration grew as no one was willing to let me in. So, forced to do what everyone else here did, I rudely pushed my way across all three lanes until—just in the nick of time—I was able to make the exit.

Now I was free. No more freeway traffic.

I happily turned right and started the zig zag through side streets, toward what I hoped was home. My mind turned to Dan as I drove, still wondering what he had up his sleeve for tonight. He was a good man, really.

As I continued to drive, the area started to look just a little familiar. Wasn't that Angelo's Restaurant just up there on the right? Now I knew where I was and couldn't believe I'd driven by that exit every day, never once realizing it would take me through this part of town, right by my favorite restaurant.

Angelo's. Just the name brought back sweet memories of all the times Dan and I had eaten there. We'd even gone there on our very first date a little over six years ago.

We liked it so much that after that, we made it a point to eat there as much as we could especially on our anniversary. Though sadly enough, it came back to me that we hadn't gone there on our last one. Of course, we'd been fighting earlier that day, the same charade as on every other day at that time.

I remembered how when Dan had first asked me out, I'd almost said no. I'd had no interest in dating anyone else after what had happened with me and Joey. But there'd seemed to be something about Dan that was special, so after a bit of hesitation, I'd finally given in and agreed to a date.

But the next day, I'd already started to have second thoughts though, about going out with him after all, the doubts nagging at me. And by the end of the day, I decided I didn't want to go and called to tell him that. Maybe he'd anticipated my cancellation, who knew, but he didn't pick up and the voicemail didn't cut in either, not like it normally would.

So, I'd ended up stuck with it then; the date would have to go ahead, and he'd shown up at my door before I'd had any chance to cancel.

I can still picture him standing there on the step, looking so excited as he waited with flowers in his hand. "You look, great," he'd said somewhat shyly. "Ready?"

I just didn't have the heart to tell him I'd changed my mind. That was it, then, I had to go, but it would be just that one time, no more dates after that. That one half-hearted date would be it.

Except, it wasn't to work out that way, of course. Surprisingly enough, I had a wonderful time that night, and by the end of the evening, I was already hoping he'd ask me out again. *Surprised* did not convey how I felt; I'd actually had no idea it was possible to feel that way about anyone but Joey.

And yet, Dan wasn't anything at all like Joey. Nothing like him at all, not in appearance or personality. He was so easygoing and laid back, where Joey was a take-charge guy. And though I'd liked that about Joey at first, I'd realized he could be a bit too controlling.

Like the way he used to insist on ordering dinner for me, as if I was helpless or something, or when he'd tried to advise me on what to wear when we went out.

Sometimes, I'd wished he'd just relax and let me make my own decisions. I'm sure that's what made it even more attractive to be with a guy like Dan, one who realized I had a mind of my own.

And though I can't even remember what Dan and I had talked about that night at Angelo's, we weren't even halfway through dinner when I'd already known this was a guy I wanted to see again.

I slowed down as a motorcycle parked out front caught my eye when I drove past. It looked like Dan's bike. But what would he be doing here? Perhaps he was meeting a new client. Or maybe he'd stopped by to pick up some dinner to take home, knowing how much I'd always loved the pasta at Angelo's. That would explain why he'd been acting so mysterious this morning. He wanted to surprise me by bringing some home for dinner tonight!

I kept going but after a moment, decided to turn around. Why not surprise him instead? But as I pulled into Angelo's parking lot, that uneasy feeling from earlier came over me again. I ignored it and parked the car, anyway, getting out and heading for the entrance.

CHAPTER 2

I HURRIED UP THE STAIRS LEADING UP TO THE FRONT door of the restaurant. At the top, I hesitated and once again wondered if I should just go home and pretend I never knew he was here.

Why ruin his surprise? But I pulled on the door anyway and headed inside. If I saw that he was with a client, I'd say hello really quickly and make up some excuse why I couldn't stay. And if he was alone, I'd suggest we stay here and eat instead of bringing it home, just like old times.

I barely had one foot inside when the old familiar garlic aroma filled my nostrils. I breathed it in and smiled.

"Welcome to Angelo's. Can I help you?" the hostess at the front desk asked.

"I think my husband is in here somewhere. I'll just go find him myself. But, thanks anyway." I excitedly breezed past her and went off to search for Dan.

I checked the main dining area first. Again, I felt a smile cross my face. I loved this place, from the red curtains, to the soft lighting, to the thick dark carpeting under my feet. And I liked how every table and booth was covered with a white tablecloth and an empty Chianti bottle with a candle sticking out of the top. It was a great place, perfect for romantic evenings with just the two of us.

We really needed to make it a point to start coming here again, now that we had been getting along better. Maybe I should make a reservation for our anniversary next month? It felt good to be able to plan again, to be able to come up with surprises to make Dan's day, the same as he was doing for me. It sure was better than fighting.

I made a mental note to do just that and to book a table for us before I left. I scanned the tables. It was still too early for the dinner crowd so there weren't many occupied, and I quickly saw that Dan wasn't there. I turned and headed for the to-go counter that was next to the bar. But he wasn't there either. I was feeling deflated.

Maybe I'd been mistaken and that wasn't his bike out front after all. But as I was about to head back to the front of the restaurant, a high-pitched giggle coming from a booth on my right caught my attention.

An attractive brunette in a sexy low-cut red dress sat in it across from a man who had his back to me. She was smiling at him and had her hand stretched across the table, resting on his.

I felt a tug at my heart. I was reminded of how Dan and I used to sit holding hands when we came here. Sadly, I started to turn away when something shiny caught my eye on the ledge behind the girl's head.

My body stiffened, and I let out an audible gasp as I recognized Dan's motorcycle helmet. The girl turned and looked at me as she slowly slid her hand off of his.

With a tilt of her head, she stared hard as if she was trying to place how she might possibly know me. The man across from her turned in the direction of her stare. I saw his mouth drop open.

"Karen?"

I stared back at him, speechless. What was Dan doing here? More than that, what was he doing here with her? I looked at his shirt, the same blue one I'd given him on his last birthday. I loved that shirt on him. The way the color made his blue eyes stand out was perfect.

I looked back at the girl. Who was she? I could see she was very pretty—and appeared to be younger than I was.

She nervously brushed a few strands of hair from her face. It was long and thick and the same deep brown mine used to be. That was, until I'd moved here and cut it all off, then dyed it blonde.

I remember how I told myself back then that it was just because I needed a change and should try and blend in with all the other blond girls in Southern California. But the truth was that I just didn't want to look like me anymore. I would be someone else—anyone else—rather than have to stare at myself in the mirror one more time.

The girl's eyes widened. Even in the dim lighting, I could see what looked like fear starting to cross her face. I looked back at Dan. So, this was why he'd been in such a good mood lately. It wasn't from going to the gym. It wasn't because we'd been getting along better. And it certainly wasn't because he'd been planning to surprise me—although, it's fair to say that he surely did, but in all the wrong ways. And now I knew it, that his good mood, was all because of her.

Dan opened his mouth as if to say something, but before he could, a buzzing sound started in my ear. It quickly grew louder within seconds, and filled my other ear, too.

The noise was familiar, but I couldn't place where I'd heard it last. Dan's lips moved some more but with the noise, I had a hard time making out what he was saying.

As I stood there, the buzzing got even louder. Several diners at a nearby table stared at me and I started to wonder if they could hear the noise too.

Suddenly, Dan jumped up. As he did, his hand knocked over a glass of wine on the table. I looked down and was briefly mesmerized as the red liquid spilled out and slowly spread across the white tablecloth.

I felt the blood leaving my face as the scene before me reminded me of the blood that had covered my brother's white shirt the day I'd found him dead up at the shooting range, followed next by a wave of nausea. I looked up at Dan and watched as he nervously dabbed his napkin over the spill.

The volume of the buzzing shot up higher and I clasped my hands over my ears in an attempt to deafen it. But it didn't help. I found it hard to breathe and looked for the exit. As I turned to leave, I took a few steps and immediately collided with a waiter carrying two steaming plates of spaghetti toward Dan's table.

I looked down at the dishes of pasta. "Sorry," I mumbled as I pushed past him and hurried to the front of the restaurant.

The hostess stared as I ran past her, horrified and panic-stricken, unsure where to run, what to do. Still with my hands pressed firmly over my ears. I dropped them to my sides again and gripped the door, bumping into a startled woman on her way in. I mumbled a "sorry" again and stepped out into the cool air that stung at my tearful eyes.

Forcing some air into my lungs, I looked around frantically for my car. I needed to get out of here, fast. Spotting it, I hurried down the steps. As I opened the door and climbed in, I thought I heard someone call out my name over the noises in my head. It was Dan who now stood at the top of the stairs motioning at me.

As he moved to come down the steps, I started the engine and put my vehicle in reverse. I hurried for the exit. But as I started to pull out, a wave of anger washed over me, and I circled back toward Dan. He stopped and stood there as my car approached him.

He had a frozen 'deer caught in headlights' kind of look. I passed by him and pointed my car in the direction of his Harley. Without pausing to think, I stepped hard on the gas and rammed right into his bike.

It disappeared underneath my hood and I could see sparks fly up, hearing the grating of metallic components catching and scraping beneath the chassis of my car. As the bike came to a rest between my bumper and the front of the restaurant, I backed up again, satisfied, and once more headed for the exit. This time as I passed Dan, instead of fear, I saw horror plastered on his face as he stared at his now crumpled bike lying on the ground. I headed toward home, my mind and heart all a blur of emotion, tension—and deep, painful loss.

My mind spun wildly as I made my way through the streets. All I kept seeing was that girl in the red dress with her hand resting there, blatantly placed on my husband's hand, in front of everyone. And I kept seeing that guilty look on his face as he tried to mop up the spilled wine while cautiously glancing up at me, unsure what to do. And again, I felt nauseous as I pictured James on the ground, his white cotton shirt a mess of bright red spilled blood.

If only I hadn't planned that stupid birthday dinner that night for Joey, then things would be so different right now. My brother would still be alive. Joey and I would most likely be married right now, and I wouldn't be going through this with Dan. Tears sprang to my eyes. I angrily brushed them away. How could Dan do this to me? How could he even think of being with someone else?

I should never have left Easley. But I had to go. It had hurt too much to be there after James died, and I'd known that if I stayed, I'd end up crazy like my mother was.

Plus, I had no reason to stay really. My twin brother was dead. I had no relationship with my parents to speak of. Even my best friend had deserted me—though to this day, I still didn't know why. And yet, even with all that, my boyfriend decided he didn't want to leave town with me and start a new life. Anything I'd thought I had to offer a man was not enough, was never enough. What else could I do but move somewhere else and start a new life?

Tears poured from my eyes. First Joey deserted me and now Dan. And there was my father and James too. Every man I'd ever known had let me down in one way or another. Well, it was only what I had come to expect.

I hurried into the house and threw my purse onto the kitchen counter, all the while asking myself who that girl was, the one with Dan. How long had he'd been seeing her? Were they in love? I turned in the direction of Dan's home office. Maybe I'd find some clues in there that would at least tell me how long this affair had been going on right under my nose.

And maybe, even if I found nothing there at all, maybe the act of just doing something would make me feel a bit better, a little less helpless and clueless.

As I passed through the living room, I noticed that the answering machine light was blinking. I stopped and hit play, half expecting it to be Dan having already called with some lame excuse as to why he was at Angelo's with that girl. But it was my own voice coming out of the speaker, haunting me, as if I was listening to a stranger. Now, it seemed like years since I'd happily called and left Dan that cheery voice message, all the while oblivious to what was going on right under my nose. Now, it seemed like everything between us had been a lie and a sham. And again, I had been made to look like a fool.

"Hi Honey, I'm stuck here on the 91 but I wanted to let you know that I took off a little early and hopefully will be home soon. Looking forward to spending a nice evening with you." Then, "I love you."

I love you.

I love you.

The words reverberated in my skull, senseless, meaningless, pointless, stupid words.

I pounded delete and continued to his office. After flicking on the light, I sat down at his desk and yanked open the center drawer.

Clawing through some paperwork, I searched for answers, my hands trembling and my eyes stinging and sore. But I found nothing. I slammed the drawer shut and opened the one below it and dug around some more.

I stopped and looked up at the sound of a car door closing out front then a car driving away. The back door slammed and several seconds later, I heard, "Karen?"

Anger started to rise up in me at the sound of his voice. No, it wasn't anger. It was rage. Rage that I'd kept bottled up for a very long time. And I was terrified, too. Terrified at the thought that once I let some of the rage out, I was sure to lose all control and I didn't know when I'd be able to get it back. My skin prickled, the red heat of fury and unfathomable hurt.

But as Dan came around the corner and stood there in the doorway, I was able to shove that rage down once again. I had to. It wasn't time to let it out. I wasn't about to let him distract me right now, so I swallowed hard and went back to the task at hand.

I looked away then after a moment, I looked up at him again. His face was as white as the sheet of paper in my hand. He pushed his hair back nervously with both hands. I could see huge circles of sweat underneath each of his arms, and that made me smile. That pretty blue shirt didn't look so pretty now, did it?

"What're you looking for?" he asked in a shaky voice as he took a step into the room.

I stared at him and wanted so badly to pummel him with my hands but would settle for pummeling him with questions instead. Like, who was she? What were you thinking? How could you?

But instead, I looked away disgustedly and went back to my digging in silence. I didn't know what I was even searching for and my eyesight blurred, so I couldn't see much anyway. But I carried on the charade since there was nothing else to do in such a scenario. I needed to appear in control, at least over this small thing.

Dan sat down in the chair next to the desk, right as I eyed a credit card statement. I glanced at him again as I slowly pulled it out.

His eyes got big. Was that an admission of guilt? I looked down and quickly scanned over all of the charges on the page but—disappointed not to find anything incriminating—I dropped the paper and lifted out a phone bill instead. As I checked it over for any repeated unfamiliar phone numbers made during the day, my pulse picked up, while at the same time Dan's breathing had quickened.

He put his hand on the desk. "Can we talk please?" he asked hesitantly.

This was it. I'd found what I was looking for. I looked at the bill before me, convinced. There were several calls to the same number made apparently while I was hard at work, one call over fifteen minutes long. He'd been talking to her. I felt sick.

"Who is she?" I asked, hurling the phone bill at him. "And how long have you been sneaking around with her behind my back?"

Dan flinched as the paper hit him. "Hold on," he said, sounding frightened. "Please. Let me explain."

I slammed the drawer shut and stood up, the blood pounding in my ears. He flinched again, as I walked around the desk closer to him. But I kept going and headed to the kitchen.

I stopped and stood there, then marched over to a cabinet and opened it abruptly. I looked in.

"What're you doing?" I turned and looked to find Dan in the doorway looking even whiter than I thought was possible. "What are you looking for?" he asked in a strained voice.

I ignored him and turned away, peering into each cabinet. Nope, not there. I opened the next one and continued down the line, looking into each one. Dan moved closer and quietly closed each cabinet door behind me.

I turned and glared at him again with hands on my hips. "Where is it?"

"Where is what?" he asked, his eyes wide.

"The bottle of Jack Daniels. I know you've got one hidden in here somewhere. Where did you stash it?"

Color came back to his face along with a look of fear.

"Hold on now Karen. I know you're upset, but please don't tell me you've started drinking again. Don't do it, sweetheart. It's not worth it."

I tilted my head for a moment, confused by what he was saying. But then I remembered that Dan was still under the impression I'd at one time had a drinking problem. It all started because when we'd first started dating, he'd mentioned finding my behavior odd, that at such a young age, I didn't drink at all. Not even a glass of wine. And he'd seen how I'd never go to a bar and in fact hated everything to do with booze, especially the smell. That was when he jumped to the conclusion that I must have had a drinking problem when I was very young.

"I'm so sorry you had to go through that," he'd said in his usual understanding way when I wouldn't answer any of his questions. "I'm here for you."

But it wasn't me who had had the problem. It was actually my mother who was the drunk, plain and simple. And I hated what her drinking did not only to me, but to James and my father, too. But that was then, that was way back, in a place and a time I had left behind. I'd worked hard to leave it all where it was—and I wasn't about to tell Dan any of it.

It was just easier to let him believe it was true and that I was the one who'd once had a problem, better that than to open up that door and let all the repercussions spill out. Though, truth be told, I'd never had one single drink in my life, except for the time I'd picked up my mother's orange juice by mistake when I was a teenager, only to find out she had poured whiskey into it. It was the same kind of whiskey that—ironically—Dan drank, Jack Daniels. My mouth soured just thinking about the disgusting taste.

No, I never did tell Dan the truth, though I did feel a bit bad especially after he was so sweet and understanding about it. He'd even offered to quit drinking himself if I'd wanted him to, but he didn't drink that often, and I didn't feel that was fair. And told him so, as long as I never had to see or smell it on him.

But as I looked at him standing there now with his eyes bulging out of his head, probably terrified at the thought that he'd driven me to start drinking again, I wondered if maybe it wasn't time to tell him the truth. "No," I told myself as I pictured him with that girl at Angelo's again. *He can just suffer, for everything he's putting me through.*

I pulled out a chair and dragged it across the floor, climbing up to stand on it. I looked down at Dan. He still wore such a panicked expression. I turned again and stuck my hand into a cabinet high over the stove and groped around in it.

"Please come down," he pleaded as he held the chair steady.

"Get away from me, Dan," I said just as my hand bumped into something tucked away in the corner. I grabbed a hold of a half empty bottle of Jack. My mind flashed back to Mother. Oh, how she had loved her Jack Daniels. I waved the liquor defiantly in his face.

"Give me that please," he said as he reached for it.

I held it high above his grasp. He dropped his hand and sighed. After a moment, I made my way back down to the floor, tentatively, all the while keeping one eye on Dan as I gripped the bottle tightly.

And though I had made up my mind a long time ago that I'd never become like my mother, right now all I wanted to do was to stop the pain. Pain of the realization that once again, I was on my own with no one to trust.

And if that meant drinking Jack Daniels of all things, then so be it. What was the point anyway? I'd been good all these years and look where that had got me. Nowhere at all.

Guarding the bottle with my body, I opened the fridge and took out a can of Coke. I opened the can and carefully poured the soda into the bottle of whiskey, stopping every second or two to allow time for the fizzing to go down just like I'd seen my mother do a thousand times before.

The bottle was almost completely filled to the brim now, so I put the cap back on and gave it a little swirl, again following the image of my mother doing the same thing. She loved Jack and Coke though she'd mix the whiskey with lemonade or iced tea, or pretty much anything else if there wasn't any Coke in the house. Sometimes, if she didn't have anything to mix it with and wanted a quick buzz, she'd drink right from the bottle. Who does that? Drink right from the bottle?

I took the lid off again, lifted the bottle to my lips and took a huge gulp. Almost instantly, my throat closed with disgust. It was horrible, just like I remembered from the time I drank from her glass of orange juice. I still couldn't understand how she managed to drink this stuff day after day.

As much as I hated the taste, I was determined to numb the pain, so I dug deep and lifted the bottle up again, forcing myself to swallow some more. As the liquid slid down my throat, I knew right then that I'd opened the door up to something I was bound to regret. But at that moment, I didn't care. I just wanted to escape.

Dan sighed again and I looked at him, almost having forgotten he was there. The look in his eyes stirred something deep in me. Not that he looked afraid, which he did, but that at least he had a reaction. Not like the blank stare Mother had given me the day I came running into the house eight years ago, screaming that James was dead. I'd never forget her face.

And I would never forget how she just sat there staring with that empty look for what felt like ages, then looked away, got up and—without saying a single word—went to her bedroom.

I followed her halfway down the hall and just watched as she closed her bedroom door and left me standing there, all alone. Alone to deal with James' death as well as my incredible, inconsolable, immeasurable grief.

I really don't know how long I stood there.

At the time I didn't have a clue what to do. Should I call my father? Or Joe? Or the police? I was frozen with indecision. Finally, I decided to call 911.

It seemed like forever until the police got there with an ambulance right behind them. They asked me to take them up to the range where James was.

It took everything I had to go back up there, but I did. This time though, I kept my eyes on the ground and wouldn't look while the officers checked over everything and talked in low voices, eventually helping the paramedics cart the bundled and covered-up body back down the hill on a stretcher. After the ambulance left, one of the policemen asked to speak with my mother. I got her to open her bedroom door, but she wouldn't talk to them. She just sat there on her bed and gave them the same blank look she'd given me.

It meant I was left to answer all their questions. There were so many. *When was the last time I'd seen James alive? Had he been acting strangely that day?*

He always acted a bit strangely, I told them, but I hadn't been around my brother that much back then and didn't notice him acting any stranger than normal when I was in his company. But I did tell them how he'd wanted to talk with me about something that morning, but I hadn't had the time. Now, I hated myself for that, probably always would.

It didn't take long for them to determine what I already knew, that James had taken his own life. They already knew about that first time he'd attempted suicide when he was younger, by taking a pill overdose, so that wasn't a huge leap to think he'd finally gone and done it later.

Before they left, one of the policemen was so kind and tried to reassure me that by the looks of the wound, James apparently had little time to suffer. I guessed it was his attempt at trying to make me feel better. But I would never feel better, and I wanted them all to say nothing at all and to just go away and leave me in peace. Platitudes meant nothing, and *sorry for your loss* meant nothing either; they were just things people said when they didn't have a clue what else to say. And in the back of their minds they were thinking how relieved they were that it wasn't *them* going through the loss.

I was devastated for sure. My only brother was gone, and I knew right then, without a doubt, that life would never be the same. And it wasn't.

And that was the last time I was with my brother except for at his funeral.

—

After the police left, I called my father and he came to the house. It was the first time I'd seen him in a while. I told him what had happened, and he just sat there without saying much. His blank look seemed to echo Mother's, then he got up and said he was going up to the range. I stayed behind.

I didn't know he'd come back when I found him in James' room, sitting on his bed and crying. I remember thinking how that was the first time I'd ever seen my father cry. And then he gave me a weak hug and he was gone. And that was it. James was dead. My mother stayed in her room and drank, and I was more alone than I'd ever been in my life.

CHAPTER 3

THOSE NEXT FEW DAYS AFTER MY BROTHER'S DEATH were a blur. I was overwhelmed as I attempted to handle everything. I had to write the obituary, set up the funeral arrangements, pick out a casket. Still, Mother barely came out of her room, only to go to the kitchen, then back to her room again.

Joey did try to help some, but he was so distraught over his bests friend's death, he really was no help at all. The only one who really tried to take some of the load off me was the pastor from the church we used to go to—Pastor Phil. He was so kind and consoling, offering me advice on what else needed to be done.

The last thing I had to do was the hardest of all. I was left to pick out the outfit my brother was going to be buried in. I just couldn't do it and put it off as long as I could. Then finally, I went through his clothes until I found just what I knew James would have wanted to wear. James was particular and always neat, so after ironing his favorite dress shirt and slacks, I dropped the clothes off at the funeral parlor, crying all the way there.

It was barely forty-eight hours since I'd found James, when the phone calls started. The house phone rang constantly, and it seemed everyone wanted to know what had happened. Of course, they acted like they were calling to offer their condolences, again to say how sorry they were and if there was anything, they could do…But I knew the truth. They didn't care about James or my family, they just wanted to know all the gory details, like bystanders at a horrific traffic accident.

And I couldn't go into town without getting stares from everyone, and several times would overhear someone talking about my crazy brother and why they thought he'd taken his own life. It killed me enough to lose my twin brother, let alone to have to listen to all that heartless gossip from people who didn't have the faintest idea.

I knew back then that if I didn't get out of that town, I was going to lose it too, just like James, and something else horrible was going to happen.

—

I looked at Dan again as he stood there staring at me. But this time, his expression had softened into what looked way too much like pity, which made me even angrier than I was.

It was that same look I'd got from everyone in Easley after James had died. I couldn't stand it then and was not about to take it now, especially coming from Dan. I looked away and took another drink from the bottle.

"Sweetheart, please. You know you don't want to do this," he said in a coaxing voice as he reached for the bottle. I pulled it from his reach.

"Don't *sweetheart* me after what you just did," I said before taking a few more gulps. Tears filled my eyes again. I looked at him and for the first time since we'd been married, felt like I was looking at a stranger. This wasn't the same man I had fallen in love with; someone I didn't recognize was standing in front of me, an imposter, cold and heartless.

"Who are you?" I asked through the tears.

"What do you mean?" he asked taking a step back, looking frightened. "I'm your husband. Please put that bottle down. You're starting to scare me. Let's go into the living room and sit down and talk about this."

"Talk? Talk about what?" I asked. "Are you going to try and tell me there's nothing going on between you and that girl? I'm not stupid, you know. I saw you with my own two eyes."

"Yes," he said sounding tired. "I know you did. But it's not what it looked like. Susan means nothing to me."

"Susan? Oh, so that's her name? Well Susan sure looked like she meant something to you with her hand all over yours," I said feeling the anger rise up again.

Dan grimaced. "I'm sorry. I should never have been there with her. I know that. I made a horrible mistake and I'm so sorry. It's you I love. Not her. You have to believe me."

"Do I? Then why were you there with her?" I asked, my voice getting loud.

"I don't know. I guess I was lonely and needed someone to talk to and she was willing to listen. You and I hadn't exactly been communicating much this past year, you have to admit. And one day we just started talking. One thing led to another. And I don't know why, but I asked her out for dinner, then before I even knew it, I started to have feelings for her. It was wrong and I'm so sorry. I guess I was lonely and needed someone to talk to, that's all."

That's all? I stared at him. Though I was hurt more than anything, all I could do was feel anger.

"Oh, so it's the old case of, *my wife doesn't understand me*, is it? That's pathetic. You cheated on me because you were lonely? Because you needed someone to talk to? You had me, Dan. Your wife, supposedly your best friend, the one who sticks by you through thick and thin. You didn't need some girl in a low-cut red dress to talk to." For a brief moment, I felt like hurling the bottle at him, but didn't want to waste it.

"And the only thing you're sorry about," I spat, "is that I found you out. If it hadn't been for that, you'd have carried on; that's how sorry you are."

"I tried to talk to you," he said his eyes now filling with tears, too. "So many times. But you'd always shut me out. And forget it if I asked you anything about your past. You acted like I was invading your privacy or something."

"So, it's all my fault, then. Well, maybe there are things that I just don't want to talk about," I replied feeling my protective walls come up.

"Some things?' he asked this time his voice rising. "You never want to talk about anything. I know little about you and you're my wife, for heaven's sake. Do you know how that makes me feel? As if you don't love me enough to open up. I want to know everything about you, good and bad. That's all I've ever wanted. Sometimes, I get the feeling that you're keeping something really big from me."

"This isn't about me," I replied quickly. "It's about you and that girl," I put the cap back onto the bottle and left him standing as I headed to the living room. I flopped down onto the couch.

He walked in and stood there for a moment looking totally exasperated. "See? You're doing it again. Every time I want to talk, you clam right up. Please, talk to me."

I looked at him and thought back to how sweet he'd been the past few weeks, how I was thrilled the other day when he'd brought me those flowers. Now I knew why.

"So that's why you were so nice to me. Those were guilt flowers, weren't they Dan? And here I was, beginning to think how you must really love me after all. You only got them for me because you were feeling guilty for cheating on me, that's all."

"That's not true," he said defensively. "I bought them because I know how much you love flowers. And I wanted to cheer you up. You seemed so down the past few months. And yes, it was easy to talk to her. But tonight, at Angelo's, all I could think of were the times you and I went there together. We went there on our first date, remember? I could never love anyone like I do you."

I looked away, disgusted.

"It's the truth," he said with a pleading tone. "I was going to tell her it was over right before you walked in and stopped me."

I rolled my eyes as he sat down on the couch. I quickly scooted to the other end.

"Have you slept with her?" I asked, bracing myself for his answer.

"Of course not," he said sliding over and reaching for my hand. I pulled away.

"Look," he said dropping his arm. "We went to a juice bar a few times and went out for dinner a couple of times after that. I swear that's all. We hadn't even done anything yet."

I whipped my head back and stared at him. I could feel the veins pop out of my neck. "Yet? You hadn't even done anything *yet*?" In a way, I almost felt sorry for him. Even if it was true, what a stupid thing to say.

Dan's face turned deep red and he started to squirm as he must have realized what he'd just said. "I didn't mean it to come out like that," he said in a stutter.

"I bet you didn't. So, what would have happened if I hadn't shown up tonight, Dan?" As I waited for his answer, I thought about Joey and how only just earlier I'd actually felt guilty for looking at his Facebook page. Maybe it was me who was the stupid one.

"I want you to go." I pointed the bottle at the door. "And take your things with you."

He gave me a hopeless look. "What do you mean? This is my home, our home. Where would I go?"

"I don't care. Go to your mother's. Get a motel. Shack up with your girlfriend. All I know is that I want you out of this house right now before I do something I might seriously regret."

"But I don't want to," he said his eyes darting around the room nervously. "I want to stay here and work this out with you. And please don't call her my girlfriend. She means nothing to me. You're my wife. She's just some girl I met at the gym."

I almost dropped the bottle as the words sank in and my eyes bulged so far out that they actually hurt.

"You met her at the gym? Oh, that's priceless. I'm so happy I was able to help set up your little romance by getting you that gym membership. Which, by the way, you never wanted in the first place."

Dan squirmed some more. As he started to say something, the phone on the coffee table rang, causing us both to jump.

"You'd better get that," I snarled as I stared at the phone. "It's probably 'Susan' looking for you."

Dan looked at the phone, then back at me.

"I guess I'll have to answer it then," I said annoyed. But before I could reach down to pick it up, the answering machine came on.

"Hello, you've reached Dan's Contracting Service and the home of Karen and Dan. Please leave a message and we'll get right back to you. And make it a great day!"

I held my breath but whoever it was hung up before saying anything. I glared at Dan. "See? It was her."

But before he could say anything, the phone started to ring again. And one more time after three rings, the recorder came on. But this time, a woman's voice came out of the speaker.

"Hello? Is anyone there?"

My heart dropped as the bottle started to slip from my hand. It was her. Mother. Dan leaned over and grabbed the bottle before it had a chance to hit the floor.

"Hello?" the voice called out again. I reached down and snatched the phone up before she had time to say anything else. There was no telling what could come out of her mouth especially if she'd been drinking, and I didn't want Dan to hear it. Out of the corner of my eye, I saw him slip the bottle behind a pillow on the couch.

"Hello," I croaked into the receiver.

"Karen? It's me."

My heart did another flip in my chest. It was amazing how after all these years, just the sound of her voice could unnerve me like that. It brought me right back to that same scared teenager I once was, wondering what I was in trouble for this time. I started to hang up but stopped.

Why would she be calling me when I'd made it very clear the last time she did, that I wanted nothing to do with her? Something had to be wrong. Maybe something happened to my father. Or maybe her liver had finally given out like we all knew it would eventually.

With the phone pressed tightly against my ear, I reached behind the pillow and tugged at the bottle of whiskey, then took it with me to the kitchen. I wanted to talk to Mother well out of earshot of Dan.

"Are you there? It's me," she said again.

"I know who it is," I growled into the phone. "I thought I asked you never to call here again."

"I know. But I knew you'd would want to know about your father. He's in the hospital. He's not well, dear," she said softly.

Dear? I flinched at the sound of her calling me *dear*. Then, a feeling of dread washed over me. My father was ill. I took another gulp from the bottle.

"Are you there? Did you hear me?" she asked after several seconds.

"I heard you, Mother," I replied, fighting the fear that was starting to grow. "What's wrong with him?"

"He was feeling dizzy and short of breath and was admitted to the hospital. They found a tumor in him. They think it might be cancer," she replied softly.

My stomach dropped. "Cancer? What kind of cancer?" I asked as if that would make all the difference.

"Lung cancer," she replied again this time even softer. "The tumor is on his left lung."

I felt sick. Lung cancer. Most people didn't survive very long with lung cancer. But he'd never smoked a day in his life and was too young to die. Hands shaking, I took another sip from the bottle as it started to sink in that I just might lose him after all.

"They're getting ready to do a biopsy. Then surgery if they need to. It's not good. I know he'd like to see you. Can you come?"

"Where is he now?" I asked, my mind racing at the thought of stepping back into that town.

"Greenville Memorial," she replied.

I could feel the bile rise to the back of my throat. That was the same hospital where they took James the time, he'd taken all those pills. The thought of walking back in there again made my stomach turn.

"Who are you talking to? Did I hear you say someone has cancer?" I looked behind me to find Dan standing there. I wondered how long he'd been listening to my conversation. Without answering, I went back to the living room again and sat back down on the couch.

"Karen?" I heard her voice coming from the phone again. "Will you come?"

A memory of my father putting a worm on a hook came to mind. It was the first time he'd ever taken me fishing and I could still picture the excitement on his face as I threw the line into the lake. But he wasn't half as excited as he was when I pulled out my first fish. My smile faded.

"Are you there?" I heard her ask again.

What should I do? I couldn't step foot into that town again. It would kill me. But how could I not go back? He could die. Though we weren't as close as I wished we'd been—especially after he'd moved out and he and Mother got divorced—he was my father after all.

Dan walked into the room, replacing my concern for my father with anger toward him. Maybe I should go. Why stay here if all we were going to do is fight? And who knew, maybe I'd get to see Joey while I was back in town. 'How do you like that, Dan?' I thought as I glared at him. 'I'm going back to where my old boyfriend lives.'

And I would like to see Joey. Not only as a payback to Dan, but to finally ask him something I'd been trying to understand all these years. How could he just have let me go like that?

"Please," Mother said, interrupting my thoughts. "It would mean so much to him if you came."

"Where is he?" I asked as I struggled to come to some kind of decision.

"I already told you," she said sounding worried. "He's at Greenville Memorial. Are you okay? You sound odd. And it almost sounds like you're slurring."

At first, I started to tell her that she was imagining things as usual. But instead, I took another sip from the bottle and smacked my lips loudly, hoping she'd hear.

"Maybe I am," I said with a sense of satisfaction. "Because right now, I'm sitting here with a bottle of Jack and Coke in my hand. What do you think of that, Mother?"

The phone line was quiet. Then after a few seconds, "just come home, please," she said in a small voice.

I let out a sigh. "Okay. But just know. I'm coming back for him. Not you." I dropped the phone onto the couch as a feeling of fear enveloped me.

"Who was that?" Dan asked as he picked it up and put it back in the cradle. "Was that your mother? Did I hear you say someone has cancer?"

I turned slowly toward him suddenly feeling more exhausted than angry. Either from the whiskey or the realization of what I had just agreed to do.

"It's my father. He has cancer. What perfect timing for you to go out and have your little affair." I stood up and got my purse.

"I'm so sorry," he said following me.

"I'll be catching the first flight back to South Carolina in the morning," I said as I made my way to the stairs leading up to our bedroom.

"I'll go with you.'

I stopped and turned around. "Are you insane? I don't want you to go with me. I want to be alone. I need to decide if I still even want to be married to you."

"You don't mean that," he said, looking panicked. "You're just upset. We can work things out. Let me go with you."

"No." I turned and walked up the stairs. When I got to the top, I turned around again.

"And don't think that you're sleeping up here with me." I marched into the bedroom, grabbed a pillow off the bed and flung it over the railing before turning around and going into the bedroom again. I slammed the door and just stood there for a moment.

I wanted to do nothing but crawl into bed and drink myself into a stupor. But I took out my phone and forced myself to make travel arrangements.

The screen blurred as tears filled my eyes. After a few minutes of searching for flights to Greenville, I gave up and dialed the airline direct. Sobbing, I told the girl on the phone that my father might be dying, and my husband had cheated on me and I needed a flight to Greenville, South Carolina.

The woman immediately sided with me and helped me out, not only with my plane ticket, but by setting up my rental car too. She said she couldn't find a room in town, but I could call her back later and she would look again. Before she hung up, she reiterated that men were pigs and that I'd be just fine without him.

I dragged my suitcase out of the closet. Just as I started to toss some things in, Dan came in and once again asked if we could talk. But as soon as he saw the look on my face, he got some of his clothes and retreated downstairs again.

The tears came. This time, I didn't try to stop them. Finished packing, with bottle in hand, I climbed into bed as anger, fear, and sadness enveloped me. As I took another sip from the bottle, once more the feeling that life would never be the same again washed over me.

CHAPTER 4

I LOOKED DOWN AT MY WATCH. IT WAS A LITTLE PAST six thirty in the morning and as I stood in line at the John Wayne airport, all I could think of was how nice it would be to just turn around and go home, head back to bed and forget everything that happened yesterday. But I couldn't.

I felt horrible. I was sick to my stomach and had one of the worst headaches I'd ever had in my life. Was this what a hangover felt like? If so, I never wanted another one.

With each step, I could feel shock waves run through my head. And it took everything I had not to bend over and get sick right there on the floor. One thing was for sure. I'd never drink again. You could count on that.

I lifted my suitcase up onto the conveyer belt as another wave of nausea hit me. I bent down to take off my shoes and once again it felt like my head was about to explode. I tossed my pumps along with my purse into another bin and made my way through the security line.

Finally, on the other side, I put my shoes back on and made my way into the terminal. The lights in the airport were so bright that my eyes hurt. So, I fished around in my purse for a pair of sunglasses and put them on before making my way to my gate. Now I knew why Mother wore her sunglasses all the time, even when she was inside the house.

Events from yesterday played through my mind as I found a seat in the boarding area. I could see Dan sitting there at Angelo's with that girl. And I could almost hear the sound of his bike scraping along the ground as I rammed it into the wall. Then, the next thing

I remembered was arguing with him before my mother called me with the news about my father. A wave of sadness came over me.

Was he going to die? I couldn't bear to lose another family member. Things from yesterday were a bit of a blur after that, though I did recall waking up in the middle of the night to find myself on the bathroom floor with my face pressed against the cold tile, and then Dan appearing sometime during the night and helping me into bed.

Then it was morning and he was standing in the doorway, telling me I was going to miss my flight and asking again if he could go with me. I didn't even remember telling him I had booked one.

He wanted to drive me to the airport. At first, I'd told him no. I didn't want anything from him. But once I found out that my car was leaking fluid most likely from running into his motorcycle, and it was too late to call a taxi, I was forced to accept his offer.

I found it sad, in a way, that I didn't have anyone else to take me there. But I had no close friends to speak of, though that was completely my choice. After what happened with my friendship with Beth, I decided it wasn't worth taking the risk of getting close to a friend like that again and chance getting hurt like I did with her.

I looked at my watch again and let out a low groan. This was going to be one long, miserable day. Between the two-and-a-half-hour flight into Dallas where I would make my connection, then another two hours into Greenville, plus, the three-hour east coast time difference, I wouldn't get into South Carolina until early evening. Then I still had to pick up my rental car and drive the half hour or so to my mother's house.

I hated that I was forced to stay with her, though she did sound happy when I called to ask her if I could. The airline reservationist was right. All the hotels in the area were full due to some cross-town rival football game being held in Easley.

There should be rooms available the following week though. So fortunately, I wouldn't have to stay with Mother more than a couple of days. Not that I planned on staying in Easley that long, anyway. Just long enough to make sure my father was okay and then leave, though I wasn't sure where I would go after that.

The line to board the plane moved incredibly slowly. *Please hurry* I thought as I stood there. All I wanted to do was get on, close my eyes and try and get rid of this horrible headache. Maybe another drink would help, I thought, but quickly dismissed that from my mind.

It didn't help that a woman in front of me dressed in an obnoxious bright pink dress had so much perfume on that she smelled like a floral shop. The smell was making me queasy and her loud humming wasn't helping my throbbing head either.

Hopefully, she wouldn't be seated anywhere near me on the plane. But once on the plane, as I looked for my seat, it was just my luck. Perfume lady was looking at the same row.

"It looks like we're going to be traveling buddies," she said in a lilting tone with a huge lipstick covered smile.

I tossed my suitcase in the overhead bin and slid past her, so I could get to my window seat. As she sat down next to me, I quickly turned toward the window hoping she'd get the hint that I wasn't in a talkative mood.

After a few seconds, I heard the humming start back up in full force. With a sigh and a roll of my eyes. I leaned back hoping I'd be able to sleep most of the way.

As soon as we were airborne, the flight attendant made her way down the aisle taking drink requests. I ordered a Sprite hoping it would help settle my stomach and perfume lady ordered a whiskey sour. Just hearing the word whiskey made my stomach turn.

The flight attendant came back a few seconds later with the whiskey sour for her and a can of soda with a glass of ice for me. After a few sips, I settled back into my seat and took a few deep breaths, looking out of the window anxiously.

I'd always been a bit of a nervous flyer and was not looking forward to this flight at all. I took another sip of the soda and squeezed my eyes shut, but as soon as I did, the image of Dan's girlfriend filled my head.

My eyes flew back open. How could I not have noticed that something was going on? The way he'd been in such a good mood the last few weeks, I should have known he was up to something.

But still, I never dreamt it was because of another woman. And here I thought I was smarter than that. I now guessed I wasn't. First Joey, then Dan. How could I have missed the signs that something was wrong with both of them?

I thought back to any other red flags I must have ignored with Dan. He had been out a lot the past few weeks, most of the time down at the gym. But I was just so relieved that he wasn't sitting around the house depressed anymore, I really hadn't given it much thought.

But now I knew the truth. He'd been cheating on me. It made sense now why, whenever I called, it went straight to voicemail. He was with her. And then there were those guilt flowers. He probably got her red roses at the same time he bought my 'friendship' arrangement.

My eyes started to water. How could he do that to me? I looked out the window again. Maybe the plane would go down. That'd fix him.

"Another drink, ladies?"

I looked up to see the flight attendant standing at the end of our row.

"Sure, I'll take another one," my seatmate giggled. "But that's it. Two's my limit." She looked at me and winked as if I was supposed to be in on her little joke.

"Nothing for me, thanks," I said as I reclined my seat back and turned to the window again.

Suddenly, the plane shuddered. My heart raced as I gripped the armrests and looked around, eyes wide with fear. The plane shook again. Nervously, I put the seat back upright.

Even the flight attendant looked frightened as she held onto the beverage cart in an attempt to steady herself.

After a few seconds, the shaking finally stopped, and she started back down the aisle again as if nothing had happened. But she didn't get too far before the plane jerked this time more violently than the first two.

"Stop," I yelled across the cabin.

Several people including the flight attendant turned and looked at me. "Yes? Can I help you?" she asked looking concerned.

"Sorry," I said lowering my voice. "But I changed my mind. Can I get a Jack and Coke please?"

"Sure," she said making her way back to me with the cart.

It's medicinal, I told myself. *Just one drink to get rid of this nagging headache and settle my nerves. Mother always said that a morning-after drink was the perfect cure for 'the hair of the dog that bit you.'*

"In fact, I'll save you another trip," I said taking out my credit card. "Bring me two, please." I handed her the card and seconds later, she set two miniature bottles of whiskey, another glass of ice, and another can of Coke onto my tray.

My hands shook so badly that I could hardly pour the whiskey into the glass of ice without spilling some.

Perfume lady smiled at me, obviously pleased to now have a drinking buddy; she raised her glass.

"Well here's to no more turbulence," she laughed and tapped her glass against mine.

"I'll drink to that," I mumbled as I took a gulp of the Jack and Coke then turned to look out the window again nervously.

I never could understand why some people enjoyed flying so much. With all the shaking, to me it was like being in an earthquake, except it was in the air.

I took another sip as my first experience with an earthquake came to mind. It was the day I'd met Dan. I'd been looking for a contractor to make a built-in entertainment cabinet when I found Dan's service online.

He came the next day and after showing him what I wanted done and agreeing on a price, I let him get started while I went back to the kitchen to finish my cup of coffee.

After a few minutes, the whole room started to shake. At first, I wondered what he was doing to cause it to do that, but when the dishes started to rattle, I knew what it was. I was in my first earthquake.

Being from the South, the only thing I knew about earthquakes at all was from what I'd seen on TV and in the movies where entire buildings crumbled and cars on the freeways were swallowed up whole. The first thing I thought of during the earthquake was how I wished Joey was there to protect me. I always did feel safe when he was around. But he wasn't there, was he? He was far away, by his own choice.

But I wasn't alone. Dan was there in the other room. And he came running into the kitchen and without hesitating, crouched under the table where I now found myself.

I remember how he kept saying, "Don't worry. I'm here. Everything's okay. You're safe."

He never once said I was being silly or overreacting like Joey would have, had he been there. Joey did like to tease me when I got frightened, like the time a snake had gotten into the house and I freaked out. I was so scared that I screamed and ran outside.

Joey laughed at me and came out, wiggling the snake in front of me before tossing it into the woods. He said it was only a Garter snake and was totally harmless, and that as usual, I was making something out of nothing.

But it wasn't nothing to me and for the longest time, I checked under my bed at night in case another snake had somehow slithered in during the day. I never did tell Joey how he'd hurt my feelings by making fun of me.

But Dan wasn't like that. He was sweet and kind. He warned me that there might be a few aftershocks and that I didn't need to be afraid. Then he went back to work but said he was just in the next room if I needed him. Fortunately, there weren't any more tremblers that day. But I really appreciated how kind he was about the whole thing. My heart ached.

Later that afternoon when he was all finished with his work, he called me in to check it out. I could still picture how his blue eyes lit up when he showed me the beautiful solid oak built-in cabinet he had built. I could tell he was proud of his work, as he should have been. He even hooked up my TV, DVD player and stereo.

And turned each one on to make sure they all worked, even helping me to store all my favorite stations.

Before he left, he gave me the bill. I found it cute the way he'd written 'guaranteed to be earthquake proof' on the bottom of it along with his phone number. It was only a few days later when he called to ask me out.

Was he in love with her? Was our marriage over? Even though I'd be totally heartbroken if it was, at least this time I'd know why the relationship ended. Not like when Joey and I split up. I still didn't understand why that happened and wondered if I ever would.

The image of Joey getting into his old pickup truck and driving away flashed before me. How could he have just given up on us like that? After all, he was the one who used to say that one day we'd get married, buy a small cabin up in the mountains, have a couple of kids and enjoy the rest of our lives together.

And yet, when he finally had his chance to be with me, he changed his mind and decided to stay back in Easley and let me go. I was devastated. I remembered how before he'd gotten into his truck, I'd let him know exactly what I thought of him.

I'd stood out in the driveway, calling him every name in the book, telling him he was not only a coward but a liar too, and how I never wanted to see or talk to him again.

It was so strange how he simply leaned against the vehicle, looking at me without saying a word, then just got into his truck as I got into my car and we both drove away. And I remember how my heart was breaking as I drove the opposite way, knowing I hadn't meant all the awful things I'd said in the heat of that moment, and hoping he knew that.

As I was leaving, I kept looking into my rearview mirror, half expecting to find him behind me, chasing me down. But he never did. I even considered turning around several times and going back, but for what? There wasn't anything left for me in Easley anymore. And for the first time in my life, I realized just how completely alone I was. And now I was alone again.

But I told myself back then, that no matter how dreadful things got, I'd never set foot back in that town again, and I meant it. And it wasn't like anyone was going to miss me much anyway besides Joey. At least in time, I hoped he would.

I left. I left Mother, who barely knew I existed most of the time. And I left my father who'd pretty much become a ghost. And I left Beth, my supposedly very best friend who hadn't even bothered going to my brother's funeral.

I left them all, though they'd abandoned me long before I went, and probably didn't realize that I'd even gone.

James' leaving was what hurt me the most of all. And though I realized he had to have been in a tremendous amount pain to do what he did, his death nearly destroyed me. Didn't he care at all what his suicide would do to me?

"Honey, are you okay?"

"Yes, why do you ask?" I asked, as I turned to perfume lady.

She took the magazine she was reading and set it on her lap, then reached into her purse to pull out a pack of tissues. She handed me the pack and smiled with a sympathetic look. I looked at her confused at first but took the tissues anyway. As I held them, I felt a tear dripping off my chin. I hadn't even realized I'd started crying.

"I'm sure it's the turbulence," I said as I dried my eyes quickly.

"I'm sure that's what it is," she agreed with a small smile. "I don't like it much either. That's why I drink these." She held up her cocktail. "How about we talk a bit and get your mind off all this nasty shaking?" she asked. But before I could answer, she proceeded to tell me her life story, whether I wanted to hear it or not. She was just one of *those* people, the annoying ones who enjoyed everything the world had to offer and couldn't bear to see someone else miserable. At least she hadn't told me to smile.

"I usually travel for business but this time it's a personal trip," she said. "I'm from San Diego and on my way to Atlanta for a family reunion. I'm so excited, too. There's going to be about eighty of us there and I haven't seen most of them in well over twenty years.

"I've been dieting all month too," she said, patting her stomach proudly, "so I can fit into this new dress. Do you like it?" But before I could reply, she took a long sip of her drink and continued. "Well, enough about me. What about you? Where do you call home?"

I stared at her. I wasn't quite sure how to answer. Home used to be in South Carolina, with Joey, and I'd never pictured it anywhere else back then. But once I realized I couldn't stay there anymore and left to start a new life, my home was California.

I hadn't planned on settling there at first, but I knew I had to find a job, and the only thing I was good at was acting. That's when, as ridiculous as it sounded, I knew Hollywood was the place for me. So, I pointed the car in that direction and drove, only stopping long enough to get some sleep, until I ended up in LA.

I was excited when I got there but wasn't totally naïve. I knew plenty of people went to Hollywood with the same dream and ended up waiting tables forever because they never did make it in acting. But I was determined to try, even if it meant sleeping in my car. At least the weather would be nice in Southern California if it came down to that.

And so, for the past eight years, Los Angeles had been my new home. But now I wasn't sure where to call home. The woman stared back at me, then after a few minutes, patted my hand sympathetically before going back to her magazine. I sadly turned away and stared out the window again as I felt the tears start to flow once more.

—

Twenty minutes later, both bottles of whiskey were empty, and my headache was gone. And sure enough the turbulence didn't seem to bother me as much. Plus, that warm feeling in my stomach was back too. Maybe things weren't that bad after all. But as I looked at my watch, I realized we had to be halfway to Dallas and that much closer to Easley. The fear set in. I closed my eyes, wishing I'd never agreed to go back.

CHAPTER 5

MY EYES FLEW OPEN AND I LOOKED AROUND WILDLY. What was I doing on a plane? But as I looked around the cabin, it all came back. I was on my way back to my hometown, and by the looks of things, we were about to land soon. My stomach knotted up.

I looked for my drink, but the tray was already up, my glass gone. Disappointed, I turned to the window and gripped the armrests as I tried to think of a way out of this. But there wasn't one.

After a bumpy landing, we pulled up to the gate. Seatbelt lights off, I tried to stand up, but my legs felt so wobbly, I had to sit right back down again. After a moment, I tried again and struggled to get my suitcase from the overhead bin. Perfume lady reached past me, took it down as if it was nothing at all and set it on the ground. Somewhat embarrassed, I thanked her and followed her and the other passengers out in the direction of the terminal.

She had helped me on that whole trip, all the way through, and I should have been thankful. But instead, I felt somehow resentful, twisted up inside. How could some people find life so easy, while for me it was always this perpetual struggle, even to the point where I couldn't get my own bag out of a bin? It seemed so unfair. I stared at the back of the woman's head, wondering if she felt my eyes boring into her, envious of her life, or the one I imagined she had.

Halfway down the tarmac, she suddenly stopped and whirled around and came back toward me. She leaned in close, too close—so close, in fact, that I could smell the whiskey on her breath.

"I hope you find your brother, sweetie," she whispered in my face. She looked at me for a second, then dropped her suitcase and reached out to give me a big hug. I felt very uncomfortable as I stood there with her arms around me with that overbearing perfume assailing my nostrils, but at the same time, a part of me never wanted the embrace to end. It was a hug at a time I really needed one, and for that I was thankful.

Finally, she let me go, wished me luck, picked up her suitcase and hurried away toward the terminal doors. As I watched her go, I tried to make sense of what she'd just said. My mind whirred.

I hadn't told her anything about my brother, had I? What did I say? Well, who knew, maybe I'd been talking in my sleep again; Joey had said I used to do that, when things got stressful. As I continued to stand there in the middle of the tarmac, the passengers still leaving the aircraft were forced to make their way around me, some glancing back. But they had lives to go to, appointments to keep. They scurried away. An airport attendant hurried up to me, probably thinking I was having a stroke or something. And to be honest, I felt very strange.

"Excuse me, Miss, you look confused. Do you need some help? He led me the rest of the way into the terminal then reached for my ticket which I realized I was clutching tightly in my sweaty palm. I looked down at it, unfurling my fingers and letting him take it for a moment. He scrutinized it, squinting. It was crumpled and looked useless now, just like I felt. "I ruined my ticket," I said in a small voice, almost feeling like I was going to cry. "I'm sorry."

Such a small, silly thing to cry about. It was only a ticket. But again, seeing it wadded up in my hand, it highlighted how utterly hopeless I felt on my own—always on my own, with no one at my side. My eyes stung. *Don't cry. Don't cry.*

"Look, it doesn't matter, honey," he said. "Ticket's fine, as long as they can read it. You won't be the first to crumple one up due to nerves. Anyway, Gate C-19…it's in the next terminal," he said pointing down the hall. "That way, where the green sign is. But you'd better hurry. It will be boarding soon."

He handed the mess of a ticket back to me and I thanked him and headed in the direction he'd pointed. Still woozy from either the flight or the drinks, I wasn't sure which, I walked half in a daze down the terminal walkways. I slowed up as I came to the women's washroom, hoping I still had enough time for a quick stop. I splashed some cool water onto my face before I got ready to leave, hoping it would wake me up. Then I looked back at my reflection in the mirror.

Up until now, I never noticed just how much I looked like my mother. I knew we were both tall and thin, but our faces were the same too. Between the high cheek bones, the square jaw and the deep-set hazel eyes, we looked more alike than I cared to admit. And other than my hair being blonde and short now, while hers when I'd left was long and deep brown, the resemblance was startling and unnerving at the same time. Was I slowly turning into her? I shuddered.

I grabbed another paper towel and dried my face, then hurried back out into the terminal. Once at the gate, I had just enough time to buy some potato chips from a nearby kiosk and got in line for boarding.

As soon as I was settled on the plane, I pictured seeing her for the first time. How was I going to feel? Would it be emotional when she opened the door and I saw her? Or would I even feel anything at all? After all, we never did have your typical mother-daughter relationship.

Between her drinking and fretting over James, sometimes I felt sure she forgot she even had a daughter. At least my father and I had been close, that was, until I got a little older anyway. But when I was young, he'd always been there for me in a way my mother never was.

He was the one who'd always been there after school, ready with something to eat for me and James. And it was Dad who asked about our day or took us shopping. He taught us how to ride a bike and do a lot of things, like how to fish and shoot guns. He'd taught me to be the self-reliant tomboy I was supposed to turn into. But somehow, it'd never happened that way; I had all the skills but none of the mental toughness. Inside, I had always been Daddy's girl and I still needed him, as hard as it was to admit.

I used to love to go up to the target range he'd built behind our house way up on a hill. He'd originally built it for James so they could have something special to do together. But between James' difficulty walking up the hill and his asthma, it became too much for him to try and go up to the range. The solution was obvious then. So, my father had started taking me up there instead.

It occurred to me now, just how much that must have bothered James that I got to go with him while he couldn't because he'd tried and failed. What had always been intended as James' treat, I'd taken away. Why had I never even realized how James must have felt about that? Was I that selfish? Maybe I was like my mother.

The flight into Greenville wouldn't be long, and as I looked out the window once again, I wondered one last time how it was going to feel when I got there and had to see her again. Hopefully, I'd have had enough time to get a drink or two down before we landed, so I could prepare myself.

By the time we started to descend, I'd managed to get down a couple Jack and Cokes and was feeling little pain once again. It was a good state to be in—at least, as far as I was concerned. I even ordered two of the little bottles to take with me and stashed them in my purse. I was as ready as I'd ever be to see her, yet my stomach was still in knots, still churning.

"Welcome to Greenville Spartanburg where the local time is 5:51 p.m. and the temperature is 72 degrees. Hope y'all enjoyed your flight. Please make sure all your belongings are with you and have a pleasant stay," the flight attendant said cheerfully as we touched down. I grabbed my bag. It was too late to turn around now.

I walked outside of the terminal, when the warm air smacked me right in the face. I'd forgotten how hot and humid the summers were in the South.

Wiping my forehead, I made my way to the car rental desk in the next building, dragging my suitcase along on its tiny wheels. I set my bag down finally at the service desk and tried to catch my breath, already feeling the effects of the humidity. And I was having a difficult time keeping my balance for some reason.

The girl at the counter looked me over, then handed me the keys to my rental, nonchalant, as if she was bored or simply couldn't be bothered.

Maybe that was a good thing, because she hadn't picked up on the condition, I was in. But as I headed for the car, the fleeting thought that maybe I shouldn't be driving came to me. After all, the only thing I'd eaten in hours was a bag of chips and a handful of pretzels on the plane—and I had been drinking, and then drinking some more. As irresponsible as my mother was, that was one thing she always stressed with me and James.

"Never get behind the wheel of a car if you've been drinking," she would say.

Her father had been a heavy drinker and was involved in a terrible car accident coming home from a bar when she was young, and it had left a strong impression on her. Not that she shouldn't drink of course, but that she should never drink and drive.

But her warning had fallen on deaf ears. After all, she didn't have to worry about me or James ever drinking, did she? But as I stood there, her words rang in my head, a warning bell. I turned around and walked back to the rental desk and handed the keys back to the girl at the counter.

"I'm sorry," I said, feeling and I was sure looking sheepish, "but I'm not feeling well enough to drive. Must have been something I ate on the plane," I quickly added feeling my face blush. "Can I come back for the car tomorrow?"

She took the keys after giving me a dubious look and explained she'd have to charge me for today due to the late notice. I nodded weakly and picked up my suitcase and slowly headed back to the terminal where a line of taxis stood out front.

After a moment, an older man in faded blue jeans and a plaid shirt walked up to me and without asking, took my suitcase and placed it in his open trunk. He opened the back door of his cab and smiled.

"Where you headed, little lady?" he asked in a thick southern drawl with a little bow.

"Easley," I replied as I wiped a bead of sweat off my upper lip.

"No problem. It sure is a hot one, today isn't it?" he smiled. "Your first time in South Carolina?"

"No, I actually grew up in Easley," I replied as I climbed into the cab. "But I moved to California years ago. Needed a change."

"Well, welcome back," he said before shutting the door. "Nice place, I hear." As I waited, he slowly got into the driver's side and adjusted the rearview mirror. He turned on the meter. "You got family here?"

"Yes," I said and proceeded to give him the address of my mother's house without going into any more detail. He punched it into his GPS then turned around.

"That's way out on the far side of Easley. Are you sure you don't have someone you can call to come get you? It's a shame to have to spend so much on a cab."

I looked at him somewhat surprised. If this was LA, most drivers would have been thrilled to take the big fare. Yet this sweet man was only concerned with saving me money. I really was in the South.

"No. I don't have anyone to call, but thanks for asking," I replied somewhat sadly.

And it was true. Once again, I had no one, and I refused to ask my mother to come get me. Besides, she was probably drunk just the same as I almost was.

And I wouldn't dare ask Joey. It was much too soon to think about seeing him, anyway. And I couldn't ask Beth since we hadn't spoken since I left. Besides, she might not even live in Easley anymore. So, just like this morning when I'd had no one to call to take me to the airport, I didn't have anyone to call now. My eyes welled as it hit me once again how lonely I was.

"It's okay," the driver said as he looked at me in his rearview mirror. "I'll give you the special friends and family fare. How 'bout that?"

I forced a smile. "Thanks," I said as I felt a tear slide down my face. Without saying another word, he headed out of the terminal and jumped on the highway leading to Easley. For the next fifteen minutes, we drove in silence and my eyes tracked the familiar and yet ever-changing landscape that we passed. As we got closer to

Easley, a feeling of dread came over me again. In less than twenty minutes, I'd be walking back into the house that held so many painful horrible memories from my childhood. I leaned my head back and closed my eyes as I fought the fear.

—

"Miss, we're here."

I opened my eyes. Where was I? But chills ran down my spine as I looked out the cab door. Though it was getting dark now, I could still recognize the single-story brick house looming in front of me. I was back at my old family home.

I sat there unable to move as the driver stood waiting, his broad hand resting on the open rear door where he was letting me out. I wanted to tell him to take me right back to the airport, when the front porch light came on and the door swung open.

Mother stuck her head out. "Karen?" she called out.

Under the light, she appeared older than when I'd last seen her. But that was over eight years ago. She hurried down from the porch.

"That will be $22 even," the driver said as he lifted my suitcase out of the trunk and set it onto the ground.

"Let me get my wallet," my mother said turning back toward the house.

"I've got it," I said as I reached for my purse. But as I pulled out my wallet, my purse fell, and everything spilled out onto the ground. I hit my head on the car doorframe as I bent down quickly to retrieve my items.

"You okay, Miss?" the driver asked, crouching to help me.

"I'm fine thanks," I said quickly tossing everything back in before he or Mother had a chance to see the two tiny liquor bottles on the ground. I straightened up and took two twenty-dollar bills out of my wallet, stuffing them into his hand. "Keep the change."

"You sure?" he asked as I walked away. I glanced back and thought he looked a little confused, here having arranged a cheaper fare for me and then I'd gone and given it back anyway.

"Yes, thanks," I replied as I hurried up the steps and right past my mother, suitcase in hand. From the corner of my eye, I saw her smile fade. I stopped at the front door, took a deep breath and opened the door.

When I stepped in, I was immediately thrown back in time as an uneasy feeling came over me. I took another step and stopped in front of the large framed photo of me, James and my parents hanging in the foyer.

Didn't we just look like the perfect, happy family standing there with our fake little smiles, I thought as I leaned in closer. Pictures could be so deceiving. I well-remembered the day it was taken, and we'd been anything but happy.

Mother had been drunk as usual and she and Dad had been fighting all morning, as they always did. And James and I had stood there miserable, listening to them bicker while the photographer snapped away, asking every few minutes for everyone to smile.

I was still not sure why Mother insisted on having that photo taken, but in a way, I was glad she did. Little did she know that this would be the last picture taken of us all together.

I touched the photo gently with the tip of my finger. Sometimes, I still found it hard to believe James and I were brother and sister, let alone twins. There I was, skinny and tall with long unruly hair, dressed in an old tee shirt and a pair of jeans. While James, on the other hand, who was shorter like my father was, had every hair in place, dressed in pressed slacks and a nice sweater.

Our personalities were just as different as our appearances, too. I was loud, a bit messy, and always all over the place, while James was organized, and typically quiet and reserved. I jumped as the front door closed behind me.

"I'm so glad we had that picture taken of all of us before James…left," Mother said softly.

I picked up my suitcase and headed toward the hallway, just leaving her standing there. I didn't know what to say and couldn't find any words.

"Are you hungry?" she asked following me. "I made you something to eat. It's your favorite, spaghetti and meatballs."

My favorite? How would she even know what my favorite was? We'd barely spoken since I was a child. Or, even when we'd spoken, her mind had not exactly been present. Besides, the word spaghetti immediately made me think about Dan and that girl at Angelo's. I turned and looked at my mother, and now the words found me.

"Thanks, but that's the last thing I want," I said firmly.

She backed up slightly and stood there looking taken aback. And I knew I had just come across as rude and ungrateful, but the words had bitten out and escaped of their own accord, and there was no taking them back—especially not for this woman. I wouldn't even try.

"Okay, how about something to drink?" she asked.

"Look, it's been a long day. I just want to get some sleep and go see Dad in the morning," I said this time in a softer tone. "By the way, how is he?"

"He's hanging in there," she said. "They're running more tests tomorrow, so we should know more then. "You sure I can't get you something to eat before you go to bed?"

I thought about Dan again and my eyes brimmed with tears. "No thanks," I said, and with that, I went into my bedroom and shut the door. She hadn't earned the right to see me cry. As soon as I knew she was gone, I slid onto the floor and let it out.

I cried over Dan, over my father, and most of all about being back in this house.

But after a few minutes, I forced myself to get up again. I might as well unpack a few things and try and get some sleep. I had a big day tomorrow.

I looked around the room. After all these years, it felt so strange being in my bedroom again. Although back then it had sometimes been a refuge from the fighting, at times it had also felt like a prison. I looked around some more and was surprised at how much smaller it was then I remembered. But otherwise, everything pretty much looked the same as when I left.

I sat down on the bed and ran my hand over my old comforter. I reached up and slid my hand up the wall. On the other side was James' bedroom. I tapped on the wall three times just like I used to when we were young, our way of saying goodnight to each other. As we got older, we didn't do it as much but every now and then, I'd hear him tap and I'd tap back, just for the sake of it, to know each other were there. I held my breath, almost expecting to hear it now. Hoping to hear it.

A sudden wave of sadness swept through me. Instead of hearing the tap back, all I heard was the echo of the many nights I'd spent listening to my parents fight right outside this door.

Sometimes, it had been so bad that I'd have to bury my face into my pillow, so James wouldn't hear me crying from his room. I'd promised myself that as soon as I was out of high school, I was going to move out and never have to listen to my parents argue again. But my father had been the one to move out before any of that happened—or, should I say, Mother had kicked him out. I can picture him now as he gathered up his clothes that Mother had strewn all over the front yard. The memory was as if it had just happened yesterday.

Our high school bus had just pulled up and James and I were about to step off when there she was, standing on the front porch in her housecoat, screaming her lungs out at my father. That was all she ever wore, too, that dirty white housecoat, unless she was going out, then she'd wear her grey velour jumpsuit that was usually stained too.

I could almost hear the kids on the bus howling with laughter right now, recalling how James and I got off and ran past both our parents and into the house, both of us mortally embarrassed. And the next day, our father was gone. He'd moved out. It was just the three of us now. James and I had finally gotten our wish and the fighting was over.

But it wasn't long before we both wondered if maybe it would have been better if our dad had never left. Now we were left on our own to deal with *her* and her non-stop drinking and mood swings.

I never could understand how our father was able to just leave so easily, without putting up a fight. Didn't he love me and James at all?

The more I thought about how he'd just abandoned us there with her, the more upset I got. Sure, Mother might have been happy to see him go so she could drink in peace without him nagging her, but James and I needed him, needed his help dealing with her. He should have thought of that—but he was gone. And after a while, I made sure to be gone too as much as I could, so I didn't have to be around her either.

And other than seeing Dad at school when he came to watch me in a play, or when I stopped at his shop, James and I had rarely seen him much after he'd left. And now here I was seeing him again after all these years, maybe for the last time. I wasn't quite sure how I felt about that but knew I was still angry.

I got up and went into the bathroom. I flicked on the light and was startled at how terrible I looked. I had dark circles under my eyes and my mascara was smeared.

My hair was a mess too. As I washed my face, I had to wonder what Mother must have thought when she saw me. But what did I care? She used to look this way all the time.

I shut the light off and put a few things from my suitcase away, then crawled into bed. I was bone-tired. But as I lay there, I started to tense up again, subconsciously waiting for the fighting to begin in the room across the hall. And even though that was a long time ago and my parents were divorced now, I put my pillow over my head and cried myself to sleep, just like old times.

CHAPTER 6

I FLUNG MY ARM OUT TO THE SIDE OF ME AND GROPED around for Dan. No one was there. I opened my eyes. It was just starting to get light and I was alone in a strange bed. Where was I and where was Dan?

But as soon as I saw the old familiar ceiling fan spinning lazily over my head. I remembered. I was back in my old bed in Easley, and he was far away in California, most likely with *her*. Sadness and anger swept over me and I lay there as I came to grips once again with what had gone down yesterday. I wished the sleep could have taken me and kept me there, the restful, peace-filled sleep. But now I'd had to wake again, to the memories, and the loneliness.

There was a blue quilt draped across my chest. Mother must have come in sometime during the night and put it on me. Another wave of sadness washed over me as I thought about her. I wished things had been different back then. But they were not different. They were as they were, and that was her choice.

My mind shifted to hunger as the scent of coffee and bacon wafted under the door and my stomach started to growl. I got up and made my way to the door.

When I opened it, she was already coming up the hall. She had on a pretty, flowery blouse with matching slacks and an apron tied around her waist. She looked so different from the woman who had never much cared about her appearance in the past. I thought of her dirty white housecoat again, wondering if she still had it.

"Oh, you're up," she said, smiling. "I just came to tell you that breakfast is ready." She turned and headed back to the kitchen. I stared at her as she walked away. Breakfast? Since when did she ever cook breakfast?

As far as I could remember, the only breakfast she made was when she put a box of Captain Crunch cereal on the counter with a carton of milk and warned me and James not to make a mess before she headed back into her bedroom with her bottle to spend the morning.

I stood there for a moment. I didn't want her breakfast. I didn't want anything from her, but the smell of bacon was too good to resist. So, I followed her to the kitchen.

She was at the stove when I walked in. "How'd you sleep? I bet it was strange to be back in your own bed, wasn't it?"

I pulled out a chair and sat down and didn't reply. I glanced over at the empty space where James used to sit. I forced myself to look away.

Mother had turned from the stove and was staring at me. I had to admit, she did look pretty this morning, and happier than I ever remembered seeing her. I wondered if it had something to do with me being here but quickly dismissed the thought. She'd never seemed to care when I was around. Why would she now?

"Why are you looking at me like that?" I asked, feeling uncomfortable as she continued to stand there staring.

"Oh, it's your hair. That's all. It's so different. Not that I don't like it..." she quickly added before turning back to the stove. She flipped over a piece of bacon that was sizzling in the pan. "How do you want your eggs? Do you still like them over easy?" she asked taking one out of the carton.

I looked at her with the egg in her hand standing there looking like Mrs. Cleaver. Who was this woman and what had they done with my mother? And how would she have the slightest idea how I liked my eggs?

"Over easy is fine." I grunted.

She turned back to the stove and cracked some eggs, dropping them in the frying pan. I watched in amazement as she removed the skillet of bacon from one of the burners. Setting several pieces of the bacon onto a paper towel, she headed to the coffee maker and poured a cup.

She set the cup in front of me and slid the container of creamer my way before heading back to the stove. She flipped over the eggs and while they cooked, she walked over to the refrigerator and pulled out a carton of juice.

I tensed up. She used to start the day with Jack Daniels and juice. She thought she was fooling everyone, but we all knew she put whiskey in it, especially after I'd accidentally tasted it that one morning and ended up spitting it out all over the table.

But surprisingly, this time she filled her glass with just plain orange juice. She poured me a glass. As I drank it, I realized this had to be the first time I could remember that she didn't put liquor in her juice. I was almost disappointed in a way. I wouldn't have minded something strong in my own juice right about now, to help take the edge off of being around her.

"What's wrong?" she asked as I set the glass down.

"Well, to tell you the truth, I'm just surprised you're not putting some Jack in there," I replied as I nodded in the direction of her glass.

This time, she looked surprised. "Don't you know? I quit drinking years ago. I told you that on one of the voicemails I left you a while back. Didn't you listen to any of my messages?"

I thought back to the couple of times she'd called. Once I saw she'd left a voicemail, I'd immediately delete it without listening. Just the sound of her voice brought back a flood of painful memories. I called her back once, demanding on her voicemail that she quit calling. After that, she had stopped, up until this last call about my father.

"No, I didn't know," I said, unable to hide my surprise as I wondered if it was really true.

"I wanted you to know," she said sounding disappointed. "Too bad you're just finding out about it now. Maybe…." Her voice trailed off.

She put the eggs onto a plate and set it down in front of me before fixing her own. She buttered some toast and pulled out a chair.

I picked up a fork and scooped some eggs into my mouth, knowing what she was about to say. Would it have made any difference had I known it back then that she'd finally stopped drinking? I swallowed the eggs along with the rather large lump in my throat. I doubted it. I still wouldn't have taken her calls. I had nothing to say to her. We were strangers.

She suddenly reached her hand across the table toward me just as I picked up a piece of bacon. "Would you mind if we said grace before we ate?"

I stopped chewing and stared at her outstretched hand. "What? Don't tell me that you started praying again. After what God did to us?"

I shook my head in disbelief. There was a time when all she'd done was talk to God and pray and drag us all to church on Sundays. I didn't like going much, but at least I knew she'd be sober for a few hours until we got back home. But when things got really bad between her and Dad, she started to change, as if she was angry with God. After that, I noticed she didn't pray anymore and eventually stopped going to Sunday service.

Several women from the church came around now and then and tried to get her to go back. Even Pastor Phil stopped by a few times. But Mother made it clear to him that she wanted nothing to do with his church or his God and to go away. Eventually, everyone gave up and stopped coming by, and I never heard her mention God in our home again.

"Things have a way of bringing us back to Him," she said with a sad smile as she dropped her hand.

"Well that won't happen with me," I said. "I want nothing to do with God after he let James die up there all by himself. Who does that?" Again, the lump in my throat was back.

"That was tragic," she said. "But James wasn't alone."

I stared at her, the anger building.

"Oh, really, Mother? And how would you know that? Were you there too?" I practically threw the piece of bacon down on the plate and jumped up as the memory of that day came rushing back.

"Oh, that's right," I continued, my heart beating faster. "You couldn't know because as usual, you were passed out in your room while my twin brother bled to death."

A wave of hurt flickered across her face. She opened her mouth as if about to say something but closed it again and, after a moment, bowed her head. I could tell she had started to pray by her mumbled words.

"Great," I said as I shoved my chair back. "Tell you what, why don't you and God stay here and have a nice little chat together? I'll finish the rest of this in my room."

She raised her head slightly then put it down again and went back to her soft mumbling. Furious, I grabbed my coffee cup along with my plate and stormed down the hall toward my bedroom.

When I got there, I slammed the door hard enough so she could hear, then set the cup and dish on the dresser. I was shaking as I sat on the edge of the bed, attempting to shove my tears down. How could she forgive God after everything that had happened? I couldn't. I wouldn't. Not ever. And I would never step foot in a church again either.

I thought back to when Dan and I had been planning our wedding, how we were at odds about where to have it. He wanted the ceremony at the same church he sometimes went to with his mother. But I begged him to keep it simple and for us to have it anywhere but in a church.

So, he agreed to have a small gathering on Laguna Beach performed by a friend of his who was an ordained minister, which was just fine with me.

I remember that even as we made our vows, I'd had a feeling God was up there, watching. But I refused to acknowledge Him even then.

I reached over and picked up a piece of toast. As I chewed it, a tear slid down my nose and fell onto the plate. What had made me think I could come back here? I should have known that being in this house again would prove to be too hard.

I thought about what Mother said about having quit drinking. Was it possible that after all those years of Dad nagging her before he started to go to Alanon meetings, that she finally decided to go to Alcoholics Anonymous herself?

I remembered how hard he'd tried to get me and James to go to Alateen at the same time, saying it would help us feel better and cope with her drinking, but we weren't having any of that.

I guessed that would explain her starting up praying again. I heard they prayed a lot at those AA meetings. Well, even if she was telling the truth and had finally quit, I wasn't so sure I liked this sober version of her any better than the drunk one. At least I'd known what to expect when she was drunk, and one thing was for sure. If she was sober, it wouldn't last. As soon as things didn't go her way, she'd go right back to the bottle again.

—

I finished the rest of my breakfast and took my cup and went into the bathroom. Once again, when I looked at myself in the mirror, I was shocked, realizing I was looking like she used to when she drank. I started the shower. Maybe that would help my disposition.

But when I got out, I realized that in my haste to leave California, I'd forgotten to pack a blow dryer. I looked through several bathroom drawers, but there wasn't one anywhere to be found. With a towel wrapped around my head, I headed down the hall to James' room to see if maybe there was one in there. But when I got there, I stopped at the doorway, hesitant to go in. I hadn't been in this room since I'd left.

With a lump in my throat, I summoned up all the courage I had and stepped inside.

The room immediately felt stuffy and depressing. Hurrying to the window, I opened the curtains hoping some light might make the room more inviting, but it didn't. I looked around. Just as in my room, James' bedroom looked like nothing much had been changed. It was if Mother thought that by leaving our rooms untouched, she could somehow stop time. But that wouldn't stop time, and it wouldn't bring James back.

I turned toward the desk where my brother had spent so much of his time and was surprised to see his old laptop was still there. Next to it was a picture of me and James taken at one of my plays. I looked at it closer and recognized it from the Wizard of Oz.

It was my first big part and I'd been terrified that I was going to mess up. But then I'd looked out into the audience to see James sitting there in the front row next to my father, and instantly I'd felt better.

Mother wasn't there, of course. She'd much rather stay home and drink than go see her own daughter in a school play. Even Joey went along to watch it most nights, but the chair next to James that had been saved for Mother was always empty.

I felt the hurt again as I set the photo down.

I sat down at the desk and lifted the lid of his laptop. As I ran my fingers over the keyboard, I could picture James in this same seat, tapping away. His fingers used to fly over the keyboard, he was so good with computers. He could fix anything, and what started as a favor here and there for a classmate or a teacher, turned out to be quite a pretty good business for him. Eventually, he was able to work on many of his client's computers remotely, right here in his room.

I got up and walked over to his bookcase and browsed some of the titles of his books. James loved to read, too. He didn't care if it was westerns or mysteries, or non-fiction. Other than fixing computers and driving his car, reading was the only other thing James liked to do.

It worked out well for him though, especially when the weather was so hot and humid that he couldn't go outside because of his asthma.

Halfway down the bookcase, I noticed a thick black book on one of the shelves. I slid it out and saw it was a bible, one book I didn't expect to find here in his bookcase. After all, neither one of us had been to church in a very long time.

I gingerly opened it and a photo fell out onto the floor. I bent down and picked it up. I was surprised to find it was a picture of my old best friend Beth. In it, she was smiling. I held it up closer. Why would James have a photo of her?

With a stab of pain, it brought back memories I'd carefully tucked away. Not only of James, but of Beth and how distant we'd become even before James killed himself.

At first when she stopped coming by the house, I assumed it was because she couldn't take being around Mother and her drinking. But then, when she stopped returning any of my phone calls and started to avoid me at school, I knew it had to be more than that.

But Beth kept insisting she was just busy with school. It was our senior year after all, and she said that as soon as things calmed down, we'd get together. But I didn't believe her. She'd changed, and I didn't know what to do. That was when it hit me. She'd just broken up with her boyfriend Steve, and it was Joey's birthday, so what if I played cupid and set her up with my brother? I thought it was a great idea at the time, but soon found out just what a mistake it was.

The whole night felt awkward at dinner, like there was an elephant in the room. And then Steve somehow found out that the four of us were at Applebee's and he showed up. Everything got crazy after that. Steve let us all know that he was upset that Beth was there without him. And he took it out on James.

I felt like jumping across the table and laying into Steve after some of the things he'd said to my brother. But fortunately for him, Beth dragged him out long before I had the chance to. And that was that.

Then Joey took me and James home and none of us talked about that night again, though I realized after the fact that maybe I should have brought it up. At least with James.

Tears pooled in my eyes. If only I'd checked to see if James was okay that night, like I'd intended to. But it was all just bad timing, that's all. After James and I had gone inside, Joey had snuck into my bedroom through the window like he often did back then, and I'd forgotten all about James and how cruel Steve had been to him.

My mind went back to how strangely Joey was acting that night, too, the way he kept saying how he needed to tell me something very important and we'd talk about it over breakfast the following morning.

Joey had mentioned several times during my senior year how he wanted to get married one day. So, I assumed between that and how he'd seemed so distracted lately, that maybe he was getting ready to ask me to marry him that next morning? It made sense, the timings all fit together.

What better place to propose than where we went to on our first date—the Huddle House? I was sure that was it and I was so excited, I barely got any sleep that night. After Joey left, I just lay there envisioning how he was going to pop the question. Would he go the traditional route where he'd get down on one knee right there in the restaurant? Or maybe he was going to hide the ring in my hash browns or grits?

Well, however he did it, I was determined to act surprised like I had no idea it was coming. I even got up several times during the night to practice my shocked reaction in the mirror when he did propose. And never once did I bother to go in and check on James to see if he was okay after what had happened at Applebee's. How could I have been so selfish? I felt that familiar pang of guilt.

Then before I knew it, it was morning. I made sure to take time to pick out something to wear that I knew Joey liked to see me in, and after carefully putting on my makeup, I headed outside to go wait for him on the front porch. That was when James stopped me in the hallway.

I could still picture his face, standing there in the hall, puffing on his inhaler. He appeared to be so nervous. I should have known something was wrong, but right as he began to tell me something, Mother started hollering that Joey was outside waiting for me. So, after promising James we'd talk later after I got home, I headed off with Joey to the Huddle House.

All during breakfast, I kept waiting but Joey never even brought up the subject of marriage. I had gotten it completely wrong. Either he had never planned to propose, or for some reason, changed his mind. Later that morning, after he dropped me off at the house again, I went straight to my room and was so depressed, I yet again forgot all about my promise to find James, so we could talk. But later that afternoon, I did remember. And that was when I went looking for him.

I remembered how his Mustang was in the barn, so I knew he had to be around somewhere. I had asked Mother if she knew where he was, but she wasn't sure and as usual she was lit, though she did say she had heard some gunshots earlier up at the range. Well, that wasn't making any sense; why would James go there? It was the last place I'd expect to find him.

James hadn't gone up to the range since Dad built it, for the simple reason it was too hard on him with his asthma and bad leg and all. So, I figured she was wrong. I hoped she was wrong. She had to be, didn't she? Because if James was at the range, there was only one reason to be—

And then it came, fragmenting my thoughts in the way I had dreaded.

A gunshot came, and I just knew. My world had imploded in that second.

I wiped my eyes, once again feeling the terror, self-blame and horror of that day. I recalled how I'd panicked and ran all the way up the stony hill without stopping, my chest hurting like it was about to cave in from the sheer effort of it all, all the while breathing hard and moaning like a wounded animal.

But when I got there it was too late. James laid there crumpled on the ground, soaked with blood. It was obvious that he was dead. I wanted to get down in the dirt and cradle him, but I couldn't. I was too terrified. All I could do was run and that's what I did, all the way back down the hill to the house.

And then came that strange buzzing sound, *buzz, buzz,* the very same noise I had heard yesterday in Angelo's, the ringing in my tormented ears. So, that was when I had heard it last.

"James sure loved to read, didn't he?" came the voice. I turned around swiftly, startled to find Mother standing in the doorway. I wondered how long she'd been standing there spying on me.

"I was looking for a blow-dryer," I stammered as I tried to clear my head of all the awful memories. As I stood there, I felt a wave of guilt now come over me like I shouldn't have been going through James' things and started to slip the photo back into the bible. When she came and gently took the picture from my hand. She looked down at it and smiled.

"He sure had a sweet spot for Beth, didn't he?"

I looked back up at her. "What makes you say that?"

"Well, you know how he was whenever Beth came to the house to see you," she replied still looking down at the picture in her hand. "He wasn't as good at hiding his feelings as you were."

"And what's that supposed to mean?" I asked, immediately feeling defensive.

She looked up at me. "You know how you could be," she said softly. "You never did like to show your true feelings." She handed the photo back to me. "Not that that's a bad thing though," she continued sounding wistful. "I wish I was able to do that more often."

I stared at her for a moment, surprised she'd even been aware how I sometimes did that, trying to hold my feelings in. I slipped the photo back into the bible and slid the bible back onto the shelf, then turned around to face her.

"I'm sure you're mistaken," I said. "James didn't like Beth that way. I'd surely have known if he had."

"Okay," she said her voice dipping. "Maybe you're right. Anyway, I've always been fond of Beth. She's such a sweet girl. Does she know that you're back in town yet?"

"I don't think so. But you know how it is around here. I wouldn't be surprised if she knew the exact moment, I stepped off the plane," I said, irritated.

"That's true," Mother said, shaking her head slightly. "News travels fast around here. Too fast, sometimes," she added with a frown. "Well, let me go get that dryer for you. I have one in my room. Is there anything else you need while you're here?"

"I don't think so. I'm going to call to have a rental car brought here this morning. If I need anything else, I'll stop by the store and get it myself on the way to the hospital."

She turned around. "Why don't you use James' car while you're here?"

I looked at her, very surprised that she'd kept the Mustang all these years after James had died. "You kept his car?" I asked.

"Yes. Your father wanted to sell it, so I wouldn't get sad every time I saw it. But I just couldn't seem to part with it. I guess it's my way of keeping a piece of James around," she said sadly.

I flashed back to the day James had brought the car home and the look on Mother's face when he told her he'd used most of the money he'd made from repairing computers to buy the car.

That money was supposed to go toward his college savings. Mother was so upset. She told him to take it right back to the dealership and get his money back. But he refused, telling her that he'd decided to stay in Easley and grow his computer repair business and wasn't going to college after all.

I was pretty proud of him for standing up to her that day, though at the same time, I was hurt he hadn't told me about his change of plans. We were supposed to be starting college at the same school together in just a few months, and yet I was only now finding out about it? I was sad, in a way; twins were supposed to share everything.

When I asked him why he hadn't told me, he said he'd only just recently made the decision and it wasn't like I was around much for him to have a chance to tell me anyway. Though that was true, it still hurt that he didn't make it a point to at least include me in his revised plans.

Mother looked around the bedroom one more time, then headed off to her room. She returned in a minute with a blow dryer and the keys to James' car. I took them from her and wandered back to my room to finish getting dressed. After putting on a blouse and pair of jeans, I headed outside.

On the way to the barn, I passed by a pair of boots in the garage along with two fishing poles leaning against the wall. The boots looked as if they hadn't been used and I could tell that they were men's boots. The poles still had the price tags hanging from them too.

This was all very strange. Since Dad was no longer in her life and Mother always hated anything to do with water, why would she have fishing gear lying around? Could it be that she had been seeing someone? Mother had a boyfriend? That would make sense with the way she'd been acting so strangely.

I didn't like the idea at all, for some reason, even though she and Dad had been divorced for a long time. The thought of her with another man was nothing less than disturbing.

But I guessed I didn't have a right to say what she did.

I continued to the barn as I tried to get the image of her and another man out of my head. As I slid the door open, those thoughts were instantly replaced with the emotion of seeing James' beautiful red Mustang in front of me. It looked so new and shiny, it was if James had never left. I envisioned him there polishing it like he often did, until it gleamed, and he could see his reflection in the shiny chrome. That car was his pride and joy, the thing he had lived for.

My chest hurt as I opened the door and got in.

CHAPTER 7

I SAT THERE FOR A MOMENT AS I TRIED TO COMPOSE myself. My breath came out in quick puffs. It felt horrible to sit behind the wheel knowing that James would never drive it again, never buff up its paintwork, never run his hand across its door handle or fill it with gas.

I breathed in the leather smell in a deep inhale and put the key in the ignition but as I turned the key, the guilt was overwhelming. Why did I get to be here, and James wasn't? It wasn't right.

I'd never even driven the Mustang. James never let anyone drive it. It wasn't that he wasn't generous with his things, but he'd worked so hard for this car and didn't want to share it with anyone. Not even with his own twin.

I felt guilty and almost shut the engine off and went back into the house, but something told me James would want me driving it. At least I told myself that. Why not take it out and show it off in his honor?

So, after a bit more hesitation, I turned the key and immediately, the engine roared to life. The vibration of the motor could be felt through the seat. The car sure was powerful, full of spirit and fire.

Excited and at the same time nervous, I put the car into reverse and carefully backed out of the barn. As I was about to turn down the driveway, I remembered I'd forgotten my purse in the house. I put the car in park and hurried back inside. Mother stood at the sink with a dish in her hand, waving it about as she spoke.

"I'm glad you're still here," she said as I walked by her. "I'm going over to the hospital in a few minutes to see your Dad.

Would you like to go with me? We can stop at the store on the way if you want."

The fishing gear in the garage flashed through my mind. She had stopped caring about my dad a long time ago, if she ever had at all. And apparently, she was seeing someone so, why go see him at all? Was she trying to impress me?

"What about your boyfriend?" I asked.

"Boyfriend? What boyfriend?" She looked puzzled.

"I came across the fishing boots and poles in the garage Mother, and I saw the men's slippers in the hallway earlier. It doesn't take a genius to figure out you're seeing someone. Where is he? Did you make him stay away because your long-lost daughter was back in town?"

She looked away. "It's not what you think."

I winced as Dan's exact same words rang in my ears.

"Oh, I'm sure it's exactly what I think," I said, grabbing my purse. "It always is."

I hurried outside as tears sprang to my eyes. Though I wanted to believe that they were out of concern for my father, I knew better. The fact was, my life was falling apart and for once, my mother appeared to have hers all together. She'd quit drinking. She had someone special, someone to love and who evidently thought enough of her to leave his fishing gear in the garage…so he could come visit, maybe even make a home with her.

It wasn't fair. Why was she the one who got to be happy?

I stepped on the gas and pulled out onto the main street. So, what was her real reason for going to see Dad? Did she feel guilty for all those years she'd mistreated him and was trying to make up for it?

As I thought more about it, my mind was not on my driving and I took the next turn a little too fast, almost sliding into a ditch. I jerked the wheel back onto the road and slowed down.

I hate this. All of this. Why did I come back here? If it wasn't for the fact that my father had cancer, I'd never have stepped foot in this town again. I already wanted to leave, desperately wanted it. Yet where would I go? I was not ready to go back to Dan, but I would go *somewhere* as soon as I knew that my father was out of the woods, though I hadn't a clue where to head this time.

I slowed down as I came to a stop sign and a familiar fork in the road. To the left was Easley Highway and to the right would take me to Finley Road. The Finley Road route was shorter and would get me to the hospital much quicker than Easley Highway. But it would also take me past Finley Church, the same church where James was buried out back.

My heart beat fast as I sat there with the engine idling for what seemed like a very long time. I turned left, having decided to take the longer route.

As I made my way through the country roads, the sky clouded up and fat drops of rain splattered the windshield which seemed to match my mood. I hadn't seen rain in some time, and it made me think of James. He had really liked the rain, said it made the world fresh and new again, like we had a fresh start on life. And though it made his asthma worse at times, he liked to go outside when it was raining and just stand there with his arms out. And he loved the way he could smell the charge in the air after a thunderstorm. Made him feel alive…

But heaven forbid if Mother found out he was outside. She'd freak out and start yelling for me to go and bring him in.

"If he gets sick, it will be all your fault," she'd always say on my way out. I had no idea how it could be my fault, but simply accepted that it was.

And even though I didn't want James to get sick, I hated to make him come in when he liked being out there so much. He wasn't happy that often. If it gave him pleasure to be out in the rain, then so be it. Sometimes, I even pretended not to notice when he snuck out again after I'd brought him in. But once Mother found out, she'd make me go get him again.

James used to get so upset with me then, as if it was my fault, he had to come in. He said he couldn't do anything without my telling on him even though I tried to convince him that it wasn't true. And forget it if he got so much as a sniffle the next day. I was the one who was in trouble with Mother. I couldn't win either way. It was my fault if he stayed out. It was my fault he came in. It was my fault she didn't know he was out, and my fault she did.

When it came to my brother, our mother blamed me for everything that went wrong with him. I suspect she even blamed me for him being born the way he was, as if it was my fault too, that I was the only one who came out strong and healthy.

Dad always said he and Mother were sure James wasn't going to make it when we were born. He was so tiny and weak. He'd even had to stay in the hospital for two weeks after he was born until his lungs got stronger. Though they never did get normal, which is why he ended up with asthma, they suspected.

I jumped as 'My heart will go on' by Celine Dion started to play from inside my purse. It was the personal ringtone I'd set for Dan's calls. I pulled the phone out and looked at it before hitting reject. I wasn't interested in anything he had to say right now.

I slowed down as I came to a Walmart up on the right.

I remembered when they'd started construction on the store right before I left town. Everyone had been so excited that little Easley had finally made it to the big time and was going to have their very own Walmart. Even I was excited, and every time I saw a 'Wally World' after that, it made me think of Easley.

I pulled into the parking lot. Maybe now was a good time to stop and pick up a blow dryer and a few other things needed for my stay. I parked the car and hurried inside, all the time glancing around, afraid of seeing someone I knew. I was determined to shop quickly and get out before I ran into anyone. Paranoia hit me as I made my way through the aisles. Worse still, what if I ran into Joey?

He was the last one I wanted to see right now, better off to wait until I was more prepared to see him. I grabbed my things and paid quickly, relieved once I'd made it out of the store without seeing anyone.

After tossing my bag onto the back seat, I headed for the exit. I looked across the street at the very same Huddle House on the corner, where Joey and I used to go. It made me smile at how odd I thought it was at the time, when Joey took me there on our first date for breakfast instead of out for dinner somewhere.

But he explained that not only did he want to end the day with me, he wanted to start it with me too. I was smitten with him by the time breakfast was over. After that, he took me there almost every Saturday morning.

My heart started to ache as I pictured sitting there with him in our favorite booth, an arm's length away from the grill. After the waitress called out our order, we loved to drink our coffees and watch as the cook put on a show.

He'd masterly flip the eggs high in the air with one hand while smashing hash browns on the grill with the other. Then he'd toss everything onto a plate before calling out that the order was ready. Eating breakfast out was dull after I moved to California.

—

I checked the parking lot in case Joey's Silverado pickup truck was there, but it wasn't, though I knew he might not even have that truck anymore. Now that he had a son, he might have been driving an SUV or some other family car. The thought made me very sad. I'd always believed when Joey had children, it was going to be with me. That was when I was still open to the idea of having a family.

'My heart will go on' started to play again from inside my purse, almost as if Dan knew I was sitting here at the very place where I'd spent many mornings with my first love.

At first, I felt guilty until I remembered it was Dan's fault, he wasn't with me. I needed to forget about both Dan and Joey for now and do what I'd come here to do. See my father. Make sure he was going to be all right. And leave.

I looked at the Huddle House again and thought about going inside, partly because I wasn't ready to deal with seeing my father yet, and partly to spite Dan and check out one of my old haunts where I used to go to with my old boyfriend. I stepped out of the car and headed inside.

"Welcome to the Huddle House," I heard a syrupy southern-accented voice say as I walked in. I turned to see a waitress with piled-high auburn hair coming toward me. She looked to be quite young. Too young to be working, in fact.

"Sit anywhere you want," she said, smiling. "We serve breakfast twenty-four hours, or you can have lunch too if you want."

My old booth was unoccupied, so I headed for it and sat down. After glancing around again at the other customers, I relaxed and pulled out a two-sided laminated menu wedged between various flavors of pancake syrups. My fingers instantly stuck to a glob of syrup and I had to smile. The menus hadn't changed. The waitress strolled over and flipped open her note pad.

"Whadyahave?" she asked as she chewed a huge wad of gum. I glanced at her pocket embroidered with the name Amber in gold letters, like out of an old TV show.

"Just some iced tea, Amber, please. Unsweetened," I quickly added remembering that in the South, iced tea came sweetened unless you requested it otherwise. "And a bowl of grits with butter."

I slid the menu back into its slot as Amber tore off a sheet of paper from her pad and hollered out, "Greasy grits" then gave her gum a pop. She filled up a plastic glass with tea and headed back to me but stopped and started talking to another customer first.

Finally, she came and set the glass down in front of me. I dumped some Sweet and Low into it when I noticed that Amber was still standing there gawking at me.

"Yes?" I asked, looking up. "Do you need something?"

She cleared her throat. "Um, I just wanted to ask you something. Is your name Karen? Karen Parker?"

I searched her face, wondering how I might possibly know her.

"It was Parker," I replied slowly, "but it's Olsen now. Do I know you from somewhere?"

"No, you don't know me, but my cousin Timmy over there knows you," she said. I followed the tip of her red fingernail to the booth she had stopped at earlier. A red-haired young man looked our way then quickly looked away again.

"Timmy said you went to the same high school that he did," Amber continued. "He said he knew you the minute you walked through the door. Though you're a little fancier now than you used to be, with the blonde hair and all. Timmy said after high school, you moved away on account of your twin brother killing himself."

Her last few words slapped me in the face. But seeming not to notice what she'd said, Amber popped her gum and continued as if nothing was wrong.

"Anyway, Timmy said you must have come back 'cause your dad's really sick. Oh, and to see your mama too, though you and her never got along good. He said he sure is glad she didn't die when she tried to off herself like your brother did, when she drove off that bridge after you moved away."

I looked at Amber aghast, not only because she could actually say all those insensitive things without skipping a beat as if merely commenting on the weather, but because of *what* she'd just said. I turned and burned a hole into Timmy. His eyes opened wide and once again he looked away.

"Excuse me," I said as I stood up and made my way to his booth. But Timmy wouldn't look at me as he busily peeled a label off a ketchup bottle.

"Please look at me," I said in a measured tone. "I hear you know me from school."

Timmy nodded but he kept his eyes looking down.

"You seem to think you know a lot about me and about my family, don't you? Well you got it wrong, FYI. My mother didn't try to 'off herself' like you told Amber. Maybe you should get your facts straight before you go around spreading gossip."

Amber walked up to us and sat down next to Timmy, catching the tail end of my conversation with him.

"Did you make that all up, Timmy?" she asked.

He looked at her. "No, it's true. I swear."

"Well you're wrong," I said again, though I was now starting to feel uncomfortable at the idea that it may very well be true. "That never happened or I'm sure I'd have known about it."

"I'm sorry," he stuttered. "It was in all the newspapers, so I figured everyone especially you, knew about it. Though I guess it makes sense now why you didn't come back after it happened. Everybody always wondered why you didn't. But hey, she didn't die so it's all good then, right?" he asked, looking hopeful.

I stared at him. So, it was true? She had tried to kill herself like my brother? She wouldn't do that. And surely, I would have found out about it somehow if she had. But Timmy said it was in the papers. Numb, I turned to Amber. "What do I owe you for the tea and grits?"

"It's on the house," she said, now looking more frightened than Timmy did.

I headed back to my booth and took out a five-dollar bill and dropped it on the table.

As I got into the car, I heard Celine Dion from inside the glove compartment. I took out my phone in time to see Dan's name flashing across the screen. Angrily, I hit reject. Then after a moment, still shaking, I googled Doris Parker, Easley, South Carolina and held my breath.

CHAPTER 8

THERE WERE SEVERAL ENTRIES ONLINE UNDER MY mother's name. But either they had to do with James' death, or it was a different Doris Parker.

Somewhat relieved that Timmy might just have gotten it all wrong, I was just about to put the phone away, when an article caught my eye. 'Woman saved from drowning at Hartwell Lake.'

My heart raced erratically as I clicked onto the title. According to the Easley Gazette, an Easley woman was pulled out of Hartwell Lake early Wednesday morning following an attempted suicide. The article went on to say how another local resident had been driving right as the car went over the side and plunged into the water.

The young man, without concern for his own life, heroically jumped into the lake and saved the woman, preventing her from a sure death, it read. The article went on to say that in a strange twist of fate, the rescuer was identified as Joey Rand. Rand was the best friend of the woman's late son James Parker, who had committed suicide two years earlier with a fatal gunshot wound to the head. I nearly dropped the phone. So, it was true. She tried to kill herself. And of all people, Joey had been the one to save her. At first, I was shocked, but then angered.

It was just like her to be so selfish! I'd had plenty of reasons to give up myself, especially after losing James, but I'd never put my father or even her through another loss like that. My mind went to Joey. And how was it that Joey of all people just happened to be there at the right time?

My head was spinning as I scrolled down to see what else the article said, but other than a few nasty comments about our family from various readers, there wasn't anything else worth noting. I sat there stunned as I tried to digest it all. A tall girl with a ponytail walked by me at a fast pace as she headed toward the restaurant. Something about her gait looked familiar.

She stopped abruptly and turned around slowly. I could see she was wearing the same colored shirt as Amber's, so she must have been another one of the waitresses. And then I recognized her. It was Beth.

I dropped the phone on the passenger seat and started the car up quickly as she started back toward me. I pulled out just as she came up to the car. When I glanced back, Beth was standing there staring in my direction.

Should I turn around and go back? This town was pretty small, so it wasn't like I could avoid her forever. Plus, she had to have recognized James' car, though with my different hairstyle, she might not have known it was me driving it.

But there weren't too many bright red Mustangs with white stripes in Easley as far as I knew, and she must have already known I was back in town. It wouldn't take long for her to put two and two together.

And once she got inside and Amber told her about the girl who was just there, who was the sister of the guy who shot himself eight years ago, she'd know it was me and that I was purposely avoiding her.

I guessed I should go back. Who knew, maybe she could fill me in on more details about what my mother had done. I was daydreaming now, and a horn from out of nowhere startled me.

"Sorry," I mouthed as a car pulled up alongside with a woman glaring at me. Once again, I'd almost got myself into a wreck and had only just arrived. I looked for a place to turn around. A flashing sign caught my eye up ahead. 'Red Penny Bar and Grill'.

Maybe that was what I needed, one drink to settle my nerves before I went back to see Beth. I pulled into the parking lot and after a moment of hesitation, decided to go inside.

Several people sitting at the bar stopped talking and turned to look at me as I walked in. I froze, hoping no one recognized me.

But within seconds, they went right back to their conversations, apparently not finding me too interesting. I looked for an empty stool and spotted one at the end of the bar.

The place was fairly dark, but light enough to make out a pool table, a jukebox, and several tables of people eating and drinking. But, thankfully, no familiar faces like Joey's were in the crowd.

I wrinkled my nose at the smell of stale beer. This was definitely somewhere I'd normally never find myself and, for a moment, I almost turned around to leave. But as I looked at all the people sitting there drinking and laughing, looking like they didn't have a care in the world, I knew that right now, there wasn't anywhere else I'd rather be.

A tall muscular bartender walked over and set a napkin down in front of me.

"Welcome to the Red Penny. What can I get for you?" he asked pleasantly.

I ordered a Jack and Coke and he returned within minutes with my drink. He set the drink on the cocktail napkin and slid it toward me.

"Here you go."

"Thanks," I said as I took out a ten-dollar bill and placed it on the bar. Moments later, he came back with my change.

Hand shaking slightly, I lifted the glass and took a sip. After a few more sips, my thoughts turned back to the newspaper article. I quickly emptied my glass looked around for the bartender again. But as he nodded and started to come toward me, guilt set in. I really should get going. I'd been here a good part of the day and hadn't even seen my father yet.

And that was why I'd come back here after all. I could see Beth some other time. I looked down into the glass of melted ice. I could always see my father another time too, when I was in a better frame of mind, but I forced myself to stand up. The sooner I saw him, the sooner I could get out of this town. I headed for the door. On the way out, the bartender smiled at me.

"Come back and see us again," he said pleasantly.

I forced a smile back. "I will." But I knew there was little chance I'd be in this bar again or any other bar for that matter.

—

Fifteen minutes later, I was pulling into the Greenville Medical Hospital. I shut the car off and sat there as I stared at the building, a building familiar from so long ago and one I'd hoped never to visit again. Thoughts of the day James was brought here whirled in my mind, recalling the time he had taken an overdose when he was much younger. How frightened we all were that he wasn't going to survive. He had taken such a lot of pills.

I could see him lying there in that hospital bed. He was so pale. My eyes teared up just thinking about it. And now I was here again but this time, to see my father who might be dying.

I put my hand on the door as I prepared to get out. What was I supposed to say when I saw him after all this time?

"Hi Dad. I'm so sorry you're not doing well. And by the way, why did you completely disappear from my and James' lives after you left Mom?" But what if he looked bad or couldn't talk? What would I do then?

I opened the car door and walked slowly toward the entrance, though it took everything I had to keep from high-tailing it right back to the car.

Maybe I should leave. It was not like I owed my father anything after the way he had left us. 'But he's your father,' kept playing in my head. I took a deep breath, prepared myself for the worst and headed inside.

CHAPTER 9

"CAN I HELP YOU?"

I looked around the hospital lobby, once again checking for anyone I knew. Relieved that there wasn't, I turned back to the woman at the counter and explained I was here to see Bill Parker, my father. She looked down at her chart then up again. I detected sympathy in her eyes.

"Oh yes, Mr. Parker. He's up in room 304," she said as she handed me a visitor's tag. "The elevator is down on the right. When you get to the third floor, turn left and it's the fourth on your right."

I thanked her as I stuck the visitor's tag onto my chest and headed toward the elevator. I pushed the button for the third floor and even before the doors opened, could hear the beep-beep-beep of the monitors. A feeling of dread washed over me as I headed down the hallway.

301, 302, 303, I stopped in front of room 304. The door was partially open. For several minutes, I just stood there bracing myself to see him. Then finally, I reached up and tapped on the door as I pushed it the rest of the way open.

"Come in," I heard a weak voice say.

A pale, older looking man was propped up in bed facing me. He had on light blue pajamas and looked very frail. Just as I was about to say I was sorry and must have the wrong room, I realized it was my father.

Shocked at how I hadn't recognized him. I stood there staring. He stared back at me. Then his face lit up.

"Karen! You made it," he said, smiling. "I'm so glad you came. I was beginning to think you weren't going to make it."

I forced a smile back. My father wasn't a tall man, but he had been stocky much like James. But not now. He was thin. Very thin, and he looked old.

I tried to hide my shock at how terrible he looked. The anger I'd harbored for him all these years was momentarily replaced by sympathy.

"Hello," was all I could seem to muster. That was when I noticed we weren't alone. There was someone in the chair next to his bed, someone in a police officer uniform who was staring right at me. It felt as if the wind was knocked right out of me. How many times had I replayed this moment in my mind, and it was finally here?

"Hi Karen," Joey said in a husky voice as he stood up slowly.

My mouth went dry. "Hi Joey," I said, my tongue now feeling huge in my mouth.

"Hi," he said again. I could feel his eyes burning a hole in me and the room suddenly seemed to get darker. I couldn't move.

"Well don't just stand there," my father said, drawing my attention away from Joey. "Come on in here."

I wanted to take a step, but my feet felt like they were buried in quicksand. My heart pounded loudly in my ears. I lifted my foot and made my way slowly to the side of the bed, all the while conscious of Joey merely feet away from me. I bent down and gave my father a clumsy peck on the cheek.

"Hi, Dad."

"Hello, dear," he said as I straightened back up. "How are you?" But before I could answer, something scraped the floor behind me, causing me to jump.

"I'm sure you need to sit down," Joey purred in my ear as he slid a chair up behind me. I sat down, grateful to have a place to sit before I fell down.

Joey's hand grazed my shoulder and I could smell his cologne which I recognized as the same brand he used to wear when we were dating. Just the scent of it made me woozy. But trying not to show how unnerved I was, I forced my attention back to my father and strained to think of something to say to him. Anything to get my mind off Joey, just inches behind me.

"So, how are you, Dad?" I asked, realizing how silly that must be to ask someone with cancer that kind of question.

"I'm okay," he replied, "though I wish I had more energy. I've been so tired lately."

"Are you in any pain?" I asked as I tried not to look back at Joey.

"Not really. Just tired and it's hard to catch my breath at times. I guess the tumor is pressing against my lung. Hopefully, the cancer is just on the surface and hasn't made it into my lungs. But enough of all this depressing stuff. How are you? How long can you stay?"

"I'm not sure yet how long I'll be here," I said getting another whiff of Joey's cologne as he moved to the side of me.

"Well, hopefully for a while so we can get to spend time together. We've all missed you. Right Joe?"

"Yes," Joey said, still staring intensely at me. He cleared his throat. "Maybe I should let you two visit, while I go get something to eat. You must have a lot to get caught up on and you surely don't need me hanging around."

Part of me wanted him to go, yet another part wanted him to stay.

I glanced down at his left hand to see if he was wearing a wedding band, which he wasn't. I looked away just as quickly, hoping he didn't see me checking. But the half grin on his face told me he had, and I felt my face get warm.

"Maybe you can come down and see me before you leave. I'd love to talk to you," he said, giving me another piercing look. "But take all the time you need with your dad. I'll wait."

My heart fluttered again.

"You hang in there, Bill," he said as he turned to leave, glancing at me one more time on his way out.

"Will do, Joey. And thanks for coming by again."

"He sure is a great guy, isn't he?" my father asked after he was gone. "It's funny, but I see him more now than when you two were dating. Don't know what your mother and I would have done without him, to tell you the truth."

I looked at him and wondered if he was referring to the fact that Joey had saved Mother's life. I found it odd that Joey would stay so close to my parents after we'd broken up and I'd left town. He never was that close to them before.

"I can tell he's happy to see you," my father added, giving me a wink. "It's obvious the guy's never gotten over you. Not that I blame him of course. But you're married now and hopefully very happy. How is that husband of yours anyway? Did he come with you?"

I looked at him, still stuck on the comment about Joey not getting over me and wondered what had made him say that. Had Joey said something to him about me?

"Is he here?" he asked again.

I looked at him. "Who?"

"Your husband," he replied. "Did he come with you?"

"Oh, Dan? No," I replied. "He's back in California. Busy on a big job," I quickly added. "He couldn't get away right now, but he said to give you his best."

"That's too bad," my father said, looking disappointed. "I was hoping to finally meet him. Well, I'm glad you could come, though. You don't know how much it means to me. And I know it means a lot to your mother too. We've both missed you so much. Just this morning, she was telling me what a blessing it is to have you staying at the house with her. I'm glad you're there, too. I worry about her being out there all alone in that big empty house."

So, apparently, he didn't know Mother was seeing someone else.

"You don't need to worry about her," I said wondering how much I should tell him without upsetting him.

"Yes, I know, now that you're there," he said, smiling again. I decided not to tell him about her boyfriend. What was the point? He'd find out soon enough. Besides, maybe he had someone of his own too.

"I have to say, I'm surprised you're so concerned about her. The last time you two were together, you made it clear that you wanted nothing to do with her."

"Things change," he said softly. He looked past me, apparently lost in thought.

"So how are things in California?" he asked, looking back at me again.

"Everything's fine," I said, finding it difficult to keep going with this small talk. I'd been wanting to tell him how I felt for far too long.

"Look, I'm just going to come right out and say it," I said. "I'm sorry you're sick, I really am. That's why I'm here. But please don't ask me to act like everything is fine between you and me. I just can't do it."

"You're right. And that's one of the reasons I'm glad you came," he said looking sad.

"I've wanted to talk to you about what happened for a very long time. When you were ready, of course. I know I was a bad father. How I wasn't there for you and James after your mother and I separated, and I don't blame you for being upset with me. I really don't. I hope you can forgive me."

For a moment, I was taken off-guard, not expecting him to admit so soon just how wrong he'd been. But I wasn't willing to let him off the hook that easily even if he was sick. It was one thing to hurt me, but he had hurt James and that wasn't something I was willing to just forget.

"Not being there for me is one thing, but what about James? He needed you. Maybe he'd still be alive today if you'd made some time for him. Do you ever think about that?"

"I do," he replied looking down. "I think about it a lot. And I hate myself for not being there and doing something, anything to stop him doing what he did. I ask myself every day what I could have done or said to keep him from making that horrible decision."

I looked away. If I was honest, not a day went by when I didn't ask myself the same thing. How if I'd said the right thing, or made more time to talk to James, how maybe he'd still be alive today. But this wasn't about me. It was about my father and how he'd just upped and all but abandoned us.

"I didn't want to leave you and James when your mother asked me to go. Believe me," he continued, "but I couldn't take one more minute of watching her drink herself to death knowing I couldn't do one damn thing to stop her. But still, it's no excuse for not being there for you and your brother. I realize that." He stopped and winced. I couldn't tell if it was from pain or from the guilt of knowing that he as a father had truly failed.

"Well, I wish you'd tried harder to stay in touch with us after you moved out," I said, feeling my heart softening a bit.

"I know," he said wincing again. "I should have made more of an effort. I tried to tell myself that you kids didn't need me anymore now that you were older and had your own lives. But going to see you in your school plays or an occasional phone call wasn't enough. I'm so sorry but I just didn't get it back then. Well, not until James called me one day and laid into me. He told me he was disappointed in me and how I'd pretty much abandoned you both. That was tough to take. But he was right, and I promised him I'd see you two as much as I could after that. James and I even made plans to go hunting together." He looked away sadly.

I looked at him surprised to hear that James had confronted him like that. I only wished my father had intended to keep his promise.

"Then James died," he said looking back at me. "And you left town and I didn't get the chance to be with either one of you after that. Not that I blame you for leaving. After everything that happened, you had to go for your own sake, and I knew that. I was just glad that you were strong enough to do it at such an early age. But then again, you always were the strong one in the family."

It annoyed me how everyone always said that about me, that I was so tough. I was, for the most part, but not all the time. No one could be strong all the time.

"Still, I hope you know that I loved you and your brother very much and I feel terrible that I wasn't a better father. I know it's too late for me to be there for James. But I'd like to be there for you, if you'll let me." He went to say something else but stopped as he started to cough. The coughing went on for minutes, each one getting harder than the last until he appeared unable to catch his breath.

I jumped up and looked toward the door, ready to run out into the hall to get help, when a nurse thankfully appeared in the doorway.

"Another one of your coughing spells, Bill?" she asked as she hurried to the side of the bed. He nodded weakly. She pressed a button that slowly lifted the head of his bed higher, until the coughing slowed and eventually stopped.

"I'm okay now," he managed to gasp.

"Sure, you are. Why don't you let me give you some meds now?" she asked patting his hand.

"No," he said firmly. "That stuff makes me go to sleep and I want to visit with my daughter some more." He took a slow deep breath and then tried to stifle a cough. "She came all the way from California to see me."

The nurse looked over at me and frowned. "It sounded like things were getting a bit heated in here when I walked by earlier. You need to not get your father too excited. He's a very sick man, you know."

"It's okay," my father said.

"No, it's not. You need to rest. Your daughter can come back and visit you tomorrow when you're stronger," she said, sounding angry.

"I'm fine. Just a little longer," he pleaded. But I could see by the way he was grimacing that he was trying hard not to cough again. I felt sure the nurse noticed too. She shook her head.

"No, I think it's time to cut the visit short. Every time you cough, that tumor pushes on your lungs." His eyes followed her as she turned a knob on the IV bag hanging near his bed and then within seconds, I could see his eyes close.

"There you go," she said in a soothing voice. "That's better. I'll come back and check on you in a bit."

She turned and gave me another frown. "He should have been resting. But he tried to stay awake all day waiting for you to get here," she said under her breath. "He kept saying you were going to be here any minute. I tried to get him to take some pain medicine several times, but he wanted to make sure he was awake for you when you finally *did* show up."

I felt my face flush. I turned and looked at him lying there peacefully, his eyes now completely shut. As angry as I was with him, it was hard to see him like that. He looked so weak. His chest rose up slowly, then back down. As it went back up again, I found my own breathing slowing to match his.

"He's going to be all right, isn't he?" I asked as I blinked back tears.

"You can talk to his doctor when he comes in tomorrow. And I suggest you spend as much time with your father while you can." She looked down at him with compassion. "You never know." She looked back at me with an annoyed expression again. "And next time, you might want to bring some mints with you. You reek of alcohol."

And with that, she turned and walked briskly out of the room. Again, I felt my face flush.

I turned and looked at my father again. Was he going to beat this? I wasn't so sure and for the first time since I'd been back in Easley, I wished Dan was here.

Not because I needed a big strong man to lean on, but because I felt stronger when he was around. Strangely, it was the opposite of how I used to feel with Joey. It wasn't his fault, but sometimes when I was with Joey, he was so overpowering that I tended to feel small.

But then I remembered the reason Dan wasn't here and felt the anger come back. I whispered goodbye and left to go meet Joey in the cafeteria. On the way down, I wondered if maybe I should just go back to the house. After all, I was drained and feeling very emotional.

The last thing I wanted to do was get into an argument with Joey. But the thought of being this close to finally learning the truth about why he had let me go all those years ago was too much to resist. I pushed my shoulders back, took a deep breath and exited the elevator. Finally, I was about to learn the truth.

—

A woman was busy clearing one of the tables when I walked into the cafeteria. I looked around but didn't see Joey anywhere. I asked her if there'd been a good-looking policeman in here earlier. She said yes, but that he'd left about fifteen minutes ago.

I thanked her and headed out to my car feeling disappointed and hurt. Why hadn't Joey waited for me? I started the car and headed back to the house feeling angry.

Mother was sitting at the kitchen table and looked up as I walked in. Her faced dropped immediately. "What is it? What's wrong? Is he okay?"

"Who?" I asked still feeling miffed about Joey.

"Your father," she replied. "Did something happen? You look upset."

"Oh. He's okay. Though he was coughing a lot. But the nurse came in and gave him something to help him sleep so I left."

"So, what's wrong? Was it just too hard seeing him like that?" she asked.

"No. It's just a lot of things. For one, let me ask you. Why did you try to kill yourself? Wasn't one suicide enough for this family?"

She stared at me and seemed at a loss for words.

"Just forget it," I said and turned to head to my bedroom. "I don't want to know after all."

"Wait," she said. But I didn't stop. When I came out of the bathroom, she was sitting on the bed.

"I'm sorry you had to hear about that from your father," she said. "I was hoping I'd get the chance to tell you what happened when the time was right."

"He didn't tell me. I had to hear it from some guy at the Huddle House. Seems everyone in town knows about it except me. How could you do that?" I asked, my voice starting to crack. I sat down on the bed and hung my head. "You had to have known what that would do to me and Dad after what had happened to James."

She put her hand on my shoulder, but I shook it off. "Don't"

"Okay. I do want to talk about this but maybe now isn't a good time. Maybe after you've had some rest. You must be exhausted."

She stood up. "Tell you what. I'm going to my AA meeting in the morning. Then to see your dad. After that, I'll be home, and I'll tell you anything you want to know. Is it a deal?"

"Whatever," I replied. She was right. I was physically and emotionally exhausted. Between seeing my father like that and seeing Joey again, and learning about her suicide, it had been a rough day. After she said goodnight, I crawled into bed, but no sooner had I closed my eyes when there was a knock on the door.

She stood at the doorway. "I forgot to tell you. I talked to Dan earlier."

I sat up. "What? You called him?"

"No, he called here looking for you. Said he's been trying to get a hold of you for the past two days and left several voicemails, but you haven't returned his calls. He was worried something had happened to your father. What's going on with you two?" she asked softly.

"Look, Mother. Let's get something straight. The only reason I came back here was to see Dad. And if it wasn't that all the hotels in the area were full, I wouldn't even be staying here with you. I'm sure you don't want me here anyway," I added.

"Besides, don't expect me to pour out my heart to you. It's not going to happen. You've never been interested in my life anyway. All you cared about was James and your bottle. I've finally accepted that. So, let's not pretend that you give a darn about me now. And please, if Dan calls again, don't talk to him about me. I haven't told him anything about my past sordid life. And I certainly don't want him hearing about it from you. Let's just get through this and I'll be gone soon enough. And you won't have to worry about hearing from me again."

She looked at me as her eyes filled with tears. "But I want to hear from you. I know I wasn't the best mother. And if I could go back and change things, I would. But you are wrong about me not caring about you. It may have seemed like I gave James more attention than you and I'm sure I did at times. But that's only because he needed it more than you did. But it didn't mean I loved you any less. I loved you very much. I still do."

"Well, I don't need your love. Not anymore," I said. "I'm grown up now."

She started to say something when the doorbell rang. She looked at me for a few seconds, then turned and headed to answer it. And after a moment, I heard her talking to someone. Then she was back at my doorway again.

"Joey's here," she whispered. "He wants to talk to you. Should I tell him you're in bed?"

Surprised, I felt a rush of excitement until I remembered how he had just dumped me less than an hour ago. "Tell him I'm asleep." I said.

She left and headed back to the front door. I jumped up and stood in the doorway, trying to hear their conversation.

"Sorry, Joey, but Karen's in bed," I heard her say.

"Oh, okay," he replied, sounding disappointed. "Please tell her I stopped by and I'll call her tomorrow. Sorry to have bothered you."

"No problem," Mother said. 'I'll be sure to tell her. Good night, Joey."

I turned around and ran to my room, jumping into bed before she got back.

"He's gone now. He said to tell you he'll call you tomorrow," she said from the doorway.

"Thanks," I said as I rolled onto my side and pretended to go to sleep.

Seconds later, I heard the bedroom door close. My eyes popped open. What was Joey doing here anyway? This was all too much, and I needed a drink.

I knew I should have picked something up while I was out, something to help me sleep. But then I remembered, I had the miniature whiskey bottles from the plane in my purse.

I got up and flicked the light on and dug the tiny bottles out. Wishing I had something to mix them with, I decided to sneak out to the kitchen and get a Coke. I stuck my head out into the hallway. Mother's room sounded quiet and she must have gone to bed. I crept down the hall and took a can of Coke from the fridge, then grabbed a glass from the cupboard and filled it with ice. I took the glass and can back to my room.

Closing the door softly, I set the glass on the dresser and made myself a drink using both bottles. As I sat there sipping, my thoughts turned back to my father and Joey.

I wondered if my father had been able to sense there was still something between us. It was crazy how strong my feelings were for Joey after all this time. I'd thought they were pretty much dead once I'd married Dan. Yet, it was hard to deny there was something still there.

But I loved Dan. I felt a stabbing pain deep in my chest. Even after what he had done, I loved this man. He'd gone out with another girl, though. I didn't know if I could get over that. I wondered if he realized that he was about to lose me. Did he even care, now that he had her? I drank some more.

Even so, I bet if he knew about Joey, he wouldn't be too happy. Like most men, just because he didn't want me anymore, didn't mean he'd want me to be with someone else. I finished the drink knowing at least I had Joey even if it was only temporary. I shut the light off and tried to go to sleep, all the while my head was spinning out of control.

CHAPTER 10

LIGHT STREAMED IN FROM THE WINDOW, HITTING MY face. Through blurry eyes, I looked over at the clock on the nightstand. I was surprised to see that it was almost nine. I couldn't remember the last time I'd slept in that late but guessed I needed it. I climbed out of bed and opened the door.

The house was dead quiet. Mother had mentioned that she was going to an AA meeting this morning, so she must have already left. When I got into the kitchen, I found a note stuck to the coffee pot.

'Breakfast is in the microwave. Coffee is ready too. Just turn on.'

I sighed. It was actually kind of sad how hard she was trying to be a good mother now. I crumpled up the note and pressed the button on the coffee machine.

The aroma of coffee quickly filled the room. When it was finished brewing, I poured myself a steaming cup and sat down at the kitchen table. Adding some cream, I looked out into the back yard.

It looked like it was going to be a beautiful day. I took a sip of coffee and wondered how many times I'd sat in this very chair watching Dad either mowing the grass or planting a tree out back.

I always did love our backyard. With well over four acres, and most of it covered with thick green grass, our yard was huge compared to the ones in Orange County, California.

There were plenty of oak trees all over it too. My father had planted every single one himself, back when I was young, about seven or eight years old.

Sometimes, James and I'd go out onto the back porch and sit together in the swing and watch him digging the holes. It was demanding work, but my father seemed to enjoy it. Then he'd gently place a tiny tree in each one before filling it in with dirt.

Each morning before it was barely light out, he'd go out and carefully water every single baby tree which at that time was barely two feet tall. I watched as over the years they grew bigger.

We were about twelve or thirteen when my father suggested James and I each pick out our favorite tree. He made signs with our names on each one and nailed the sign to the tree we'd picked out. I loved having my own tree.

Sometimes, I'd go out in my pajamas and sit under it either reading, or daydreaming, or writing. My father was so attentive to our trees, always making sure they were well watered and that no weeds grew around them. That was back when he seemed to enjoy doing things for us. I sighed and got up to refill my cup.

Before going inside, I stood there in the back yard and breathed deeply, savoring the fresh, clean air. It did smell wonderful. So much better than the ammonia smell in LA.

And I loved all the sounds coming from the woods, especially in the morning when the birds were calling out to each other or there would be the occasional barking dog. These were some more of the things I missed about living here, things I'd forgotten about.

I headed outside with my coffee and made my way barefoot through the grass to my oak tree. It was surprising how much it had grown in eight years.

'Karen's Tree.' I smiled at the piece of wood with my name etched deeply in it. Though it was now a bit worn from all the sun and rain, it still made me happy.

I ran my hand over the engraved letters. Then, finding a dry spot under the tree, I sat down, careful not to spill any of my coffee and leaned back against the trunk.

Memories of all the journaling I'd done back then, came back to me. I'd sit right here and write about everything from my spats with Mother to how I felt when she and dad would fight. And I wrote about Joey. And about James too, and how I hated when the kids at school picked on him, especially Steve. I wrote a lot of things about James. Some good, some not so good, but writing made me feel better, at least for a while.

After James died, I felt bad about some of the things I'd written about him and burned the journal not far from this spot in a big pile of leaves. I'd gotten James a journal too around the same time I'd bought mine. I gave it to him on our birthday. I'd thought it might help him deal with his feelings, too. But he didn't want it. In fact, he acted like he was offended when I gave it to him.

"What do I want this for?" I remembered him asking as he dropped the journal into his bottom desk drawer. "Just because you want to write about your 'perfect' life, doesn't mean I want to write about mine."

"I thought it might help when you get...depressed," I tried to tell him.

"Well it won't," he had said sounding angry. "My life is bad enough without having to relive it again by putting it down on paper."

My feelings were hurt but I never mentioned the journal to him again. But after he died, I wondered if maybe I should have encouraged him more to write in it. It might have helped him deal with things and let it out like it helped me. I sighed as I stood up and brushed the dirt off my pants and headed back inside.

After eating some of the breakfast Mother had left for me, I headed back to my room to get dressed. It was 10:30. That should have given Mother plenty of time to spend with my father so hopefully I could go see him without her there.

I checked my phone as I got ready to leave. Three voicemails. Two were from Dan asking me to call him and the third from my supervisor wanting to know when I planned to be back at work. I called her back and left a message that I needed some more time to be with my father and would get back to her with an update as soon as possible.

—

On the way to the hospital, I slowed down as I came to the Huddle House. Maybe Beth was working today. Now might be a good time to stop and ask her what she knew about Mother driving off the bridge. But truth was, it was just an excuse. Though I was curious about what she knew about Mother, I really wanted to ask her what had happened to us. Why did we stop being friends?

I sat there staring at the building, trying to make up my mind whether to go in or not when there was a rap on my window. I turned to find Beth standing there. I rolled the window down.

"What're you doing sitting out here?" she asked. "Aren't you coming in?"

I took a deep breath and looked at her. Of everyone I'd seen so far, Beth hadn't changed much at all. She was still strikingly beautiful with her long dark hair tied back in a ponytail.

"I wasn't sure if you wanted to see me, so I was trying to get up the nerve to go in," I said, feeling somewhat embarrassed.

She smiled. "That's what I figured. Come on in. I get a break in a few minutes."

I looked at her for a few seconds then rolled up the window and got out.

"Joey said he thought he saw you sitting out here," she said as we walked toward the front door. I stopped.

"He's here?"

"Yes, but come on," she said taking my arm. "You're going to have to talk to him sooner or later."

I allowed her to drag me inside. "I'll be back in a few minutes," she said as she gave me a slight nudge toward the booth where Joey was sitting. He smiled at me.

Trapped, I walked toward him but stopped. He wasn't alone. The young boy from the Facebook photo, Joey's son, was sitting next to him. I wanted to run out of the restaurant.

"Well, this is a pleasant surprise," Joey said, standing up.

I walked closer and sat down, all the while trying not to stare at the boy. Finally, I got the courage to look at him. He was definitely cute, just like his dad. I swallowed the lump in my throat and looked away.

"I didn't expect to see you here," Joey said. "Are you stalking me?"

"No, I came by to talk to Beth," I said. I could hear my voice shaking.

"Well I'm glad you did," Joey said. "I wanted to talk to you since I didn't get a chance to last night. This is TJ, by the way." He put his hand on the boy's shoulder. "Say hello, TJ."

TJ looked at me and smiled. "Hello Ma'am," he said politely with a slight drawl then went back to doodling on his placemat.

"TJ? What does that stand for?" I asked, trying not to show how rattled I was.

"Thomas Jay," Joey replied. "Thomas after my grandfather. And Jay after my great grandfather. But everyone calls him TJ. He's adorable, isn't he? Everybody says he looks just like his mother."

I glared at Joey, surprised that he had the nerve to mention the boy's mother around me.

"Oh, and by the way, I'm sorry I had to leave like that last night," he continued. "I got a call from dispatch while I was waiting for you in the cafeteria. I tried to call you on your cell phone, but you must have had it turned off. That's why I came by the house. I wanted to tell you why I wasn't there. Like I said at the hospital, I'd really like to talk to you. Can we get together later? I need to leave in a few minutes to drop TJ off at school before I go back to work. But I get off at four and can come by the house if you want. I promise I won't stand you up this time."

"I don't think so, Joey," I said, looking at TJ again before looking away quickly.

"Come on," he said with an innocent look. "It's harmless. Just two old friends getting together."

"Excuse me," a woman from the next booth said. We both turned and looked at her.

"I hate to interrupt you, but I can't help but notice what an absolutely adorable little boy you have. He's the spitting image of both of you," she said smiling.

"He's not mine," I snapped back at her.

Her eyes flew open. "I'm so sorry," she said as she turned back to her food.

"Karen," Joey whispered. "She was just trying to be nice."

Just then, Beth walked up and slid onto the seat next to me. "I only have a few minutes. Did I miss anything?"

I looked at her, then at Joey and TJ. "I'm sorry," I said. "I can't do this. Let me out, Beth."

Beth looked at Joey then back at me. "What's wrong?"

"Please, just let me out," I said this time firmer. She stood up looking confused. I squeezed by her and hurried for the door.

"Karen, wait," I heard Joey call out, but I kept going until I got to the car. As I got in, tears poured down my face. Joey had a son with someone else while my own marriage was falling apart. How did this happen? I put the key into the ignition just as I saw Joey and TJ walking out. Joey lifted his hand up as if trying to stop me, but I ignored him and continued to back out as fast as I could.

Not sure where I was headed, I jumped on the main road. Too upset to go see my father now, I decided to stop at the first liquor store I came to, so I could buy a bottle of Jack and several cans of Coke. I found one, and before leaving filled a plastic glass from the soda fountain with ice. I jumped in the car and started driving again. As I passed by Finley Church, I decided to pull in. What better place to have a drink than here?

I parked and made myself a healthy whiskey and Coke which I sipped as I thought about Joey's son. That could have been our son. Back then, I was willing to have a child before the fear of having one had time to set in.

Car after car pulled into the church parking lot as I continued to sip on my drink and think about what might have been. It was funny how often things worked out the complete opposite of how you thought they would. I used to drive by this church all the time picturing my wedding here. Instead, I was there for my twin brother's funeral.

I squeezed my eyes shut as I tried to erase the image of them lowering him into the ground and gulped down the rest of my drink. I made another one, this time much stronger.

By the time I had drunk it, the parking lot was almost completely full. There must have been some kind of service here today.

I mixed myself one more Jack and Coke and took my glass with me as I walked slowly around to the side of the church where the cemetery was.

Most of my relatives, along with James now, were buried there. I stopped and looked around. It was a nice cemetery as far as cemeteries went. Butted up to a thick wooded area, it even had a little stream running alongside it. I gathered up some courage and walked up to where James' headstone was. There were what appeared to be flowers only a few days old, lying next to his grave. Someone had been here recently. It must have been Mother. I looked at the headstone as my throat tightened up.

James Parker—1990 - 2008. Cherished son, brother and friend.

Taking another gulp of my drink, I sat down in a matted area of grass next to his grave and took off my shoes.

"Hello, brother," I said. "I made it back to see you. I didn't think I would. I haven't been here since I left and drove all the way to California all by myself eight years ago. Joey chickened out and for some reason didn't go with me. But that's okay. I met someone else. His name is Dan. We're married. I think you'd like him," I said, deciding not to mention that Dan had been unfaithful to me. James wouldn't like that.

"Dad's sick, James, I mean really sick. That's why I came back here. I'm staying at the house with Mother if you can believe it. I think she quit drinking. And guess what? I think she has a boyfriend too. Is that crazy or what?" I asked taking another sip.

As I lowered the glass, I swear I could hear music coming from the church, but it didn't sound like funeral music. It sounded like wedding music. I squeezed the glass as I thought about Dan and Susan again and how I wished I'd never gotten married. And now some girl was in this very church and about to make the biggest mistake of her life. Maybe it was up to me to let her know what she was about to do. I stood up, took a big gulp nearly draining the glass, and turned.

"I'll be right back," I said walking barefoot, toward the front of the church.

As I got closer, I could see a black limousine with a 'Just Married' sign on its back window and white streamers hanging down from the bumper parked in front of the church. The driver looked at me as I stumbled by and made my way up the church steps. As soon as I walked through the doors, I stopped, feeling as if I'd just been punched in the stomach as once again, I pictured James' casket in the front of the church.

I tried to erase the sight from my mind and walked into the hall. A girl in a long white dress was making her way down the aisle toward the front of the church. She had an older-looking balding man at her side. With one last swallow, I took several more steps into the hall.

"Don't do it. You're making a mistake," I yelled out.

But apparently no one could hear me over the music.

"Stop!" I screamed at the top of my lungs.

The music suddenly stopped, and the bride and her escort turned around to see where the hollering was coming from. Several people up near the front turned around too and looked toward the back of the church. More and more heads turned until nearly everyone in the church was staring at me.

A woman from the front called out, "who are you and what do you want?"

"Hi," I said now realizing that I've might have made a mistake but knowing that it was too late to back out now. "Sorry to interrupt, but I wanted to let you know," I looked toward the bride, "that marriage never works. Trust me, I know." I could detect a bit of a slur in my voice.

There were several loud gasps from around the room. I reached out with my free hand to steady myself and held onto one of the pews before continuing. "Believe me, it might look like one big fairytale right now, but he'll end up breaking your heart. If you're smart, you'll run for your life." Now even more gasps filled the room along with murmuring.

"Karen? Karen Parker. Is that you?" I looked around trying to see where the voice was coming from. A man stepped down from the front and made his way toward me. As he got closer, I recognized him. It was Pastor Phil.

"I thought I recognized your voice," he said as he continued toward me and then stopped. "But I guess it's not Parker anymore."

"Karen Parker?" I heard someone close by say. "Isn't that the girl whose brother hung himself?"

"Shot himself," I snapped back loudly. Again, the church buzzed with loud murmuring. I looked at Pastor Phil, remembering how kind he was to me at James' funeral.

"What're you doing, dear?" he asked in a soothing voice. "This couple is in love. I see no reason why they shouldn't be married."

I looked at the bride again with the groom now standing next to her with his arm around her shoulder protectively.

"But she needs to know the truth, Pastor Phil," I said, this time in a little lower voice. "I have to warn her about what she's getting herself into."

"Hush now," he said gently taking my elbow and leading me out to the foyer. "Why don't you sit down here?" He pointed to a bench near the door.

"Karen?" I looked up to see Joey standing in the doorway and he did not look happy.

"Well if it isn't Officer Joey," I said as I started to get up. But as I stood, I felt myself immediately start to tip forward. I quickly reached down and scratched my bare foot in a futile attempt to make it look like I planned to bend forward. But one look at Joey's face and I knew he hadn't fallen for it.

"So," I said, trying to act nonchalant, "what brings you here? Oh, I know. You changed your mind. You realized that you wanted to marry me after all. So, where's the ring?"

Joey looked at Pastor Phil with raised eyebrows, then back at me. "Someone called the station to report that a drunk woman was causing a disturbance at the church and I happened to be close by. It's you they called about? What's going on?"

Pastor Phil patted me on the arm. "You're in good hands now. So, I guess I'd better get back inside. I have a wedding to attend to.

And please say hello to your mother and father for me. We're all praying for him."

As he shut the hall doors, I could hear voices coming from inside the church. I turned back to Joey who was now staring at the tumbler in my hand. His eyes made their way down to my bare feet.

"What happened to your shoes?" he asked.

"I left them with James," I said with a sarcastic grin.

He looked at me strangely. "What? Never mind. Let's go outside," he said, taking my arm and leading me down the steps. He walked me over to his police car parked in front of the limousine and opened the passenger door. Joey gently pushed me down into the seat as he took the glass from my hands. I started to protest as he dumped the ice on the ground. "I can't have this in my car."

I looked down at the wet spot, sadly.

"So why are you here?" he asked.

I looked back up at him. "That girl has a right to know what she's getting herself into." And then as if on cue, the wedding music started to play inside again.

"I should get you home," Joey said. "Where's your purse?"

"In the car," I said. I watched as Joey got my purse out of the Mustang. I prayed that he didn't see the bottle of whiskey I'd left on the passenger side floor. Apparently, he didn't and as I watched, he locked the car and came back with my purse. He handed it to me and leaned in close. Alarmed, I pulled back.

"I wasn't going to kiss you if that's what you thought," he said as he buckled my seat belt. "Come on. I'll take you home and I can bring you back to get the car tomorrow."

Embarrassed, I looked away as he shut the door and got into the driver's side. After saying a few words into his CB, Joey pulled the car out slowly and headed toward home. We drove for several minutes when he turned to me.

"What's going on with you? First, you bolt out of the restaurant this morning like a crazy woman, then you show up at the church making a scene. And it's obvious, you've been drinking. I can't believe you started doing that after what you saw your mother go through."

I looked at him. "What's going on? You want to know what's going on?" I took a breath and it all came spilling out. How my father might be dying, and my husband had been cheating on me.

"Oh, and let's not forget the part about seeing my ex-boyfriend, the guy who broke my heart," I said glaring at Joey. "Or that I'm forced to come back to deal with my mother in the very town where my only sibling shot himself. How's that for starters?"

Joey looked at me and for the first time, I could see the deep lines etched in his face. He was just as handsome but looked much older than the man I had left behind eight years ago.

"Karen, I'm sorry about your dad. You know that. I do know he's going to beat this. And it doesn't make me happy to hear that your husband has been cheating on you, believe it or not. And I do realize it must be difficult to come back here and see your mother again. But maybe it's time you and she talked. Especially since she's doing so well now. Straighten some things out with her."

"Like why she tried to kill herself? Why didn't anyone call to tell me that happened? I guess I can see why she didn't tell me, but my father knew how to get a hold of me. And you could have tracked me down if you'd really wanted to," I said feeling hurt.

"Your Mother asked everyone not to tell you," he said. "She was afraid that if you knew what she had tried to do, you'd think about coming back. She didn't want you to until you were ready, not just because of what she had done. But she's doing a lot better now like I said. I think going to AA has a lot to do with it."

"And maybe the fact that she has a lover," I blurted out. Instantly, the car slowed down.

"What makes you think she has a lover? "he asked turning and looking at me again.

"Oh, I guess that's one thing that I know that you don't," I gloated. "There's been some guy hanging around the house. I know because I found some of his things he'd left."

"I think you must be confused," Joey said.

"Whatever," I said leaning my head back. "I just wish I didn't have to find out about her driving off that bridge from 'Timmy' at the Huddle House."

"Timmy? Who's Timmy?" he asked.

I didn't reply, and suddenly felt very sleepy. I turned away and closed my eyes. The next time I opened them, I was surprised to find I was sitting in front of the house in Joey's police car. I looked at him and tried to remember why I was there. Then, feeling embarrassed as it came back to me, I put my hand on the door, anxious to go inside.

"Wait," he said. "We need to talk some more. I wanted to explain some things to you. I hated the way things ended up between us, you know. I never meant to hurt you. I loved you. You know that."

My heart beat faster, and I took my hand off the door. Finally, I was about to learn the truth. "So then why didn't you go away with me if you loved me so much, Joey?"

He looked up toward the ceiling then back at me. "Because I thought I was doing what was best for you."

"Best for me? How was ripping my heart out, best for me?" I asked angrily. He looked away.

"Oh, just forget it," I said opening the door. "It doesn't matter now. You and I have our own lives now. I have a husband and you have your new little family."

"My family?" he asked. "What does my family have to do with this?"

The porch light went on and we both turned to look toward the front door. Mother came out and stood there looking in our direction.

"I better go," I said quickly. "And don't worry about taking me to get the Mustang tomorrow. I'll find my own way. I always do."

Mother hurried toward the car and before I could get out, she leaned in.

"Where's James' car?" she asked looking over at me.

As I racked my brain to try and come up with a plausible answer, Joey jumped in.

"I was making my rounds earlier and happened to notice the Mustang at Finley's Church with the hood up," He looked at me then continued. "Apparently, it was having engine trouble. So, I suggested that the best thing to do was to leave the car there overnight and have it checked in the morning."

I could see her eyes narrow briefly. "Well, I was going to call you anyway, Karen. The hospital called, and your father isn't doing well. I'm heading there now."

"What's wrong with him?" I asked as worry set in.

"They said he was having a tough time breathing again. That tumor must be pushing on his lung," she replied anxiously. "Do you want to go with me?"

I hesitated. I wanted to go. But if I went with her, she was bound to know I'd been drinking. And I didn't want to get into it with her.

"Why don't we all go?" Joey suggested. "Karen can ride with me. This way, I can lead the way and we'll get there faster."

At this point, if I hadn't been so angry at Joey, I'd have kissed him.

"Thanks Joey," Mother said.

"Wait. I'll be right back," I said remembering I didn't have any shoes on. "I just have to use the restroom real quick." While Mother headed to her car, I hurried inside and grabbed another pair of shoes I'd brought and made my way back outside again. Mother was waiting in her car behind Joey's, as I jumped back in his passenger seat.

Joey glanced in his rearview mirror as he turned on his sirens.

"Thanks for covering for me," I mumbled as we sped down the driveway. "I'm sure she would've jumped all over my case if she knew the real reason you had to drive me home."

"That's okay," he replied turning onto the street. "I just figured she has enough to worry about with your dad and all. I just hope he's going to be all right."

"Me too," I said as I shuddered at the thought of having to plan another funeral.

CHAPTER 11

WE MADE IT TO THE HOSPITAL IN RECORD TIME AND after dropping me off in front, Joey parked the car while I hurried inside. Either from the bit of time that had passed, or all the excitement, thankfully, I felt a little more sober as I walked into the hospital.

Mother was just getting her visitor's sticker when I walked in. I fished around for a piece of gum and made sure to keep a safe distance from her, so she wouldn't be able to smell the whiskey on my breath.

As soon as we got to his room, she rushed to the side of his bed. My father was lying there with a breathing mask over part of his face.

"Bill, honey. I'm here," she said as she leaned in close. "Karen's here too."

He turned his head slightly in my direction then back at Mother. I could see her eyes fill with tears as she tenderly rubbed his arm and once again, I was taken aback by how loving they were toward each other.

Maybe there was hope for me and Dan. After all, if they could feel this way after what they went through together, anything was possible. Though as I stared at them, I couldn't remember the last time Dan and I had looked at each other as lovingly as they were doing now. The same nurse from earlier walked in and adjusted my father's mask.

"What happened?" I asked nervously. "We heard he was having a hard time breathing."

"Yes, he woke up and had another bad coughing spell after you left, one that wouldn't quit," the nurse said giving me one of her looks. "We figured it was best to call you and your mother in case it got any worse. But it looks like he's doing better now. But he always does better when you're here," she said to Mother. "Isn't that right, Bill?"

I saw my father's eyes blink several times in agreement. "I'll leave you all alone, but I'll be right outside, if you need anything," the nurse said before she left.

Mother sat down in one of the chairs by the bed and took my father's hand. "You're going to be okay, Bill. You just have to be. I need you." I stared at her. She really did love him, then. But what about the fishing gear I'd seen over at the house?

"How is he?" Joey asked, walking in briskly.

"Better," I said, though I was more worried than I'd been since arriving in town.

Joey looked at me and put his arm around my shoulder. At first, I stiffened up, but then it felt so good to have his strong arm around me that I closed my eyes and leaned against him.

"Joey, can I talk to you for a moment please?" I heard Mother ask. I opened my eyes quickly just as Joey took his arm away.

"Sure, Doris," he said. "What is it?"

"Out there if you don't mind," she motioned toward the hallway. "We'll be right back," she said, I imagined to my father.

I watched them leave as I wondered why she needed to talk to Joey in private. What did she have to say that she couldn't say in front of me or my father? Did it have to do with Joey's arm around me and she didn't like it? So, what, if she didn't approve? She didn't have any room to talk.

I heard a moan coming from the bed. "James?" my father called out. "James, is that you?"

His eyes were open wide, and he was staring right at me.

"No, it's me, Dad," I said nervously.

"James," he said this time even louder, and grabbed at my arm. Startled, I jerked back, almost losing my balance. He reached up and pulled his mask down below his chin.

"Where did you put it James?" he asked.

"It's me, Dad. Karen," I said again frightened. What was wrong with him?

"Oh, Karen," he said as he settled back into his pillow. He closed his eyes and after a few seconds, his breathing slowed, and I could tell that he'd fallen back to sleep.

What was that all about, I wondered. As I stared at him, the nurse came into the room quickly, followed by Joey and my mother.

"What happened?" the nurse asked in a loud whisper as she walked briskly over to the bed and pulled my father's mask back up. "We heard someone yelling all the way down the hall. And why is this off? What did you do?" she asked accusingly.

"I didn't do it," I said as I looked at Joey and Mother. "He woke up and pulled it off himself. He thought I was James, I think. He was trying to ask him something." But everyone looked at me skeptically, especially the nurse.

"Like I told you earlier, this excitement isn't good for him. Maybe it would be best if you all visited a little longer than let him try and get some sleep. Just go home for now. I'll call you again if I think you should come back. But he really needs his rest."

We hated to leave but after a few minutes of watching him as he laid there lifeless, plus another trip back from the nurse eyeing us, we decided she was right and that it would be best if we headed back home.

"Okay," Mother said as she touched Dad's hand gently and whispered goodnight in his ear. And told him that she'd only be a phone call away. I whispered goodbye to him as well and we all headed out of the room.

I let Mother get a few feet ahead before I tugged on Joey's arm. "What did she want to talk to you about?"

"Nothing much," he said, though he looked guilty and continued out to the parking lot.

"Thanks for coming, Joey, and leading the way," Mother said as we got outside the car.

"No problem," Joey replied. "I'll talk to you tomorrow," he said to me before he left.

As soon as I got in the car with Mother, I asked her the same thing. "What were you and Joey talking about?"

"Oh, just something that's been bothering both of us," she replied. "What happened in there with your father?"

"I don't know. It was really strange. Like I said, he thought I was James, and was trying to tell him something."

We didn't say much to each other the rest of the way home. And I couldn't wait to climb into bed when we got there.

The next morning, I awakened to the smell of fresh coffee. Once again, it took me a minute to remember where I was. My clothes were in a pile on the floor. I must have been too tired last night to even put them away. I picked them up and got dressed, then made my way to the kitchen.

"Good morning," Mother said, looking up from the kitchen table. She had a cup of coffee in her hand. "The hospital already called. They plan on doing that laser surgery today. Where they make a small incision in his chest and go in with a tiny camera and laser off any cancer. It's supposed to be fairly simple and much less invasive than regular surgery. And the recovery time is a lot shorter too. They just need to make sure he's strong enough though, before they do it, "she added.

"It's set for three this afternoon and will take about an hour. I'm going to head out there early. Do you want me to take you to get the Mustang, so we can drop it off at the shop? You can ride with me to the hospital or I can come back and pick you up later. Or maybe we should just call the shop and have a tow truck get it."

I looked at her confused for a moment, until I remembered that the Mustang was still at the church because I'd had a little too much to drink and Joey had had to take me home...but she didn't know any of that. So, I'd just ride with her now to the church and make up some excuse as to why it was suddenly running just fine, after we got there.

"Maybe it was just overheated or something," I said acting surprised when it started right up.

But Mother insisted we take it to the shop anyway to get it checked out, so I kicked the bottle of whiskey under the seat and backed up. Remembering that I'd left a pair of my shoes at the cemetery, I decided to get them some other time when she wasn't around.

She followed close behind me all the way to the shop. As I drove up, the sign on the building filled me with memories.

—

Bill's Auto Repair. James and I used to love hanging out there when we were young. Dad would order a pizza and James and I would eat while we watched our father tinkering on a car. The last time I was here though, wasn't under the best of circumstances. It was right after James' funeral and I was raw with grief and anger.

I'd been angry that no one had stopped James from doing what he did, especially my father. And I told him just that, how I blamed him for James' death and that I was leaving and never wanted to talk to him or Mother again. And I didn't, except for a couple of times when he called around the holidays.

"You can go now" I said to Mother as I got out of the car and headed inside. "I'll have them give me a loaner if they are unable to repair it right away."

"That's okay," she said, "I'll wait until you find out what they say one way or another."

Groaning, I headed inside so I could pretend that I was really getting the car checked out. A bell over the door rang as I walked in. The last time I'd heard that bell was when I'd stormed out of here eight years ago.

I stepped into the shop stopping to look around. Everything looked exactly the same. Same posters and same pictures on the walls. It even had the same tire smell that strangely enough I used to like. Ever since then, every time I smelled rubber, I thought of my father.

"Hi there. Can I help you?" a young man in blue overalls asked as he came walking in from the back. I turned and looked out the window again and waved frantically to Mother, telling her that it was okay to go. Thankfully, after a few seconds, she waved, backed out and left.

"No thanks," I said, turning quickly and heading for the door. But before I could open it, I heard someone else call out my name.

"Karen?"

I turned around again. Another man, a little older and also dressed in blue overalls stood staring at me. He had short brown hair and a stocky build. Though I didn't recognize him at first, there was something familiar about him. But then I knew. It was Steve, Beth's old boyfriend and the boy who used to terrorize my brother back in school.

"It's you," I said gritting my teeth.

"Hello," he said. "Nice to see you again."

Well, it's definitely not nice to see you again, I thought as we stared at each other. The other mechanic excused himself and made his way to the back. Steve cleared his throat and looked out the window.

"Is there something wrong with the Mustang?"

I stared at him a few seconds longer. "You actually work here at my father's shop?" I asked in disbelief.

"Yes," he replied sounding almost apologetic. "I'm the head mechanic."

"Oh, so what happened to your moving away and becoming a big-time attorney? Things didn't work out like you planned, then?" I asked, relieved to find out that his dreams didn't work out like he'd hoped.

Steve's face turned red. "I decided to stay here in Easley and do something else. But it's okay. Everything worked out for the best. And I like being a mechanic, especially working for your dad."

"Well there's nothing wrong with my brother's car and I wouldn't let you touch it if there was," I snapped, as I opened the door to leave again.

"Wait," he said. "Before you go, do you think we can talk?"

I turned around again. "Talk about what, Steve?"

He looked down at the floor. "About James," he replied softly. "Can we talk about James?"

Just hearing him say my brother's name infuriated me.

"I don't think you want to go there," I warned him.

"Please. I'd really like to talk to you about that. I won't take up much of your time, I promise," he said.

As much as I wanted to leave and never see his face again, I was curious what he could possibly want to say to me about my brother.

"Okay. What is it?" I asked, crossing my arms.

He looked around nervously. "Can we go somewhere private to talk? How about your dad's office?"

I uncrossed my arms and left him standing there as I marched toward my father's office in the back. I sat at my dad's desk and I waited for Steve to tell me what he had to say. He sat across from me and cleared his throat, again.

"First of all, I wanted you to know that I appreciated the fact that you never told your parents how I treated James so poorly back in school. I tried to talk to them about it one day so I could apologize, and they had no idea what I was talking about. I'm really grateful to you for doing that."

"I didn't do it for you," I said. "There just was no reason to upset them."

"Well, I appreciate it," he went on, "Anyway, I know I was a real jerk back then and there's no excuse for the way I acted toward your brother. And to tell you the truth, I wouldn't blame you if you never talked to me again. The other day when Beth got home and told me you were in town, I knew I just had to see you while you were still here and tell you just how truly sorry, I was."

When Beth got home? That meant they lived together. That's too bad. I'd hoped by this time she had dumped him and was with someone nice.

Like I did with Joey, I glanced down at Steve's hand, hoping she hadn't been dumb enough to marry him at least. I hadn't noticed a wedding ring on Beth, but I hadn't really been looking, either. And though Steve wasn't wearing a wedding band, that didn't necessarily mean anything. Mechanics didn't normally wear jewelry when they were working on cars. I knew my father didn't.

I stood up. "Okay, so you apologized. Do you feel better now? Because I sure don't. All the apologies in the world aren't going to bring my brother back."

"I know that," he said. "I just wanted you to know how I felt. And one day, I hope you'll find it in your heart to forgive me."

"Well, don't hold your breath," I said, turning to leave one more time.

The bell jingled again as I headed out to the Mustang. As I got in the car, I could see Steve's face in the window looking out at me. Disgusted, I backed the car up and headed for the road.

I'd never forgive him for the way he treated my brother, especially that last night at Applebee's when he said all those horrible things about James in front of all of us. I stepped on the gas and headed for the hospital.

—

I was only a few miles down the road when I heard a horn honking behind me. Irritated, I looked in my rearview mirror to find flashing red lights behind me.

I lifted my foot off the gas and glanced at the speedometer. I must have been speeding. The police car pulled up close behind me with its lights still flashing. I couldn't see who it was but hoped it was Joey just messing with me. But to be on the safe side, I pulled over anyway.

As I reached for my purse to get my driver's license out, there was a rap on my window. And there he stood with a big silly grin on his face.

"You scared me half to death," I said as I rolled down the window. "I thought for a moment that I was getting pulled over by a real cop."

Joey raised his eyebrows. "I am a real cop and you really were speeding. Have you been gone from here so long that you forgot that the speed limit's thirty-five on this road?"

"I guess I was distracted," I said, still annoyed. "I just had a little chat with Steve at the shop and I'm still fuming. I can't believe my father actually hired him."

"Oh, so that's what's got you driving like a crazy woman?" he asked. "Yes, Steve's been a mechanic there for a few years. He's good too. He's pretty much been your dad's right hand since he found out he had cancer. I'm assuming your talk with him didn't go very well?"

"You got that right," I said angrily. "I can't stand the sight of him after the way he treated James. And he had the nerve to think that an apology would make everything okay. It's a little too late for apologies as far as I'm concerned."

"I don't blame you for being upset," he said leaning against the car. "But I do know that he does feel bad for how mean he was to James in school. And believe it or not, he's changed. That was a long time ago and he's not the same jerk he used to be. He's actually a good guy. And we've gotten to be pretty good friends, too. And most importantly, he's a good husband to Beth, which makes me very happy."

"Oh, so she did end up marrying him after all?" I shook my head. "That's too bad. I was hoping she'd marry a nice guy."

"They got married not too long after you left. They're really happy too. He *is* a nice guy. But I didn't pull you over to talk about Steve. I wanted to know how your dad was doing and get you to slow down."

"He's okay, I guess," I said feeling the worry come back. "Though Mother said they want to operate on him later today."

"Oh no. What time are they planning on doing that? Maybe I can stop by for support."

"About three o'clock, I think she said." I replied.

"Good, that will give us time to go somewhere and grab a drink. Non-alcoholic that is," he added quickly, "so we can talk."

I looked at him, annoyed by his non-alcoholic comment. "That's okay. Some other time. I thought I'd head over there early, anyway."

"Come on. No use waiting there and worrying. You can spare a half hour for me, can't you? I'm sure you have plenty of things you're dying to ask me."

He was right about that. "Okay, but I'm not going to stay long."

"Great. I'll see you at Larry's Diner. It's on the way to the hospital. You remember the place, don't you?" he asked.

"Of course," I replied as I thought about the killer hot fudge cake they made there.

Joey and I went there on every birthday, both his and mine, to have a piece. Though, we didn't make it there for Joey's last birthday, when I still lived here, after what happened at Applebee's.

"I'll see you there," he said as he hit his siren one more time then pulled out onto the street. Knowing I should just head in the other direction and stand him up like he stood me up, I followed him anyway.

CHAPTER 12

WHAT WAS I DOING, I ASKED MYSELF AS I DROVE BEHIND him? Did I really need to make things any more complicated than they already were? *Turn around*, my brain screamed. But I couldn't. I'd been waiting too long to talk to him face to face.

The parking lot at Larry's was fairly empty, which was a good thing. If anyone saw us there with each other, it wouldn't take long before rumors would start about how Joey and I were back together.

He walked with me inside. The hostess led us to a small table by the window where we both ordered coffee and, against my wishes, Joey ordered a hot fudge cake with two spoons. He stared across the table at me as we waited for our drinks.

"Quit looking at me like that," I said. "You're making me nervous."

"I can't help it. You're even more beautiful than you used to be, as if that's even possible," he said as the waitress returned with our cups and a huge piece of chocolate cake dripping with hot fudge and smothered with whipped cream.

Joey slid a spoon over to me as the waitress walked away.

"But if it's making you nervous, I'll change the subject. How do you like living in California? I imagine we all look like a bunch of hicks here, now that you live there."

"Not really," I said. "I'm still a country girl at heart. I like it there, but I miss a lot of things back here, too. Like the empty roads. And how quiet it is. I'll never get used to all that traffic in LA."

"I bet," he said spooning a huge bite into his mouth. "I've seen on the news how bad the traffic jams are there. I could never live in a big city like that where it's always congested. Is your husband from California originally?"

I looked at him feeling a bit uncomfortable talking about Dan, but I answered him anyway. "Yes. He was born and raised in LA."

"He's a contractor, right?" he asked.

I stopped with my spoon in midair and looked at him suspiciously. "How'd you know he was a contractor?"

Joey smiled mysteriously. "I'm a cop, remember?"

I waited for him to tell me how he really found out, and eventually he sighed and put his spoon down.

"Okay. So, I admit I might have peeked at your Facebook page once or twice over the years."

I tried not to smile so I wouldn't let on that I'd done the same thing and looked at his page too—and much more than once or twice.

"Well you're right. He's really great with wood. He can build anything. He's done very well with his business, that is except for this past year. The slowing economy's hit him hard which has been difficult on us both of us," I said sadly.

"That's too bad. The recession has hurt a lot of businesses here in Easley too. Except in my line of work, of course. The worse the economy gets, the busier I get unfortunately. Job security, I guess. Maybe this is none of my business, but yesterday you mentioned something about him cheating on you. What's that all about?"

I felt myself blush. "I did? Never mind. It was nothing."

Joey reached out and touched my hand. "Nothing? I don't know if I believe that. But we don't have to talk about it if you don't want to. Just remember, if you ever need a shoulder to cry on, you can always count on me."

I pulled my hand away and thought back to how Joey *wasn't* there for me when I really needed him, when I'd decided to leave Easley eight years ago and move away. So, they felt like empty words, the sort of words a man could conjure up just to try and hook a woman again.

"Let's talk about something other than my husband," I said feeling angry again.

"Okay. Let's talk about me and you then," he said.

I looked him square in the eyes. "Okay. Let's do that. So, tell me, Joey. When did you stop loving me? I thought we were going to spend the rest of our lives together but apparently you had other plans. Tell me the truth. What happened? Was it that you couldn't handle all the drama with my family and figured you'd better bail while you still could?"

Joey rubbed a spot between his eyebrows. It was something I remembered he did whenever he was feeling pressured. "What are you talking about? It wasn't that at all."

"So, what, then. Another girl?"

"No," he said. "I'll tell you the truth. But you're not going to like it."

I put my spoon down. "So, it was because of another woman. Just admit it."

Joey looked across the table with surprise. "There was no other woman. I've never loved anyone but you. Don't you know that? It was because of James. It's funny. Your brother was the reason we got together as well as the very reason we aren't together anymore, too."

I stared at him blankly. "What on earth do you mean?"

He pushed the half-eaten cake aside. "Several weeks before he died, James called me asking if we could talk. We hadn't seen each other much at the time, so I knew it had to be important. So, I suggested that we meet at your house which we did. And that's when he told me that he was in love with Beth."

My jaw dropped. "What? I don't believe it."

"I know, I was just as shocked as you are now. And at first, I thought he was messing with me, but he wasn't. He really liked her and wanted to ask her out. I guess he wanted my blessing or something. I still can't believe that I never noticed that he had feelings for her. You didn't know?"

I flashed back to Mother's comment about how James had always acted odd when Beth was around. She was right, and here I'd totally missed it. Just like I'd missed all those signs with Dan.

"No, but my mother noticed something. But even if it was true, which I find extremely hard to believe, I still don't get it. What's all that got to do with you not wanting to be with me?"

"Because…" he said slowly, "when he told me how he felt about my sister, well, it caught me by surprise, and I didn't know how to react. I ended up telling him that I didn't approve of him asking her out. And that I wanted him to have nothing to do with her. At least not, romantically." Joey looked down at the table.

"What? Why on earth would you tell him that? You liked James. Ever since you protected him from Steve and the other bullies at school, you were best friends. He was good to you too, helping you with all your homework. Why wouldn't you want him dating your sister?"

"You're right. He was the best friend I ever had. But still I thought Beth would be better off with someone else. Not someone like James."

I felt the hair bristle on the back of my neck. "Someone like James? What's that supposed to mean?"

Joey's face turned even redder. "I meant someone who was in better health and could take care of her, that's all. James was a great guy and all. And it's not that he wouldn't have been good to her, because I know he would have. It's just let's face it, he could barely walk up a flight of stairs without gasping for breath. You said it yourself."

Now it was my face that got red.

"I just wanted to know that she would end up with someone who'd be there for the long-haul," he continued. "I couldn't bear the thought of her being alone like my mother was after my father died."

I stared at him. "So, what you really were afraid of was that he was too unstable to go out with your sister. Isn't that right? That maybe he'd try to kill himself like he'd tried once before?" I felt the anger building. "What else did you say to my brother?'

Joey squirmed in his seat, then looked at me with tears in his eyes. "I told him that if he really cared for Beth, he'd realize that she'd be better off with someone else." He looked away for a moment. "I'll never forget the look on his face. I really hurt him. But I honestly thought that I was doing what was best for her and for him too. It wouldn't have lasted long and they'd both have ended up getting hurt. They were too different. You have to admit that."

They were completely opposite, that was for sure. But still, for Joey to say that to James was nothing short of cruel.

"Things were never the same between me and James after that," he continued. "That's why when you put that birthday dinner together and told me that you'd invited him, I tried to talk you out of it. The only reason I went was because I thought he'd never show up anyway after our argument. But he did. Maybe because he knew Beth was going."

I thought back to that night again. Now it all made sense why James and Joey both were acting so strange all evening. And why Steve came barging into the restaurant, saying those horrible things about James. Maybe Steve knew how James felt about Beth. Maybe Beth told Steve. Poor James, he had to have felt like such a loser when Beth ended up leaving with Steve that night.

I looked across the table at Joey. He looked so lost and broken, I couldn't help but feel sorry for him. This clearly must have been eating him up all these years. "Why didn't you tell me about this back then? I'd never have invited James or Beth to begin with."

"I know, I should have, but every time I thought about telling you, I just couldn't. I knew you'd be angry. And then when James killed himself and I realized it was partly my fault, I just couldn't think of spending my life with you after what I'd done. I knew you'd never be able to forgive me, either. I know I can't even forgive myself."

I thought about it. *Could* I have forgiven him if I'd known? It would be hard, but if the shoe was on the other foot and it was my sister we were talking about, I'm not sure if I wouldn't have felt the same way. I loved James, but Joey was right. He wasn't the healthiest guy around and I had worried that he might not live to be a ripe old age with all his health issues.

"You should have told me anyway," I said. "Maybe you and I would still be together if you'd been honest with me. Instead, you were a coward and just let me go on wondering all these years, if maybe everyone was right. That I was damaged goods too, doomed to end up like James or my mother. How could you have let me go on thinking that?"

"What're you talking about?" he asked with a look of amazement. "I never thought that about you. I loved you. I still do."

"I should go," I said reaching for my purse.

"Listen to me Karen. I love you," he said. "And I want you back."

I headed for the door.

"When are you going to stop running away every time you don't want to face the truth?" he called out as I hurried out of the diner. I jumped into the car and started it up. Maybe he was right. I did run away when things got tough. As I started to back up, the phone rang. I stopped long enough to look at the number. I froze. It was Mother.

"Is he all right?" I asked before she had a chance to say anything.

"Yes, but his blood pressure went up, so they had to postpone the surgery. They said if it goes back down, they can try again tomorrow. I just wanted to let you know so you didn't rush out here."

"Thanks." I said as out of the corner of my eye, I saw Joey coming out of the diner. He headed for my car. "Tell Dad I'll see him later," I said, hanging up quickly.

Joey stood there watching as I drove away.

CHAPTER 13

"JACK AND COKE, PLEASE," I SAID, SLIDING ONTO THE same stool I sat in last time I was there. I set my purse on the bar. The same bartender who had waited on me yesterday walked over and set a napkin down. "Sorry, but today's Sunday."

"What, people around here don't drink on Sunday?" I asked slightly irritated.

He laughed. "What I meant is, we can't serve hard alcohol on Sunday. This is a dry county. Beer and wine only."

He was right. I remembered now. Easley was in Pickens County. Pickens was one of the few counties around here that weren't allowed to serve hard alcohol on a Sunday. That was why Mother made sure that she was well stocked up every Saturday night. That also meant that unless I wanted to drive to another county, I'd have to settle for beer or wine. I'd never tried either.

"Okay, wine then please."

"Red or white?" he asked, reaching for a wine glass.

I flashed back to Dan's red wine spilling onto the table at Angelo's and the image of the blood all over James' shirt.

"White," I replied quickly.

A few minutes later, he was back with a large goblet filled almost to the brim with white wine. I took a sip and although I didn't exactly care for the taste, I took several more. As I sat there sipping on the wine, my mind went over my conversation with Joey.

So, he'd wanted me back all along, and was just afraid I wouldn't want him after what he'd said to James. He knew I'd be angry. And I would have been. Did what he said to James drive him to take his life? There had to be more to it than that.

Maybe it was because of Beth and how he knew he couldn't have her. I was still baffled that he had feelings for her to begin with, and how I never realized it. As far as I could remember, when she used to come over to the house, he barely said two words to her and went right to his room.

Did she know how he felt about her? Maybe that was the reason she'd stopped coming over to the house and avoided me. Maybe she'd known how he felt, and it made her uncomfortable. She would have known that I'd be concerned she was going to hurt him.

I'd have to ask her about all that when I saw her next. What a colossal mess all this was.

Glass almost empty, I ordered a refill. Shortly after the bartender had brought a fresh one, I lifted the now full glass to my lips and stopped. I stared at my reflection in the mirror across from me.

Was I really that naïve to have thought that just by changing my hair, I could be someone else and forget my past? What had I been thinking? I'd never be able to hide where I'd come from and who I was. I was stuck with it for the rest of my life.

That was the beauty of acting, and one of the reasons I'd signed up back in high school. Acting allowed me to be someone else. People didn't see me anymore, didn't see the girl with the alcoholic mother and the brother who was a bit odd. They saw Dorothy or Alice, or whoever else I was playing at the time. And while up there on stage, I could forget who I was too. At least for a few hours.

"Ready for another?" the bartender asked. As I looked down at my glass, I was surprised to see it was almost empty again. As he reached down, I noticed a rather large tattoo on his arm.

"Who's Sandy?" I asked, tilting my head to read the name.

He looked down at his forearm. "Oh, that's my wife. She wanted me to get it. I guess it's her way of making sure I'd never forget about her. As if I could," he laughed as he picked up the glass and headed off for more wine.

I thought about James. At first, after he'd died, I couldn't stop thinking about him. I made up my mind then, to bury the memory of him because it had hurt too much to think about him and the way he'd died. And though I often asked myself how I could have prevented his death, I tried to forget everything else about him, even though I felt guilty about it. How could I allow myself to forget about my brother like that?

"Where'd you get it done?" I asked when the bartender returned with my glass.

"Right down the street," he said setting it down. "Why? You're not thinking of getting one, are you? People tend to do some pretty crazy things when they've been drinking. Things they end up really regretting. You might want to think about this."

I ignored his advice, determined to do something about this guilt I'd been carrying around for way too long. "Is it within walking distance?"

"I guess if you have comfortable shoes on," he said. "Two blocks down on the left." He turned and took a card from the pegboard on the wall, handing it to me. "This is the place. But don't blame me if you're sorry about it tomorrow."

I took the card from his hand. "I won't."

The name of the shop was 'Tattered'. There was a picture of a muscular, flexed and tattooed arm above the phone number.

"Ask for Bobby Junior. Tell him Big Al sent you," the bartender said as I stood up. I placed a napkin over my half-full glass of wine.

"I'll be back," I said and headed for the door.

After walking for about a block, I started to question what I was about to do. Since I'd been in town, I'd found myself doing some things really out of character for me. Drinking, hanging out in a bar, and now I was off to get a tattoo. I felt out of control, but it felt liberating at the same time.

I opened the door and walked in. Every inch of the walls was covered with photos of various tattooed body parts. A man with a beard and goggles on looked up at me briefly before bending down again and drilling on a young man's arm. I took a seat nearby and watched until he was finished. After about fifteen minutes, he turned the drill off, stood up and took the goggles off.

"Are you Bobby Junior?" I asked staring at the drill which was much larger than I'd expected. "Big Al sent me."

"That's me," he said as he snapped a photo of the tattoo he'd just completed.

"I'm here to get a tattoo." I said quickly before I changed my mind.

"Okay." He pointed the drill toward a stack of photo albums. "I'll be finished here in a few minutes. You can take a look through those if you want some ideas."

I browsed through one of the albums, and as soon as I saw a photo of a horse galloping, I knew exactly what I wanted.

James used to love to watch the horses run around in the corral next to our house. He often said how he wished he could run fast and effortlessly like they did. I, on the other hand, had wished I could fly like a bird, so I could fly away anytime I wanted to.

"I want a horse right here," I pointed at my wrist, "with a bird circling overhead. And make it look like the horse is running like in this photo," I said, holding up the photo album.

"Sure," he said then walked over to a desk and scribbled on some paper. He came back and showed it to me. "Something like this?" he asked as I looked at the drawing.

"Perfect." I nodded. After putting on a fresh pair of plastic gloves, he wiped the inside of my wrist with a cotton ball and turned on the drill. It sounded quite loud as he brought it in close. I jerked my arm away from him.

"What's wrong?" he asked, looking alarmed.

My eyes teared up not only from the thought of the drill digging into my skin, but as a memory popped into my head. It was from when James and I were around five years old. It had been raining for a solid week and finally when the sun did come out, Mother laid a blanket on the grass, tossed some toys down and told me and James to get out of her hair and play so she could take a nap.

While out there, several bees started buzzing around – it was the same buzzing noise the drill just made. One of the bees landed on James' arm. I can still see the fear on his face as he stared down at it.

Without thinking, I brushed the bee off his arm, and it landed on my leg and stung me. I screamed, and waved my arms causing the other bees to get agitated and swarm around us more.

When Mother came out to see what all the noise was about, she saw James crying and snatched him up and brought him inside. I remember waiting for her to come back for me. But she never did.

Eventually, I made my way inside the house and there she was, asleep on the couch with James on her lap. I remembered thinking, even at that early age, that she couldn't possibly love me like she loved him for her to abandon me like that.

I pushed the memory out of my mind and gingerly held my wrist out to him again, squeezing my eyes shut as the drilling began. I didn't open them again until I heard the drill finally come to a stop.

"Whaddya think?" he asked, looking down at my arm with a look of pride

"I love it," I said staring at the tattoo on my very pink wrist as tears sprang to my eyes.

"Okay, I'm going to clean you up and put some ointment on it and a bandage. Keep the bandage on for a few hours then you can take it off. It might be a little sore for a few days, but after a week it should feel fine. If you have any problems, just come back and see me."

I thanked him and let him take a photo of my new tattoo before he covered it with the bandage. On the way back to the Red Penny, my wrist started to sting. But I knew the pain was worth it. It felt good to do this in honor of my brother. And the fact that getting a tattoo was something I'd never have thought of doing before, somehow made it more meaningful.

I picked up the pace, anxious to get back to the Red Penny not only to show Big Al, but to finish my glass of wine. But when I came upon a hair salon on my right, I paused. Why stop with just a tattoo now that I was feeling so brave?

—

Two hours later, I was on my way back to the bar again, not only with a tattoo but now with very dark brown hair. Big Al blinked several times when I walked in.

"I thought you'd changed your mind and weren't coming back. Now I see what took you so long. I guess you decided to get your hair done instead of a tattoo. Smart idea." He set down a fresh glass of wine in front of me. I looked at my reflection in the mirror and this time I liked what I saw.

"I got a tattoo as well," I said, taking a sip then turning my wrist over and gently lifting the bandage, so he could see.

Big Al let out a whistle. "So, you did do it. It's a horse," he said.

"With a bird soaring over it," I added as I covered it back up. "The bird is for me and the horse is for my brother."

"Oh, I heard about your brother. He was your twin, right? "I'm sorry for your loss."

I looked at him sharply. "How'd you know that?" I asked.

"Oh, one of the customers in here earlier recognized you and mentioned he knew your brother who had passed away some years back."

"What else did he say?" I asked wondering if he had mentioned how James had died. I immediately felt defensive. Seemed like the whole world knew the story of the loser boy who had killed himself.

"Just that your brother had fixed his computer for him a few times. And that he was a really nice guy."

I picked up my glass and took a sip. At least it wasn't anything negative about James for a change. Big Al walked away just as my phone started to ring. This time, I recognized Beth's number.

"Hello?"

"Hi. It's me. Are you okay?" she asked. "I was worried about you after you ran out of the restaurant the way you did. And Steve said you stopped by the shop and seemed pretty upset."

Someone down at the end of the bar laughed loudly and I turned to look.

"Where are you?" Beth asked.

I turned my attention back to the call. "I'm at the Red Penny."

"Oh. Are you with someone?" she asked.

"No. I'm by myself," I replied, knowing how it must sound for me of all people to be in a bar all alone.

"See, I do have reason to be concerned," she said. "I can't believe you're in a bar."

"They do serve food here too," I quickly added.

"Are you drinking?" she asked.

I hesitated. 'Yes, but I'm fine, really. I just needed something to clear my head."

"I'm coming down," she said.

"You don't have to. I'm fine, really. Plus, I won't be here that long."

"I'm coming anyway," she said before hanging up.

I was actually glad she was coming. I needed someone to talk to, and Beth was always a great listener.

I'd just finished my wine and ordered another one when she walked in. She looked around the bar and then in my direction. At first, she didn't appear to notice me. Then after a few seconds, she smiled and walked over, pulling out a stool next to me.

"I see you went back to your old hair color. I like it. You look like your old self again."

"Thanks, I guess," I said, looking at myself in the mirror then back at Beth. "I'm glad you came. I wanted to talk to you."

"Me too," she said. "Do you mind if we move to a table where it's quieter, though?"

"Sure," I picked up my glass of wine and followed her to a table. No sooner did we sit down when Big Al set down a couple of cocktail napkins in front of us.

"Welcome," he said, smiling at Beth. "What can I get you? Would you like to see a menu? We have the best burgers in town"

"Just a Diet Coke for now, thank you," Beth replied.

"How about you?" Big Al asked me. "Are you hungry?"

"No, I'm good. Thanks Al. I'll just take another one of these," I said, holding up my glass. Big Al gave me what appeared to be a look of concern before leaving to get our drinks. In a few minutes, he returned with Beth's Diet Coke, my glass of wine and a huge bowl of pretzels which he set down right in front of me.

"How's your father?" Beth asked as he walked away. "Anything new?"

"He was supposed to have laser surgery today, but they put it off. Something about his blood pressure going up. Mother thinks they're going to try again tomorrow, though."

"Let me know if they do. I can take a couple of hours off work and come down and sit with you."

"Thanks," I said. "But I should be fine. So, tell me, how long have you been working at the Huddle House?" I asked as I pushed the bowl of pretzels away and lifted my glass.

"A couple of years, I wasn't planning on working there that long, just a few months to bring in some extra cash. But I like getting out of the house. So, I plan on doing it for a while longer. What about your job? Joey mentioned you're an acting teacher, right?"

"Well, really a coach," I replied, wondering what else Joey had told her about me.

She looked at my glass. "I hope this doesn't upset you, but I do have to admit I'm surprised to see you sitting here in a bar drinking. I remember when you said that you'd never drink. How you'd do anything to keep from ending up like your mother."

I put my glass down. "I never thought I would either. But then I found my husband cheating on me. That's a pretty good reason to start, wouldn't you say?" I asked as I thought about Dan at Angelo's again. My eyes teared up.

"I'm sorry," she said looking startled. "That's terrible."

I looked at her. "I'm the one who should be sorry," I said in a softer tone. "Here, I haven't seen you in all this time and I dump this on you. It must be the wine talking."

"It's okay," she said touching my hand. "I'm glad you did. You can tell me anything, you know. You always could." She picked up her soda and took a sip, then looked at me again. "What happened to us, Karen? We used to be so close."

"I don't know," I said. "That's what I wondered. You're the one who pulled away. And then you didn't even bother to go to my brother's funeral. That really hurt, Beth. You were supposed to be my best friend. You should have been there for me."

She looked down at her glass. "I know. I just couldn't."

"Why?' I asked feeling the old hurt come back. "Because Steve wouldn't let you? Is that why? Since when, did you let someone tell you what to do?"

"Steve had nothing to do with it. In fact, he said I should go and that he'd go with me if I wanted him to. But I knew that wouldn't go over well with you if he was there."

"You're darn right," I said getting angry. "Steve's the last person I wanted to see that day. But you, you were like family. You should have gone. And then you just go and leave a message on my cell phone about how sorry you were. As if that was supposed to make up for you not being there. Well, it didn't."

"I'm sorry," she said again. "I did go by the house later that day and look for you. But your mother said that you had left town. You didn't even say goodbye. That made me sad.

After that, I tried to get a hold of you, but always got your voicemail. Then you changed your number. And once I realized that you'd blocked me on Facebook, I got the message that you didn't want anything to do with me. But I thought about you a lot Karen, and hoped you were okay."

"It was the worst time in my life. I just wish you'd been there," I said, my eyes filling with tears again.

"I know," she said her eyes tearing up too.

Big Al appeared out of nowhere and set a box of tissues down on the table in front of us, then slipped away. I flashed back to the pink perfume lady on the plane and how she'd handed me tissues too. I sure was crying a lot lately which I found odd. I never was much of a crier before.

"I felt so bad for you, and know I should have been there," Beth said, taking a tissue before pushing the box toward me. "And then you and Joey split up. What happened with you two anyway? I've always wondered. I asked him, but he always would give me some lame excuse about needing to stay here to take care of me and Mother. But there had to be more to it than that. He loved you way too much to just let you go like that."

"For the longest time, I wondered what happened too. But I found out earlier the reason he didn't go with me," I said.

"You did?" she asked her eyes widening. "What was it?"

I paused. "It had to do with James."

"James?" she asked sounding surprised. "What about him?"

"Joey told me about something that happened between him and James. But I need to ask you something first, Beth. And I want you to tell me the truth."

Beth's eyes widened. "What is it, Karen?"

CHAPTER 14

I TOOK ANOTHER SIP OF THE WINE. "DID YOU KNOW James was in love with you? Is that the reason you didn't want to be my friend anymore?" I watched her face closely.

She looked at me, then looked away, which was answer enough for me. She did know how he felt. That was why she was acting so strange back then.

"Why, Beth?" I asked. "Why didn't you tell me? Why would you let something like that get in the way of our friendship? I don't understand."

Beth looked down at her wedding ring and twirled it on her finger. Then she looked up again.

"I'm sorry. I didn't think it was a big deal. What does that have to do with you and Joey breaking up anyway?" she asked.

"Because James told Joey that he liked you. And that he wanted to ask you out. But your brother didn't want him to. And he told James exactly that, to basically stay away from you. Joey knew that once I found out what he said to James, I'd be angry. Which I am.'

Beth blinked several times. "Joey told James that? But why?" She looked away then back at me. "Now it makes sense why Joey and James stopped hanging out together. I always wondered what happened between them. They used to be so close."

She was right. Now that I thought about it, Joey and James hadn't been hanging out like they used to. I thought it was because Joey wanted to be with me all the time, not because they had a falling out.

"That makes me really angry. What right did Joey have to say that to him? Though you know how Joey can be," she added, shaking her head.

"He always did think it was up to him to protect everyone. He's been like that ever since our father died. But, poor James. It had to kill him to have his best friend say something like that to him." Beth put her hand up to her mouth, apparently realizing too late her poor choice of words.

"Kill him?" I asked. "I guess you could say that it did kill him," I said. "Literally."

She looked at me. "I didn't mean that. Surely, you don't think James' death had anything to do with what Joey said, do you?"

"Why not? Between that and Steve showing up at the restaurant that night, and saying all those nasty things to James, I'm sure it all played a role in his death. Joey said so himself, that he knows he had a part in it."

Beth looked away again and it made me think there was something she was keeping from me.

"What is it, Beth? What aren't you telling me? Is there some other reason Joey didn't go away with me? What do you know? Was he seeing someone else? You can tell me."

She looked back at me with a shocked expression.

"You mean while he was dating you? Of course not. There's never been anyone but you. He was crazy about you. Really devastated when you left."

"Not that devastated apparently," I said picturing TJ. "It didn't take him long to find someone else once I was gone."

"What're you talking about?" she asked, this time looking confused. "He's barely dated in the last eight years."

"Then what about TJ?" I asked feeling the hurt come back. "He's got to be what, seven or eight years old? Apparently, Joey didn't waste any time getting some girl pregnant once I was out of the picture. Or was he seeing someone when we were together?"

Again, Beth looked confused then her eyes slowly opened wider. "You don't think that TJ is Joey's son, do you? He's my son, not Joey's. Mine and Steve's."

I sucked my breath in quickly and felt the blood rush to my face. I had it totally wrong. Joey was TJ's uncle, not his father.

"So, that's why you were acting so strange at Huddle House yesterday," she said. "You thought TJ was his son. Joey has never been serious about anyone and certainly not enough to have a child with her. Every time a girl starts getting close to him, he dumps her. I've always believed it's because he's clinging to the hope that someday he'll have another chance with you. But I guess it's too late now."

I sat there a moment, trying to add it all up in my head. "TJ is your and Steve's son. So that means you got pregnant soon after I left." This time, my eyes opened wide. "Or, were you pregnant while I was still here? Is that why you pulled away?"

"No. It wasn't until after you were gone that I found out I was pregnant. I only wished you were still here, so I could have told you." Beth's eyes teared up. "I was so young and so scared. And things weren't good with Steve. It was a tough time in my life. I wasn't even sure if I wanted to keep the baby. But I'm so glad I did," she said her eyes watering even more.

"That little boy means everything to me. And Steve's a great father, too." She wiped her eyes and looked at me. "He's changed, Karen. He really has. I know you don't want to believe it, but he's a good man, now."

"Good for him," I said taking another sip of my wine as a time Steve mocked the way James walked came to mind. That was a long time ago, I had to admit. But I was still bitter about it. I set my glass down.

Beth eyed my wrist. "What's that?"

I turned it over and lifted the bandage. "It's for James. He's running like the wind now," I said, my throat tightening up. I wondered if it was really true and James was up in heaven with a perfect body and didn't hurt anymore. I hoped so.

"Oh," she said. She now had tears running down her face. Somewhat surprised by her emotional reaction, I pushed the box of tissues back toward her.

She pulled one out and wiped her eyes. "He was a great guy."

Seeing her cry, made me cry too. Beth let out a little laugh and slid the tissues back toward me.

"Look at us," she said. "Sitting here in a bar, crying. Who would have thought that would ever happen?"

"I know, right?" I said pulling out a few more of the tissues and wiping my eyes. As I looked at my old friend, I was overwhelmed at how much I had really missed her.

"I missed you," I said but as I did, she said it at the same time. We both laughed again.

"I'm so glad you came back," she said, smiling. "I know you and your dad haven't been close ever since he and your mother got divorced, but it's a nice thing you did for him, coming back here. I know it couldn't have been easy."

She looked at her watch. "Uh oh, I need to get going. How're you getting home? You're not planning on driving, are you?" she asked, glancing at my glass of wine.

"Don't worry," I replied. "I'll call a cab if I need one. I think I'm going to swing by the hospital to see my dad before I go back to the house anyway."

"Let me drop you off there, then," she said. "It's not that much out of the way. I'll call work right now and let them know I'll be a little late."

Before I could stop her, she took out her phone and after explaining that she needed to drop a friend off at the hospital, she took out her wallet and some cash.

"Ready?" she asked as she left the money on the table along with mine.

"Sure," I said, standing up. But as we both started to leave, I stopped. There was still a little wine left in my glass, so I picked it up and drained it. As I put the glass back down, I noticed Beth watching me. I was turning into my mother, after all. Embarrassed, I grabbed my purse and hurried out of the bar.

On the way to the hospital, I found myself doing most of the talking. My tongue felt looser, most likely because of the wine and it felt good to finally let some things out.

"Do you think you and Dan are going to make it?" she asked when I'd finally stopped long enough to take a breath.

"I don't know," I replied, feeling a tightening in my chest. "He really hurt me. I never expected him of all people to do something like that."

"I can imagine," she said sadly. "I'm so sorry. You don't have to talk about it anymore if you don't want to."

But I did want to talk about it, especially with her. She knew me better than anyone. As we drove on, I told her everything that had happened after discovering Dan and Susan together at the restaurant, including smashing into his motorcycle.

"I'm sorry you had to go through that," she said. "But I'm not sorry you ran over his motorcycle."

I smiled. Now that was the Beth I remembered.

"Is he serious about that girl?" she asked softly.

"He says he isn't. He tried to say he was just lonely and that's why he started talking to her. That he and I never talk. And though he's right about that, it's still no excuse. I just don't know. Things had been strained ever since the recession. We just couldn't seem to get along, anymore."

"Steve and I went through the same thing when he lost his job at BMW years ago," she said. "Once money got a little tight, we started to argue about the pettiest things, especially over bills. But fortunately for us, he was only out of work for a couple of months before he got that job at your dad's shop, thanks to your mother."

I looked at her. "Thanks to my mother? What did she have to do with it?"

"One afternoon, TJ and I were at Walmart when we ran into her. I mentioned how Steve had just been laid off and your mother told me to tell him to call your dad. She was sure he could find Steve something to do at the shop. That next day, Steve called him, and your dad hired him right over the phone. He even paid for Steve to take a mechanic's course. It was a godsend. He loves working for your dad, too. And I know it's been good for your father to have someone to rely on like him, especially since he's been sick."

—

We pulled up to the hospital entrance and Beth put the car in park. She touched my shoulder. "I'm so glad I called you and we got to talk. I'll call you tomorrow."

"Me too," I said as I watched her drive away. And I was glad. Glad that we'd finally broken the ice. Maybe we could be friends again, after all, even if it was long distance.

My father was sitting eating a bowl of Jell-O when I walked in. He looked alert and better than I'd expected.

"Hi, honey," he said, "I'm so glad to see you. I see you got your hair done. I like it. You look so much more like your mother, now."

"Thanks," I said, not sure if I should take that as a compliment or not. I sat down in the chair next to the bed. "How are you? I heard they postponed the surgery until tomorrow."

"Yes," he replied. "And I'm glad they did because I've been wanting to talk to you when your mother wasn't around. I really need you to do something for me in case I don't make it out of surgery."

"You're going to make it," I said firmly, even though I was scared too.

"Well, anyway, if something happens to me, I need you to do something really important for me."

I looked at him. "What is it?"

He paused. "James had a journal. I need you to go and find it and get rid of it. I don't want your mother to come across it. Promise me you'll look for it for me and if you find it, destroy it."

"What're you talking about Dad? James didn't have a journal. It was me who had one, remember?"

"I know you did. But he had one too," he said. "I know because I found it one day when I was in his room looking for the keys to the Mustang. I know it was wrong for me to read it. I only read the first few pages before he walked in and caught me. But even that was bad enough."

I looked at him, shocked to learn that not only had James kept the journal I'd given him, but that he'd started writing in it. Though I wasn't surprised my father looked at it when he'd found it. I know I would have.

"What did he say in it?" I asked now curious.

"He was angry back then. About a lot of things. Your mother's drinking, and our fighting. I'd just hate for her to find it and read it.".

"Maybe she should read it. Show her how her drinking affected all of us," I said.

"She knows it did, believe me. And she feels horrible about it. I think that's one of the reasons she drank even more after he died. Out of guilt. But she said she learned in AA that guilt and shame will lead her right back to drinking again. So, she's been working really hard on trying to forgive herself. Just find the journal please, and when you do, burn it."

"Okay. I'll look for it for you," I said but it was really mostly out of my own curiosity than for him. I wondered if James had written anything about me in it. He must have.

"Thank you," he said, his face relaxing. But then a look of concern crossed his face. "You shouldn't read it either, for your own sake. He was in a dark place and that's all in the past. No reason to upset yourself more."

So, there *was* something in there about me.

"I hope I'm not interrupting."

I turned around. Joey was standing in the doorway, looking as handsome as ever in his police uniform. My pulse quickened as usual.

"No, not at all Joey," my father answered. "Come on in."

Joey came in and sat down in the chair next to me. His eyes opened wide as he looked at me.

"Wow, I like your hair. It's the same color as when we were dating. Makes you look more like your mother, too."

"Thanks," I said unnerved at the comparison. "I'm surprised to see you here."

"I stopped at the Huddle House for coffee like I normally do before my shift. And they told me Beth was coming in late because she had to drop some friend off at the hospital. I knew that friend must be you, so I thought I'd stop by and see you both," he said.

"You have visitors, I see." Mother came bustling into the room carrying a stack of magazines. She set them down on the table next to my father's bed.

"You changed your hair," she said.

"I got a tattoo too," I blurted out before I could stop myself. Everyone looked at me.

"And before you ask, Mother, yes I had a glass of wine before I came here."

"A tattoo?" Joey asked.

"I didn't know you drank," my father said. "I'm kind of surprised," he said glancing at my mother.

Mother looked at Joey and mouthed something. He mouthed something back.

"What's going on?" I asked. "What are you two talking about? First yesterday, and now again today. I know it's got something to do with me."

"I'll tell you later," Joey said under his breath.

"I want to know now," I said loudly.

"What's going on?" My father asked from the bed.

"Okay," Mother chimed in. "I'll tell you now though I didn't want to worry your father. It's just that Joey and I have both noticed that you seem to be drinking quite a bit since you've been in town. And we're concerned, that's all."

"You've been drinking quite a bit?" my father asked. "You need to keep an eye on that, honey. You know how that can get out of hand."

"I'm fine, Dad," I said. "It's not that bad." I looked back at Mother. "And you. If that isn't the pot calling the kettle black. I can't believe you of all people have the nerve to tell me that I'm drinking too much. At least I'm not home passed out on the couch like you always were. Remember the day James died? Maybe if you'd been sober, you'd have seen him leaving with that gun."

"Now, Karen," my father said in a firm voice. "That isn't fair. James' death wasn't your mother's fault."

"That's all right, Bill," Mother said, patting his arm. "No need to get excited. Karen's right. I was drunk a lot." She turned to me again. "But that's why I'm so worried about you, don't you see? I don't want you to go down the same path that I did."

"Well, you don't need to worry about me," I said. "I'm not like you." I glared at Joey again as tears filled my eyes.

"And you. You saw what I had to go through with her drinking, all the times I had to put her to bed when she was drunk or had to clean the kitchen stove after she almost burned the house down. You should know that I'd never let myself get that bad."

"I remember," he said. "And I know you think you're strong enough not to let that happen to you, but no one is immune. I just don't want to see anything bad happen to my girl."

"I'm not your girl," I said, my tears drying up instantly. "I'm not anyone's girl."

"Okay, let's not upset your father," Mother said. "All I was saying is that we've already lost one child. We couldn't bear to lose you too. Let me help you."

I stared at her. "Help me? I quit expecting help from you a long time ago, Mother."

"Karen," my father said sternly from the bed.

"Beth?" Joey said as he turned toward the door.

I looked to find Beth in the doorway. She was still in her waitress uniform and it was obvious by her face that something was very wrong.

"We need to talk," she said, looking at me.

"What's wrong, sis?" Joey asked.

"I just need to talk to Karen," she replied, motioning me out into the hallway.

I hurried over to her. "What's wrong?" I asked.

"It's Dan," she whispered back. "He's coming."

CHAPTER 15

"I TRIED CALLING YOU," BETH CONTINUED AS SHE stood there looking nervous. "But it went to voicemail. I knew you probably wouldn't have your phone on in here. That was when I figured I'd better come down and tell you myself. Dan's on his way here."

"You mean to Easley?" I asked.

"No. I mean here to the hospital," she replied.

"What?" I asked. "How do you know that?"

"He came to the Huddle House earlier and happened to be seated at one of my tables. We got to talking and he said he just flew into town to surprise his wife who's here visiting her father in the hospital. I just knew who he was when he said that. I told him I used to be your best friend and he started asking me all kinds of questions. Karen, why didn't you tell him you had a twin brother?"

I grabbed her arm. "What did you say about James? You didn't tell him James committed suicide, did you? I hope you didn't say anything about Joey." My mind whirled as I imagined what Dan may have just learned about my past. She looked down at my hand still on her arm. I let go of her.

"I told him that your brother and my brother were best friends, that's all. And once I realized he didn't even know you had a brother, I clammed right up. I didn't say a word about Joey, I swear."

"How do you know he's coming here?" I asked, looking down the hall nervously.

"Because he asked for directions to the hospital. That was while he was paying the bill, so I took off and drove here. I knew I'd better warn you that he was on his way, especially if Joey was around."

As if on cue, Joey stepped out of the room and walked toward us. Mother was close behind him.

"Who's on his way?" he asked.

"No one," I said, looking anxiously down the hall again, then back at Beth.

"Karen?" I froze as I recognized Dan's voice.

This time, we all turned and looked down the hall at the man stepping out of the elevator.

"It's your husband," Joey whispered as Dan got closer. I looked at him surprised that he'd automatically knew it was Dan.

"Hi Karen," Dan said, now only a few feet away. I looked back toward the elevator. Maybe I had enough time to dash inside before the doors closed and avoid all this.

"I almost didn't know it was you," Dan said, standing there awkwardly.

I looked back at him.

Your hair..." he continued, but mother cut him off.

"You must be Dan," she said. "It's so nice to finally meet you face to face."

My heart sank as I heard the elevator doors shut with a ding. I'd missed my opportunity to make a run for it.

"I'm Karen's mother, Doris," Mother extended her arms out as if to give Dan a hug.

Dan stood there for a few seconds, then let Mother wrap her arms around him.

"I can see that," he said when she let him go. "You almost look like sisters. Nice to finally meet you, Doris."

I heard the elevator ding again. I turned toward it and watched as several people filed out. If I hurried, I could still get in it and get the hell out of here. But if I left Dan here with all of them, surely, he'd learn more about my family and possibly about Joey. Better he heard it from me. Even so, my heart sank as the doors closed again.

"What're you doing here?" I asked, resigned to the fact I was stuck here to face the music.

"I thought that I'd come and surprise you and make sure you were okay." He glanced at Beth. "But I guess you're not so surprised I'm here, after all. Hello again, Beth."

"Hi Dan," she said, her eyes darting back to me.

"You two know each other?" Joey asked.

"He was at the Huddle House earlier," Beth replied.

"Why are you here?" I asked Dan again.

"To be with you," he said, looking Joey up and down.

"Oh, this is Joey," Mother said, apparently noticing Dan's curiosity. "Joey is Beth's brother." I glanced at Mother, grateful she didn't add that Joey was also my old lover.

"Oh yes," Dan said extending his hand to Joey. "Beth said you're Karen's brother's best friend. Nice to meet you."

Joey glanced at me as he shook Dan's hand.

"I'm looking forward to meeting her brother. Is he here?" Dan asked letting go of Joey's hand and looking around. "Oddly enough, up until today, I never knew she even had one."

My stomach dropped. Everyone looked at Dan then back at me.

"Did I say something wrong?" Dan asked, his eyes widening.

"James passed away some years ago," my mother said softly.

Dan's face turned red. He looked at me, at first with confusion, then disappointment. "I'm so sorry," he said in a whisper.

I could feel everyone's eyes back on me, as if waiting for me to explain why I hadn't told my own husband I'd had a brother, let alone that he had passed away. Wishing I could just run away, I was relieved when Mother spoke up.

"Well, let's not all stand here in the hallway. Dan, why don't you come and meet Karen's father?"

Dan looked at me again, then followed Mother into the room. I started to follow them when I felt a tug on my arm.

"You didn't tell him you had a brother?" Joey whispered into my ear. "What's up with that?"

"I can't talk about this right now," I whispered back as I shook his hand loose.

"Well, I guess I should be getting back to work," Beth said. She looked at me. "I'll call you tomorrow."

"Okay," I said as I hurried into the room and left them both standing there. Dan was by my father's bed when I walked in.

"I was just telling Dan how nice it is to finally meet him," my father said. "And how much we appreciate him taking the time off work to come all the way out here, especially with that big contracting job he's been busy with."

Dan gave me a look then smiled at my father. "Glad I could come, sir."

"I hope you both can stay at least for a while," my father said. "I'm sure Karen's anxious to show you around where she grew up."

"I don't think he has time for all that," I said, giving Dan a look of warning. "He has to get back soon."

"Yes, Karen's right," Dan said his smile fading. "I should get back to work. Besides, I only booked my hotel at the airport for a few days."

"You booked a room?" Mother asked. "Why did you do that? You must stay at the house with Karen and me."

I looked at Dan, then back at her. I was stuck. If I told Dan he couldn't stay at the house, I knew I'd only get barraged with all kinds of questions from my parents, asking what was wrong with my marriage. I wasn't about to get into all that with them just yet.

"Yes, of course you should stay there, Dan," I said, forcing a smile. "I'll give you directions and meet you there." But then I remembered that I'd left the Mustang at the Red Penny.

"In fact, better yet, I'll go with you to the hotel and after you check out, we can ride together to the house. It can be kind of tricky to get to if you're not familiar with the area, especially at night. I can get the Mustang tomorrow when I come back here. We probably should get going now, though," I said anxious to get him out of here.

"Good idea," Mother agreed. "Before it gets too late."

"Well, I hate to cut this visit short, but I'm sure I'll be back to see you tomorrow. It's nice to meet you sir," Dan said to my father, reaching out his hand.

"You too," my father replied, shaking it. "And please call me Bill. We're family."

As soon as Dan and I were inside the elevator, I pushed the button and turned to him. "Why did you come here? I told you I didn't want you to. And now you're staying at the house with me? Things are hard enough without you coming back here and making them worse."

"I hoped it would make it easier on you by my coming here," he said. "Besides, I couldn't just sit at home knowing you were here dealing with all this by yourself, plus with what we're going through right now. I had to come."

Annoyed, I followed him to his rental car and didn't say anything else.

"If you want, I'll stay at the hotel," he said, opening my car door. "But I'm still driving you to the house. I didn't want to say anything in front of your parents, but it's obvious you've been drinking." He turned to me as he started the car. "It kills me to see that too. I know it's all because of what I put you through."

I got in and he shut the door then got in the driver's side. As we started to back up, I got the uncanny feeling someone was watching us. I looked around to find Joey standing a few feet away, staring in our direction.

I glanced at Dan but fortunately, he didn't appear to have noticed Joey. When I looked back out my window, Joey was gone.

I still didn't say anything as we headed to the house, except for telling him when to turn. Dan kept glancing over at me during the drive, however.

"So, this is where you grew up?" he asked as we pulled up the driveway.

He pulled the car up close to the house and shut it off.

"Yes," I replied softly. "Lived here for eighteen years until my brother died and I left and moved to California. And met you," I added with a bite to my voice.

"I'd like to know why you never told me you had a brother," he asked in a low voice.

I looked over at him. As much as I didn't want to get into it right now, I knew that being here in Easley, sooner or later he was bound to find out how James had died. And he might as well hear the truth from me.

I looked out into the dark. "I'll tell you. But there's something you need to know first."

I heard Dan suck in some air. "I think I already know what it is," he said his voice dipping. "You're in love with Joey, aren't you? You didn't have to tell me. I could see it in your eyes at the hospital. The way you looked at him."

I felt my face get warm at how obvious it was that I still had feelings for Joey.

"No," I said. "That's not what I was going to say. It's about how my twin brother died."

"You're a twin?" he asked sounding surprised. "Wow."

"Yes," I said, feeling my eyes well up. "James was older by a little more than a minute, though he always felt like my younger brother. He had problems. Physical and mental. Sometimes he got depressed. Really depressed. When he was fourteen, he almost died from taking a bunch of painkillers."

"Oh," Dan said. "That's horrible. I'm so sorry."

"But he got through that time. Or at least I thought he did," I said sadly. "Our dad built a shooting range behind our house," I said swallowing hard as I tried to fight the tears. "And one afternoon, James went up there and shot himself."

"Oh my God," Dan said. "I don't know what to say."

"It was the worst day of my life," I said, feeling my chest tighten. "And what made it even worse was that I'm the one who found him up there. It was two weeks before our 18th birthday."

"Oh no. No wonder you always hated it when I'd try and make it a big deal about your birthday. I'm so sorry," he said again. "Why didn't you ever tell me any of this?"

"I don't know. I guess I just wanted to try and forget it ever happened. That's one of the reasons I moved to California. I needed a fresh start. And to tell the truth, I was afraid to tell you."

"Afraid? Why?" he asked, looking at me.

"After James died, people treated me differently. Like they were afraid I was going to do something crazy like he did. I was scared you'd look at me differently too, once you knew about him and what he'd done. I didn't want that."

"That's crazy. I'd never think any less of you no matter what happened in your past. If anything, it makes me love you even more, knowing what you went through and yet still came out to be the wonderful, caring person that you are. The way you love to help others. Like all those hours you put in down at the elementary school in Anaheim on weekends, helping the teachers with the school plays. You don't have to do that. But you do." He paused for a moment. "Your poor parents," he said turning away. "I feel so bad for them. It must have been devastating losing their only son."

"My dad wasn't around much once they got divorced, right before James died. And Mother was a drunk so I'm not sure how it affected her," I said bitterly.

Dan looked at me. "Your mother has a drinking problem too? I'd never have thought that by looking at her."

I didn't say anything. Should I finally tell him the truth, how it was always her with the problem, not me?

"I'm sorry if that came out wrong," he said. "What I meant is that sometimes, alcoholism can run in families or, so I've heard."

I sighed. "I guess I might as well tell you. It's my mother who is the alcoholic. Or was, I should say. According to her, she doesn't drink anymore. But I've never had a problem with liquor, myself. In fact, I've never wanted to drink at all. That is until a week ago."

"What? What do you mean?" he asked sounding confused. "You lead me to believe that you had a problem with alcohol."

"Well, I never actually said that," I replied, my voice dipping. "You just assumed that when you wondered why I hated alcohol so much."

"I don't understand," he said sounding hurt. "So, what, you made that all up? Why would you do something like that?"

"Because I didn't want to get into it, Dan. Like I said, when I left here, all I wanted was to start a new life. Forget about her, and James and everything else."

"Wow," he said shaking his head. "You had a brother. A twin brother to be correct, who I knew nothing about, and who died, tragically. And now I find out you're not a recovering alcoholic like I'd always believed. I knew you were keeping things from me, but I didn't realize just how many things."

"I'm sorry," I said. "I know that must make you mad, but I couldn't tell you."

"I'm not mad, I'm actually sad," he said. "That you had to go through all that, let alone feel you couldn't talk about it even with me. You can talk to me. I want you to know that. I'll never judge you for anything in your past or for what your family did,"

I looked at him and for an instant, felt the love that I had for him surface again. But I pushed it away.

"I guess I should go inside before Mother gets home," I said, opening the car door. I shut it quickly and hurried inside before I weakened and ended up inviting him to stay.

CHAPTER 16

IT WASN'T LONG AFTER DAN HAD LEFT BEFORE I HEARD Mother's car pulling in. I knew she was going to ask why Dan wasn't staying here. To avoid her interrogation, I got undressed and climbed into bed quickly.

I'd just shut the light off next to the bed, when my cell phone started to ring. I turned the light back on and answered it right away.

"Hello?" I whispered.

"It's me. I need to talk to you. Can I come by?"

"What? Now, Joey? No. I'm in bed," I whispered back.

"Why can't I? I know that Dan isn't there."

Spooked, I glanced toward the window. "How do you know that?"

"Because I followed you home and watched him leave. I'm parked down the street on Alpen Road," he replied. "Please, I need to talk to you, I'm coming over, anyway. Look for me at your window in five minutes."

Before I could tell him no, the phone went dead. I jumped up and threw on some clothes and flew to the bathroom to put on some makeup. Listening for Mother, I swiped on some lipstick too, then checked myself in the mirror before shutting off the bathroom light.

But as I walked over to the window, I felt foolish. Why should I care how I looked for him? But I did. After a moment, I could see headlights as a car was coming slowly around the bend.

Heart beating faster, I watched as the car's lights went off. Suddenly, Joey's face popped up in the window, startling me.

Annoyed, I still couldn't help but smile as the memory of all the times he'd pop up in this same window—scaring me just like that—came flooding back.

"Shh…" I said, holding my fingers up to my lips as he slid the window up. "Mother will hear us."

Joey climbed over the ledge, slid the window shut and dusted his pants off. He stood there staring at me.

"Sit down. You're making me nervous," I said.

He plopped himself down on the quilt and patted the bed next to him. "It's been a long time since I was on this bed," he smiled.

I hesitated, then made my way over to him. I could feel the hair rise on the back of my neck as I sat down.

"You look nice," he said sniffing toward me. "You smell good too. Did you put perfume on just for me?"

I felt my face flush. "No," I replied, annoyed to have been found out. "Why are you here, anyway? Did you come to badger me some more about my drinking? Or was it because you wanted to know why I didn't tell Dan about James? If so, none of that is any of your business."

"Well, I have to admit I am curious about all that, but it's not the reason I wanted to talk to you," he said. "I've been thinking a lot, and then seeing your father the way he is, well, it reminded me that we never know just how long we have left. Not that anything's going to happen to any of us," he quickly added.

"But life is short and there are no guarantees. I've decided that whatever time I have left, I want to spend it with you. And I don't want to go another minute without you in my life."

"What're you talking about, Joey?" I asked, sliding away a few inches. "I'm married."

"Yes, I know. But your husband did cheat on you, don't forget. You don't deserve that. I'd never do that to you. And besides, I don't think you could possibly love him as much as you loved me. If you did, he'd know about your brother."

I stood up, my heart racing. "You have to stop all this crazy talk. You should go."

"Why?" he asked, grabbing my hand and pulling me back down onto the bed. "Does it scare you? Maybe it should. Just tell me you don't love me, and I'll leave right now. And you can go back to California with Dan and will never have to see or hear from me again."

I looked at him. I had to admit that I did still feel something for him. But was it love? Or was it memories from how much I used to love him? As I sat there trying to sort it out, I heard a knock. Startled, we both turned to look toward the door.

"It's Mother," I whispered. "She must have heard us. You have to go."

Another two raps came. This time louder.

"Karen? Are you awake? Dan's here," I heard her say hesitantly.

Wide-eyed, I looked at Joey and pointed to the window frantically.

"Just a moment," I replied, my voice shaking. I nodded toward the window, but Joey just sat there. "What're you doing?" I whispered pushing him. "You have to go."

"Maybe it's time he knows about us," he whispered back a little too loudly.

"There's nothing to know. Please, Joey. You have to go. Don't do this."

Joey got up slowly but just stood there. Frantic, I shoved him toward the window. My hands were still on his back when the door opened. Dan stood there staring at us with shock on his face.

Mother stood behind him and she looked equally shocked. I watched as Dan's eyes moved to my hands which were still on Joey's back. I slid them off slowly.

"What's going on here?" Dan asked, stepping into the room. "Why are you in my wife's bedroom, Joey?"

"He just stopped by to talk," I said, realizing as soon as the words were out of my mouth how lame they must sound. "I thought you went back to the motel."

"I did," Dan replied, his eyes still boring a hole in Joey. "But after what you shared with me earlier, I thought I should come back here and be with you." His eyes moved to the wrinkled bedspread. "But apparently you had other plans."

I looked at the bed, then back at Dan. "It's not what you think." Another lame thing to say that I wished I could take back. And even worse, I realized I'd used the very same words back to Dan, when I'd found him with that woman.

"Joey, I think you should go," Mother said from behind Dan.

"Okay." He walked over to the window and slowly slid it open. He was about to put one leg over the ledge when he stopped and pulled it back in. He slid the window shut again and turned and walked toward the bedroom door. Dan stood there blocking his way, but after a few seconds, stepped back to let Joey go by. Moments later, the front door closed. Dan turned back and looked at me.

"I think we need to talk," he said.

"Let's all go into the kitchen. I'll make some tea," Mother said nervously.

Anxious to get away from Dan's glare, I slid by him and followed her down the hall. As my mother put on the kettle, I sat down at the table. Dan came in and sat across from me in James' old seat. He didn't take his eyes off me.

Mother took out three cups and set them on the counter. She took a plate of muffins and uncovered them and placed them on the table, as if we were having some strange tea party. "You must be hungry, Dan," she said. "Please help yourself."

"Thank you," he said in a monotone as he continued to stare bleakly at me.

The kettle started to whistle and after filling the cups with water, Mother put them on the table along with an assortment of tea bags, honey and spoons.

"I think I'll just have my tea in my bedroom," she said after fixing herself a cup. She looked at me, then turned and left.

Dan just sat there staring at me. Finally, he cleared his throat. "Are you going to tell me why he was in your bedroom?"

"Now you know how it feels," I said before I could stop myself.

"Okay. You were trying to get even. Well still, I don't get it," he said, sounding very tired.

"You come back here, which I could understand, because you wanted to see your father. And although things have been bad between us, earlier you'd opened up and I thought we were getting somewhere. And then, you go off and invite a man into your bedroom? What's going on?"

"I didn't invite him," I said defensively.

"Whatever. He was there. I really don't understand. Remember when you told me the other day how you didn't know me? Well, I'm beginning to wonder if I really know you either. Maybe you're right and it was a mistake coming here."

"So, why did you come? Was it because things didn't work out with you and Susan or because you felt guilty?"

"I haven't even talked to her," he said. "I came because I love you," he said. "I wanted to be here for you with whatever you were going through. Isn't that what married people are supposed to do? Be there for each other when things get tough?"

"Cheating isn't being there for me," I snapped back.

"You're right," he said. "There's no excuse for what I did. I was wrong, and I'll regret it for the rest of my life. But a wife isn't supposed to get all dolled up and invite a man into her bedroom in the middle of the night either."

I felt my face flush again. "I didn't get dolled up."

"Whatever. Let's not argue anymore," he said. "I'm going back to the hotel. And then, I'm going to go back to California. But before I do, we need to sit down and talk. I'm not giving up on us yet."

He started to leave, then reached down and snatched up a muffin before heading for the front door. I followed behind him and watched as he stopped in front of the family photo in the foyer. He stared at it, shook his head, then opened the door and left.

I wanted to run out and stop him. But I didn't. I just stood there for a moment, then turned and went back to my bedroom. Mother's door was open, and she was standing there waiting.

"Did he leave?" she asked softly.

"Yes," I replied.

"I'm sorry," she said. "Are you okay?"

"Great," I said. I looked at her and had an urge to tell her what was going on. But instead, I turned, heading into my room and closing the door, leaving her standing there.

That night as I lay in bed, all I could see was Dan's hurt face when he found me with Joey. If I had a car right now, I'd run away. But deep down I knew I couldn't, not until I knew my father was going to be okay. But once I knew that, I was gone.

CHAPTER 17

THE NEXT MORNING, I AWOKE FEELING MORE TIRED than I had when I went to bed. I'd barely slept at all and when I did finally doze off, I had nothing but horrible dreams. In one of my dreams, this time it was me up at the range, holding a gun pointed at my own head. I tried to erase the terrible image from my brain. As I lay there, my mind went back to last night.

I should never have let Joey come over. That was dumb. And though nothing happened, it only made Mother and Dan think there was something going on. So what, I told myself as I headed toward the kitchen. Let them think it.

The house was quiet. Obviously, Mother had already gone to a meeting or to see Dad. So, I turned the coffee on. As I sat there watching the coffee drip slowly into the pot, my mind turned to my father. What if he didn't make it? I tried not to think about it and took my cup back to my room to get dressed. The first thing I needed to do was get the Mustang and go see him.

I looked on my phone for a local cab company. While I'd been known to take Uber on occasion, I still felt safer with a cab.

I'd barely finished putting on my makeup when I heard a honking out front. The cab was running, and its rear door was open. A tall, dark-skinned man stood next to it. He gave me a toothy grin.

"Morning, Miss. It's another wunnerful day in Easley. Where is it I can take you?"

"Good Morning," I said somewhat amazed at how cheery he was at this time of morning. "Can you drop me off at the Red Penny over on Main Street? Do you know where that is?"

He closed my door and walked around to the driver's side and slid in.

"Sure do. Everyone knows the Penny," he said, pressing the meter on the dash. "The place has been there for years. Have you there in fifteen minutes, tops."

As we started to move, I noticed he kept looking at me in the rearview mirror. Could he possibly know me? He stopped at the end of the driveway and turned around to face me.

"You're Doris's daughter, aren't you?"

I looked at the name on the ID badge hanging from the mirror. Charlie Bangs. It didn't ring a bell.

"Yes," I replied hesitantly. "You know her?"

"Sure do. I used to be her driver," he said, turning back around. "She called me anytime she needed a ride. Well, I should have known, you look just like her. Haven't seen her in years but I like Doris. We got to know each other pretty good. How is she anyway?' he asked.

"She's okay," I replied. More than ever, I was beginning to see what a mistake coloring my hair was.

"She sure was proud of you," he said, chuckling. "Talked about you all the time. Sorry about your brother by the way," he added shaking his head. "That was a darn shame. Yes," he said again, "she sure was proud of you."

"Thanks," I said very surprised that Mother would say something nice like that about me to a stranger.

"So, she's okay?" he asked again.

"Yes," I replied, wondering if he knew she had a drinking problem. He had to. Everyone in town knew she was a drunk.

"That's good. I was worried about her when…when I heard about the thing that happened on the bridge," he said, pulling out onto the highway.

I felt my face get hot. Was there anyone in this town that didn't know about that?

"She always asked for me when she needed a ride," he said, sounding proud. "We got to be friends. Said I was the best driver she'd ever booked."

So that was how she got her liquor back then. James and I always wondered how she managed to get to the store, since she wouldn't drive drunk and was drinking most of the time. But the only time I remembered seeing her take a cab, was when she came to school the day James had that asthma attack.

"You're the one who took her to the grocery store, I guess," I said, fishing to see if he knew what she was really going there for.

"Yep. She didn't like to drive herself if she was… under the weather." He glanced in the mirror again. "But a lot of the time, I took her to the school."

"The school?" I asked.

"Yes. The high school. To see you in your plays. She loved going to them. I remember how she was always happier on the way home after seeing one. She would go on and on about how good you were. She was so proud of you," he said again. I stared at the back of his head as I tried to make sense of what he was saying.

"Are you telling me that my mother went to see my plays?" I asked, certain that Charlie must be mistaken. He looked in the rearview mirror again.

"You didn't know she was going?" he asked, sounding surprised.

"No," I said. "Are you sure? I asked again.

"Sure, I am, picked her up all the time. Took her to the store sometimes, but to the school mostly. I remember the first time I brought her there. But that wasn't to see a play. I think your brother was sick with asthma or something. You were there. You were both quite young as I recall."

He turned the wheel and continued. "Your mother wasn't feeling too good herself that day. I felt so bad for her when she fell like she did. After that, she made sure I always dropped her off around back, when she went to see you act. You know, in case she fell again." Charlie looked at me briefly in the mirror.

He went on to say something else, but I was no longer listening. She went to my plays? But that couldn't be. The only ones that went, were James, Dad and sometimes Joey. They sat right there in the same place in the front row every time. Mother's seat…it was always empty. So, if it was true and she did go, why not sit with them? And why would she keep it a secret she was going? I looked out the window more confused than ever.

"Hope I didn't say anything I shouldn't have," Charlie said glancing into the mirror again.

"No, it's fine," I said. "I'm just tired."

"Didn't you move to California?" he asked. "Always wanted to go there. Looks to be a pretty exciting place with all those movie stars all over the place, by what I've seen on TV." He slowed the car down and pulled into the Red Penny parking lot.

"Well here you are. You don't need a ride back home?" he asked.

"No, my car is right over there," I said. I paid him and got out.

"Well, good to see you again. Enjoy your visit," he said smiling as he shut my door. "And please be sure to give your mother my best."

"I will," I said. I stood there and watched him leave. *Why didn't she tell me she'd been going*, I was still asking myself when I heard a voice behind me.

"Hi there." I spun around to find Joey standing there.

"What're you doing here? Are you checking up on me again?" I asked.

"I knew you'd say that," he said, laughing. "No. I figured you'd be here to pick up the Mustang sometime this morning, so I came by. If I'd known you were going to have to take a cab though, I'd have offered to give you a ride myself."

Before I could say anything, as if on cue again, 'My heart will go on' started to play from inside my purse. I didn't move to answer it.

"Maybe you should get that," Joey said. "Nice ringtone."

The song stopped playing as the recorder picked up.

"The real reason I'm here, is that I was hoping we could pick up from where we left off last night. I'm not giving up."

"Joey," I said, feeling alarms going off in my head like they always did when he was around.

"Come on," he pleaded. "You know we have to talk about this. I know just the place to talk, too."

My heart beat faster. And though I knew the smart thing to do was to leave and go see my father right now, I couldn't leave things like they were. I needed to know for my own sake if I still had any feelings for him.

"Come on," he said again.

I hesitated another few seconds, then followed him around back to his car. But once again, as we pulled out onto the road, I knew I was making a mistake. I turned and looked out the window and reminded myself of what Dan had done, hoping that would make me feel less guilty. But it didn't.

We drove in silence for several minutes, then Joey turned on the radio and the car filled with music. I looked over at him and had to smile as he tapped his hand on the steering wheel to an old country song. He always used to do that when we went on long drives.

"Remember this song?" he asked smiling at me again.

Of course, I did. It was 'I need you' by Faith Hill. That was our song and I hadn't listened to it in a very long time. Every time it came on the radio, I'd always turned it right off. I even made sure not to listen to any country music after I'd moved away from Easley because it reminded me too much of Joey.

I turned and looked out the window again, staring out at the rich, green hills. It was so nice to see green again. The few hills near my house in California were dry and brown. The green was something else I missed about the South. Everything looked so alive around here.

After a while, Joey turned the radio down and looked at me. "Anything starting to look familiar yet?" he asked as he took the next turn onto a dirt road.

"All that's missing is that ugly old fishing hat you used to wear," I replied trying not to laugh.

"You know you loved that hat," he said, chuckling himself.

I rolled my eyes dramatically. Actually, I had hated that hat. But Joey had a way of looking good in anything. I looked out the window at Lake Jocassee which was one of my favorite places in the whole world. Yep. Joey still knew how to get to me.

"When's the last time you went fishing?" he asked as he pulled in and found a parking place.

I tried to remember but couldn't. I hadn't been near any type of water in a long time, let alone fishing. The beaches in California were too crowded. And the few lakes we had outside Los Angeles were too far and too low to fish in because of the drought we'd experienced the past few years.

"The last time I was here with you, I guess," I said, feeling a bit sad.

"Hmm. And believe it or not, that's the last time I've been too," he said.

I looked at him. "Really? Why don't you come here anymore? You used to love this place."

He looked away. "Too many memories, I guess." He opened the car door. "Anyway, guess we'll have to do something about that. Still remember how to bait a hook?"

I flashed to the secluded spot out on the lake where Joey and I used to stop to fish. But it always would lead to making out on the blanket we'd laid out on the shore. I felt a tingle run through my body as an alarm went off in my head again.

"I don't think this is such a good idea," I said, not moving.

"Come on. What's wrong with spending a few hours on a pontoon feeding some fish with an old friend? That is, unless you're afraid to be alone with me." He smiled mischievously.

I looked at him and opened the car door to get out. Though I felt guilty, I wasn't about to let him think I was afraid to be out there alone with him. Because I wasn't.

We headed into the bait shop. And as soon as I walked in, I was flooded with memories of all the times we'd come here. Joey would rent the pontoon, while I'd go next door and pick up lunch. Back then, we even used to have our own fishing poles. But since we didn't have any now, Joey looked through a rack of reels to rent. I flashed back to the fishing gear at the house.

"Why don't you go next door and get us a couple of sandwiches while I grab some bait and finish up here?" he said.

"Just what I was headed to do," I replied and headed next door.

The girl behind the counter was just putting our sandwiches and waters into a bag, when Joey walked in carrying a brown bag and the fishing poles. On top of his head was that same silly hat he used to wear.

"Don't worry," he said, reaching into the bag and pulling out another one. "I got you one too." He dropped it on my head. "Wouldn't want you getting your pretty face all burned out there."

I grabbed the bag with our lunches, and we headed outside. As Joey and I made our way to the boat, the wooden planks made the same old familiar sounds under our feet as they used to do. Finally, Joey stopped in front of one of the pontoons and set the poles and the bag on the ground.

"This is the one," he said as he held his hand out to me. I ignored his hand and climbed up onto the pontoon. He handed me the poles and our lunches and followed me onto the boat.

A cooler filled with ice sat ready for us in the middle of the deck. I put the bag of sandwiches and bottled waters into it and closed the lid as Joey set the bait and poles down and climbed into the captain's chair. He ran his hand over the controls, and I could see him smile.

After a moment, he looked at me, turned the key, and within seconds the engine roared to life. As we took off, I was forced to grab the railing to keep from falling back. I looked at Joey and he gave me a big grin as he stepped on the gas even more.

As we sped through the water, the warm air hit my face and it was exhilarating. It felt great to be out here on the lake again. After a while, Joey slowed the boat down until finally we were barely coasting.

"It feels good to be out here again, doesn't it?" he asked, his eyes twinkling.

I kicked off my shoes and reached down to roll my pant legs up but didn't reply. No reason to give him false hope. We cruised for a while, then Joey slowed the boat down some more, then shut the engine off. He got up and came and sat down next to me. "You look happier than you've looked since you got back to town."

"What did you want to talk about anyway?" I asked, changing the subject even though he was right. I was happy. Happier than I probably should be.

Joey moved closer. "What was bothering you when you got out of the cab earlier? You looked upset."

I sighed, thinking back to what the driver had told me about Mother attending my school plays.

"Is that what you brought me out here to talk about?" "I asked.

"No, but I do want to know."

I hesitated, then looked at him. "It was something the driver said about taking my mother to the school to see me act. He said he used to take her to all the plays. Isn't that strange?"

"Was he sure?" Joey asked. "I never saw her there. Maybe he's confused. After all, that was a long time ago."

"He was sure. And he remembered our house, too. And he remembered the time when we were young when James was sick, and Mother had to come to the school and get us. The time she fell out of the cab drunk in front of everyone. You remember me telling you about that, don't you?"

"Yes, I do. Well, why don't you just ask her about it then? I'm sure she'll tell you why she felt the need to keep it a secret from you."

"I'm planning to. I have a lot of things I want to know before I leave town."

"Are you already thinking about going? I was hoping I could talk you into staying longer," he said, sounding disappointed.

"I wasn't planning on being here more than a few days to begin with. Just long enough to make sure my father was okay. But I don't want to leave until I know he's out of the woods. No use going only to have to come right back if he…" I didn't finish my thought.

"He's not going to die, if that's what you think," Joey quickly added.

"I hope not. But I'm scared." I looked at him again. That was the first time I admitted out loud just how frightened I really was that my father might not make it.

"It's all right," Joey said, putting his arm around me. "He's going to be fine." But I could tell by the look on his face that he didn't believe it any more than I did.

"What else did you want to talk about?" I asked, changing the subject once again.

"About last night. And about us. I've never stopped thinking about you since you left. Wondering if you were happy and if you missed me like I missed you. All I really knew over the years was that you got married. Little else, since you cut off all ties with your parents. You know, just what I could find out on Facebook, things like your job and then how you met someone and got married. I'd have thought with the way you loved acting so much, that you'd have become an actress and I'd have seen you on TV or in a movie by now."

I thought back to the time I heard about an open casting call at the Greenville Playhouse and wanted to try out for a part, and how Joey had quickly squashed the idea. He said although he was proud of me for getting as far as I did, acting was just a hobby for me and I shouldn't get my hopes up for it being anything more than that. Besides, he didn't want me doing anything that would tie up my weekends and take me away from him.

I never did try out at the Playhouse, but always wondered what would have happened if I had. Who knows? Maybe if Joey had supported me more, I might have gotten a job there and never left Easley. And we'd be married by now.

That was another difference between Joey and Dan. Dan had always encouraged me to follow my dreams while Joey often appeared to be threatened by them.

"So why didn't you become an actress since you loved it so much?' he asked.

"You're right. I sure did love acting. My plan was when I got to California, I'd do what every other kid with dreams of becoming a star did. I'd get a job as a server at one of the restaurants in LA while I went out and auditioned. And I did just that. One day," I continued, "one of the girls at the restaurant I worked at told me how she'd been trying for over a year to get a part in a soap opera. But every time she went to audition, she bombed. I offered to run some lines with her and after a little advice from me, she went out and nailed her very next audition and got a big part. She was thrilled and told some of the other struggling actors at the restaurant. And some of them came to me asking for advice too.

That was when I figured that maybe I should apply for a teaching position. I teach, and I coach young actors there. But you're right, acting is my first love and hopefully, one day I'll get back to it."

"You were good at pretending, that's for sure," Joey said. "Even when you weren't on stage."

"What's that supposed to mean?"

"You know, like how you'd act like everything was just fine even when it wasn't. Remember the time we were watching TV and your mother came out of her room totally smashed and practically fell on top of me?" He looked away.

"I could tell how embarrassed you were, but you acted like nothing was wrong. In fact, you made a little joke before you escorted her back to her room. I doubt she even noticed that you were upset," Joey looked at me again. "But I knew. I guess I'm just surprised that you didn't follow your dreams, that's all."

"Maybe one day I will," I said. "So, what about you? You said you'd never become a cop after what had happened to your father and, yet here you are. What made you change your mind?"

"Your mother actually had something to do with it," he replied.

"My mother?" I asked, surprised.

"Yes. After I pulled her out of the lake, I knew I was meant to be a cop just like my father was. She could have died if I wasn't there." He looked at me. "Are you sure you're okay, talking about this?"

"I was going to ask you what happened anyway," I replied. "Like how you managed to be there just at the right time to save her."

"Steve was partially responsible for that actually," he replied.

"What did Steve have to do with it?" I asked, now more curious than ever.

"What happened was, after you left town, I made up some excuse to stop at the shop and have my truck checked out, every now and then. But, mostly to see if I could find out from your dad if he'd heard from you. And after Steve started working there, I had an even better excuse. To stop and see him and at the same time, stay close to your Dad in case he had any news about you.

That day when I went by, Steve said that your mother had just been there and how she was acting even stranger than usual, and how he was worried about her. He asked me if I'd go find her and make sure she was okay. So, I took off in the direction he'd said she gone, and just as I got to Shoeless Jack's Bridge over in Greenville, I saw her car go over the edge.

"It was horrible," Joey continued grimacing. "If Steve hadn't noticed something was wrong and suggested I go after her, I don't know what would have happened."

The image of my mother's car hitting the water made me sick. Joey touched me on the shoulder gently.

"Are you okay? I'm sure this isn't easy for you to hear."

"I'm fine," I said. "Go on. I want to know everything. I can handle it."

"That's pretty much it. I pulled her out. It was strange how she kept saying she wasn't alone down there. That God was with her."

I thought back to the other morning when she'd insisted James wasn't alone when he had died. Maybe that was why she believed it, because she was sure God was with her down there. I wondered if it was possible that it was true. After all, it was pretty strange that everything worked out the way it did.

"After I saw she was going to be okay," he said, "I knew right then what I wanted to do with the rest of my life. I wanted to be a cop like my dad and help people. So, I went right down to the Easley PD and signed up and it was the best decision I ever made. I love it." He took my hand. "But let's talk about something else."

Suddenly, he turned my wrist over. "I forgot that you mentioned at the hospital, you got a tattoo. A tattoo?" he asked sounding surprised as he lifted it closer to his face.

"James always wished he could run like a horse," I said, as he peered at it. "The bird represents me."

Joey moved my hand to his lips and kissed the tattoo gently. I looked at him, moved more than ever at how sweet he was being. It reminded me of why it was so easy to fall in love with him. And if I was honest, why I loved him still a little.

"Let's eat," I said as I pulled my hand away quickly and stood up. Joey looked at me with surprise, then stood up too.

"Good distraction," he said with a grin and got the bottled waters from the cooler alongside the bag with our sandwiches, I'll put my jacket down on the seat here and we can eat and relax."

For the next ten minutes, we both ate our lunches in silence. Finally, I could eat no more and wrapped the rest up and put it in the bag. As I went to put the bag back into the cooler, Joey stopped me.

"Wait," he said touching my leg lightly.

"What?" I asked making sure not to look at him.

"Look at me, please,'" he said.

I slowly turned and looked up at him. The intensity of his gaze was almost too much to take.

"I know you don't want to talk about this, but we have to. You can't deny there's something very strong between us. And you never did answer me last night. Do you still love me? I need to know."

"No, Joey. But even if I did, it's too late for us. I have Dan now."

"Then why are you out with me right now? And what kind of marriage do you have when you never even told your husband about your own brother? And then he goes and cheats on you? You don't deserve that."

As I tried to think of an answer, the sound of a boat coming toward us caused us both to turn around. Another pontoon was heading straight for us at what appeared to be a very fast clip. As it got closer, several bursts of laughter could be heard coming from a couple on deck. It pulled right up to us and the driver, a young man, shut the engine off.

"Finally, signs of life on this deserted lake," he said. "We have some wine coolers and tequila. What will you have?" The girl next to him in a bathing suit giggled and took a sip from the bottle in her hand.

"Nothing, thanks." Joey replied as he glanced over at me.

"You sure?" the young man asked. He looked in my direction. "Maybe your girlfriend would like something. She looks thirsty."

"She doesn't want anything," Joey said rather firmly.

I looked at him, annoyed. "I can speak for myself. No thanks," I said, though a wine cooler did sound good.

"If you don't mind, we're trying to have a private conversation," Joey said.

"Hey man, I was just trying to be hospitable," the boy said, sounding offended. "No reason to be rude." He snatched the wine cooler from his girlfriend's hand and drank the rest of it down before tossing the empty bottle into the lake.

I could see Joey's jaw tighten as he watched the bottle floating away.

"Come on," the girl said as she tugged at her boyfriend's arm. "Let's go. They're no fun. Let's go find some people who are."

"Okay," the boy said as he started the boat up again. As he took off, he turned the wheel sharply causing water to spray over both me and Joey as they sped away.

"Jerk," Joey said as he wiped the water off his sunglasses. "You okay?"

I looked at the empty wine cooler bottle almost out of sight now. "I'm fine. But maybe we should get going," I said.

"We haven't even fished yet. Don't let those punks spoil it for us," he pleaded.

"I should get to the hospital to see my father, anyway," I said. "Please, Joey. I just want to go."

"Okay," he said as he tossed the rest of his sandwich over the side. Looking disappointed, he climbed back in the captain's chair and started up the engine. I could see he was upset as he angled the pontoon back toward the dock.

"Did those kids say something to upset you, or are you just looking for another reason not to face things?" he asked as we slowly headed back toward the marina.

"I just need to get back," I replied.

"You know, you may not realize it, but you've let your guard down a few times around me since you've been in town, and I can see you still have feelings for me whether you want to admit it or not. I don't know why you just won't admit it."

I looked away. He was right. I did have some feelings for him. But why wouldn't I? I was madly in love with him at one time. But that was a long time ago.

"Okay, have it your way," he said as we picked up speed and headed back to the dock.

—

After returning the unused fishing poles and pontoon keys back to the bait shop, we headed back to the Red Penny to get the Mustang.

Joey didn't say a word the entire way there. He walked me to the car, and after saying goodbye, he said he hoped I would think about things. Then he left. I started up the car, but instead of heading to the hospital, I decided it would be best to go home and clean up and change my clothes first.

When I got to the house, I grabbed the bottle of Jack and headed inside. As I made my way through the garage, I was relieved to see that Mother's car wasn't home.

But as I stepped into the kitchen, I stopped abruptly. Dan was sitting at the kitchen table and he didn't look happy at all.

"Where have you been?" he asked as he stared at me.

CHAPTER 18

"WHERE WERE YOU?" HE ASKED AGAIN AS I FIDGETED and attempted to hide the bottle behind my back. "Your mother and I have been trying to get a hold of you all morning. I left you three voicemails."

"Sorry, I didn't have my phone on," I replied nervously, wondering why he was there. "Is my father alright?"

Dan looked at me skeptically. "Yes, but the hospital called, and they've decided to do the surgery on him today. Your mother left to go there about a half hour ago. She thought that you'd want to be there for the operation, so she asked me to wait here for you, so I could tell you when you finally *did* come home."

"Oh. Okay, thanks for telling me," I said, anxious to get to my room before he had a chance to notice the bottle of Jack.

"I told her I'd take you over there when you got back," he said as he stood up.

I looked at him. Maybe it would be best if I let him drive me there. Ever since I saw that wine cooler at the lake, I'd been craving a drink. This way, I could have at least one before we headed to the hospital.

"Okay," I said backing up toward the hallway. "That would be great. Just give me a few minutes to wash my hands and put on some lipstick. Why don't you wait outside, in fact? I'll be right out."

Dan looked at me again then turned and made his way out the same way I'd come in.

As soon as he was gone, I grabbed a can of Coke out of the fridge and made myself a strong drink. As I hurried down the hall, I spilled some of it onto my shirt. I tried to wash the stain out but ended up soaking my blouse. Annoyed, I took it off and quickly put a fresh blouse on. I chugged the last of the Jack and Coke and hurried outside. Dan was waiting in the car with it running.

Still breathing hard, I popped some gum into my mouth and climbed in the rental car. I could see him eyeing my blouse, but he didn't say anything, and we headed to the hospital.

"So, you never did say where you were," he said as we turned the corner. "You look like you've been out in the sun. I sat there with your mother talking for a good two hours. Where were you?"

"What did you talk about?" I asked, avoiding the question again and nervous that she may have told him something else I didn't want him to know. Like how Joey and I almost got married.

"Oh, all kinds of things," he said. "But why aren't you answering me?"

I sat there for a moment, debating if I should tell him the truth. I hated to get into an argument on the way to the hospital, yet at the same time a part of me wanted him to hurt him like he'd hurt me.

"I needed to clear my head, so I went fishing"

"Fishing? Unbelievable. Your mother told me that you know how to shoot a gun which I never knew, and now I found out that you like to fish? What am I going to learn next? That you're an expert at milking cows too? You went with him, didn't you?"

"Yes," I replied.

"That's just great. I thought you came back here to see your father, not hook up with your old boyfriend, Karen. That's what he is, right? Your ex-lover?" Dan's face was red with anger.

"We did date back in high school," I said.

"So, that's why you were so anxious to come back here," he said angrily. "I knew it had to be something more than just seeing your father since you haven't even mentioned your dad once in the whole time, I've known you. So, you're paying me back by sneaking around with him? Is that it?"

"Don't you talk to me about sneaking around," I said, my voice going up.

"Fair enough," he said. "I deserve that. But if you and I are going to have a chance of working things out, we're going to have to be honest with each other and that means no sneaking around. I'm willing to do my part, but you're going to have to be straight with me too."

"Okay, fine," I said. "You want me to be honest? Then answer me this. How long have you and Susan been sleeping together?"

Dan looked away.

"See? Just as I thought," I said disgusted. "You're incapable of being honest."

Suddenly, he jerked the car over to the side of the road and shut off the engine. Then he turned to me and for the first time in a very long time, I saw the same fire in his eyes that he'd had back when we first started dating. I loved when he was passionate about things.

"Okay, you want to know everything? Fine. Here goes," he said taking a deep breath. "I met Susan at the gym as you know, and we started talking. Just about working out and our jobs and stuff. After that, whenever I was there, we seemed to bump into each other. Then one afternoon, we decided to have a juice together after working out. Then the next thing I knew, we were making plans to go out for dinner. But we never had sex, I swear."

"Like I believe you," I said feeling sick. "How could you, Dan? I trusted you. Doesn't that mean anything to you?"

"Sure, it does and I'm so sorry for hurting you. It was a terrible thing to do. I realize that now. I don't know how it managed to go that far. I don't know, I guess I felt like I was somebody when I was with her. For the past year, I felt like nothing but a failure not only in my eyes, but in yours too."

"I never said that," I said angrily. "I always tried to encourage you and tell you that things would get better. Besides, you hadn't exactly made me feel so great this past year either. But you didn't catch me hooking up with someone, though I certainly could have if I wanted to. There are plenty of male students in my classes."

Dan looked hurt. "Well, you're the only woman I love and ever will. You have to know that." This time, I looked away.

"Say something," he said.

I looked back at him. "What do you expect me to say?"

"I don't know," he replied, his voice choking up. "Tell me that I'm a jerk. Or that you hate me. Just say something, please."

I swallowed hard. "Can we get going please? I don't want to miss the surgery."

He shook his head and started the car up again. "Just what I figured."

He pulled back onto the road. "We can't go on like this, you know. This must be eating you up as much as it is me. And you know you can't keep holding everything inside like you do."

I looked back out the window. Joey had said pretty much the same thing to me. And so did Mother. Maybe I did keep things bottled up. But what was the alternative?

After about fifteen minutes, we pulled up to the front of the hospital, and I got out while Dan went to park the car. When we got to my father's room, a nurse was talking to my parents.

"Hi, sweetheart," my father smiled. "Hi Dan.".

"This is our daughter and her husband," Mother said, introducing us to the nurse. "She was just going over all they'll be doing to your father," she continued looking over at me with fear in her eyes.

"Yes. As I was just saying," the nurse went on, "the doctor will make a small incision in the left lung and slide a tiny camera inside which will help us see exactly where the cancer is. Don't worry, you won't feel a thing," she quickly added, looking at my father.

"Then we laser off any of the cancerous areas and we'll have him back in his room within a couple of hours. If all goes well, he'll be out of here within a couple of days."

"I don't want anyone to worry," my father said bravely, though I could see he was worried too. "I'm not going anywhere just yet."

"You better not. I need you," Mother said in a shaky voice.

"It's time to go," the nurse said, reclining his bed and lifting the side rails up. "Why don't you all go and wait in the visitors' lounge? I'll come and get you as soon as he's out of recovery."

Mother leaned down close to my father. "Don't worry. Everything's going to be fine."

Another nurse came in and the two of them wheeled him out. As I watched them take him away, a feeling that it wasn't going to go as smoothly as the nurse had suggested came over me. We walked back together to the visitors' lounge and sat down. Mother flipped nervously through a magazine and stopped. She closed it and looked at me.

"I was beginning to worry that you weren't going to get here in time for the surgery. Were you out with Beth? I called you several times but kept getting your voicemail."

"I had my phone off," I said, avoiding looking at Dan.

"Well, it gave Dan and me a chance to have a nice little chat, anyway. I see you never told him that you were the best actress Easley High ever had," she said, sounding proud.

"No, she didn't," Dan glanced over at me. "Something else I'm just now learning about my wife." He looked back at my mother. "Tell me more, Doris."

"Oh yes. Karen was a born actress. She was so good that she always got picked for all the lead parts. Isn't, that right, dear?"

"I guess you should know," I said, once again feeling hurt that she didn't tell me she was there. "Oh, and Charlie said to give you his regards."

Her eyes opened wide. "You met Charlie? I haven't seen him in years. He's such a sweet man."

"Who's Charlie?" Dan asked. He looked at me. "Was he your drama teacher?"

"No. Charlie is a cab driver," I replied, looking at Mother again. "He was the one who drove my mother to see me in my school plays. Though, for some strange reason, she didn't want me to know that she was there. Isn't that right, Mother?"

My mother looked down at her hands. Dan looked from her back to me. "Did I say something wrong again?"

"No, you didn't, Dan. What Karen's referring to, is that I went to all her plays, but at the time felt it best to keep it a secret."

"Yes, what was that about Mother? "I bit my lip. "Was it just one more way for you to mess with my head?"

"Of course not," she said. "I thought it was best that you didn't know I was there. I thought it might upset you if you knew I was. But are you sure you want to get into this right now?" She looked over at Dan.

"Oh, Dan and I don't have any secrets, do we?" I asked with sarcasm. "Besides, I have a feeling with you around, there's not much he won't find out about me before too long anyway. So, go on. Enlighten me. Why go if you were just going to hide in the back somewhere? Or was it that you just wanted to be alone with your bottle?"

She looked hurt. "I didn't tell you because I didn't want to embarrass you, like I had so many times before when you were young. So, I went but I sat in the back where I knew no one would know I was there, especially you. That was your time. I didn't want to ruin it for you."

I thought back to all the plays I'd been in over my high school junior and senior years, and there were quite a few. And I pictured her sitting in the dark somewhere, most likely pulling out a bottle every now and then and taking a sip. For a moment, I actually felt sorry for her. And she was right. If I had known she was there, I was sure I would have been so distracted, I'd never have been able to focus on my lines. Maybe she did do me a favor. But still, if only she could have stayed sober and sat up front with James and Dad.

"Did Dad know you went?" I asked in a softer tone.

"No. I never told him."

She started to say something else, but the ringing of my cell phone cut her off. I thought I had it on silent. I dug it out of my purse and glanced at the screen, I could see Dan watching me.

The call was from a local number, but I wasn't sure who it was. Maybe it was Joey calling from the police station. I put it on vibrate and slipped it back into my purse. A moment later, it started vibrating loudly.

Dan looked at me again, almost certainly thinking it was Joey calling.

"I'd better get this," I said, standing up. "It might be my boss. I called her earlier and asked if I could take a few more days off." I hurried out of the room and went a ways down the hallway.

"Hello?" I said in a faint voice.

"Hi, it's me. I was just wondering how your dad's doing. The front desk wouldn't give me any information since I'm not immediate family," Beth said, sounding worried.

"He's in surgery right now," I said, relieved but at the same time disappointed that it wasn't Joey.

"Do you want me to come down and sit with you?" she asked.

"No, it's okay." I was touched by her offer. "Mother and Dan are here and..." As I started to say more, Dan hurried up to me and I could tell something was wrong.

"You need to come back in right away," he said.

"Why? What happened?" I asked frightened by the look on his face.

"I'm not sure. The nurse came back, and she and your mother talked in the hallway for a few moments, then your mother asked me to go find you."

"Beth, I have to go," I said quickly. "Something's wrong with my father." I hung up and followed Dan back to the waiting room as a sick feeling came over me.

CHAPTER 19

MOTHER WAS PACING THE ROOM, STOPPING EVERY NOW and then to look toward the door.

"What happened?" I asked as soon as I walked into the waiting room.

"They hit a vein when they were taking the camera out, and your father started bleeding heavily. And his blood pressure shot up, too. The nurse left a few minutes ago but promised to return soon with an update."

"Oh no," I said as I collapsed onto the chair next to her. Though I'd known things were serious from the moment I found out he had cancer, the reality that he could die while I was here, hit me very hard. Especially now that we were just getting to know each other again after all this time. I wasn't ready to lose him now that I knew there was a chance, we could be close again, like we were when I was young.

Dan sat down on the other side of me and we all took turns looking at the door, as we waited anxiously for the nurse to return. Finally, it opened. But as I started to get up, I saw it was only Beth, with Steve close behind her.

I was glad to see Beth here, but wished she hadn't brought Steve. Even though according to Joey, Steve had a big part in saving my mother's life, I still couldn't get past how he'd treated my brother. I doubted I ever would.

"Is your father okay?" Beth asked, sitting across from us.

"We're waiting to hear back from the nurse. There were complications after the surgery," I replied.

"Oh no," Steve said, sitting next to Beth.

"Hi, I don't think we've met," Dan said as he reached out his hand to Steve. "I'm Dan. Karen's husband."

Steve jumped back up. "I'm Steve,' he said, "Beth's husband. I work for Bill at his shop, too." He sat back down only to have Mother jump up this time.

"This is taking too long," Mother said. "Maybe I should go and try and find out what's going on."

Beth leaned in and whispered into Steve's ear. "I told you we should have brought TJ."

"You're right. I'll go get him," he whispered back.

I looked at Beth. "If you two need to get home to TJ, go right ahead. You can't do anything here anyway. I can call you later with an update."

As Beth started to say something, the door opened, and the nurse walked in. "Can we talk out in the hall?" the nurse asked my mother.

I stood up. The nurse looked at me. "I'm sorry. Just his wife for now."

Mother looked at me somewhat apologetically and followed the nurse out. I stood there and watched them leave, feeling angry. Dan got up and put his arm around me.

"Why don't you sit down for now? I'm sure they'll be right back."

I shook his arm off. "No. He's my father. The nurse should be talking to me not her. She's not even technically related to him anymore," I snapped.

"Well, actually she is," Steve said. Out of the corner of my eye, I saw Beth give Steve the elbow.

"What?" he asked, looking at her.

"Obviously, she doesn't know yet," Beth whispered.

I looked at her, "I don't know what?"

Steve rubbed his side, looking embarrassed.

"Know what?" I asked again, impatiently.

"I'm sorry, Karen, but they got married again," Beth replied softly.

"You mean to each other?" I asked incredulously.

Beth nodded. I looked back out the window at my mother standing there, talking with the nurse. So, that was why she and my father had been acting so strangely since I'd been here. They were husband and wife again. But then who did the fishing gear and slippers belong to? I sat down slowly, when it hit me. Of course, they belonged to my father.

He was the one who'd been staying at the house. I couldn't believe they got remarried. But why keep it from me? Through the window, I saw the nurse nod and walk away. Mother opened the door and came back in looking somewhat relieved.

"They stopped the bleeding," she said, "and it looks like his blood pressure's going back down. They want to make sure he's stabilized before we can see him."

"That's wonderful news," Beth exclaimed as she reached over and squeezed Steve's hand.

As relieved as I was, I also couldn't stop thinking about my parents getting married again.

"Yes, that's great news, Mrs. Parker," I mumbled as Mother sat down.

Steve cleared his throat nervously as my mother turned and looked at me.

"Oh, so you heard?" she asked.

"You can go see him now—both of you," the nurse said, sticking her head back into the room. "But please keep it short. He's not out of the woods just yet. They're setting him back up in his room now."

I jumped up and pushed past Mother and followed the nurse down the hall. This time, there were even more tubes coming out of my father. Tears welled up in my eyes. Mother came in behind me and rushed to the side of the bed.

"Hi, sweetheart."

My father looked at her and smiled weakly. He tried to say something, but no words came out.

"Don't try to talk," she said, looking down at him. "Just rest. You had us worried, but you're okay now." She was biting her lip and I realized that I was biting mine at the same time. I quickly stopped.

"You're going to be okay, Dad," I said, though I wasn't quite sure I believed it by how horrible he looked. He was very pale.

"Yes, you are," Mother agreed as she touched his cheek gently.

I looked at her again, this time with some compassion. No wonder she'd been so worried. She had almost lost the man I'd just discovered to be her husband again. She had to be scared to death. Dan's face came to my mind and even as angry as I was, I couldn't help but think at how horrible I'd feel if it was him lying in this bed instead of my father. My eyes teared. Mother touched my arm.

"Don't cry," she said. "He's going to be fine as soon as he gets his strength back. Your dad's a fighter. And the nurse said the cancer was only on the surface which is wonderful news."

I didn't bother to tell her the tears were about Dan, not my father.

"I hate to disturb your visit, but he really needs to get some rest," the nurse said as she walked in again.

"We'd better go back to the waiting room," I said.

"Maybe it would be better if you both went home for now and got some rest and let him get some rest too. We don't want him moving around or getting excited. You can come back later if you want or even better tomorrow morning. We'll keep an eye on him and I promise to contact you right away if there's any change," the nurse said.

"Maybe we should," Mother said as she bent down and kissed my father on the lips. "We're going to go now Bill, so you can get some sleep. I'll be back first thing in the morning, though."

My father smiled again faintly and closed his eyes. After saying our goodbyes, Mother and I headed back to the waiting room.

"Is he all right?" Dan asked, jumping up as we walked back into the waiting room.

"I think so," Mother replied. "Just very weak. The good thing though, is the nurse said they think they got it all. And the cancer that was there was only on the surface, which is great news. But he needs his rest and the nurse suggested we all go home and get some rest too. But I think I'm going to look in on him one more time before I go. Thank you so much for coming, Beth and Steve."

Beth gave me and Mother a quick hug before she and Steve left.

"Karen, why don't you let Dan take you back to the house?"

"No, I'll wait for you," I said. I felt bad to see her so shaken up.

"Okay," Dan said. "I guess I'll head back to the hotel then. I'll come by the house tomorrow. In fact, why don't we go out for breakfast, Karen?"

"That's a great idea," Mother said. "I don't think you've been eating enough since you've been here."

"We can come back here to see your father after that," Dan said.

I looked at him. He really was trying to be there for me.

"Okay. You can pick me up at 8:30," I said, giving in.

"Great," he said. "See you then."

After he left, Mother and I went back and checked on my father again. He was out like a light. We headed out to the car after reminding the nurse on duty to call us if there was any change in his condition.

—

On the ride home, my mother kept saying how she knew my father was going to be just fine, as if she was trying to convince herself. "He has to be. I want to spend the rest of my life with him," she said staring straight ahead.

"I need to ask you something," I said. "What made you two think it was such a good idea to get married again? Why not just date? And why not tell me that you got remarried? Why do I have to keep hearing things from other people?"

She pulled into the garage and looked at me. I could see the weariness in her face.

"Let's talk inside."

I followed her in and sat down at the kitchen table while she made some tea. She set the cups down on the table and pulled out a chair.

"Your father did call you some time ago to tell you our plans, you know. He said he left several messages for you to call him back so he could tell you himself, but you never did."

"Even so, I've been here for days. You could have told me about it since I've been back."

"You're right. But I knew you had more than enough on your plate right now and hated to spring this on you. And he asked me to wait until we could tell you together. When he was back home."

"Well, I have to tell you, I think it's a big mistake," I said, spooning some honey into my tea. "You know as soon as you start drinking again, it's going to be just like it was before. You're both going to fight and hurt each other again."

A look of resolve came over her face. "I intend to keep doing everything I have been doing these last four years to stay sober. Which is, go to my meetings, work the twelve steps with my sponsor, and do anything else it takes to never drink again. I'm never going back to that life."

"I wish you would have thought of that sooner," I said sadly. "If you had, you'd still be married, and at least James and I could have had some kind of chance at a normal childhood."

"I know. I tried to quit back then," she said, '" believe me, I tried many times. I never thought it would get bad like it did so quickly. But as much as I thought I could control it, it ended up controlling me. I never drank until you and James were born, you know.

I just needed something to help me sleep. But it gradually turned into needing something during the day to help me unwind. Then something for sleep. Then to get me going in the morning. Then if I was upset, I'd drink. Or worried. Pretty soon, there wasn't any reason not to drink. Most of all though, I think I drank to try and stop my feelings of guilt."

"Guilt? About what?" I asked.

"From thinking that somehow I caused James to be born the way he was. Maybe if I'd eaten better, or gotten more rest, or done something different. I don't know what, but something… Yes, I blamed myself for him being the way he was."

I looked at her with surprise. All those years, I thought she blamed me for everything that was wrong with him—and here it sounded like all that time she had only blamed herself.

"So, I drank. And before I knew it," she continued, "I'd crossed that invisible line they talk about in AA, where drinking had become such a part of my life that I felt like I couldn't go a day without doing it."

I felt a shiver of fear. Even though I'd only been drinking for a brief time, I could see how easy it would be to turn to alcohol if I was feeling uncomfortable or stressed. In fact, I was already doing that, and often telling myself I could stop whenever I wanted. But wasn't that what everyone said? But still, I *was* sure I could still stop if it meant losing everything.

"Why didn't you just quit? That's what I could never understand," I said.

"I did try," she said again, her voice rising with emotion. "Every night, I swore I wouldn't drink again. But by ten o'clock the next morning, I was already making up an excuse why I needed one, even though I knew I was going to lose everything important to me if I didn't stop.

And I did lose everything. Your father was gone, James died, and you left, and I was all alone—which all just gave me more reason to feel sorry for myself and drink some more, until one day, I woke up and realized I was nothing but a drunk and had no reason to live as far as I could see.." I could see the pain in her eyes as she went back to that horrible time.

"That was when I went by the shop to see your father one last time. But he wasn't there. I figured it was just as well and drove down to the lake with the intention of ending my life. Even after what had happened to James, I just wasn't thinking straight. And... I drove off the bridge.

But just as the car went over the side, I realized I didn't want to die after all. But at the same time, I knew it was too late."

She looked at me, hard now, as if staring right into my soul. "Alcohol – it takes you over, as you know. It makes you do things you never would."

I looked away, quickly, her words replaying. *It takes you over, as you know.* Hell, what was that supposed to mean? Why would *I* know?

And now it struck me, the irony of it all, that the roles seemed to be reversing. Now, it was my mother worried sick about me, not the reverse. I felt stupid—and at the same time, thought *she* was stupid too. Nothing had taken me over, and nothing would. I felt irritated by the hushed accusation that had passed between us both.

"So, you thought it'd be a good idea to kill yourself, just to make us all feel that much worse," I said, regretting it immediately. I knew how that feeling went, and it was plain she had been so unhappy, felt so alone. Like I did.

"No. I did not think it was a good idea at all," she said, her voice rising with upset and pain. "I never said it was *a good idea*. It's a permanent solution to a temporary problem." She looked away again.

"And I've wondered so many times since then how many others felt the same way I did. And at the last second regretted the decision to take their own life and at the same time realized it was too late to prevent it?" She looked at me again earnestly.

"Had they only known the things I know now," she said, eventually, "I mean, if they'd given things a little more time to work out, those people would find that things always get better in time."

She looked down at her cup then back at me. "Do you think James realized that he was making a mistake at the end?"

"I don't know," I replied sadly. "But it doesn't matter now, does it?"

"No, I guess not." She looked up at me earnestly. "Promise me you'll never do anything like that. It would kill me if I lost you too. And your father…I don't have to tell you what it would do to your father. Promise me."

"Mother, if you knew me at all, you'd know I'd never do what James did. I still can't believe he did that, anyway, knowing what his death would do to me. He had to have known." I looked at her as the anger grew. "Or didn't he care? Didn't he love me at all?"

"I'm sorry," Mother said softly. "I didn't mean to upset you. Of course, he loved you."

"And he didn't even bother leaving a note," I went on. "Didn't he know how I'd blame myself for his death? Or is that what he wanted? Was he trying to hurt me at the end? Did he resent me that much for the way things were?"

"I'm sure he didn't," Mother said her eyes widening.

"As much as I loved him, sometimes I hated him for what he did!" I said even louder unable to control the bottled up hurt and anger. I stood up suddenly and smacked the back of my cup of tea, sending it hurtling off the table onto the floor. There was a shattering sound, bits of china scattering across the floor in all directions.

"How could he?" I cried out. I fell back into my chair and clutched my head. After a moment, I looked up. Mother was staring at me with a shocked expression. Then she slowly rose and walked over to the sink, and without saying a word, she bent down and took a trash can and brush from underneath.

I watched as she slowly swept up the broken pieces of the cup. Then, wiping the tea up with a paper towel, she tossed everything into the trash can and straightened up.

She filled a new cup with some water and set it down in front of me along with a fresh teabag. Then she sat back down as if nothing had happened.

I looked at the cup, then back at her. Now I was the one who was shocked, not only at what I'd just done, but at her reaction to it. This...this was a mother. A *real* mother. A mother I had never seen before, one with endless time and patience for her daughter, even when her daughter messed up.

In the past, if I'd done something like that, she'd have gone into a drunken rage and yelled at me to clean it up. Yet here she was, looking at me with what I could only describe as pure love, something I had never seen coming from her.

"You need to hear this," she said to me very slowly. "James did not know what he was doing. He was hurting. He didn't realize how his death would affect you. If he had, he'd have never gone through with it. He loved you, Karen. He loved you very, very much. All he wanted to do was stop the pain and he didn't know how. But all this - it was his choice, not yours. You must stop blaming yourself. He wouldn't want you to."

"But maybe if I'd been around more, he might have felt he could confide in me and I could have stopped him. How am I supposed to get over the guilt?" I could hear the pain in my own voice.

"It's not easy," she said. "But you must. Otherwise, it will destroy you like it almost did me."

I stood up again. "I can't talk about this anymore." I turned and headed down the hall to my room. My nerves were frayed. I got the bottle of Jack out of the closet and took the lid off, my hands shaking uncontrollably. Up until just now, I hadn't realized just how angry I was at my brother. Now, I not only had to deal with the guilt, but also the rage I felt too. I lifted the bottle up to my lips and closed my eyes. 'God help me' ran through my mind as I took a huge gulp.

CHAPTER 20

I AWOKE TO A RAPPING SOUND. THE DOOR OPENED AND Mother peered in.

"Sorry to wake you," she said, "but Dan's here waiting for you."

I drowsily looked at the clock, then back at her. "What's he doing here?"

"He came to take you out for breakfast, remember? You said you'd go with him then you were both going to the hospital together."

I groaned. "Please tell him that I changed my mind and I'll go to the hospital by myself."

She hesitated, "It would be good for you to get out. And I can tell he really wants to talk to you. Besides, I talked to the nurse and your dad is doing fine and can't see anyone until they feed him and get him up. Shall I tell him you'll be out in a bit?"

I lay there regretting that I'd ever agreed to go with him this morning. I couldn't take another emotional day, though we did need to talk and figure out where we were going to go from here.

I got dressed and headed out to the kitchen. Dan was sitting at the table talking to Mother, with a cup of coffee in his hand. He looked up and smiled.

"Good morning. Ready to go have a good southern breakfast?"

As I looked back at him dressed in a plaid shirt and blue jeans—something he'd obviously bought since he'd gotten here, to try to fit in with the rest of the Southerners—I felt a tugging at my heart. He was cute. And I had to admit I still loved him. Even after what he'd done.

But then I felt the wall come back up. Even more reason not to go out with him this morning. It was much safer to stay angry than to get hurt again..

He stood up. "Thanks for the coffee, Doris. Ready?" he asked, smiling again.

I headed out to the car. Dan followed me and hurried to open the passenger door.

"You sure look nice," he said as I got in. "Did you get some sleep last night?"

I ignored his compliment. "Where're we going? Not the Huddle House, I hope," I said putting on my seatbelt.

"I thought we'd go to the Cracker Barrel in Greenville. The girl in the lobby at my hotel recommended it."

The Cracker Barrel. Was there anywhere I could go that Joey and I hadn't been to?

"I'm glad we're going to get a chance to be alone and talk," Dan said as he headed toward the highway. "I wanted to run something by you. It's about me going back to California, tomorrow."

I looked at him quickly. "What's your hurry?" I asked with a bite in my voice.

"It's for work. But let's talk about it over breakfast," he said as he followed the directions of his GPS.

I sat there, angry. *He wants to get back to Susan.* Why did he bother to come here then? Unless it was only out of guilt or a sense of obligation. After driving for a while, we came to the exit leading to the restaurant.

As we pulled the car into the Cracker Barrel parking lot, memories came back of all the times Joey and I had eaten here. That life back then had been so simple compared to now. I followed Dan in. A hostess led us to a table in the back.

"Brenda will be right back to take your order," she said. "Enjoy your breakfast."

We sat down and as Dan flipped through the menu, I just stared at mine. After a moment, he closed his menu and looked at me.

"Are you upset that I said I might go home early?" he asked.

"Look, do what you want," I replied as I opened the menu and pretended to read it.

"It really is for work. You remember Jon Dye, don't you? The supervisor in charge of that new retirement home that's going up in Fullerton? Well, his original contractor is retiring early due to medical reasons and Jon asked me if I wanted to finish the job for him."

"Great," I said still pretending to study the menu.

"It's a huge job and it pays well. I thought it might be good for us. What do you think?"

I looked up. "What do I think about what?" I asked.

"What do you think about me going back and taking it? I wanted to make sure it was okay with you before I committed to Jon. But if all goes well and he likes my work, there will be plenty of more jobs like this with him after that. You know how we can really use the money. But if you want me to stay here longer, I will."

I didn't say anything and continued to look at the menu that I already knew very well from all the times I'd been here.

"I'm sorry to spring it on you like this," he continued, "but I got the call from Jon late last night on the way back to the hotel. I know you're dealing with a lot right now, between your dad's illness, seeing your mother again and what I put you through. And although you seem to be holding up well, though I don't know how, if you want me to, I'll stay."

The waitress appeared, carrying a pot of coffee. She turned our coffee mugs over and filled them to the top, then set the pot on the table. "I'll be right back to take your order."

Dan opened a pack of sugar and emptied it into his mug. "So, what do you think? I'd feel a whole lot better leaving if I knew you and your mother were on better terms though, and you at least had her to lean on."

"She's the last person I'd lean on. She's never been there for me. So, no reason to expect her to be now. I'll be fine," I said.

He picked up his cup and took a sip of coffee as he searched my face. "Really? That's too bad. I wish it wasn't like that. Maybe I should just pass and tell Jon I've decided to stay here longer. It sounds like you need me."

"I don't need you. Just go. I'll be fine."

Dan looked at me. "Now, it almost seems like you're anxious for me to go. Are you? Does it have something to do with Joey?"

"Of course not," I replied, though I did have to wonder myself if it was easier to let Dan leave knowing Joey was here.

"Are you sure?" he asked. "Because I get the feeling there's something going on between you two."

"I told you, he's just an old boyfriend. That's all," I said, staring at my untouched coffee.

"I don't know if I believe you. Look at you. You can't even look at me when you say his name."

The waitress came back before he could say anything else and asked if we were ready to order. But one look at our faces, and she said she'd come back later.

"So, just how serious were you about him back then?" Dan asked, once she was gone. "Serious enough to marry him?"

"Well, we did talk about it," I said, remembering the time I thought Joey was going to propose.

"So, why did you break up? Why didn't you get married?" he asked.

"Because my brother died, and I left town and moved to California and met you. And up until last week, I hadn't seen or talked to Joey since I left Easley over eight years ago."

"But you still have feelings for him. I can tell," he said softly.

"Whatever feelings we had for each other died a long time ago," I replied, trying to sound convincing.

"Well, even if that's true for you, which I'm not so sure about, I don't think it's true for him. I saw the way he looked at you. Then he shows up in your bedroom the other night. He's obviously still in love with you."

"Well that's not my fault if he is," I said looking away.

"Spending time with him like you've been doing isn't helping. It's only going to make it harder on him and on you too. And on me as well. Is that why you've been so moody this past year at home, because you still have feelings for him?"

I began to answer when the waitress timidly came back for our order again.

"You're the one who's been out of sorts this past year," I said after she was gone. "I figured it was because your business was slow. But we both know the real reason you were so moody. It was because you wanted to be with her."

"That's not true," he said. "Sure, I felt bad about being out of work. But you were different, too. Distant. You rarely talked to me and then started making up excuses why you had to come home late. I could tell you didn't want to be with me."

"Well why should I hurry home if all we were going to do was argue? I grew up watching my parents fight all the time and I refuse to live like that."

"I'm sorry," he said. "I didn't know you had to grow up with that. I'm sure that was rough. But we're not like that. We may have some heated discussions from time to time. But at least when we did, we were communicating. If it was up to you, we wouldn't talk at all. It's like living with someone who's in the witness protection program or something. Since I've been back here, I've learned more about you in three days than in the entire time I've known you. I just want to know you, that's all. How you're feeling, what you're thinking."

"If I told you what I was feeling and thinking all the time, you couldn't handle it," I said.

The waitress came back with our breakfasts, set the plates down in front of us and left as quickly as possible.

"Try me," Dan said as he lifted his fork. "I may not always like what you tell me, but if this is going to work out between us, you need to open up. That is, if you still want to be married to me." He looked at me. "Do you?"

"I don't know what I want right now. You really hurt me, Dan. And you broke my trust. I don't know if I can ever get past that."

"Sure, you can," he said his voice cracking. "I'll help you. We'll get through this together. I love you so much. Please, don't give up on us. I promise I'll never do anything to betray your trust again. I love you."

He looked broken, and the idea that our marriage could very well be over, broke me too. My cell phone started to ring, and I reached into my purse for it in case it was my mother. But it was Beth.

"Did I catch you at an inconvenient time?" she asked after I said hello.

"No, it's fine. Dan and I are at the Cracker Barrel having breakfast. What's up?"

"I just talked to your mother and she said your dad was doing pretty good, thank God. I wanted to go see him. I thought maybe if you weren't on your way, we could ride together. So, we can talk some more."

I looked at Dan again. Maybe he was right, and I needed to talk to someone.

"Sure," I said. "I was going to ride with Dan, but he's thinking about going home early. I'll call you when he drops me back at the house."

"Sounds good," she said. "Talk to you then."

I set the phone down. "That was Beth. I'll just go with her to the hospital."

"Okay," he said, sounding disappointed. "I guess since it appears you don't care if I stay or go, I'll just go back to the hotel and book my flight back." He looked at me as if waiting for me to tell him to stay, but I went back to my breakfast without saying a word.

As we headed back, Dan said little until we got back to the house.

"I'm not giving up on us," he said as I got out of the car. I hurried up the porch steps as the tears streamed down my face.

CHAPTER 21

MOTHER WAS IN THE KITCHEN AS I HURRIED ON BY. I wiped my tears quickly, so she wouldn't notice I'd been crying.

"How was breakfast?" she asked. "Where's Dan? I thought you two were going to the hospital together after you ate?"

I stopped at the doorway and turned around. "I decided to go with Beth a little later. Dan went back to the hotel," I said, "so he can work on moving his flight back to California up."

Oh, honey," she said pulling out a chair. "Sit down and talk to me."

I hesitated, then pulled out the chair across from her and sat down.

"So, what happened?"

"He needs to get back right away. *Said* it's for work," I said, feeling the tears come again.

"And you're not going with him?"

"No. I'm not leaving until I know Dad is going to be alright. But don't worry, I'm sure there are hotels available now that I can go stay in for the rest of the time I'm here."

"Oh honey, don't do that. I like having you here," she said. "Please stay. So, tell me, what did he do? He seems like a nice guy, but apparently he did something to upset you." I saw a flash of anger in her eyes.

"I caught him having dinner with another girl that he'd been seeing."

"I'm so sorry," she said with a pained look.

"He said he doesn't love her and that he loves me very much. But I just don't know. Sometimes, I think I should never have left here. Joey would never have done something like that," I said bitterly.

"You're probably right, I've always liked Joey. But maybe Dan really means it and is telling the truth when he says he won't ever do it again. But only you can decide if you think you can believe him. I can see how much he loves you and that you love him too. Just follow your heart is the only advice I can give you."

"Following my heart is what got me into this mess to begin with," I said, looking away.

"Well, you deserve the best. And I want you to know how proud I am of you coming back here for your dad. I know it couldn't have been easy with all the painful memories here. And now to find out what you've been going through with Dan, and you still came. Well, you're an amazing young woman, is all I can say."

My eyes misted again. I so wished she'd said something like that to me when I was growing up, but it still felt good to hear it now. Yet, I felt conflicted. I loved her, I wanted nothing to do with her, I loved her…

"Try not to worry," she said sympathetically. "Things will work out. I promise."

I looked at her and though I wished it was true, I knew all too well that things rarely worked out like I'd hoped.

"Well, I guess I'll be heading off to the hospital. I'll tell your dad you and Beth will be by later. I'm just going to grab a few more things to take for him to read, to keep him busy while he's there."

When she said that, I was reminded about the journal and how my father had wanted me to look for it again. And of how I'd promised to do just that.

As soon as she was gone, I hurried off to James' room. I'd have a little time to look before I called Beth. As I looked around, the memory flooded back, of that time Mother had found some magazines with pictures of half-naked women in there. After that, James made sure to never leave them where she'd be sure to find them.

I headed for his closet and after scouring through it and ending up finding nothing, I closed the door and turned to the bookcase. Maybe I'd missed something the other day, and he had the journal somewhere slid in between all his books.

But after looking through each row again, I decided it wasn't there either. I stood up and looked around some more. Where would he have hidden it? Maybe he'd destroyed it once he had made the decision to end his life. But if he hadn't, that meant it must still be somewhere in this room.

I had to find it, not only to keep Mother from coming across it, but because there had to be something in there that would give me a clue what had made James do what he did. And I was willing to take the chance and find out, no matter how insistent my father was that I shouldn't read it.

As I pulled open a dresser drawer, the doorbell rang. I shut the drawer and headed to the front door. When I opened it, Beth was standing on the doorstep.

"I thought I'd just come by instead of waiting for you to call," she said, walking in. "I really want to talk to you." She stopped in the foyer and stood there, staring at the family photo. "I haven't been in this house for a long time. It feels kind of strange being in here again."

"I know," I said. "I felt exactly the same way when I first walked in. Well, come on. Mother just left to go see Dad. We can talk and have some peach tea she made. It will give her a chance to visit before we head there."

Beth followed me down the hallway into the kitchen. "She's been cooking a lot since I've been here. Kind of strange seeing her do that," I said, smiling.

"Maybe she's just trying to stay busy because she's worried about your dad. I'm so glad he sounds like he's doing better."

I filled two glasses with ice, then with the tea and handed her a glass before sitting down at the kitchen table with mine.

"So, how'd things go at breakfast with Dan? Did you talk things out?" she asked, taking a sip of her tea.

"We talked some. But nothing was really resolved. He's going back home, he says, for work," I replied as the sick feeling of disappointment came back.

"Sounds like you don't believe it's just for work. Are you worried he wants to be with that girl?" she asked.

I put my glass down. "I don't know. But if he is, there's not much I can do. Right now, all I can focus on is my dad and seeing that he gets through this. I'll have to deal with Dan and all of that when I go home. *If* I go home."

"Where else would you go?" she asked. "At least with him gone, it'll give you time to sort out your feelings about Joey."

I raised my eyebrows.

"Anyone can see how you two still feel about each other. I'm sure even Dan had to notice, which actually serves him right," she said.

I smiled. It felt good to have someone else on my side.

"Do you still have feelings for Joey?" she asked.

"I don't know. Maybe it's because things aren't great right now between me and Dan or maybe because coming back stirred up a lot of old feelings, but I'm not sure how I feel. It's not that I'm ready to give up on my marriage quite yet, but what if I'm making a mistake by not giving Joey another chance?" I asked.

"Just take your time and don't rush things," she said. "See how you feel. You don't have to make any decisions right now. All I know is that you deserve to be happy and if that means staying with Dan or getting back with Joey, I'll support you either way. And who knows, maybe you can work things out with your mother too, while you're back here."

"Well, she has been nicer, that's for sure. But still, I can't forget how mean she was back when she was drinking. I wish she could have been there for me, you know, like a mother should be."

"I know. James used to say that even when she was there, she wasn't really there. Though your father wasn't much help to you or James either after he and your mom got divorced and he started seeing that woman. That really bothered James."

I stopped and stared at her. "What woman?"

Beth looked surprised. "You mean you didn't know about her?"

"No, James didn't tell me," I said feeling hurt that one more time, my twin had kept something else from me. And yet, he was willing to tell Beth about this woman?

"I'm sorry,' she said. "I'm sure he intended to tell you. I guess he found out from one of the boys at school, that your dad—and Gloria, I think her name was—were dating. We heard she'd lost her husband right before she met your dad. No, James wasn't too happy that your father was seeing someone so soon."

I looked at her. "You and James sure talked a lot, didn't you?"

Beth looked away quickly.

"What is it, Beth? What aren't you telling me?" I asked.

She looked back at me. "Okay but promise me that you won't get upset."

I braced myself, knowing full well that anytime someone says, 'promise you won't get upset', it meant they were about to tell you something bound to upset you.

"What is it?" I asked with trepidation.

She hesitated. "Remember when you asked if I knew that James liked me?"

"Yes," I said slowly, with an uneasy feeling.

She looked down at her left hand and gave her wedding ring a twirl. "Well, actually I did know how he felt."

I waited for her to go on.

"The fact is," she continued, "I liked him too."

"I know you did," I said impatiently, anxious for her to get to the point. "And?"

"No, what I mean is that I *really* liked him," she said putting the emphasis on *really*.

"Just spit it out, Beth. What exactly are you trying to say?"

"I'm trying to tell you that I was in love with your brother, Karen."

"What?" I gasped.

"Yes," she replied softly. "We were in love."

"Wait," I said, trying to wrap my head around what she was saying. "When did all this happen?"

"Back when we were seniors. Back when Steve and I had split up for a few months. Remember? Or maybe you don't. You were pretty wrapped up in Joey back then," she said sounding hurt.

"I knew you were upset. And I felt really bad for you. But I knew you'd find someone else. All the guys liked you," I said. "But you decided to go back to Steve anyway."

"I was heartbroken when Steve and I broke up. But you didn't seem to care at all. And if it wasn't for James, I don't know how I would have made it through all that. James was there for me when no one else was. He even called every night to check up on me. That's when it happened. Before I knew it, I'd fallen for him really hard."

I thought back to the terrible night at Applebee's and how Beth took off with Steve. It sure looked like she was still with Steve.

"If that was true, why did you leave Applebee's that night with Steve?"

"Because I didn't want Steve to find out until I had a chance to tell him about me and James. That was the least I could do. That wasn't the time or the place to break it to him. Just because I'd fallen in love with James, didn't mean I didn't still have feelings for Steve. I'm sure you of all people can understand what it's like to care strongly for two guys at the same time."

This time, I looked away. She was right. But still, how could she just sit there and pretend she didn't have any feelings for James at all, that night?

"But you were willing to just sit there and let Steve say all those horrible things about James. How could you do that if you loved my brother like you say?" I asked, in turmoil.

"I just wanted to get Steve out of there before he did something stupid. You know how he could be impulsive."

"You sure that's the reason? Or was it because you wanted to keep your little affair with James secret? I wonder if you ever intended to tell Steve about James. You were just stringing James along, weren't you? After all, you were Beth Meyer and only dated good-looking jocks like Steve. You'd never let yourself be seen with someone like James."

"Someone like James?" she asked looking angry. "You make it sound like there was something wrong with him."

I felt my face get warm. "I'm just saying, James had to be very hurt when he saw you leave with Steve. And he must have figured that you'd been using him all that time. Why wouldn't he? He knew the truth, and he couldn't take it."

"I wasn't using him, I loved him. In fact, I told Steve on the way home that very night that I wanted to be with James. I left my cell phone in Steve's car or I would have called James and told him what I'd done that night. I figured I'd wait until morning and go by the house and tell him then. But when I got there, no one was home except for your mother, who was asleep on the couch. That afternoon, I got my phone from Steve and left James a message."

I stared at her. I wanted so badly to believe that she was telling the truth and really did love James, but I just couldn't. If she'd loved James as much as she said she had, then why not just come right out and tell Steve that she'd fallen in love with someone else? Why keep it a secret for so long from not only Steve, but from me and Joey too?

Was she just keeping her options open until she'd made up her mind if she really wanted to be with James? I thought about Joey and wondered if I wasn't doing exactly the same thing with him. Could I be waiting to see how I felt about Dan before deciding if I wanted to be with Joey?

The thought that I could be possibly doing the same thing that Beth did with James, made me even more angry with her.

I set my glass down hard on the table. "You should go," I said. "I don't want to hear any more. You broke my brother's heart and now he's dead. I hope you're happy."

"That's not true," she said.

I got to my feet. "Just go before I say something I'm going to regret."

Beth stood up too. She looked at me and shook her head. "Please, you're wrong. I loved your brother." I walked swiftly to the back door and opened it. I just stood there.

"You don't understand," she said. "It wasn't like that."

"Please, go," I said, tearing up.

Beth looked at me one more time, then walked past me with her shoulders slumped. I almost felt bad for her, until I thought about how James must have felt the exact same way as he watched her walk out of Applebee's with Steve that night. I closed the door and headed to my room, going straight for the bottle of Jack.

CHAPTER 22

THE TEARS RAN DOWN MY FACE AS I HEADED BACK TO the kitchen with the whiskey bottle. Eyeing my peach tea still on the table, I filled the glass to the top and took it with me back to my room.

The mixture wasn't great, but the more I thought about my poor brother, the more I drank. All he'd ever wanted, all anyone wanted, was someone to love who loved us back, and Beth had destroyed that dream.

He'd never get another chance to love someone. I would, though I wasn't so sure if it was worth the pain. At least now, I finally knew why he had taken his life, but knowing didn't make me feel any better like I thought it would.

In fact, the idea that Beth was the cause made me feel even worse. If only she hadn't left with Steve that night, maybe James wouldn't have taken it so hard. But then again, if only I hadn't set that night up to begin with.

I took a few more sips of the Jack and tea, when the doorbell rang. Beth was back. "Please go away," I shouted. "I don't want to fight anymore,"

But the doorbell rang again followed by a pounding on the door. Annoyed, I set my drink down and got up to answer it.

"What do you want now?" I asked, whipping the door open. But it wasn't Beth, it was Joey.

"Oh, hi," I said stepping back with surprise. "I thought you were your sister."

"That's why I'm here. She called me just now, said that you and she got into an argument."

He came in and shut the door, then sat down on the living room couch.

"What were you two fighting about?"

I sat down across from him, wishing I could get back to my whiskey and tea. "She didn't tell you? It was about her and James."

"What about them?" he asked.

"They were seeing each other all that time," I replied.

He looked at me. "You're crazy."

"It's true," I said. "She told me."

"I don't believe it. You sure you aren't imagining things? I can tell you've been drinking again. I can smell it on you," he said.

"It's true! Beth and James were not only seeing each other, but according to her, they were madly in love. And they didn't want anyone to know. Not you or me."

"I don't believe it," he said. "She was with Steve the whole time I can remember."

"Except their senior year when they split up for a few months, remember? That's when she started seeing James. But I guess eventually, she decided my brother wasn't good enough for her. So, she dumped him and went back to Steve. What a mistake," I said with disgust.

Joey looked stunned. "So, the night at Applebee's? Were they seeing each other then? Is that why James went, because Beth was going?"

I shrugged.

"This is all very confusing," he said, rubbing his hands together nervously. As he started to say something else, his cell phone beeped. Joey stood up and unclipped the phone from his belt, then took a few steps away.

"Hello," he said, keeping one eye on me. "Yes. I'm not far from there right now. Sure. I'll be right there." He put the phone back onto his belt and looked at me.

"That was dispatch. There's a car broken down on the 135. I have to go and direct traffic. But stay put. We need to finish this conversation." He started for the door but stopped and turned around. "And please don't drink anymore while I'm gone."

As he opened the door to leave, a memory of my father came to mind, of how every morning before he left for the shop, he'd say the exact same thing to my mother. And no sooner was he out the door, when she'd run and make herself a drink. Oddly enough, hearing Joey say that made me want to do the same.

And sure enough, just like Mother, no sooner had I heard him drive down the driveway, then I hurried back to my room. But instead of finishing my drink, I took out my phone.

"Hello, Charlie? This is Karen Parker."

"Well, hello Miss. What can I do for you? Do you need a ride somewhere?"

"Yes. Can you come and get me? I'm at my mother's house."

"Sure," he said.

"I looked at my watch. "How soon can you be here?"

"In fifteen minutes or so," he replied.

"Great," I said. "I'll be waiting. Please hurry." I hung up and went into the bathroom and put on some fresh makeup.

—

As I slipped on my shoes, I heard a car coming up the driveway. I prayed it wasn't Joey back already, and when I looked out the window, I was relieved to see it was Charlie.

"Hi," I said, jumping onto the now familiar backseat. Charlie shut my door and got back in.

"So, how's your visit going so far? Is your dad doing better?" he asked.

"He's fine," I said nervously as I glanced down toward the end of the driveway. "Can we get going please? I'm kind of in a hurry."

He turned back around and put the car into reverse. "Sure. So, where do you need to go?"

I hesitated for a moment. "To the Greenville Hospital, but can we stop at the Red Penny first?"

"Okay," he said, putting the car in drive and slowly heading down the driveway. He glanced in the rearview mirror at me several times.

Quit worrying, Charlie, just drive, I wanted to tell him. *I'm not like my mother.* But even I was starting to wonder if maybe I wasn't more like her than I was willing to admit.

We pulled out onto the main road and by the lights on the top of a car coming toward us, I knew it was Joey returning to the house. I ducked down quickly. After a few minutes, I straightened back up.

"Everything okay, Miss?" Charlie asked, glancing in the mirror again.

"Yes, fine," I said, picturing Joey's reaction when he got to the house only to discover that I was gone. That was what he got for standing me up at the hospital the other day.

We finally got to the Red Penny, and Charlie parked the car while I promised to be out soon before running inside.

And no sooner did I walk in, when someone called my name. I froze, but it was only Big Al saying hello. I took a seat in my usual spot, all the while knowing it couldn't be a good sign when the bartender knows you by name.

Big Al held up a bottle of Jack. I nodded and waited anxiously for my drink. As he set it down, the phone on the wall started to ring.

"Red Penny," he said. I sipped my drink.

"Okay, no problem," Big Al said as he glanced over at me. "I'll be sure to let you know." He hung up and walked over to me. "Guess who that was?"

I had no doubt it was Joey.

"It was Officer Joey looking for you. But don't worry. I didn't tell him you were here."

"Thanks, Big Al," I said, relieved as I picked up the glass again.

"That poor guy's never gotten over you, has he?" he asked as he started to walk away.

"What do you mean?" I asked.

He turned around. "He used to come in here all the time before he was a cop. He'd sit right there by the wall," he said pointing. "It never failed. By the third drink, he'd start talking about *the girl he let get away*. I'm guessing now that girl was you."

I stared at him. "What else did he say?"

"Just that he was going to California to try and win you back. Sadly, he came back all alone. I felt bad for the guy.

I sat there with my mouth open.

Big Al's eyebrows went up. "Oh, I guess you didn't know. Well, no harm in telling you now, I suppose. Yep. He said he was going to ask her to marry him and bring her…I mean you…back home."

"What?" I gasped, my heart starting to beat faster.

"That's what he said. After he came back without you, he never mentioned you again and I didn't see him much after that. Then I heard he started working for the police department."

Big Al glanced at my hand. "It looks like things worked out for you, though."

I looked down at my wedding ring numbly.

"Anyway, I haven't seen him in here since. Not until yesterday," he said.

Someone called out for another beer, and Big Al left me to go wait on him. I sat there stunned, unable to believe Joey actually went looking for me. My phone beeped with a new text. I felt guilty to see that it was from Dan giving me the details of his flight home tomorrow. And more than that, I was surprised at how disappointed I was that he still planned on leaving.

I dropped the phone back into my purse just as Big Al walked up. You okay?"

"Sure," I replied.

"He's here," he said, cocking his head toward the door.

I turned to see Joey standing in the doorway, frowning in my direction.

"I knew I'd find you here. Why didn't you wait for me back at the house?" he asked, sounding annoyed.

"Can I get you anything?" Big Al interrupted. "A Coke for you Joey? You ready for a refill?" Big Al asked me.

"I think she's had enough," Joey said firmly.

"Yes, I'll take another one, please," I replied, once again miffed that Joey was answering for me.

"Can we just go?" Joey asked as Big Al walked away. "I'm still on duty. I shouldn't be in here, let alone it bothers me that you are. Let's go back to the house and finish our conversation."

"Wait. Sit down. I have something I'd like to ask you," I said, thinking about what Big Al had just told me about Joey going to California.

"Sure, anything. But not here," he said.

"Okay then," I said. "You can drive me to the hospital to see my father. We can talk on the way."

"Do you really want to go there after you've been drinking? You'll only worry him. Maybe you should just wait and go later. Let's go back to your house and you can have some coffee. Then if you still feel like it, I'll drive you there," he said.

"Okay," I finally agreed as Joey laid some money on the bar. Big Al watched as I followed Joey outside. After explaining to Charlie that I didn't need a ride to the hospital after all, I paid him and climbed into Joey's car.

"So, what did you want to ask me?" Joey asked as he headed for the house.

"Why didn't you tell me that you'd come looking for me in California?" I asked.

He sighed. "I see Al told you about that. I guess it was because I was embarrassed. Especially since when I got there, I saw Dan kissing you on the front porch. I knew I was too late, and you'd already found someone else, so I left."

That must have been some time ago, I thought to myself, back when things were good with Dan. He made it a habit of getting up before I left for work, so he could walk me out to the car and kiss me goodbye. He hadn't done that for a long time.

"I left and came back here and tried to forget all about you," Joey continued. "But, as you can see, that hasn't worked out too well. I'll never be able to forget about you."

I didn't say anything.

He turned toward me. "What would you have said?"

I looked back at him. "What would I have said about what?"

"If I'd showed up at your door and asked you to leave Dan and go back to Easley to marry me. What would you have said?"

I looked away as the image came to me of the doorbell ringing and opening up the door to find Joey standing on the doorstep. I wasn't sure what I would have done.

"I don't know," I replied just as softly.

"Well that's promising," he said. "At least you're not sure you'd have told me no. Maybe I shouldn't have given up so quickly. Who knows? You could have been my wife right now and not married to him."

Joey pulled up to the house and turned the engine off. As I opened the door to get out, he grabbed my hand and pulled me toward him.

"What're you doing?"

"I'm asking you now, what I should have asked you a long time ago. Will you marry me?"

"Are you crazy? What about Dan?"

"Divorce him. I know you still love me," he said.

"You're not making sense right now. I can't marry you. Besides, my job is there."

"So, get a job here. Not that you need to work. I can support you. Or what if I went back there? I can transfer to Los Angeles. I'll do anything, as long as we can be together." Without warning, he leaned in and kissed me square on the lips.

I pulled my head back. "You have clearly lost your mind."

"Maybe I have," he said. "But I've wanted to kiss you from the moment I first laid eyes on you at the hospital."

"This isn't right. I can't do this." I opened the door and got out. Leaving it open, I ran up the front porch and went inside, all the while my heart was leaping out of my chest. I closed the door and leaned my back against it, breathing hard as I asked myself what the heck just happened.

Dan was right. Being around Joey was just intensifying both Joey's and my feelings for each other. And that wasn't good. My life was complicated enough right now. I heard a car door close, then another, and turned around and watched through the side window as Joey's car backed out and drove away.

Heart still racing, I headed to my room. But, halfway down the hall, I stopped.

I could hear what sounded like crying coming from the kitchen. I turned around and headed there, only to find Mother standing by the kitchen sink holding a bottle of Jack in her hand.

I stopped in the doorway stunned, even though I knew I shouldn't be that surprised. I'd figured she was bound to start drinking again. She turned and slowly looked at me with tears running down her face.

"I'm so sorry," she said.

I pictured how disappointed my father was going to be when he found out she'd started drinking again. I'd told her this would happen. She put the bottle down onto the counter.

"I'm so sorry," she said again. "You'd never have started if it wasn't for me."

Confused, I looked at her, then at the bottle. It was when I noticed the pitcher of tea next to it that I realized that it was my bottle of Jack in her hand. I must have left it there earlier when I'd made myself a drink. I walked over and took it from her hand.

"I'm the one who is sorry, Mother," I said, feeling horrible. "I didn't mean to leave this out where you could find it."

"Won't you let me help you?" she asked in a pleading voice.

"I'm fine really," I replied. "I guess it has been harder than I realized coming back here, and maybe you are right, and I've been drinking too much. But it's not that bad."

Embarrassed as well as ashamed, I took the bottle and headed to my bedroom, and tossed it into the closet. My eyes filled with tears. How could I have been so careless and risked her sobriety like that? She could have started drinking again because of me. What was wrong with me? Or could that be what I'd wanted all along, for her to fail? No. I may have been bitter about how she raised me, but I hoped I'd never stoop that low.

I shut the closet door and as I turned around, I could hear banging in the kitchen followed by the scent of something cooking. There she was again, cooking. I was sure it was because, once again, I'd upset her. At least cooking was a far healthier thing to do than drinking, when she was nervous. But still, I felt bad. She had enough to worry about with my father.

I grabbed my jacket and quietly let myself out the front door. I needed some air. I walked around to the back yard and headed in the direction of the trail that led up to the shooting range.

Careful not to trip over any holes or rocks on the dirt path, I made my way up the hill. As I climbed, I got more and more anxious. I hadn't been up here since James had died.

Halfway up, I stopped to catch my breath. I could hear dogs barking wildly, somewhere off in the distance. As I started to walk again, the barking took on a more frenzied tone, the same sound I knew they made when they'd cornered some poor animal. Right now, I knew just how that poor animal felt.

I continued my climb as my mind went to how James must have struggled that morning, not only physically but emotionally too, knowing what he was about to do, as he'd made his way up this very same hill, for the last time. I took a few more steps and prepared myself as I got to the top.

CHAPTER 23

A CHILL RAN THROUGH ME AS THE MEMORY OF FINDING James on the ground, not far from where I was standing, ran through my mind. And I considered going back to the house, but I took a deep breath, and slowly looked around.

On one side were the three targets my father had built. And on the other side, was a starting line of rocks guiding us where to stand when we were shooting.

I walked closer to one of the targets. It had many holes in the center of it, and I wondered if any of them were from James the morning he'd died.

I turned around slowly and looked down at the spot where I'd found his body. Shuddering, I could almost see him there right now on his back, blood covering the front of his shirt and the side of his head where the bullet must have entered. And that halo of deep red that spread all around him, soaking into the grass and the earth.

For the 100th time, I asked myself what I could have done to stop him from wanting to kill himself. I sank to the ground, leaned against a log, and moaned out loud.

"I'm sorry, James. I loved you so much. I wish I'd told you that more."

I tried to imagine what had been going through his mind that morning. Was he thinking about Beth? He had to be. Had he thought at all about me? Tears flowed down my face and I leaned back and closed my eyes as I tried to remember some of the happier times with James.

—

I opened my eyes and sat up for a moment, confused as to why I was even up at the range. It was much darker than when I'd come up here.

Realizing I must have dozed off, I stood and zippered my jacket up higher. It had gotten colder too and now the little light there was, came only from the moon that was now out. As I started toward the hill to go back down, I heard a voice and froze.

I thought I must have been imagining it but then I heard it again, sounding as if someone was calling my name.

"Karen," I heard again, this time louder.

"Karen? Is that you?" This time, I recognized my mother's voice. She was now at the top of the trail and was pointing a flashlight in my direction. She lowered it as she walked toward me.

"There you are. When you weren't in your room, I went looking for you and somehow guessed you'd come up here. I was worried. What are you doing up here all by yourself in the dark?"

I looked toward the spot where James had taken his last breath. "Looking for answers I guess."

She stared at the same spot. "I understand. I come up here doing the same thing sometimes." She sat down on the log I was just leaning against.

I hesitated, then sat down next to her.

"I wasn't happy when your father built this up here," she said in a hollow voice. "I was always afraid someone was going to get hurt. And I hated it even more when James came up here by himself. It was bad enough when you and your father or you and Joey came up here. But when James started coming, I wasn't happy at all."

I looked at her. "I don't remember him coming up here except for that one time when he went with Joey and Dad, and they almost had to carry him back, his asthma was so bad."

"For some reason, he started coming here again before he died," she said. "I'd hear him up here shooting for hours. I'd sit in the house and listen until I knew he was back home safe. He said he wanted to get good at using the pistol, so he could go hunting with your dad. I guess they had a trip planned at the time."

I sat there shocked. I'd had no idea James had been coming up here. How did I not know that? Was I that out of touch with my brother?

"I was a terrible sister," I said to no one in particular.

"What makes you say that?" she asked, sounding surprised.

"I was so caught up in my own life, I didn't know half the things he was doing. One of them being how he was coming up here to shoot."

"You can't blame yourself," she said. "You were young. You were living your own life. That's what teenagers do. We all missed the signs that he was depressed enough to do that. In fact, I thought he seemed happier than he'd been in a while at the time. But I was wrong."

"I feel so guilty though," I said, feeling my chest ache. "When does the guilt go away?"

She looked at me. "I want you to know that I feel guilty too. I've never told anyone this, but after James died, the guilt was unbearable. Not just for being drunk the day he came up here and thinking that maybe I could have stopped him, but because I knew what a terrible mother I was.

It was my job to protect my children and I had failed miserably. And what's worse is that when he died, there was a part of me that actually felt relieved. And I hated myself for feeling that way."

Shocked, I stared at her. "Relieved?"

She looked away. "I know what you're thinking. What kind of mother would even think something like that? But it's true. I was glad in a way. Not because he was gone. But because I loved him so much and it killed me watching him struggle day after day. So, when he died, as devastated as I was at losing him, there was also a part of me that was relieved.

He was finally free. And selfishly in a way, so was I. I didn't have to anguish over him anymore. Or lie in bed at night wondering if he was in pain. So, if anyone should feel guilty, it should be me, not you. I want you to know that. You have nothing to be guilty about. He loved you."

I continued to stare at her, speechless, not only because she was willing to admit such a thing, but that she was willing to admit it to me of all people. And yet, as horrible as it sounded to hear her say she'd felt that way, I understood exactly how she felt.

As much as I adored my brother and would do anything to have him here with us right now, there were moments when I'd wondered if my life wouldn't have been easier if I didn't have a brother so emotionally and physically challenged.

How many times did I have to turn down doing things with my friends because if James couldn't go, it meant I couldn't either? Like the time I wanted to join the junior softball team. But since James couldn't play any sports at all, it meant I wasn't allowed to either. I was devastated, but Mother didn't want him to feel bad, so she told me any sport was off-limits to me too. She did suggest I try out for the drama class, however. At least that was something James would be able to do.

But he wasn't interested in it like I was. It was funny. I'd never realized until now that I had Mother to thank for my love of acting. I looked at her in a slightly different light. Maybe she wasn't so bad after all.

"You must be freezing," she said, standing up. "I know I am. Let's go back down"

"Okay," I said, standing up again.

As we started to leave, her flashlight slid from her hand and onto the ground. She bent down to pick it up. "What's this?" she asked, pulling something shiny out of the ground.

I took it from her hand and scraped some of the dirt off and held it up close to my face. "Oh, it's James' inhaler."

"But it's round," she said. "I don't remember his inhalers looking like this."

"He was trying that new kind that had just come out right before he died. Remember?"

My throat got a lump in it as I pictured him standing in the hall, trying the new inhaler, right before I ran off to be with Joey. I stared at it a little longer, then stuck it in my pocket, and we headed back down to the house, neither one of us saying anything.

"Would you like some hot chocolate?" Mother asked once we got back home, as she stripped off her jacket.

"Remember how much you and James loved hot chocolate covered with those tiny marshmallows?" she asked opening a kitchen cabinet. "I don't have any marshmallows, but I do have whipped cream."

I'd almost forgotten about that. On rare occasions when Mother wasn't completely wasted, she'd fill our cups halfway with hot chocolate and the rest of the way with marshmallows. James and I were high on all the sugar for the rest of the night.

I sat down and was thinking about what Mother had confided to me up on the hill, when she placed the cup of hot chocolate overflowing with Cool Whip onto the table in front of me.

She sat down with her own cup with just as much Cool Whip. After eating several spoonsful of the whipped cream, I got up and went to get my phone to check messages.

I brought it with me and sat down, taking another sip of my hot chocolate. I turned it on. I had two texts, one from Joey and one from Dan. I looked at Joey's first.

"I meant what I said," it read. "I'll go anywhere to be with you. Call me."

I felt my heart skip a beat as I pulled up Dan's text.

"I'm back home. I start the new job in the morning. Hope your dad is doing okay. Remember, I love you very much. We can work things out." I set the phone down sadly and stared into my cup.

"A text from Dan?" Mother asked, nodding at the phone.

I stirred the hot chocolate sadly.

"You look sad. You miss him, don't you?" she asked.

"I guess a little. Though I don't know what I feel anymore," I replied with a sigh.

"It's hard to be torn between two men," she said.

I set my spoon down and looked at her. She sounded as if she was speaking from experience. How could she possibly know how that felt? She'd never been with another man other than my father as far as I knew. They'd met way back when she was in high school at the same age, I'd met Joey.

My mother's eyes got a faraway look. "There was someone else at one time, you know. A boy back in high school. His name was Brian. He was good-looking and very popular." She looked at me. "Joey reminds me of him a lot."

She looked away again. "I felt lucky just to be with him. I was sure he was the one at the time. That was, until I met your father. When I was around your dad, I felt different than when I was with Brian, as if I was the most important person in the world.

I didn't have to be anything but be myself when we were together. I didn't have to pretend I was one of the popular girls in school to get him to like me. He liked me the way I was. Do you know what I mean?"

I stared back at her and thought about how lucky I'd felt too, when Joey asked me out. And as much as I loved him, it was sometimes a lot of pressure to be his girlfriend. It felt like I always had to look and sound my best if I wanted to keep him.

With Dan, it was different. Right from the start, I'd felt comfortable with him. I didn't have to put on any airs. I somehow knew that he'd love me no matter what. I felt an ache in my chest. Did he still love me? Was it really over with that girl? I had to admit, I did still love him. If only he hadn't hurt me. Mother reached her hand across the table and put it on mine.

"I know it's difficult to know what the right thing to do is. I remember how hard it was when I had to tell Brian I wanted to be with your father. Even then, I wondered if I was doing the right thing. But I found out that I did make the right choice.

"I know your dad's not perfect, but he's a good man. And he loves me unconditionally even after all that we've been through. I can't picture myself with anyone else but him."

"So, how did you get past knowing that he was seeing another woman? I'm not sure I can do that with Dan." She slid her hand away.

"I wondered if you knew about her," she said sadly.

"Yes. I just found out. Beth told me. Apparently, James found out Dad was seeing someone and told her about it. I'm sorry. I know you guys were split up at the time. But how could you take him back after that, knowing he turned to someone else so soon?"

"It was hard, I can't lie. And yes, though I knew he didn't start seeing her until after we divorced, it hurt anyway, that he could care for someone else like that, so quickly.

And yet, it was me who pushed him away at first. Nothing was more important than staying numb with alcohol back then. Not even my marriage. It's what they call in AA, incomprehensible demoralization. You know, sometimes we push people away and then wonder why they aren't around anymore."

Her words hit me. Was that what I'd done, kept everyone at a distance after James had died and if they tried to get close, pushed them away? But, for me it wasn't due to alcohol. It was out of self-preservation.

"Anyway, we made it through the storm," she continued, "and your father and I love each other more than ever. That's what matters now. I just pray he kicks this cancer in the butt and that I get many more years with him. I pray too that if it's Dan you want to be with, that you can work things out, too. I just want you to be happy."

I looked across the table at her as I wondered if it was too late for me and Dan.

"But how will I know when it's time to walk away?" I asked sadly.

"Oh, honey," she said, tearing up. "You'll know. You always do."

My eyes filled with tears too and she reached out to touch my hand again. After a moment, she dried her tears with her napkin and pushed her chair back.

"Well, I guess we both should think about getting some sleep. I'm going to the early bird meeting tomorrow at the Fellowship Hall in Powdersville, if you want to go. It starts at seven." She got up and placed her cup in the sink.

"I think I'll sleep in, I'm exhausted," I said as I put my cup in the sink next to hers. I filled them both with water.

"I bet you are. Well, I'm glad we had a chance to talk," she said. "It's funny, I don't remember us ever having conversations like this."

"We never did," I said sadly as I turned and headed for my room.

Mother stopped when she got to her doorway. "Goodnight. Sleep well."

"You too," I said as I shut the door behind me and got ready for bed. As I lay there, I went over all the things we'd talked about this evening and how open she'd been.

After a few minutes, I got back up, opened my bedroom door and glanced across the hall. Her light was off, but she'd left her door open. Leaving mine ajar too, I said goodnight again and climbed back into bed.

CHAPTER 24

IT WAS MORNING AND I COULD TELL BY HOW QUIET IT was throughout the house, that Mother must have already left for her AA meeting before heading off to see my father.

As usual, there was a pot of coffee already prepped, and this time, a cup and spoon next to it too. I smiled. As the coffee started to brew, I checked the microwave in case she'd left me anything to eat while she was at it.

I smiled again. There was a bowl in there, of oatmeal covered with raisins. As I ate my breakfast, I went over the talk Mother and I had had last night once again. How surprised I had been to learn, how she'd loved someone else before my father, and that she'd pushed everyone away like I had been doing too.

It was beginning to look like we were more alike than I'd thought. Maybe that wasn't such a terrible thing, though I didn't want to follow in her footsteps—at least not when it came to drinking.

Maybe I should have gone to the AA meeting with her. I considered it for a moment, but it was still pretty dark outside, and I didn't know Powdersville that well, so I decided not to. But the longer I sat there, the nagging feeling that I should - propelled me to take out my phone.

"Charlie? Good morning. I hope I didn't wake you. This is Karen again."

"Oh no, I was up already. Good morning," he said sounding awake and pleased to hear from me.

I hesitated. "I was hoping you were free to give me a ride this morning. Do you know where the AA hall is in Powdersville?

"Yes," he replied quickly.

"Can you pick me up at the house and run me over there? There's a meeting at seven I'd like to try and make."

"Sure thing, miss. It's six twenty now. I can be there in fifteen minutes. That will get us there right near seven o'clock."

"Great," I said. "See you soon." I poured myself another cup of coffee and for a split-second, the thought of pouring some Jack into it to stop the butterflies crossed my mind. I was already feeling nervous at the thought of walking into an AA meeting, which made me even more determined to get there. Although. I didn't exactly feel like sitting in a room full of drunks. I got dressed and headed outside to wait for the cab.

—

"Morning," Charlie said cheerfully as he held open the back door and waited for me to get in. "Looks like it's going to be another wunnerful day in South Carolina. So, you're headed to the hall, huh?" he asked, glancing in the rearview mirror. "Good for you."

"Yes," I replied, not willing to go into any detail about why I felt I needed to go at this insanely early hour to an AA meeting way over in the next town.

I imagined Mother's surprised reaction when she saw me walk in; and though I was sure she'd be relieved, I hoped she wasn't going to now assume that meant I was an alcoholic like her and wouldn't try to drag me to more meetings while I was in town.

It was almost light by the time we pulled up to the front of the AA hall. Several people standing out front smoking with coffee mugs in their hands, turned and watched as Charlie came around and opened my door.

"Here we are," he said. "I'm proud of you."

I glanced at him and felt embarrassed that he assumed I had a problem.

As I turned and looked at all the people out front, I started having second thoughts. Was I going to have to admit to anything when I was in there? Maybe I wasn't ready for this. If I had a problem, which seemed very unlikely, I could handle it myself.

"I'm sorry, Charlie. I've changed my mind. Can you take me back home, please?"

He looked at me. "You sure, Miss?"

"Yes.

I got back inside the cab and looked away as Charlie shut my door. He got back in and glancing into the rearview mirror before putting the car in drive, we headed in silence back to the house. Even when I got out, he didn't say anything other than to give my mother his regards and that he wished my father all the best. As he drove away, it felt like I'd just disappointed someone else in my life, along with myself.

As I watched the cab go down the driveway, I thought about my father. I needed to remember that he was the reason I was here, and just focus on that.

I went inside and got the keys to the Mustang. It was light now, and I started the car up and headed to the hospital. But when I got there, I barely could get in two words with my father, between all the nurses coming in and out of his room and him dozing off every few minutes.

I ended up cutting my visit short. I'd come back later when things had calmed down and he was more awake. Disappointed that the morning was already starting out as a failure, I decided to stop by the cemetery where I'd go pay my respects to James.

I thought about my father again as I came to the headstones. Was he going to be in here next? I quickly shook the thoughts from my head. He was going to be just fine, I had to believe that.

I was almost at James' gravesite when I noticed a shaggy-looking Golden Retriever lying on the grass next to James' headstone.

The dog was chewing on her paw. It looked like she had something in it that was irritating her.

"What's wrong, sweetie?" I asked, slowly approaching her.

The dog looked up at me as I bent down and glanced at her paw. An object was sticking out of it. It appeared that a twig had gotten lodged in her right front paw.

"Let me help you," I said tenderly as I lifted her leg. I pulled the twig out and the dog jerked to her feet. She wagged her tail several times as a sort of thank you and trotted toward the woods.

"I see you met Goldie." I turned around as Pastor Phil approached me. "At least, that's the name we gave her yesterday. She's been here the last few days. Not sure where she goes at night but she's here in the morning, come what may. Our grounds-man Jeff gave her the name. We asked around, but no one seems to know who she belongs to, though by the looks of her and lack of a collar, we are assuming she's a stray.

"I heard that your dad is doing better, praise God. You have to be relieved about that."

"Yes," I replied.

"I imagine you'll be leaving soon and going back home to California, as soon as you know he's back on his feet. Your mother's going to miss you, I'm sure. Though I imagine you'll be glad to get back home."

"I guess so," I replied, not too excited at the thought of having to make a decision about my marriage.

"You don't sound happy about it." He paused. "Marriage isn't always easy, is it?"

I looked at him, surprised by his comment.

"Did my mother tell you I was having marital issues?" I was disappointed that just when I'd finally confided in her, she'd run off and told Pastor Phil my problems already.

"No, she didn't mention it. But she didn't have to, after what happened during the wedding ceremony. By the way, I have your shoes in my office. I'll get them for you before you leave, today.'

'Oh." I said as I looked away in embarrassment. "I'm sorry about that, Pastor."

"It's okay. Do you want to talk about it? Maybe you'd like to tell me what drove you to say those things?" he asked softly.

I didn't say anything.

"What's bothering you, dear?" he asked gently. "Why don't we go inside and talk?"

Without waiting for an answer, he turned and headed toward the church. I watched him slowly walk away. I was tired of talking. What was the point? But for some unknown reason, I followed him anyway.

I walked up the same steps I had walked up the other day and stepped into the hall. But, no sooner had I stepped inside the church, when I felt like turning right around again, not only because I was ashamed of my actions the other day, but even more because I didn't belong here. Especially not after what I'd said to God after James had died. How I'd told God about how I felt about Him in no uncertain terms. I stood there frozen.

"Come," Pastor Phil said, holding his hand out to a front pew. He disappeared and came back a few seconds later with my shoes in his hand. He handed them to me, then sat down next to me. We sat there in silence. The church was empty, and still I found the silence deafening.

"I'm not sure I want to be married anymore," I finally said in a soft voice.

"I'm sorry to hear that," Pastor Phil said just as softly. He sat there as if waiting for me to go on.

"My husband was seeing another woman. He said she doesn't mean anything to him, but I don't think I can ever trust him again after that," I continued.

"It takes a long time to rebuild trust once it's been broken," he agreed. "Do you still have love for him?"

"I guess so. But every time I look at him or even think about him, all I can do is picture him with her. And it makes me so angry," I replied.

"Sometimes, it takes a long time to forgive," he said.

I looked at him. "Why should I forgive him at all after what he did? He doesn't deserve it."

He looked back at me with kind eyes. "The forgiveness isn't for him, dear. It's for you. What he did was wrong, there's no way around that. But if you want peace, which I'm sure you do, the only way you'll have that is to try and forgive him.

"Whether you stay with him or not, if you can't do that, you'll carry anger around for the rest of your life. I'd hate to see you go through that."

"But what if he does it again?" I asked, feeling the anger come back. "I refuse to be one of those women who takes their husband back only to find out he cheated again. How can I be sure he won't do it again? And how do you expect me to forgive him, when I can barely look at him?"

He sat there for a moment. "Can you try and remember what he looked like before he did what he did to hurt you?"

I looked at him confused. "What do you mean?"

"Think back to when you first knew that you were in love with this man. Can you do that?"

I looked away. I knew I was in love with Dan the day he saved the bird, the one that had flown head first into my living room window, hitting so hard it left an imprint of wings on the glass.

I felt horrible. Dan was with me and he jumped up and ran outside barefoot in his underwear. I watched through the window as he picked up the bird that was now lifeless on the ground and held it in his hand.

Here he was, this big strong man, outside in his underwear holding this tiny bird up to his mouth and blowing on it. And after a moment, to my amazement, the bird started to shake then flew away.

I knew right then that Dan was the man I wanted to spend the rest of my life with, someone who could finally make me forget about Joey. I looked back at Pastor Phil with tears in my eyes. He had a small smile, almost as if he'd been able to see what I had been remembering.

"That's who you need to picture when you think about your husband and get angry. That man. The man you fell in love with before he got so lost and hurt you the way he did.

It won't be easy, and it will take time, but with God's help you will be able to forgive him eventually."

I thought about what he was saying, but instead of making me feel better, his words made me angry.

"I don't want God's help. Where was He all the times, I needed Him? When I begged Him to stop my Mother from drinking and to let my brother find some sense of happiness in his life? You tell me, where was He then?"

Pastor Phil looked at me sadly. "I'm sorry you had to go through what you did. Life is hard at times. I am glad your mother was able to see the light and get sober, though. And I don't know why James had to die. But I do know he was happy. Though sadly for only a short time." He looked toward the cross with Jesus hanging at the front of the church.

"I know what it feels like to be angry with God," Pastor Phil continued. "I too, had a tough time dealing with your brother's death and the way he died. God and I have had plenty of heart to heart conversations about that very thing. At the time, I even questioned my faith and wondered how I could have not seen that coming."

I was somewhat surprised by how deeply James' death seemed to have affected Pastor Phil. After all, as far as I knew, James hadn't been to church or talked to Pastor Phil since we were both very young. But perhaps this was just something else I hadn't known about my brother.

"There was no way you could have predicted any of this would happen, Pastor."

He looked at me and started to say something, when someone called his name. We both turned around.

"Oh, Mrs. Connors," Pastor Phil said, standing up. "I'm so glad you came by." He leaned down and whispered, "I have to go. Her husband died unexpectedly a few days ago from a massive heart attack and I need to speak with her."

I looked back at the young woman who didn't appear to be that much older than I was. Surely, much too young to lose her husband. It made me think of Dan and how devastated I'd feel if something like that happened to him. As she walked closer, she looked at me and I could feel the depth of her grief in her sad eyes.

"I'm sorry," I said in a whisper. She smiled faintly and nodded. I picked up my shoes and hurried outside, glancing at the woman once again on my way out.

I sat in the car for a few moments, imagining once again how sad it would be if it was me standing there instead of her. I jumped at the sound of my cell phone ringing. I could tell it wasn't Dan by the ringtone, and I was disappointed.

"Can we talk? Please. I want to explain." It was Beth.

"Let's just leave things as they are," I said, reaching down to start the car. "I don't have the strength to fight with anyone anymore."

"Please. I have to talk to you before you go back to California."

I hesitated. Though I didn't want a repeat of yesterday, I could clearly hear desperation in her voice and after what I'd just seen in the church, I was reminded once again that we never know when someone could be taken from our lives.

"I'm at the church. I'll call you when I get home," I said before hanging up. I backed the car up, still feeling angry at Beth. She'd hurt my brother. Could I ever forgive her for that? I thought about what Pastor Phil had said about forgiveness. There were so many people in my life I was angry at; I had my work cut out for me if I was going to try to forgive them all.

And there was Joey. I was still upset at what he'd said to James and over how we broke up. Maybe that was what Beth wanted to talk about. Maybe she had some dirt on Joey.

—

As soon as I got back to the house, I got the bottle of Jack from the closet and went to the kitchen and made myself a drink. I had a feeling I was going to need it by the sound of Beth's voice. I had barely taken a few sips when I heard a message pop up on my phone.

I picked it up. It was from Joey.

"How R U?" it read.

"Fine," I texted back and took another sip.

"Where R U?"

"Why?" I texted back.

"Need to see U."

"NO." I waited. Finally, a new text popped up.

"How's your dad?" But this time, the text was from Dan not Joey.

The word *forgiveness* popped into my head. Yeah right. "Better. Thanks," I texted back.

A new text from Joey popped up. "Can I C U?"

"NO!" I texted back.

"Why? Afraid U might want to kiss me again?" the next text read.

Annoyed, I quickly responded with, "I didn't kiss you. You kissed me"

I waited for his reply and after a few seconds, "What????" popped up.

I started to text back, "You kissed me!" again when I stopped. Heart pounding, I looked at the last text I'd sent to Joey. But my reply wasn't there. I looked at my last text to Dan. I almost got sick when I saw I had texted him by mistake.

Panicked, I grabbed my glass and drank nearly all of it down. As I stared at the phone, a new text popped up. I was afraid to look but sure enough, it was from Dan.

"CALL ME." I stared at the phone some more.

"Well?" a new text from Joey popped up. As I held the phone, wondering what to do, it started to play Dan's ringtone.

I quickly hit reject and set the phone down, just as I heard a car pulling up the driveway. Grabbing the phone along with my glass and the bottle of Jack, I hurried off to my room. On the way down the hall, the house phone started to ring. As I turned the corner into my room, I heard Mother talking.

"Hi Joey. Yes, I'm just getting back from the hospital in fact. He's doing well, thanks for asking. He might even come home tomorrow. Okay, I will. Let me get Karen for you. I think she's in her room. Karen?" I heard her call out as she came down the hallway, "Karen, are you here?"

Still shaken, I put the glass and the bottle in the bathroom and shut the door just as Mother came in holding the phone.

"It's Joey," she said, handing it to me. She stared at me. "Are you alright? You look upset."

"I'm fine," I replied, trying to appear calm as I took the phone from her. "Hello?"

"Where'd you go? I texted you again," I could hear Joey say. "But you were gone. Please, can I see you?"

I waited for my mother to leave before I answered him.

"Thanks a lot, Joey," I replied in a hushed tone. "I texted Dan back by mistake and now he knows you kissed me."

"You kissed me," he said again.

"Whatever," I said a little too loudly.

"Well, maybe he should know about us," Joey said sounding unapologetic.

"I keep telling you, Joey. There is no us."

"Karen?" I looked up to see Mother back in the doorway, again. "Beth is here."

"I have to go," I hung up and followed Mother to the door.

By the look on Beth's face, I could see something was bothering her.

"Can we talk? It's really important," she said.

My mother started to walk away.

"No, Mrs. Parker. You don't have to go. I'd like you to hear this too," Beth said, stopping my mother.

Mother looked at me, then back at Beth. "Sure. Let's all go to the kitchen. Can I get you something to drink, Beth?"

"Just water would be nice," Beth replied, sitting down at the table. I hung the phone up and sat down while Mother poured Beth a glass of water. Beth sat down and nervously took a sip.

"There's something I've been wanting to tell you, both of you," Beth said, setting the glass down, "for quite some time." As she lifted the glass again, the phone on the wall behind my head started to ring.

"Excuse me," Mother said, getting up. "It might be someone from the hospital calling about Bill."

"Hello? Oh, hello Dan," Mother said, glancing at me. "Are you back in California yet? Yes, she's right here."

But before I could say that I didn't want to talk to him, Mother handed me the phone. I stared at it, then slowly lifted it to my head.

"Hello?"

"What the heck is going on out there? Did I get that right? You kissed Joey?" he asked sounding angry.

"I didn't kiss him. He kissed me," I replied as I glanced at Beth and Mother, both of whom were staring at me looking surprised.

"I can't talk about this right now," I said lowering my voice.

"You sound like you've been drinking again, too," he said. "I can't believe this. Here I felt bad about leaving you, but it appears that you wanted me to go home all along. I bet your father's illness was just an excuse, so you could go back and see Joey. I guess you've managed to pay me back."

"If you hadn't cheated on me, we wouldn't even be having this discussion. You'd be here with me," I hissed into the phone.

"Fine. Go ahead and be with him if that's what you want. I'll talk to you later." The line went dead. I slammed the phone into the holder.

"I think I should leave," Beth said. "We can talk some other time."

"No. You wanted to tell us something, go ahead," I said, sitting back down.

"Maybe I should just come back when you're feeling better," Beth said as she stood up.

"Nice," I said, the anger growing. "That's the same thing you used to say when you'd come over and Mother had been drinking. How maybe you should come back another time when she was *feeling better*. I've barely had a thing to drink."

Beth looked at my mother then back at me. "I'm going to go," she said, grabbing her purse. "I'm sorry Mrs. Parker. Karen, I'll call you later."

I stood up too. "Don't bother. I'm going out anyway," I said, storming back to my room. I quickly chugged some more of the Jack down and grabbed the keys to the Mustang.

As I came down the hallway again, I overheard my mother say, "I'm sorry Beth. She's dealing with a lot right now. She's not herself."

Annoyed and upset, I slid out the front door and marched out to the car. It felt like my world was crashing down again, much the same as eight years ago. I jumped into the Mustang and started it up.

Out of the corner of my eye, I saw my mother come out the back door. I shoved the gear into reverse, anxious to get away when suddenly, I felt the car slam into something. My head lurched forward, and I felt the side of my face hit the steering wheel hard, then heard a car alarm go off.

The driver's door opened, and I turned to see Mother staring at me, her eyes wide with fear.

"Shut it off," she said.

I looked at her somewhat in a daze. "What?"

"Shut the engine off," she said. I stared at her and she reached past and turned the key in the ignition. The engine was suddenly quiet, but the alarm was still sounding.

"Can someone stop that noise?" I yelled touching the side of my face. Beth appeared behind Mother. She disappeared and minutes later, the car alarm went silent.

"Here, let me help you out," Mother said. As I got out, I noticed that my ears were buzzing. I shook my head.

Mother and Beth led me to the front porch and sat me down on the bottom step.

"Are you okay?" Beth asked, looking worried.

I reached up once again and touched the side of my face and winced.

"You hit your cheek," Mother said touching the side of my face gently.

"I hate that noise. Can't you make it stop?" I asked pushing her hand away.

"What noise?" Beth asked.

"That darn buzzing noise," I said, trying to stand up.

"What're you talking about?" Mother asked. "Maybe we should call an ambulance."

"I'm fine," I said, trying to keep my balance. "Just make those darn bees go away."

"What bees?" Mother asked, sounding concerned. "Maybe we should go inside the house."

I looked at her than pointed at the front lawn. "It's just like I remember."

"What is?" Mother asked now looking frightened.

"You remember, don't you? Right there. James and I were playing right there," I pointed more emphatically. "Then the bees came. You took him inside, but you left me out there with them all. One stung me." I looked at her and tilted my head. "Why did you do that? Leave me there? Didn't you love me too?"

Mother glanced at Beth then her gaze fell back on me. "Let's get her inside." She grabbed my arm. "Come on, dear. The bees are all gone now, and they aren't coming back. I won't let them. And yes, I love you very much," she said as she led me up the stairs.

And just like that, the noise was gone.

—

Beth and Mother sat me down at the kitchen table and Mother brought me an icepack for my cheek.

"We should get her checked out," I heard Beth say.

"I'm fine," I said, my head starting to clear. "I just want to lie down."

"Maybe we shouldn't let her lie down," Beth said as I got up and headed to my bedroom.

"I'm okay, Beth, really," I said. "I just hit my cheek on the steering wheel."

"I'll stay with her to make sure she's alright," Mother said. After tucking me in my bed, Beth asked Mother to call her later and let her know I was okay.

"I love you," Beth said as I closed my eyes.

CHAPTER 25

THE ROOM WAS DARK WHEN I WOKE UP. BUT I COULD tell I wasn't alone.

"Who's here?" I asked, feeling afraid.

"It's just me," Mother said as she turned the lamp on by the side of the bed. She was seated in a chair next to me with a quilt over her legs.

"What're you doing in here?" I asked. I touched the side of my face which was now throbbing.

"You backed into Beth's car earlier tonight, remember?" Mother asked. "You have a nasty bump on your cheek. But other than that, I think you're fine."

I sat up, making my cheek throb even more. "I did? What happened? Is Beth okay?"

"Yes," she replied. "She wasn't in the car, thank goodness. It was parked in the driveway behind the Mustang."

"Oh, good," I said relieved. "I'm glad no one was hurt. I guess besides me. What about James' car? Is it alright?" I asked, knowing how upset James would have been if anything happened to that car.

"Both cars are a little banged up, but the main thing is that you're okay," Mother said "Why don't you get some more rest? We can talk about this in the morning after I get back from my meeting. If you're up, and feeling ok, I'd love to have you go with me."

"Some other time," I said and closed my eyes again.

"Okay. You just rest. I'm going to call and check on your dad, now. But I'll be right in the next room if you need me."

She headed to her room and I opened my eyes again, trying to remember everything that had happened. Beth had wanted to tell me and Mother something, I remembered that much. Then Dan had called, and we'd argued over the text I sent him by mistake. I winced as I remembered how I'd done that.

Then the next thing I knew, Mother and Beth were helping me out of the Mustang. Had I been drinking? Yes, I remember now. What was wrong with me? I knew better than that.

I could have hurt someone. That was it, then, I was through with that. I'd never touch another drop. I closed my eyes once more and tried to go to sleep, knowing that I'd now come much too close to that invisible line Mother had talked about.

It was nearly eight o'clock when I woke up the next morning. I felt sick to my stomach as the memory of what I'd done last night ran through my mind. I got up and dressed.

Mother wasn't home, and I knew she had gone to her meeting then off to see my father. I poured myself a cup of coffee and put my shoes and a jacket on. I might as well get it over with and go out and see what kind of damage I had done to James' car.

The Mustang was parked at a strange angle close to the barn. I walked around the car and was dismayed to see the back fender and the broken tail light. Ashamed, I went back into the house and had another cup of coffee while I searched for a nearby collision repair shop on my phone.

There was one in Anderson, about fifteen minutes away and it opened at nine. Maybe if I was the first one in line, I might be able to get someone to look at it and possibly get it repaired right away. As I put my phone away, Mother walked in.

"How are you feeling?" she asked, pouring herself a cup of the coffee and sitting down with me at the table.

"I'm fine. I thought I'd take the Mustang today to be fixed at a repair shop I found over in Anderson. I'll be leaving in a bit since they open at nine. How's Dad? Did you go see him?"

"No, I wanted to stop here after my meeting first, and check on you. I'm sure he knows someone who could fix it, though," she said.

"That's okay," I said. "I'll handle it. I'd rather that he doesn't even know what happened, if you don't mind. He has enough to worry about. If they can take it in today, I'll get a loaner and come by the hospital."

"Okay but call me if you need me. Otherwise, I guess I'll see you there. By the way, I'm going to a noon meeting at the hall if you want to go after we visit him. I don't normally go to two meetings in one day but it's my AA birthday. Four years today. I'm going to pick up my chip."

"Your chip?" I asked.

"Yes, it's a token they give for different lengths of sobriety. My sponsor will be there. I'd love for you to go and meet her."

I looked at her skeptically. "Are you sure it's not because of what happened last night, that you're asking me to go? If so, you don't need to worry. I've already made up my mind not to drink anymore."

"I just thought you might want to see me get my chip. But that's okay if you don't want to go," she said, sounding disappointed.

I looked at her and thought it was ironic that she seemed to want my approval. That was all I'd ever wanted from her.

"Maybe I'll go if I have time," I said.

Her eyebrows shot up. "Really? I'll give you directions to the hall just in case."

"That's all right. I know where it is," I said.

"You do?" she asked looking surprised. "Okay well, try to get there early. Birthdays are always crowded. I'll save you a seat in case you come."

After she headed off to the hospital, and just as I was about to leave for the collision repair shop, my phone rang.

"Are you okay? Steve told me what happened," Joey asked in a panicky voice.

"I'm fine. But before you start to lecture me, I want you to know that I'm going to an AA meeting this afternoon."

"Thank goodness," he said, sounding relieved. "Want me to go with you?"

"No. I don't need anyone holding my hand. Besides, Mother will be there. But please let's not make a big deal about this."

"Okay," he said. "How about we get together after the meeting for lunch, then? You can tell me how things went at the meeting."

"That's not such a good idea," I said.

"Why not?"

"Because I don't think we should keep seeing each other, Joey. I've decided to go home in a few days, anyway."

"I knew you'd run away again and go back to him. Typical."

"I'm not running away. And I haven't decided if I am going back to him. The only reason I came back here was to see my father. And now that he's doing better, and hopefully coming home soon, it's time for me to go. That's all."

"Here you go," he said. "Whenever things get tough, you run. Just like you did eight years ago."

"I didn't *run* away. I just couldn't stay here any longer after what happened with James. You're the one who decided not to go with me."

"Whatever. Okay, go ahead. Go back to the guy who cheated on you. But don't think I'm going to wait for you this time."

The line went dead before I could say that I didn't want him to wait, anyway. I flung the phone into my purse, started the Mustang and headed to the repair shop, anxious to get the car fixed, see my father and get far away from this place.

CHAPTER 26

"CAN I HELP YOU?" THE GIRL BEHIND THE COUNTER asked as I walked in. I was still fuming over what Joey had said as I walked up to her.

"Yes, I need to get my brother's car repaired as soon as possible. It was in a little accident. The rear bumper's smashed, and the tail light needs to be fixed," I pointed out the window to the Mustang parked out front.

"I'm so sorry, but we're swamped today," she said. "We couldn't even look at it until tomorrow at the soonest, I'm afraid. And there's no telling when we could repair it."

"Oh, that won't work. I'm leaving town soon and need it repaired before I go. Is there another shop around here you can recommend? I asked, disappointed.

"Well, there's Mike's Body Shop up in Greenville. But I know they're pretty busy right now too. It's always busy during the rainy season. Everyone just drives too fast when the roads are wet."

"Never mind," I said. "My father owns a repair shop in Easley. I guess I'll just leave it there and let them get it fixed for me."

She looked out the window at the Mustang again then back at me.

I turned around to leave, when I heard her say, "You're not talking about Bill Parker's Auto Shop, are you?" she asked. I turned around again, slowly. "Are you by chance James Parker's sister?"

"What if I am?" I asked defensively.

"Hold on a minute," she said. "I'll be right back." She left, and I could see her outside standing by the Mustang, talking to one of the mechanics. He nodded and after a few minutes, she came back inside.

"We have everything we need to get it fixed for you right away," she said. "And don't worry, I'll make sure you get a good price for the repair. We have a complimentary loaner car too, if you need one."

"Really? That's sure nice of you," I said as I wondered why all of a sudden, she was being so accommodating. "And a loaner car would be great, thanks."

"No problem. Glad to help." She leaned across the counter. "Betsy Carlyle. Your brother was in one of my classes and he was the nicest guy."

She stood there looking at me as if expecting me to recognize the name. But I didn't.

"Anyway," she continued, "you probably don't remember me, But I remember your brother. He helped me with my computer all the time. I felt terrible when I heard what happened to him. I was at his funeral. Maybe you saw me there?"

I stared at her blankly.

"Anyway," she said again, "I couldn't believe the way you stood up there in front of everyone and said all those wonderful things about him. To tell the truth, I don't know how you did it. I know I couldn't have gotten up there and been able to talk, if it was my brother. You're really brave, you know."

"Thank you for your kind words," I mumbled.

"He was a great guy, that's for sure," she went on as she took out some paperwork. "He helped a lot of other kids at school, too, sometimes fixing their computers for free if they didn't have any money. Everyone liked him. He talked about you a lot, you know. I could tell he really loved you a lot. But I guess you know that."

She kept saying 'you know', but in fact, I didn't know any of it.

I stood there stunned again, not only that James had told people how much he loved me, but at how well he'd been liked in school. All that time, I thought most everyone looked down on him.

"Thanks again," I said as I started to get choked up.

"No problem," she replied. "Just sign right here and leave your cell phone number. I'll get the loaner keys for you and you can be on your way. I'll call you as soon as the car's ready. Should be later today or tomorrow at the latest."

I signed the paperwork and took the keys for the loaner from her.

"It's the white Escort out there," she said. "And don't worry about filling the tank with gas. We'll take care of that, too," she said. "Talk to you soon."

I thanked her once again and feeling a lot better than when I walked in, headed outside and got into the white Ford Escort. As I passed by Finley Church on the way to the Fellowship Hall, once again I felt an urge to stop and go talk to James.

Goldie was back. She seemed happy to see me and got up, limping slowly over to me. I bent down and checked her paw again. It looked fine, though was probably still sore from the twig in it yesterday.

She stayed by me for the next hour as I sat there with her and talked, sometimes to James but mostly to her, about everything I had been going through and the decisions I needed to make. Goldie seemed to listen, and by the time I got ready to go, I hated to leave her.

After all, she was the only friend I had right now. But I got up knowing that if I didn't leave soon, I'd miss the meeting and I knew how much Mother was looking forward to me going.

Goldie trailed behind me as I went back to the car. As I opened the door, she gingerly jumped up and laid down on the passenger seat.

"What're you doing?" I laughed surprised. "Sorry, but you can't go with me."

The dog looked over at me with her huge, sweet brown eyes but didn't budge.

"Come on girl," I said again halfheartedly. "You have to get out."

But she still didn't move. Finally, after some coaxing, she hopped back onto the ground. As I backed up, I could see her watching me. And as I drove away, I felt lonelier than I had in a long time. It was strange how quickly I'd taken to this shaggy dog. But there was something about her that spoke to me.

—

When I got to the hall, I forced myself to go inside. I looked around the room for Mother and found her talking to another woman by the coffee area. She saw me and waved, and they both walked over to me.

The woman looked to be close to the same age as my mother and had a beautiful smile.

"So, you must be Karen?" she said, reaching out to hug me. "I've heard so much about you. I'm Peggy—your mom's sponsor. So nice to finally meet you."

"Oh, hello," I said back. There was something kind about this woman and I immediately liked her.

Mother pulled out the chair she had saved for me, and we all sat down. I looked around the room again.

There were all kinds of people in the huge room, from men in business suits to young girls in jeans and even a few grandmotherly-looking types. Most of them didn't appear to look at all how I'd imagined alcoholics to look.

Mother leaned in toward me. "It's starting," she whispered.

"Good afternoon," a man sitting at a table up front said in a loud voice.

I glanced at the poster on the wall behind him. *12 Steps to Recovery* it said, with a list of twelve suggested items to do if you wanted to stay sober.

"My name is George and I'm an Alcoholic," he bellowed.

"Hi George," everyone in the room chanted back.

"Let's go around the room and introduce ourselves," George said, "starting on my right."

One by one, each person said their name followed by, "and I'm an alcoholic." I could feel myself growing more and more uncomfortable as the introductions moved down our row and closer to me.

"Hi, my name is Peggy. And I'm an alcoholic," Mother's sponsor said.

"Hello, my name is Doris and I'm an alcoholic," my mother said, almost sounding proud. She turned to me.

I sat there not sure what to say. The room was silent.

Finally, I said in a soft voice, "I'm Karen. I'm just here for my mother."

The introductions continued and went around the room until they ended back up front with the man called George.

A man next to George stood up. "This is a chip meeting. Will Mary O. give out the chips today?"

A young woman with long blond hair hurried to the front of the room and flipped open a plastic container. She took out a silver chip and held it up for all to see.

"Are there any newcomers here today with less than thirty days of sobriety? If so, would you come up and get a chip and a hug?"

She looked around the room. Mother glanced at me and I gave her a stern look. I watched as several people stood and hurried to the front. And one by one, Mary O. handed them a silver chip and gave them a hug each, just as promised.

"How about anyone with thirty days of continuous sobriety?" Mary O. asked after they'd sat down, and this time she held up a green chip.

Thirty days of continuous sobriety? I hadn't even been drinking for thirty days. Did they give a chip for that, I wondered?

Several more people scurried up to the front of the room to get their chips and hugs and then sat down. This continued until Mary O. held up a bronze chip. "One Year?" she asked. "Two years? Three years? Four years?"

Mother stood up and after glancing at me, walked to the front as everyone clapped wildly. Mary O. handed her a chip and hugged her tightly.

"Hi. I'm Doris and I'm an alcoholic," Mother said in a loud voice, as she held up the bronze chip.

"Congratulations," Mary O. said as Mother made her way back to our seats. "Any other birthdays? If not, Doris, would you like to tell everyone how you did it?"

"Sure," Mother said as she stood up again, and faced the room.

"First off, I'd like to thank my sponsor for all her support for the past four years. I don't know what I would have done without her. And," she looked at me again, "I want to say how proud I am to have my daughter here with me today. We haven't been close for some time because of my drinking. But I'm sober now and I'm so glad to get another chance with her."

She looked like she was about to sit down again, but she continued. "How did I do it? Well, I did it one day at a time with the help of all of you," she said. "And since this program is about rigorous honesty, I have something else I'd like to say." She looked at me before continuing.

"I may be sober today, but I almost drank a few days ago."

Someone said, "oh no," in the back of the room. I felt uncomfortable as I realized that she was probably referring to how I'd left the bottle of Jack out.

"I came across my favorite bottle of whiskey," Mother continued. "I have to say it was inviting. But I didn't drink it."

Someone yelled, "way to go," from the back.

"Do you want to know why I didn't?" she asked, looking at me. I could see tears in her eyes.

"Because of my daughter, here. Because I know she needs me more than ever right now and the only way I can be there for her for once, is if I stay sober. So, honey," she handed me her chip, "this is for you." She looked around the room again. "Thanks for letting me share," she said and sat down. Once again, the room was filled with loud clapping.

—

I sat there for the next twenty minutes halfway listening to other people share as I turned the chip over in my hand. Once the meeting was over, I dropped the chip into my purse and looked for the exit.

Mother and her sponsor were busy talking to a group of people gathered around them, so I was able to sneak off and make a beeline for the door.

As I walked out to the car, I had to acknowledge that everyone seemed nice and all, and I was glad they were able to help Mother, but I hadn't been drinking that long, so I doubted I was one of them.

I got into the car and before starting it up, checked my cell phone. I had one missed call. It was Cindy from the repair shop, already calling to let me know they were almost finished with the Mustang and it would be ready later today.

I headed to the shop and they were just washing it when I got there.

"They were able to push the bumper out and replace the light, and it's as good as new," Cindy said as she handed me the bill. She'd kept her promise too. The bill was surprisingly low.

"Thanks again," I said, handing her my credit card. She ran it through and handed it back to me along with the keys to the Mustang.

"Would you mind if I gave you a hug before you go?" she asked. But before waiting for an answer, she hurried from behind the counter and gave me a tight squeeze. "I'm glad you're doing well," she whispered. "Take good care of yourself."

"Thanks," I said, touched by her warmth. Why did it take me coming back, to find out there were actually some nice people here after all?

As I headed home, I passed by the Huddle House and thought about Beth. She'd appeared to be so worried about me last night and it was obvious how much she truly cared. And who knew, if all that hadn't happened between her and James, maybe we'd have never stopped being friends. I decided to go in and see her. Who knew if I'd get a chance again before I left town?

She was setting some plates of food down in front of a couple at a booth. She looked up and gave me a relieved-looking smile when she saw me walk in.

"I'm so glad to see you. I was going to call you when I got a break to see how you were doing," she said, but frowned as she looked at my cheek.

"I'm fine. I just wanted to stop in and say hello. I'll be leaving soon now that my father's coming home in the next few days and I wanted to get a chance to see you."

"I'm glad he's going to be okay," she said, "I do hate to see you go already, though."

"I need to get back to my life, whatever that is," I said. "I'll be sure to text and let you know where I end up. By the way, I want to pay for whatever it costs to fix your car."

"Don't worry about that," she said. "Steve will get it fixed. I'm just glad that you're okay. So, you're not sure if you're going back to Dan?"

"No, not just yet. I was thinking that I might go to Florida or up north and take a few weeks to try and figure things out."

"Are you sure you're alright, Karen?" she asked, and by the way she was looking at me, I could tell she wasn't talking about the bruise on my cheek.

"Sure I am. You know me, Beth, I'm strong. I can take care of myself."

"Being strong all the time isn't always such a good thing. We need to lean on other people sometimes. You never could allow yourself to do that. I know I'm not right around the corner, but I'm only a phone call away. You can always lean on me, you know."

I looked at her and smiled. "I know that now, Beth."

"Well," she said, "I should get back to work. Promise me you'll keep in touch."

"I will," I said, though I knew that keeping in touch with her would only keep the door open to Joey. I needed some time away from both him and Dan. I said goodbye and gave her a quick hug and left.

—

"There you are," Mother said as soon as I walked into the house. "What happened? Where'd you go? I turned around after the meeting and you were gone."

"I went to get the Mustang," I said. "It's all fixed."

"Oh good," she said, "that was fast. So, what did you think of the meeting?" she asked watching my face I'm sure to see if the meeting resonated with me.

"It was fine," I replied uncomfortably. "I was happy to see you get your chip."

"Thanks," she said smiling. "By the way, I have some wonderful news. The nurse called, and your father gets to come home today. Isn't that great? They said he's strong enough to come back here and recover. I'm so happy. I'm leaving in a few minutes to go and pick him up. Do you want to go with me?"

"That is good news," I said, though I knew it also meant I'd really have to kick it in gear and decide what I was going to do about Dan. I wasn't ready to go back home just yet, but it was time to leave here. I hated to admit that maybe Joey was right, and I did tend to run away. But why not? It had worked for me last time, at least for a while.

Florida did sound good but then again, I'd always wanted to go to New York City. They had a lot of plays there, and maybe I could even get a short part in one for a while.

I was so glad I'd kept open the bank account I had before Dan and I were married. Somehow, I must have known I'd need it one day in case of an emergency. It was certainly going to come in handy now.

I emailed my boss with a lengthy explanation of why I needed some more time off and suggested maybe she should find a temporary replacement for me, since I wasn't quite sure when I'd be back. I closed the lid on my laptop with the realization that I was committed to figuring out my next move now.

After that, I took a stroll out into the back yard and sat under my tree for a while, one last time. Strangely enough, I was going to miss it here after all, but it was time to go.

I headed back inside and took out my suitcase and started to pack. With Dad coming home today, I might as well see him get settled in, then leave early in the morning. The sooner I was gone, the better for everyone.

As I was putting some things in the suitcase, I heard a car coming up the driveway. After a few minutes, I heard my mother's voice.

"I can't believe you're finally home," she said, sounding very excited.

"Me neither. I'm so glad to be out of that place and back in my own bed. I've missed sleeping next to you, too," he said. "Don't forget that we're still newlyweds."

"Shhh," Mother said with a giggle. "Karen might hear you. Let me go tell her that you're home."

"Not until you give me a kiss," I heard my father say in a weak voice.

"Stop that, Bill," Mother said with a laugh in her voice. "You know you aren't supposed to be getting excited. Besides, the nurse said it's going to take weeks for you to get your strength back."

"I'm not too weak for a kiss," he said. This time, I could hear them both laughing. The laughter seemed out of place in this house, let alone from the two of them. And though I was happy for them, it only reinforced in me how very lonely I was.

After a few seconds, I heard another, "stop that," and another giggle from my mother.

I smiled sadly. Yes, it was time for me to go and let them get back to their own lives. The tears started as I thought about Dan and what a mess my marriage was in.

The urge to run away was stronger than ever now, and I decided not to wait until morning after all to leave. But I was sure if I told them that, they'd just try to talk me into staying longer so I might as well go now without telling them. They had each other. They didn't need me hanging around.

I opened the door slightly and heard some pots and pans, then another round of laughter coming down the hallway.

Tossing the almost empty bottle of Jack into the suitcase, I zipped it shut quickly and grabbed my purse. No, there was no reason to make a big fanfare about my leaving. I never was good at goodbyes anyway.

I quietly went outside and made my way across the lawn to the Mustang. After dropping the suitcase into the trunk, I looked back at the house. It didn't seem as foreboding as when I had first arrived. In fact, as much as I didn't want to admit it, this place had started to feel like home—a proper home.

I got in the car and shut the door. But what about the Mustang? I started the car up anyway. I'd find a way to get it back to them after I was planted somewhere. I looked out at the house one last time and with a knot in the pit of my stomach, I backed up and drove away.

CHAPTER 27

SEVERAL MINUTES LATER, AS I DROVE DOWN FINLEY Road, it was hard not to sob, partly because I was going to miss some things about this place and partly because I felt so lost.

My thoughts turned to Goldie and how I wished that she was leaving with me. Maybe if she was, it would be easier to go, but I couldn't take her with me.

As I rounded the corner I thought, but why not? According to Pastor Phil, she didn't really belong to anyone as far as he could tell. She needed me as much as I needed her. Feeling slightly better, I stepped on the gas. When I got to the church, I hurried to the cemetery.

I was thrilled to see her sitting by James' gravestone as if she knew I was coming. She jumped up and started wagging her tail.

"How's your paw? Want to go for a ride, girl?" I asked looking down at her paw as I petted her head.

Goldie wagged her tail harder.

"I'll take that as a yes," I laughed.

After saying goodbye to James, I led Goldie to the car. I looked around nervously as I opened the door to the Mustang, feeling a bit like a dog thief.

Goldie climbed into the car and started dancing around on the passenger seat excitedly.

"Hold on," I laughed. "Let me get you something to sit on before you scratch my brother's leather seats all up. I just got this car back to pristine condition."

I opened the trunk and looked in. I'd noticed a crate in the back of the trunk earlier. Maybe there was something in it that Goldie could sit on for the ride. I took my suitcase back out and slid the crate toward me.

I opened it up and quickly looked through it. There were several cloth towels and what looked to be a folded-up blanket. Perfect. I grabbed the blanket and started to put the lid back on the crate. But as I did, I spotted a plastic bag in the bottom of the crate.

I pulled it out. In it were several flares and another plastic bag with some inhalers in it. James must have kept some backups in there in case of an emergency. I thought about the last time I'd seen him using an inhaler, the morning he'd died.

I put the bag of inhalers back into the larger bag and set it back into the crate. As I did, I noticed a book at the bottom. I pulled it out, and almost dropped it when I saw what it was.

It was a journal; *the* journal!

It had been here in the car all the time. Well, of course, James must have known it was safer than keeping it in the house. I opened it up. As I looked at James' handwriting, my heart beat so fast that it felt like my chest was going to explode.

Here it was, what I'd been looking for ever since my father first told me about it.

A car pulled into the parking lot. I set the journal down and put the lid on the crate and slid it back into the trunk. I needed to get out of here before Pastor Phil came out of the church.

I threw my suitcase back in and slammed the trunk shut, took the journal along with the blanket and got back in the car. Without waiting to put the blanket onto the seat, I tossed it onto the back seat along with the journal and started the car up quickly.

Goldie looked at me as I backed up hurriedly and headed for the exit. I needed to get someplace where I could read the journal in private. My mind raced. But, where could I go? Maybe it was best to get some distance between me and Easley, so wherever I stopped to read it, I knew I wouldn't be disturbed.

I jumped onto the I-85 going north, having decided to head to New York. I'd drive a bit, then find somewhere to stop and read. My heart was still racing as I stepped on the gas.

—

After driving for almost an hour, I couldn't take it any longer. I had to see what James had written. Taking the next exit, I looked at the sides of the road when I noticed a motel sign on the left. Maybe I should just get a cheap room for the night and read the journal there.

It would be getting dark soon and maybe Goldie and I should just spend the night somewhere safe and get a fresh start in the morning.

The Bluebird Inn, the sign said. I pulled in and parked the car quickly. Leaving Goldie in the car, I hurried inside.

"Welcome to the Bluebird Inn," the elderly clerk at the desk said as I walked in.

I checked in quickly and headed back out to the car.

The motel room was old and run down, smelling like a combination of cigarettes and Lysol. But it didn't matter. I just wanted somewhere I could read the journal, get a few hours' sleep and be on my way.

I brought in the suitcase before going back out and getting the blanket and journal from the back seat. Laying the blanket down on the motel floor for Goldie, I filled the ice chest with water and set it down for her.

I was sure she was hungry, so I found a vending machine and bought some beef jerky and some other snacks for both me and her, along with a couple of waters and Cokes.

I fed her some of the snacks and made myself a drink, then sat down in the chair by the bed. I took a sip and with hands shaking, opened the journal again. I hesitated. Maybe my father was right, and I shouldn't read it. What good could come from reading it now anyway? James was dead and we all knew that he wasn't happy before he died, and surely had written about it.

It would only make me sadder to read his thoughts on the days leading up to his death. I looked down at the journal again. Who was I fooling? There was no way I wasn't going to read it. I had to, not only to try and find out what was going through James' mind when he killed himself, but maybe why he'd shut me out of his life the way he had those last few years he was alive.

I took a deep breath. Once I started, I knew there'd be no turning back. I glanced at the first page and got nervous again. What if he made it clear in here that there was something I could have said or done to talk him out of ending his life?

Then again, what if I found out I had nothing to do with it and it was Beth's fault? Or Joey's? At least I'd be off the hook then. But was that what I really wanted—to be off the hook? Was it?

As crazy as it sounded, guilt was the only thing that seemed to have kept me connected to my twin brother. I glanced down at my wrist. I needed more than just a tattoo. I took another sip and started to read.

CHAPTER 28

THE NEXT DATE MADE MY PULSE QUICKEN AGAIN. IT was the year James and I had graduated, and the year James died.

4-21-09

'They're at it again,' the journal started out. *'It's all they do· Always starting out the same way and by the end of the night, finishing the same way· 'If you don't stop drinking, I'm going to leave you,' he shouts and then Mother cries like there's nothing she can do about it· 'If you don't stop, I'm leaving you·' There, he's said it again and Mother cries some more· But she won't stop· And he won't leave her· It's a farce· Sometimes I think he is just as sick as she is·'*

My heart ached as I thought back to how many times, I'd heard the same thing night after night and thought the exact same thing.

'Last night, I heard her saying how it's my fault that she drinks like she does· Because it isn't fair that I didn't turn out normal like Karen· So, I'm not normal than, Mother? Nice!'

My heart sank again. I hadn't known she'd even said that sort of thing, let alone that poor James had to hear her say it. I sadly went back to reading. All the while, my heart thumped in my chest.

'It's all a lie· She doesn't drink because of me· She drinks because she wants to· Or as she likes to say, because drinking keeps her from going insane· Maybe that part is true at least· Maybe

she has those same voices in her head that I have and truly believes that's the only way to quiet them· But if that worked, I'd have taken up drinking a long time ago, too· No·

The truth is, she drinks because she doesn't love us enough to stop, whether she wants to admit it or not· Why doesn't she love us?'

I looked at the page as a lump formed in the back of my throat. Even after taking another sip of my drink, the lump was still there. This was going to be even harder than I imagined it would be. I turned the page.

'The fighting is getting to Karen too, I know it is· Though she tries to pretend it doesn't bother her· But I hear her crying in her room· I want so bad to go in there and tell her how everything will be okay· But that's a lie· Things will never be okay, not as long as Mother drinks like she does· I can't wait to be gone·'

I lifted my eyes from the page. Had he already been thinking of killing himself, I wondered? And, I didn't know James had heard me crying in my room. I had tried so hard to be quiet and keep it from him. He was right though, about me trying not to let him know how all the chaos in the house was affecting me. I remembered wanting to be strong for him but guessed I didn't do such a good job of that after all. I looked down at the journal again, almost sick at the thought of reading more, but my eyes seemed unable to move from its pages. It was a horrible position to be in.

4-23-09

'So, he's gone then· That's it, at long last, no more fighting· Mother booted him out! It's so nice and quiet in the house now· But who is going to take care of her now that he's gone? Karen's never home· She doesn't care that I'm left alone with Mother· And how her drinking has gotten even worse with him gone·

Yesterday when I went to check on her, she was so drunk she actually thought I was Karen· I had to listen to her go on and on about how wonderful I am and how proud she was of me. And how she loves going to my plays. All the while knowing it was my sister she was talking about.

And up until yesterday, I had no idea she even went to see Karen act. That was a shocker. I'm sure no one else knew she did either. Though I shouldn't be too surprised that she was there. Mother hates to show it, but we all know how she loves Karen more than anything in the world. Except her drinking of course. That is her true love.'

I sucked in my breath. So, James had known Mother was going to my school plays and didn't tell me? Why not? And, what was that about her loving me the most? Everyone knew Mother loved him much more than she could possibly have loved me. Besides, he had to know you couldn't believe anything Mother said when she was drunk! There was no telling what would come out of her mouth. Once again, I wondered why he wouldn't tell me that she'd been going. It sounded like he was jealous. Was that it? The thought made me sad.

I wondered how it had felt for James, stuck there alone with Mother and in that environment of constant stress and arguments. And from the journal, it sounded like the drinking had only been getting worse and worse, and the next thing was, Dad had filed for a divorce! Unbelievable! And poor James, in the middle of all that and I was only concerned about myself as usual, while he stressed about what Mother was going to do.

'She's going to go off the deep end, I just know it,' he wrote in the journal. *'I'm scared to death that she's going to do something really bad and hurt herself. I should stay home from school this morning and keep an eye on her. But I have all those tests today. I'll tell Karen. Maybe she will stay with her this once.'*

But he never did tell me, and I now wondered why he didn't. I could have done that for him, sure; yes, I could have stayed with her. But it had turned out okay anyway, by the sound of what he'd written after that. How he'd gotten home early and oddly enough, Mother had seemed to be alright. She hadn't taken the news of the upcoming divorce hard at all. In fact, James thought she'd even seemed in a better mood those next few days than she ever was. But then a few days after that, he came home to find Mother lying on the floor.

'Mother looked dead. It was horrible. Her face was so white and her lips were completely blue, and she smelled like alcohol and vomit. Karen wasn't home as usual. She must have snuck out sometime during the night like she always did and was at Joey's. I really wish she was there this once. It was rough.'

I felt so bad reading that and began to understand why my father hadn't wanted me to see any of this. He'd known it would only make me feel bad, but I'd blamed myself for so much anyway, it couldn't really get that much worse had I known all this.

'The sight of Mother made me almost pass out. She looked like a corpse and I didn't know what to do but finally called 911. I could tell the paramedics were scared for her too but then she woke up. All of a sudden, there she was again, large as life, almost like nothing had happened! Well, she was pretty out of it at first and they tried to get her to go to the hospital but of course she wouldn't. After they left, she was so mad at me and told me never to call 911 again and if I found her there, just let her be, and that it was none of my business. And then she went right back to drinking.'

I felt sick to my stomach. Poor James had to have been scared to death when he'd found her looking like that. Why didn't he tell me any of this had happened?

And to think he'd had to go through it all by himself because I wasn't there to help. And yet, I'd always knew that was going to happen to her sooner or later. How one day, a teacher with a look of pity on her face would come into one of my classes to pull me out gently and tell me that something had happened to my mother, and how my father was coming to pick me and James up to take us home. And then the teacher would say how sorry she was, and what a lovely woman my mother was, and if there was anything the school could do…

Yes, it was only a matter of time her drinking would take her from us. We'd all known that, hadn't we? We'd all known it, for sure, every single day we lived there with Mother in that house. Yet, I'd never once stopped to think that if I wasn't around to find her when she died, it meant James would be left to discover her body. It always was James who got the bad deal in life, the bad hand.

Again, I was filled with guilt. Yet I read on. Thankfully, though, the next few parts didn't mention Mother much. They were mostly about what James did over the summer, and how he'd found the thankful distraction of working on computers or reading. It appeared that he was beginning to enjoy writing in the journal. That it was somewhere he felt safe to let his thoughts out. I was grateful for having given him this, at least.

Maybe it was a good thing after all that I'd made him that small gift, though the relief he found in his writing apparently was short lived. Once again, I felt guilty for not being there for him. And for the first time, I realized just how incredibly lonely my brother was. Maybe he had been even more lonely than I was now - if that was possible. And I well knew how horrible it was to be lonely and wouldn't wish that on anyone, especially not on my James. And slowly, page by page, I saw the slow and pain-filled destruction of my beautiful brother, line by tormented line.

> *'I'm having second thoughts about going to college,'* the next entry started out. *'Whatever's going to happen to Mother? Who's going to keep an eye on her if I'm not here?'*

Not only was he concerned about what was going to happen to our mother, but he was now starting to question if he hadn't made a mistake by joining me at the same college.

'I should never have let Karen talk me into going to Clemson with her. For once, I'd like to be on my own without her or anyone else looking over my shoulder. I can take care of myself. But I hate to hurt her feelings.'

Hurt my feelings? Really? That was crazy. The only reason I'd suggested that we go to the same college was because I thought James would want to have someone there on his side, someone like me. I'd much rather have gone to a different college and not always have had to worry about him. Didn't he even realize I was only trying to look out for him?

Again, I wondered why he hadn't just told me the truth, though I guessed I could have told him how I felt, too. I wondered how many times we'd both tried to spare each other's feelings by not sharing what we felt and suffered, only to end up hurting each other's feelings in the long run anyway.

I also thought about how I tended to do that with Dan, not tell him how I was really feeling. And look where that had gotten me. My eyes stung as I turned the page.

'Ran into Beth today, sweet Beth! I've always liked her. I remember how I used to make excuses as to why I had to go into the room whenever she was over. She has the most beautiful and intense eyes I've ever seen. I could get lost in them. I can see everything she's feeling by looking into them, too. Today when I saw her, her eyes were telling me she was sad. I wonder why? I know I should have asked her, but I didn't have the nerve.'

I had to smile. James was right. Beth's eyes always did tend to give her away. Maybe that was another reason why she avoided me back then. She knew I'd be able to tell there was something going on with her, and that she liked James more than I knew.

'Saw her again, the beautiful Beth, during lunch. Asked her what was wrong. She told me she'd broken up with Steve.

Well, I'm glad! He's a real jerk· Though I do hate to see her so sad· She said she was glad to finally be able to tell someone what was wrong· She said she couldn't talk to Karen anymore· That Karen never liked Steve anyway and would just make Beth feel worse·'

I felt a pang of regret reading that. I should have been there for my friend, no matter what I thought of her boyfriend, shouldn't I? But it was true, I didn't like her with Steve at all. It was not only because of the way he treated James but because I didn't think he was good enough for Beth. Plain and simple, the guy was a loser. He was shallow, callous and mean. I flashed back to the day James had come home and told me that Steve was picking on him again, but this time one of the sophomores had told him to lay off. That sophomore was Joey.

And how as a thank you, James had offered to fix Joey's computer and after that spent time teaching Joey how to use it. And then they'd become friends, and then best friends. That was how I'd met Joey and then Beth too.

I still couldn't believe it when Beth told me she'd agreed to go out with Steve later that year when he asked her. But she said he felt bad about the way he'd treated James and was different than everyone thought. And though James did say Steve had quit hassling him at school, I still didn't like the idea of Beth dating him. I mean, a person couldn't change that much, especially not in so short a time. He was still mean and cruel as far as I was concerned. No matter what excuses Beth chose to make for him.

'Can't believe she called!' the next entry read. *'We talked for a long time· Beth's so easy to talk to· Can't wait to meet her at Starbucks tomorrow·'*

It felt good to read the excitement in James' voice, but it was also alarming the more he talked about her, since I knew full well how it would all end up.

Pretty much every entry was about Beth now, how great she was, and about the things they did together, where they went and how they laughed and shared things. It was obvious, James was falling for her fast and everything he did was centered around making her happy, as if he now had a new mission in life.

'She gets me. She really gets me. We have a lot more in common than I thought. And she understands how it feels to be angry with your parents and at the same time to feel guilty for feeling that way.

Beth told me that she was so mad at her dad when he died. Even though she knows it wasn't his fault that he died. I feel the same way though my father is still alive. But he is never around, which is almost the same. She said I should tell him how I feel and maybe I will. She said she's never told anyone any of the things she's told me and that's because she has strong feelings for me. I kissed her when she dropped me off at the house today and I could tell she liked it. I know I did!'

It made me feel strange reading this. It was hard to picture James and Beth together romantically, and it wasn't long after this that James wrote they'd slept together for the first time.

I took a few more sips of my drink as I quickly skimmed over the details, feeling even more uncomfortable as James recounted how he had snuck Beth into his bedroom while Mother was passed out, and made love to her.

After that, I could see he was walking on clouds. He was thrilled that he finally had someone he cared about and someone who cared about him just as much. But in the next few entries, I could see how he was starting to have his doubts whether Beth did actually feel the same way about him, or was it all for show, all a game?

I shuddered, my body trembling at the thought that my best friend might have used my own brother like that. I wanted to give her the benefit of the doubt. Relationships did go wrong, and I was the first to admit that. It was never just one person's fault.

'She's acting strange. We don't see each other as much either. She claims she's busy, but I know there's something else going on with her. And why hasn't she told Steve about us yet? Why is she hiding it? Is it because she still likes him? Beginning to think maybe I was just a rebound.'

That last line hit a chord. I thought back to when I agreed to marry Dan. I did love him, but also wondered if maybe I wasn't rushing things. I'd thought maybe being with Dan would help accelerate getting over Joey, and it did. But sometimes, I had caught myself wondering if Dan wasn't just a rebound for Joey.

But I grew to love Dan very much, just as much as—if not more than—I'd ever loved Joey. Now I wondered, when had I stopped feeling that way? It didn't happen overnight. If I was honest, I'd started pulling away from Dan months before I ever bought him that gym membership. Before he met Susan, even, I was ashamed to admit. And now it came back to me how he'd said he just wanted some attention…

I hadn't pulled back because I didn't love him, it definitely wasn't that, but I was tired of being hurt, every time he was in one of his moods. So just like I did with my mother, I shut down. I had to close myself away in my own safe space before I got hurt. But I got hurt anyway, didn't I?

Maybe if I hadn't tried so hard to protect myself, Dan never would have turned to someone else. But no—that wasn't how it worked. It wasn't my fault. We were married and what he did was his own choice. He could have persisted in finding out why I was becoming so closed, instead of running to another woman like that.

I flipped to the next page.

'Maybe Joey was right. Maybe I am crazy for thinking she could ever go for a guy like me.'

I felt myself wince again. I could see by the next few entries that James was sinking deeper into depression as Beth pulled away even more.

I felt apprehensive knowing I was about to come to the part where James decided he didn't want to live anymore. I braced myself and questioned if I should go on. But the next entry was about the day Pastor Phil stopped by the house.

'Pastor Phil came today after school to see Mother. She wouldn't talk to him of course. But he stayed anyway and talked to me instead. He could tell that something was bothering me. I guess it's pretty obvious that I'm miserable about Beth.

I can't believe I opened up to him. I haven't been able to talk to anyone like that except Beth. Though we don't talk that much lately. In fact, we don't talk at all. It tears me up how she just isn't interested in me anymore.

But Pastor Phil listens. And he cares, I can tell. I told him everything. About Beth and how I love her so much but I'm afraid that she doesn't feel the same way about me anymore and how it's killing me.

I told him about how her brother said I'm not good enough for her. My 'best friend' said that. I asked Pastor Phil if maybe Joey wasn't right, and Beth was out of my league and that I should just accept it.

But Pastor Phil said no. He said it doesn't matter what Joey or anyone else says about me. How what they think about me, doesn't make it so.

He told me that he was there at the hospital the day Karen and I were born. How Mother was frightened and asked him to come to the hospital and pray over me. He said I was in really bad shape. And how he'd never seen such a tiny baby fight so hard to survive.

Pastor Phil said he knew right then that I was a fighter and something really special. And so, Joey and everyone else had it all wrong. If they could only see me through Pastor Phil's eyes, they would see just how strong and kind and special I was. No one's ever said things like that to me. But that's what he said.'

I felt tears burning my eyes. That was just not true. I had told James many times how special he was. Why didn't he believe me? I guessed he had to hear it from someone else, because maybe sisters always said that kind of thing.

But I was happy that Pastor Phil told him that and was able to be there for James.

And by what James wrote on the next few pages, he took what Pastor Phil said to heart. So much so, that I immediately could see all the changes he was making in his life for the better.

One of the first things he did was to tell Beth he loved her and was tired of waiting for her to tell Steve about them. No more secrets, he said. If she loved him too, she needed to tell Steve before James did. *Good for you James*, I said out loud, feeling proud of my brother.

He wrote how he had called our father and told him that he didn't like how he was already seeing another woman especially when he didn't even have time for us. Then how Dad broke down and said he was sorry and swore he'd spend more time with both James and me. He even promised to take James on his next hunting trip.

I guessed Dad was telling the truth when he'd told me the other day how he'd been planning on taking James out with him. Next, James decided to buy a car, as it seemed he didn't want to have to depend on Beth or anyone else to get around. And he wanted not just any car either, but a car that would get attention when he drove it down the street with Beth in it. A few days later, he went and found the perfect one.

'I bought my first car, a beautiful red Mustang. It's amazing. I'm sure Mother will be upset when she finds out I used most of the money I was saving for college to buy it. But I don't care. I earned that money and don't want to depend on anyone anymore. And I need a car to do that. And I'm not going to college either, I've decided. I'm sure that will upset her even more. But I've got plans. Plans to grow my computer business. Get my own shop one day and marry Beth.'

My eyes welled up with pride again. James was becoming independent. Thank you, Pastor Phil, for helping my brother believe in himself, at least for a while. I turned the page and once I saw the date at the top, I instantly felt ill. It was Joey's birthday and that horrible night at Applebee's. Then the next day, James was dead. I forced myself to go on.

09-07-11.

'We're all going to Applebee's tonight for Joey's birthday. I wasn't going to go but Joey did say he was sorry when I ran into him the other day, for what he said about not wanting me to date Beth. I feel kind of bad that I've kept it from him that we are seeing each other. But Beth said she'd be going tonight so it will be the perfect time to tell Karen and Joey the truth.'

I was taken by surprise to learn that Joey had apologized to James. Joey hadn't mentioned that to me. Maybe he'd forgotten or perhaps he'd known that, at this point, it didn't really matter. But at least he did it. That counts for something.

James wrote that evening after dinner how beautiful Beth had looked that night, and how apparently, I and Joey were oblivious to how James and Beth felt about each other.

'I can't believe Karen and Joey couldn't tell how much in love we are. Couldn't they see it in our eyes? Especially Beth's? Her eyes were beaming. And then when she slipped up, or maybe it was on purpose, and called me 'honey' right in front of everyone, I was sure they had to know then. Steve did. He knew. I actually felt so sorry for him.

It was all over his face that he knew she loved me, and he'd lost her. I almost wanted to rub it in his face after the way he treated me, but I couldn't. I know what it feels like to be humiliated in front of everyone and I don't wish that on anyone, even Steve. Besides, it doesn't matter. She's mine. All mine. And for the first time in my life I know that everything's going to be all right.'

Now, I looked up from the page with confusion. I didn't understand…I really didn't. That night, James had left Applebee's happy and convinced that Beth really did love him. So, what happened between then and the time he'd decided to kill himself? Heart pounding in my chest, I turned the page.

'Woke up to a gorgeous sunrise right outside my window· Why have I never noticed that before? It must be because I'm in love· Oh, how I wish Beth was here to see it with me· But we'll have plenty of sunrises to watch together· We should watch the sunset together tonight, though· That's it· I'll pick up some roses and swing by her house and surprise her·

We can go to The Cliffs restaurant and sit outside on the patio and watch it· She loves going there· God, I love her so much· I can't wait to tell Karen that we're in love· Why wait? I'm going to tell her right now·'

And that was it. The rest of the page was blank. I flipped to the next one, but it was blank also. And all the pages up to the back of the journal were blank. I went back and reread the last few sentences.

'I can't wait to tell Karen that we're in love· Why wait? I'm going to tell her right now·'

I stared at the page and my mouth dropped open. I couldn't believe it. I was wrong! We'd all been dead wrong. I was completely blown away. I knew the truth finally, and it wasn't what I thought at all. It was not at all what any of us had thought.

CHAPTER 29

I SAT THERE FROZEN, FEELING LIKE I'D JUST BEEN struck by lightning. So, James wasn't depressed that morning at all; on the contrary, he'd been so happy, probably happier than he'd ever been. He was in love and knew that Beth loved him too. That was what he'd wanted to tell me that morning in the hallway. He was nervous all right. But nervous with excitement.

But I didn't stay to hear what he had to say, I left with Joey. And though I imagined James was disappointed that I didn't stick around to hear his wonderful news, he'd figured he'd tell me when I got back. And that was when he must have decided to go kill some time up at the range. He had that hunting trip with Dad coming up, and I was sure he wanted to impress him.

I could see it like it was almost happening right before my eyes. He decided to go up to the range. So, he went into the safe where we kept a few guns for when Joey and I went shooting, he got one out, and headed up the hill with it.

I had imagined him struggling up the hill all this time, but that morning, he was so happy and excited about Beth, plus the fact that he'd been going up there a lot lately, he probably didn't even struggle that much. He probably was so excited, he practically ran up there.

But something must have gone wrong while he was up there shooting. Maybe he tripped, and the gun went off. Or he had one of his asthma attacks. I thought back to the inhaler Mother and I had found up in the dirt yesterday. James must have dropped it while he was getting it out. Or trying to use it.

Whatever the case, the gun must have gone off accidentally and hit him. He didn't mean to kill himself. It was an accident! All this time, we'd all thought it was suicide when it was nothing but a terrible accident!

I held the journal like it was the most precious thing in the world. And right now, it was. I looked at Goldie who was now staring at me as if confused by my excitement.

"He didn't do it, Goldie," She looked at me and tilted her head and I got the impression that somehow, she already knew that. "I mean, he did do it, but he didn't mean to!" I ruffled her fur and her ears shook from side to side. She jumped around, picking up on my high mood.

It was unbelievable. I thought again how all this time, we'd been telling ourselves James took his own life and we'd each believed we were responsible, when all along no one was. I started to shake. I had to tell them, all of them. Beth, Joey, my dad, Mother. I had to tell Mother! She, more than anyone, needed to know it wasn't her fault. I got up and dug my phone out of my purse and turned it on. There were quite a few missed calls from my parents' house. I hit dial to return the call. But as it started to ring, I hung up.

This was too important to tell over the phone. I needed to tell her this in person.

I grabbed the journal again and put it along with my phone, into my purse. As I glanced at the half-empty glass of Jack and Coke on the night stand, I realized that I'd been so overwhelmed by the journal, I never even finished drinking what was in my glass. I picked it up but stopped.

Grabbing the almost empty bottle of Jack, I took it along with my drink to the bathroom, and with resolve, dumped the contents of them both into the toilet. As I pushed the handle down, a huge sense of relief came over me as I realized that I may have very likely just dodged a bullet myself. I tossed the empty bottle into the trash, zipped up my suitcase, grabbed my purse and headed for the door with Goldie close behind me.

As we pulled out of the parking lot, I felt my body start to tremble uncontrollably, not only because of what I'd just discovered in the journal, but because I knew with certainty that I was about to rock everyone's world.

As I drove, I thought about Beth and how she really had loved my brother. Maybe that was why she didn't go to his funeral—maybe it had been just too much for her. After all, she'd just lost the boy she loved, and from all things, she'd lost him to suicide. And I knew, she too had been blaming herself all these years for his death, just like I had.

As I came to the Red Penny, I started to regret pouring out the whiskey. I would need something strong to drink if I was going to tell my parents something that would surely shock them as much as it'd shocked me. Yet, just minutes earlier, I had made up my mind I wasn't going to drink anymore. Well, I'd just run in really quick and say goodbye to Big Al, anyway. That's all.

Al's back was turned as I walked in. I pulled out a stool and sat down. Just being there made me crave a drink.

Big Al saw me, and reached for a glass, the same as he always knew to use when he saw me. Before I could tell him no, he'd already poured me a Jack and Coke and was setting it down in front of me.

I stared at it. I guessed a few sips wouldn't hurt. As he stood there watching, I lifted the glass to my mouth. But before I could take a sip, my cell phone rang. I put the drink down and groped in my purse for the phone. My fingers felt something round on the bottom of my purse and I pulled it out just as the phone stopped ringing.

It was the AA chip that Mother had given me this morning. As I stared at it, I thought of James and how proud he would have been to see her get this. And how disappointed he'd be if he knew I was drinking. My eyes teared up.

Big Al looked at the coin in my hand, then back at me. Without saying a word, he reached down and picked up the glass.

"This one is on me," he said as he walked away with my drink and poured it down the sink. I smiled at him and stood up.

"Thanks for everything, Big Al," I said.

He gave me a wink. "Anytime. Good luck, kid."

I got my purse and headed for the door. It was dark as I made my way back to the house. The lights were on at the Finley Church as I drove by. I couldn't help but think of Pastor Phil and how kind he had been to James. No wonder he was so upset when James had died, especially believing that he'd killed himself. I jerked the wheel and pulled into the parking lot. Here was someone else that really deserved to know the truth - Pastor Phil.

"Is everything okay?" the pastor asked looking concerned as I hurried up to him slightly out of breath.

"I need to tell you something," I said as I tried to slow my heartbeat.

"What is it, dear?" he asked, looking more alarmed.

"I don't know how else to say it Pastor Phil, but James didn't kill himself like we all thought he did. It was an accident."

Now Pastor Phil looked stunned. "What makes you say that?"

I pulled the journal out of my purse. "Because of this. He kept a journal."

"He did?" he asked staring at it.

"Yes, and he wrote down everything. How he was in love with Beth. And how you helped him believe in himself. Thank you for that, Pastor Phil."

"I wanted to tell you the other day about Beth, but I'd promised James that I'd always keep it a secret," he said, still staring at the journal.

"That's okay. He was planning on telling me anyway, that morning he died. But I was in a hurry, so I didn't give him a chance. And that was when he went up to the range to do some target shooting and wait for me to get back. But something went very wrong up there. The gun must have gone off."

I waited for a reaction from Pastor Phil. He just stood there so I continued. "It's true. There's no doubt by what he wrote that he didn't want to die. He was happy, Pastor Phil. Happier than he'd ever been."

This time I could see tears in his eyes. "I know he was," he said softly. "That's why it just didn't make sense that he would do a thing like that. I'm so relieved to know the truth even though I know it doesn't bring him back, but at least it helps to know he wasn't in turmoil."

"Yes, it does," I said."

After a moment, I put the journal back into my purse. "Well I just wanted you to know. I have to go tell my parents now." I turned for the door and stopped. "And again, thank you for everything you did for my brother. All he wanted was to be loved and accepted and you helped give him that."

Pastor Phil walked me outside. "That's all he ever wanted for you too, you know. He used to tell me how he wished you'd find someone like he did. Someone who loved and appreciated you for just who you were."

I opened the car door. "I had someone like that," I said softly.

"Oh, but I was under the impression he didn't think Joey was that guy," he said.

I looked back at him. "I wasn't talking about Joey," I got into the car and drove away.

CHAPTER 30

AS I PULLED UP THE DRIVEWAY, JUST LIKE WHEN I'D first arrived, Mother's head was sticking out of the front door. But this time, I was excited and happy to see her as she hurried down the steps to greet me.

"You're back," she said as I climbed out of the Mustang. "Where'd you go? I tried to call you. You took all your things, so I was afraid that you'd left without even saying goodbye."

I reached out and hugged her. And when I let her go, she was smiling but looked apprehensive.

"Is everything okay?" she asked as I walked around and opened the passenger door.

Goldie hopped out and ran up to my mother, her tail wagging as if Mother was the best thing she had ever seen.

"I see you've brought a friend," Mother laughed as Goldie licked her hand. "Isn't she the dog from the church? I saw her the other day when I stopped in to see Pastor Phil." She bent down and rubbed Goldie's back.

"Yes," I was surprised to see her being so affectionate with Goldie. She never did care for dogs as far I could remember. But as I had been finding out, there was a lot I didn't know about my mother. "Let's go inside," I said getting my suitcase out of the trunk.

My father opened the door as I walked up. Though he looked thin and tired, it was good to see him back home again. I hadn't seen him in this house for a very long time and it just felt right.

"Where'd you go?" he asked as I walked past him. "Your mother was frantic."

I looked at him and set the suitcase on the ground. "I found it, Dad."

"Found what?" Mother said from behind me. She filled a bowl with water and set it on the floor for Goldie.

"Can you and Dad sit down, please?" I asked nervously as I headed to the kitchen table. "I have something very important to tell you."

My father's eyes were wide as he pulled out a chair for my mother, then slowly lowered himself into the other chair.

"It's okay, Dad," I said patting his hand. "It's all good." I reached into my purse and slowly slid out the journal and set it on the table. I heard an intake of air from my father.

Mother looked down at the journal. "What is that? Isn't that the journal you were always scribbling in?"

"No. This one belonged to James," I replied.

"Oh. I didn't know he kept one too," she said looking at my father. "Did you, Bill?"

My father didn't answer. His face looked pallid and tense.

"I went somewhere to read it. That's where I've been. And that's what I wanted to talk to you both about. I guess there's no other way but to just come out and say it. James did not commit suicide."

Mother's face turned pale. "Why are you saying that?"

"It's true, Mother. It's all in here. Some of it was hard to read, but the fact is, James' death was nothing but a terrible accident. I'm quite sure of it."

They both looked at me with stunned expressions.

"James was happy," I went on. "Probably happier than he'd ever been. He was in love. With Beth. You were right, Mother. He did have a crush on Beth. And she loved him too. He had no intention of shooting himself when he went up to the range that day. He wanted to spend the rest of his life with her."

"What? Are you sure?" Mother asked, her voice trembling. "How do you know for sure that it was just an accident?"

"Because, he wrote about everything in here. How he was getting ready to tell me all about him and Beth that morning he died. And how he wanted to grow his computer business and one day marry her. He even wrote about what he was going to do that very day. Pick up some roses for Beth and watch the sunset with her. It's all in here.

So, you see, he didn't want to die. He wanted to live. He must have tripped or had an attack or something up there and shot himself accidently. But it's clear by what he wrote in this journal, he had no intention of killing himself."

"That's why we found that inhaler up there the other day," Mother said looking at me her eyes widening even more. "He must have been trying to use it. Oh, poor Beth. She was in love with him. Have you told her? Does she know?"

"No. The only people I've told so far was Pastor Phil on the way here, and now you and Dad."

"You should call her," my father said. "She needs to know."

"And Joey too," Mother added. "I'm sure he will be just as relieved as we are. Call them now."

"Okay. I'll see if they are both up," I said taking my cell phone with me into the hallway. But instead of calling Beth or Joey, I dialed Dan.

He picked it up on the second ring. "Karen? What time is it? Are you okay?"

"Yes," I said, my voice choking up.

"What is it? Is it your father?" he asked, sounding worried.

"No," I said, tears coming as the rollercoaster of a day started to wash over me.

"Tell me. What's wrong? You sound upset."

"It's about my brother," I said trying to compose myself.

"James?" he asked. "What about him?"

"I just found out that he didn't kill himself like we all thought, all this time. It was an accident."

"Wow. How'd you find that out?" he asked.

"James had a journal like I did when I was young. It's all in there. And from what he wrote, it's clear he was in love with Beth and had no intention of killing himself. Do you know what that means?" I asked, tears now running down my face. "It means he was happy. And it means it wasn't my fault."

"Of course, it wasn't your fault," Dan said soothingly. "Look, I'm coming out on the next flight."

"No, you don't need to. I'll be fine," I said trying to stop the tears. "I don't know why, but I just wanted you to know."

"I'm glad you called me," he said. "But I'm still coming out."

"No, Dan really, I'm okay. Stay there and work. I'll be coming back soon anyway."

The other end of the phone was silent.

"You're coming home? I was so afraid you weren't," he said, his voice cracking.

"I'm not sure what I want to do about us yet, but I am coming back to California. We can sort it out when I get back. Well, I better go. I need to call Beth and let her know the news." I was careful not to mention anything about calling Joey too.

"Okay sweetheart, I'm so glad you called.," he said softly. "And so happy for you. I'll talk to you tomorrow. Goodnight".

I said goodnight and hung up the phone and dialed Beth's cell next. When she picked up, by all the noise in the background, I could tell she was still at work.

"Beth, it's me," I said. "How late do you work tonight? I need to talk to you."

"I was just getting ready to clock out. Why? What's wrong?" she asked, I was sure assuming—just like Dan—that something had happened to my father.

"Can you come over to the house on your way home? I want to tell you something face to face. Don't worry, it's all good. I'm going to call Joey too and ask him to come by."

"Sounds serious," she said. "Sure, I can be there in about fifteen to twenty minutes."

"Okay, I'll see you then."

Joey didn't answer so I left a voicemail asking him to call me as soon as possible, and if he was in the area, to come by the house.

When I got back to the kitchen, Mother was busy mixing up something in a large bowl.

"Did you get a hold of them?" she asked, setting the bowl down to turn the oven on.

"Yes. Beth's coming over now and I left Joey a message," I replied. "Are you baking at this hour?"

"Yes, it helps me relax," she said, dropping balls of dough onto a pan. "I was just going to heat up some meatloaf too and make a sandwich for your father. Do you want one?"

"I don't think I can even eat right now," I said. "I'm too excited."

But she made me a sandwich anyway and while my father ate, I sat with him and dug into mine. Mother took the end of the meatloaf and dropped it in a bowl for Goldie.

As I took another bite, my phone rang. It was Joey.

"What's up?" he asked. "I just got your message. Is everything okay?"

"Yes, but, where are you? Do you think you can come by the house tonight? Beth's on her way and I need to talk to you too."

"What's going on?" he asked again. I could hear the anxiety in his voice.

"I'll tell you when you both get here."

"Okay," he said. "I'm on my way." He hung up and I went back to my sandwich. My father excused himself and went to his room.

"I was thinking," Mother said as she put the pan of cookies in the oven, "how, if you'd never come back here to see your father, we might never have found out the truth about James. Funny how things work out, isn't it?"

She was right. If she hadn't called to tell me about Dad's cancer, and if Dan and I hadn't been fighting, I may not have come back. And what was even stranger, was that if I hadn't met Goldie and taken her with me, I might never have found the journal and then, who knew what might have happened?

I looked at Goldie licking the bowl clean as if she wanted to try and see her face in it. There was something odd about this dog, as if she'd been sent to help me. Did James send her? Or maybe God did. I smiled at the thought.

"We would have all gone on living our lives believing that we were responsible for his death and could have somehow prevented it. Well, what a gift to know the truth," Mother said as she turned the timer on for the cookies. "I feel so much…lighter…if you know what I mean."

"I know what you mean, Mother. I do too," I said, a warmth spreading throughout my body.

I looked at Goldie again. Yes, I had to admit, it was all a gift. The doorbell rang, and as I started to leave to answer it, I heard my father's voice.

"Hi Joey, come on in."

"How are you doing?" I heard Joey ask. "You look good, Bill. I bet it's good to be home."

"Sure is," my father replied. "I'm going to sit down though for a bit. I'm a bit tired. The girls are in the kitchen waiting for you if you want to go in."

A moment later, Joey appeared in the kitchen doorway.

"I came as fast as I could," he said, pulling out a chair. "What's going on?"

"Would you like a cup of coffee, Joey?" Mother asked. "I was just about to put a pot on."

"Sure," he said eyeing the journal that was still on the table. "What's that? Your old journal?"

Before I could answer, the doorbell rang again, and once more I heard my father's voice. Seconds later, Beth walked into the kitchen. And once again to my disappointment, Steve was with her, holding the hand of a half-asleep TJ.

It would have been a lot easier to tell Beth the news without Steve around. But as I thought back to some of the things James had written in the journal, I kind of felt sorry for Steve, though he did end up getting Beth in the end instead of James.

"I stopped by the house and Steve wanted to come with me," Beth said. TJ opened his sleepy eyes and started to shut them again but opened them wide as he noticed Goldie in the corner.

TJ pulled his hand from Steve's and ran over to Goldie who gave TJ a huge lick, sending him backwards on his behind. Everyone laughed, including TJ.

"I just made some chocolate chip cookies," Mother said as she pulled the pan out of the oven. "Maybe TJ should stay here with Goldie and have a cookie and some milk while the grownups go talk in the living room."

Mother filled a cup of coffee for Joey and got out a container of milk. She filled a glass and set it on the table along with a warm baked cookie on a plate for TJ.

Steve pulled out a chair for TJ and TJ climbed up in it. "We'll be in the next room buddy,"

I picked up the journal and followed everyone into the living room where my father was already seated. I felt a pang in my heart. He looked exhausted, though I was sure it was partly due to all the excitement. After I was gone, I hoped he'd be able to get plenty of rest.

Everyone found somewhere to sit and looked at me with anxious expressions. I took a deep breath. Everything I said from this moment on was about to change their lives drastically, and I knew it.

CHAPTER 31

ONCE AGAIN AS I HELD THE JOURNAL, MY HANDS WERE shaking. I could feel everyone's eyes on me and the silence in the room was deafening.

"This," I said clearing my throat, "is James' journal." I looked around the room at everyone's faces. My gaze stopped on Joey. His eyes were huge, no doubt from the fear of what James might have written about him, especially after the argument they'd had. I looked at Beth whose face was simply downbeat and sad.

"I didn't know he had one," she said. Steve looked down at the floor briefly.

I took a deep breath and set the journal onto my lap. I looked at Beth.

"Like I told my parents earlier, there are some things in here that were difficult to read. But what's important, and the reason I asked you and Joey to come over, is to tell you that James was happy at the end of his life. And it's totally clear by what he wrote in here that he didn't intend to die that day up on the hill. It was an accident."

I heard a couple of gasps.

"Are you saying that he didn't kill himself?" Beth asked her voice sounding pinched.

I looked at her with compassion. This news, though it was good, would only open up old wounds. But she had to know

"Yes, Beth. It's all in here. What he was thinking and how he was feeling that morning. He even wrote about all the things he planned to do later that afternoon," I looked at her and saw her eyes soften as she stared at the journal.

"He was getting ready to tell me something the morning he died," I continued, "but I was in a hurry, so he didn't get a chance to. I figure he must have decided to go up to the shooting range for a while. He wanted to practice because he was excited about going hunting with my father soon." I looked at my dad and saw his eyes get moist.

"Anyway, there's no doubt in my mind, from everything he wrote in here, that his death was nothing more than a horrible accident. I just wanted you all to know the truth. It was an accident," I said again as I looked around the room.

Joey sat there looking stunned. And Beth's eyes were so big now, they looked like they were about to fall out of her head. Even Steve looked shocked as he stared straight ahead. He looked up as TJ came walking into the room with Goldie close behind.

I could see chocolate on TJ's face. TJ stopped and looked around the room innocently, then headed for his mother. He sat down at her feet and looked up at her.

"Mommy why are you crying?" he asked as he reached up and wiped at her tears with the back of his hand.

His gesture reminded me of how James had done the exact same thing the day that bee had stung me. He had reached up just like TJ just did, and wiped my tears with the back of his hand.

A bolt of electricity shot through me. I looked at Beth, then at TJ again, and then at Beth a second time. She was looking at me and her eyes were filled with tears. She nodded her head slightly and smiled. I could see something in her gaze that told me everything. No! Surely not!

"It's okay Beth," I heard Mother say. "Go ahead, dear. It's time."

I turned, confused, and looked at my mother. "You knew?" I asked in a whisper.

Steve stood up slowly and took TJ's hand. "Hey buddy, what do you say you and I go have another cookie together, so the grownups can finish talking?"

He looked at Beth and nodded. She smiled back at him. I could see in her eyes how much she loved Steve and it warmed my heart.

"Okay," TJ said, quickly forgetting all about his mother's tears as he pulled Steve toward the kitchen eager for another cookie.

Once again, Goldie followed, trotting behind like the two were surgically attached. I wasn't sure if it was the cookie or the boy, she found more alluring, but either way, it made for a cute sight.

"You knew?" I asked Mother again, this time louder.

"Knew what?" Joey asked as he looked from person to person then back at me. "What's going on?" He seemed utterly confused.

"I had a suspicion," Mother replied. "But I wasn't sure. And I was afraid to find out if it was true in case, I was wrong. I wanted so badly for it to be true. TJ gave me a reason for living when I needed one, and another reason for staying sober too."

"What're you two talking about?" Joey asked, sounding frustrated. "Will someone please tell me?"

I looked at Beth again. "Does Steve know?"

"Yes," she said softly. "But he loves TJ just the same as if he was his own son. See, I told you he was a good man."

My father turned to my mother. "Why didn't you tell me, Doris?"

"I wanted to be sure before I did. I didn't want to disappoint you if I was wrong. Plus, I figured that Beth and Steve would tell us when the time was right, and when they were ready—if it was true," she said. "I'm sorry, honey."

"So that's why you wanted me to hire Steve," my father said softly. "You wanted to make sure TJ was well taken care of."

"Yes," Mother said.

"Steve and I felt bad keeping it from everyone," Beth said, looking at my parents as if for approval. She still had doubt written across her face, like a child who was in deep trouble for keeping a secret.

"But we were worried about how the kids at school were going to treat TJ once they found out James was his father and how he'd died," she continued. "It could be horrible, how cruel kids can be, as you know. I never wanted him to have to go through what James did. So, Steve and I decided to wait until TJ was a little older before we told anyone the truth. Though, we almost did tell you at the hospital the other day when you were having complications. She looked at my father.

I thought back to how strange I'd thought it was when Steve and Beth had kept whispering about going to get TJ. That was why they wanted him there; they were afraid my father might die without ever knowing he had a grandson.

"A few times, I started to tell you and your mother, too, but something always stopped me. I'm sorry," Beth said again looking apologetic.

Joey looked at Beth. "Are you saying that TJ is James' son?"

"Yes," she replied looking at her brother and holding his gaze. Steve walked into the room and sat down next to Beth.

"The third cookie and glass of milk knocked him right out. He's curled up on the rug next to the dog." Steve put his arm around Beth and looked around the room. "You okay?"

"Yes," she replied softly. "I told them. I explained too, how we wanted to keep it a secret until TJ was older. They understand."

"We'd still like to wait a little longer, before we do tell him if everyone doesn't mind," Steve said. "It will be easier on him. But you're all his family, now. And we couldn't ask for a better family for the little guy." He looked at my parents. "You can see him anytime you'd like, of course, Grandpa, Grandma..."

"We'd like that," Mother replied smiling as if her face was not wide enough to accommodate her grin. She looked at my father. "We have a grandson, Bill. Can you believe it?"

"Yes, honey," he said his voice choking up. "I know. It's a miracle. Especially for an old man who almost wasn't going to be sticking around."

"Oh, shush," Mother said, digging him in the ribs playfully with her elbow. "You're not going anywhere."

Mother looked at me. "And you have a nephew."

I looked at her as it all started to sink in. I did have a nephew. James' son. And while it was sad that James would never get to know his son, a part of my brother would always be with us.

"Well, maybe we should get TJ home to bed and let Bill get some rest, too. I'm sure it's been a long day for him," Steve said as he stood up. "We can talk about all this more tomorrow."

"Good idea," Mother said, standing up. "I'll wrap some chocolate chip cookies before you go. You can take some home with you for TJ."

As Beth and Steve started to follow Mother to the kitchen, I stood up to stop them.

"Steve, before you go, I'd like to say something in front of everyone."

Steve looked at me.

"I just wanted to say that the past is the past. I can see how much you love Beth and TJ. And how you've been there for them. And in a way for my brother, too. And for that, I want to thank you."

"It's okay," Steve said, looking down shyly. "Beth and TJ are my world."

"Yes, thank you Steve," my dad said holding his hand out. "You're a good man."

Beth looked over at me and smiled faintly, before going with Steve back to the kitchen to get TJ. My parents went with them.

I looked back at Joey who was left sitting there still looking just as confused. For a police officer, he sure was slow to catch onto things!

"Are you all right?" I asked as I got up and took a seat next to him.

"Sure," he replied. "But you have to admit it's a bit overwhelming, Shocking actually. First, to learn that James' death was an accident and then to find out he's TJ's father. It's wild. Couldn't write it, could you?"

We both looked up as Beth and Steve stopped in the doorway on their way to the front door, Beth with a plastic bag full of cookies in her hand and Steve with TJ now slung over his shoulder like a big sack of potatoes. After saying goodnight again, they turned, and my parents walked them to the front door. You could feel the warmth in the air—the warmth of love, of promise and of better times to come.

Once again, I was left there all alone with Joey and there was something I needed to say to him.

CHAPTER 32

"WELL, I GUESS ALL THE SECRETS ARE OUT," HE SAID, looking at me. "You don't have any more hidden away, do you?" he asked, taking my hand. "You are quite the detective, you know."

I thought of Dan and how I'd been keeping so many secrets from him, all the things I'd known and never shared with the one man I was supposed to share them with. Being here had made me realize that I didn't want to keep any more from him. I could almost understand now why he'd messed around. It was no excuse, of course, but I now kind of knew how pushed out he must have felt. The husband who was the last to find out anything. I suddenly felt ashamed and, in a way, cruel.

"Well, I think I'm going to turn in," my father said, interrupting us as he stood leaning against the doorway. I pulled my hand away from Joey abruptly.

"Goodnight, sir," Joey said, standing up. "I hope you can get some rest."

"I'm sure I will," he replied. "Tonight, of all nights, I will."

As Joey and I watched, my father made his way slowly over to us. It made me sad to see how much pain he was still in. He shook Joey's hand, then leaned over and kissed me lightly on the top of my head. "Goodnight sweetheart," he said as he straightened back up.

My eyes started to water as he slowly walked away, not only because of how weak and frail he looked, but because it was the first time I could remember since I was very young, that he'd kissed me like that. After he had left, Joey sat down again.

"I guess I should be going," he said, though he didn't move.

I stood up. "Yes. I'll walk you to the door." I let him out but not before he looked at me one more time. I could tell he wanted to kiss me, but I just smiled, said goodnight and closed the door softly.

As I headed to bed, I noticed Mother standing in the hallway. She reached up and pulled a box down from a top shelf in the hall closet. She set it on top of another one that was on the floor.

"What're you doing?" I asked as I walked up to her, resting a hand gently on her shoulder.

"I figured since I won't be able to sleep now with all the excitement, I'd go through some old photos of you and James," she replied. "Do you want to look at them with me?"

As tired as I was, I knew I wouldn't be able to sleep either. I picked up the boxes and headed to the kitchen with them. As I set them on the table, Mother filled the tea kettle with water and set it on the stove.

For the next few hours, we went through every photo, sometimes laughing, sometimes crying, especially when we'd come across a picture of James. I pulled one out of the stack and looked at it, running my finger lightly across his face as if he could feel it.

In it, James looked to be around the age TJ is now. I was blown away at how identical they looked. How could I not have seen that TJ was James' son? Now, it seemed impossible that I hadn't pieced it all together. Turned out I wasn't much of a detective after all.

As I put the photo back onto the stack, Mother put her hand on mine and held it there. I loved feeling her warmth and softness, the touch of a real mother, the one I had wanted all my life till now.

"Keep it," she said. I picked the photo back up and saw that my hand was trembling.

"I'm so grateful that you found his journal," she said as she looked through another stack.

Once again, I thought of all the coincidences that had led me to finding it. Coming back here. And Goldie. I looked down at her, now curled up at my feet. There was something truly special about this dog.

"Oh, and about the journal. I don't need to read it. At least not right now," Mother said. "I don't know if I ever will. I know what I need to know. Because of you."

"Okay," I said. "I'll put it in James' desk just in case. But you're right. The main thing is that he didn't kill himself, and that he was happy."

"I know," she said with tears in her eyes. "That's all I ever wanted - I'm sure you too, just for him to be happy."

"Yes," I said.

We finished going through the rest of the photos and it was well past midnight when we were finally done. Mother stood up and stretched.

"I guess we should see if we can get some sleep now."

I got up too and followed her down the hall. As she turned to go into her bedroom, I said, "goodnight, Mom."

I stopped as I realized that this was the first time, I'd ever called her Mom instead of Mother. A shiver ran through me. A shiver of happiness and in a way - closure. I looked back at her to see if she'd noticed what I'd called her, and by the look on her face, I knew that she had.

That night, as I started to drift off, I kept thinking about how ecstatic James would have been to know he had a son. But somehow, I was sure that he did know.

—

The next morning, I awakened to the sound of heavy breathing and at first was alarmed, until I remembered that Goldie was in the room. I patted her and got dressed before we both headed to the kitchen.

My father was at the kitchen table already, eating a bowl of oatmeal. I was glad to see there was a little more color in his face this morning.

"Good morning. How'd you sleep?" he asked, looking up. "Your mother is off to her meeting. But she prepped the coffee for you and left a bowl of oatmeal in the microwave. She also left the last of the meatloaf in the fridge for Goldie."

I smiled as I poured myself a cup of coffee, all the better for the fact she had made it for me. This was just another thing I was going to miss, having the coffee prepped for me. Dan used to do that until I told him not to bother, that I'd do it myself. What was I thinking?

I let Goldie outside to relieve herself and sat down at the table with my cup.

"How're you doing this morning Dad?" I asked.

"Better, though exhausted. Are you going to have some oatmeal with me?"

"I think I'll just get something at the Huddle House. I want to stop and see Beth one more time before I leave tomorrow."

"Oh, so you are going already? I sure wish you'd stay longer. But I understand. Just promise me you'll come back and visit us, soon."

"I will," I promised, knowing that I would. "Just try and keep me away," I laughed.

He pushed his bowl away. "Your mother and I were talking last night, and we decided that we'd like you to have the Mustang. We considered giving it to TJ but thought that you might like to have it instead, since he won't be able to drive for quite some time. That is, if you want it."

I mulled over how I felt about keeping the car. I liked the idea, if only because it was one more way to keep James' memory close. "Thanks Dad. I'd love to have it."

"I can have it shipped to you," he said.

"That's okay. I can drive it back myself," I replied. "It will be fun. Especially now, now that I know James was happy...it will feel different driving it."

"It's still a long drive," he said. "Why not just let me get it out to you?"

"Don't worry," I replied. "I've made that drive before. Besides, it might help clear my head out. I need some time to think. Besides," I looked down at Goldie, "I thought that maybe I could take Goldie with me. She really doesn't belong to anyone as far as I know."

"That would make me feel better if you weren't alone," he agreed. "I'll have Steve look the Mustang over thoroughly before you go, though. We definitely need to do that. The car's no spring chicken, like me." He laughed to himself and I joined him. "I'm sure he can do it today," he added.

"Great," I said. "I'll run it by there later."

After a second cup of coffee, Goldie and I headed for the Huddle House. On the way, I decided to stop by the cemetery. I wanted to tell James everything that had happened as well as saying goodbye to him.

Goldie trotted ahead of me. As we came to James' grave, I was surprised that this time, the heaviness I'd felt each time I came to visit wasn't there anymore.

"Hi, Brother," I said as I sat down on the grass next to Goldie.

"Found your journal. I know you probably wouldn't be happy that I read it, but I'm glad I did. At least now I know that you were happy and that you didn't mean to die. I'm sorry that I thought you were pulling away from me, Brother, when I can see now that I was the one who had pulled away first. Your journal showed me how I do that a lot with people. I'm going to try really hard not to do it anymore.

And guess what? You have a gorgeous son. Or maybe you already know that. His name is TJ. He looks just like you and he's such a happy little boy. Beth is a great mother too, but I'm sure you're not surprised to hear that. And I have to admit, that Steve isn't such a bad guy, after all," I added.

"I promise even after I go back to California, I'll keep in touch with TJ and Beth. Mom and Dad, too. Well, I have to go. But I'll be back here again, soon. That much I know for sure."

As I headed to the car, I noticed that this time, Goldie wasn't following me.

"Come on, girl," I said, hitting the side of my leg. But she just stared at me with her beautiful brown eyes. Then after a moment, she trotted toward the woods and stopped, turned around and looked at me one more time and then she was gone.

Tears filled my eyes. Somehow, I just knew I wouldn't see Goldie again. She'd come to help me and now it was time for her to go. As I continued to stare at the woods, I wondered once again if James had sent her or maybe it was God who did? I guessed it didn't matter, though. She'd done what she came for and I'd never forget her.

CHAPTER 33

BETH LOOKED EXHAUSTED, BUT ALSO VERY HAPPY TO see me. I sat down in my old booth and turned over a coffee cup.

She reached for a coffee pot. "I could use one too," she said as she filled my cup. "I'll join you in a few minutes."

When she came back, instead of having oatmeal, I ordered eggs, bacon and a side of toast. I was famished. "Some grits too," I added before Beth called out my order.

As I sat there sipping my coffee while she waited on another customer, I stared out the window at the occasional car driving by. I was really going to miss this slow pace.

Beth came back and set my breakfast down, then after pouring herself a cup of coffee, she slid into the booth across from me.

"Crazy night, huh?" she asked as I put a dab of butter into my grits.

"Yes," I agreed. "This whole trip has been wild."

"I'm so glad you came back and found that journal. The fact that he didn't take his own life means everything to me, as I know it does to you and your parents. I'm so relieved that it's finally out about James being TJ's father, too.

"We felt so bad that we couldn't tell anyone. I wanted to tell you for so long. It was hard, you know? Every time we were together, I almost blurted it out. But I guess I was scared and all. Of what, I don't honestly know. But I'm sorry, Karen."

"Hey, I'm the one who should be sorry, Beth," I said as I reached out and touched her hand. "That's one of the reasons I wanted to come by this morning. I wasn't there for you like I should have been. I let my feelings about Steve get in the way of being a true friend to you. I feel horrible about that."

"It's true, it was hard when I didn't have you, especially after James died," she said. "I really loved him. But you'd lost your brother too. We should have been there for each other."

"I'll be there now. No more pushing people away. James showed me in the journal how much I've done that. Whenever you need me, all you have to do is call. I'll only be a plane flight away."

"Oh, so you are leaving?" she asked looking sad. "I feel like I just got you back in my life, and now you're leaving again."

"I need to go back and deal with things. Though I'm still not sure what I'm going to do about my marriage. I'm going to miss you though," I said feeling emotional. "But I'll keep in touch."

Beth stood up and held her arms out and we hugged each other for what felt like a very long time. Finally, she let me go.

"Don't forget, you're an aunt now. Your nephew needs to see you too."

"Your table is asking for their bill," someone said from behind me. I recognized Amber's voice and turned to look.

"Oh hi," she said with a wave. "Beth told me this morning that your brother didn't shoot himself on purpose like everyone thought he did. I bet that sure makes you happy knowing he wasn't such a loose cannon like everybody thought." Amber smiled and walked off to take an order from another table.

I shook my head. "You told her of all people?" I asked Beth after Amber was gone. "You realize everyone in town is going to know, now."

"That's precisely why I told her," Beth replied. "This way, by the time we tell TJ that James is his father, everyone will already know his death was just an accident and hopefully it will be easier on TJ. Besides, Amber can't help it. She comes from a pretty messed-up family. Hopefully, she'll learn how to filter herself, so she doesn't keep blurting things out and upsetting people all the time."

I looked over at Amber again. A memory popped into my head about the time a boy was making fun of James for walking too slow, and before I could stop myself, I blurted out that if he'd had a bum leg like James, he'd be walking slow too.

I'll never forget how embarrassed James looked when I said that in front of everyone. I guessed we all had things we needed to learn. And one thing I'd just discovered, was that I was still learning.

Like how up until now, I was sure everyone was going out of their way to hurt me when they were all just dealing with their own stuff. Mother with her drinking. Dad with the divorce. Even Joey, when he'd decided to stay back in Easley, and it was all because he was ashamed of what he'd said to James.

I took it all personally even though everyone just did what they had to, out of the need to protect themselves. It was like some stupid game. Each of us dancing around the truth and hiding our vulnerabilities from one another. Well, we shouldn't. That much was clear now, and I, for one, wasn't going to play that game anymore. It was time to take responsibility and to be honest with myself and everyone else - even when it wasn't always easy.

Beth looked out the window. "Wasn't that Joey driving by just now?"

I looked out too. It was him. So, I took out my wallet and laid some money on the bill. "I should go out and talk to him. I'll call you before I leave town, I promise."

Joey rolled his window down as I walked up.

"Hi. I was driving by and saw James' car," he said.

"Hello," I said back. "It's actually my car, now. My parents gave it to me. In fact, I'm driving it back to California tomorrow."

"So, you're still going back?" he asked. "That's too bad. I keep hoping you'll come to your senses and stay here with me. But I guess it was just wishful thinking. You're driving back? By yourself? I don't think I like that idea."

"I did it before, remember? You didn't seem too worried about me doing it then."

"And back *then*, I didn't know you were driving clear across the country," he said defensively. "Isn't there anything I can say to make you see you're making a mistake?"

I stared back at him, in a way wishing there was something he could say to convince me to stay. Because I wasn't sure that I wasn't making a mistake, not sure at all, but I did know I wasn't ready to give up completely on Dan.

"I'm sorry. I have to go," I said. And with a heavy heart, I got into the Mustang and just like eight years earlier, I drove away.

CHAPTER 34

I WAS STILL THINKING ABOUT JOEY WHEN I WALKED into the house. Mother looked up. She was sitting at the kitchen table with a pad and pen, making what looked like a list.

"Your father and I decided we'd like to have a goodbye dinner for you tonight. I hope you don't mind but I invited some people over."

"You don't need to do that," I said.

"I know, but we want to. I haven't asked Joey yet, I wanted to see if it was okay with you. But Beth and Steve are for sure coming. Steve said if we bring the Mustang by the shop today, he'll check it all over and bring it with him to dinner tonight. I thought we could drop it off before we go to the store. I need to pick up some more groceries for the dinner."

I started to say I didn't want a goodbye dinner but caught myself. I needed to stop pushing people away and maybe this was a good time to start.

"Okay, that sounds good," I managed to say. "Thank you!"

"So, what about Joey, then?" she asked again. "Should I invite him?"

After the way we'd just left things in the parking lot, I didn't think it was a good idea to ask him, let alone that he'd even come, but if there was any way to leave things on better terms than the first time I left town, it was worth a try. And it'd be mean to leave him out when his sister would be there. It would only make things awkward for them both.

"Why not," I said, "though I'm not sure he'll come."

"He'll come," Mother said as she jotted something else down on the pad.

As we rode to the shop, I told Mother about what had happened with Goldie. She didn't seem too surprised and said something about God working in mysterious ways.

I was still thinking about what she'd said as I went into the shop to give Steve the keys. Seeing Steve this time felt different and I was glad that nearly all the resentment I'd had for him seemed to have just melted away.

He promised to check the car over thoroughly and Mother and I headed to the store. It felt odd shopping with her, but at the same time felt nice.

When we got home, she got busy right away preparing the spaghetti sauce while I prepped several large bowls of green salad. I then went to my room and packed a few things to get a jump on tomorrow.

A few days ago, I would have thought I'd be happy to be leaving, but instead I was sad at the thought of not seeing my parents again for a while. Strange how things could turn around like that in such a brief period of time.

I sent out a few emails and headed back to the kitchen. It smelled like sausage and garlic which sadly brought me back to that day at Angelo's.

After helping Mother with the dessert, I headed back to my room and changed. As I got dressed, I wondered if Joey would have the nerve to show up. But I had my answer when on my way back to the kitchen, I passed by the living room and Joey was sitting there along with Pastor Phil, talking to my father. I was glad Mother had thought of inviting Pastor Phil.

I said hello and before I could say much more, the doorbell rang.

It was Beth and Steve along with little TJ.

"Goldie?" TJ asked, looking around.

"No," I said sadly. "Goldie had to go back to where she came from."

TJ frowned.

"The car's all set," Steve said, handing me the keys to the Mustang. "I checked it top to bottom and put air in the tires. The tank's full too."

"Thanks, Steve," I replied smiling as I took the keys from him. "What do I owe you?" I asked, reaching for my purse. He just shook his head.

"This one's on me."

I almost wanted to hug him, which felt strange, but I was seeing this man in an entirely new light. Beth had done well. Not as well as she would have done if she'd had her future with James, but not bad. Not bad at all. I smiled a broad, warm smile at Steve. "Well, thank you," I said, blushing slightly, knowing we had made our peace then and there.

"Why don't you all go relax in the living room with Joey and my dad, while I help Mother with dinner?" I suggested.

"I'll help you," Beth said and followed me down the hall.

Finally, the table was set and ready for everyone to sit down and eat. As the food was passed around. Joey kept glancing at me. Before anyone could dig in, Pastor Phil asked if it would be okay if he said grace.

Mother reached out her hand to me hesitantly, but this time I was willing to take it. I no longer felt angry with God. And if I'd lived here, I'd even consider going to Pastor Phil's church.

Joey took my other hand and I jerked at his touch. The electricity between us was still there, causing me to once again question if I wasn't making a mistake.

—

While everyone was having dessert, Joey asked if he could talk to me outside. I took my cup of coffee with me and followed him onto the porch.

We sat down on the top step side by side, and as I sat there sipping from the cup, I waited for Joey to speak first.

The sun was starting to set, and it reminded me of all the times we had watched it go down together while we were out on the lake. Finally, Joey cleared his throat.

"I'm sorry I took off like I did earlier. I was just upset. Are you absolutely sure this is what you want? How can you leave me again? I really thought you still loved me."

I looked at him. "I do love you. You know that," I said. "I always will love you. But I can't be with you."

"Why not? Is it because you can't get over what I said to James?"

I thought about how my brother's death had caused a wedge between me and Joey. A wedge that I wasn't sure would ever go away. Yet, in a strange way it had also kept me tied to Joey all these years, too.

"I love you but getting back with you is not what I want right now," I said. "And I honestly believe it's not what you want either."

"How can you say that?" he asked, his voice getting a little too loud and irritated. "Of course, it's what I want. Why else do you think I've been hanging on, all this time? Don't you think I'd have let go by now if I didn't feel that way?"

As I looked at him, it hit me. It hit me why neither one of us has been able to let go.

"Joey, for the past eight years we've been living our lives based on a lie. You, me, my parents, Beth, Steve, even Pastor Phil. We've all been telling ourselves we were to blame for James' death, when none of that was true. It was all a lie. We didn't have *anything* to do with his death. It was nothing more than an accident."

Joey stared back at me.

"Don't you see?" I asked feeling a wave of emotion. "Now we know the truth, it's time to stop blaming ourselves. Especially you. It's not your fault James is dead. It never was. Arguments happen in life, and God knows, I've caused enough of them myself over the years. And it's not as if I never argued with James myself, is it? So, let it go. You're free now, Joey."

"Free? What do you mean, free?" he asked sounding confused. "Free from what?"

"Free from guilt," I said, seeing things clearly for the first time. "There's no blame in this anymore, Joey. Not for any of us."

He looked down and shook his head, as if he couldn't accept my words. I carried on.

"That's the real reason you've never been able to let go of me. I understand that now. You convinced yourself that because of his death and what you believed was your part in it, you owed me and my family something. But you don't. It wasn't your fault. You're free now. Free to go on with your life."

Joey shook his head again. "But maybe I don't want to be free. Not without you in my life, anyway."

"But don't you see?" I asked, feeling as if my heart was about to break in half. "I need to be. *I* need to be free."

As we looked into each other's eyes under the porch light, I could see such raw emotion coming from Joey's eyes that it nearly took my breath away. After a moment, he looked away.

"Well, Dan had better be good to you or he's going to have one bad cop to contend with," he said softly.

I tried to force a laugh. "I'll be sure to tell him that. Or maybe I won't." I looked at him again. "Please don't worry about me, Joey. Haven't you learned by now that I can take care of myself?"

"I'll never stop worrying about you. Never," he said. "Will you let me do one thing before you go? Can I at least give you one last hug?"

"Sure," I said and for the last time, I let Joey wrap his big strong arms around me as I tried to choke back the tears. After a moment, he loosened his grip.

"I love you, Karen, and I always will. Don't you ever forget that." And with that, he turned and headed down the stairs and out to his car without looking back once.

"I love you, too," I said after he was well out of earshot.

I watched his car go down the driveway and as he rounded the corner, the doubts crept back as I asked myself if I was making a mistake by not stopping him.

But I knew that even though Dan had hurt me very much, I wasn't ready to give up on my marriage completely.

Joey's tail lights faded away and I turned and slowly walked up the steps. But as I opened the door, I heard a car coming up the road. I turned around, trying not to get excited. He had come back.

But as the car turned into the driveway and got closer, I could see it wasn't Joey's car after all. It was a taxi cab. Why would a taxi be here at this time of night? I watched as it pulled up close and stopped several yards from me.

The driver's door opened, and a man got out. I could tell even from here, that it was Charlie.

Charlie opened the rear door and another man got out, carrying a small suitcase. He shut the door and they both walked toward me. As I tried to figure out who was with Charlie, I suddenly knew. It was Dan. My heart swelled.

The front door opened behind me and Mother came out and stood next to me. "Charlie, is that you? I couldn't believe my eyes, so I had to come out and check!"

"Well, hello Doris," Charlie said, smiling as he looked past me toward my mother. "My, it sure is good to see you again."

"You too, Charlie. You too! Is that Dan with you?'

"Yes, it is," Dan said, walking closer. "Hello, Doris," he said, his eyes still on me.

"Well come on in, both of you. What a pleasant surprise. Charlie, I haven't seen you in years. Come. I want you to meet my husband," she said, holding the door open.

"Love to," he replied as he walked slowly up the porch steps. After they both went inside, I turned back to Dan who was still standing there staring at me.

"What're you doing here?" I asked, my heart beating fast.

He walked closer and set his bag down on the steps. "I had a feeling you needed me."

I stared back at him, at a loss for words.

He took a step closer. "Do you? Need me?"

Shock. Happiness. Confusion. Every type of emotion ran through me, including anger at what he'd done.

So, it was true what Pastor Phil had said, that if I didn't find a way to forgive Dan, I'd always feel anger whenever I looked at him. I hoped that wasn't the case. I was tired of being angry. It was exhausting. But was it really possible to be able to find forgiveness after what he did? Or was I just fooling myself?

Maybe it would be easier to stay here with Joey after all. If I went back with Dan, I knew that he'd want to get inside my head and—now more than ever—want to know everything I was thinking and feeling. I wasn't so sure I was ready for that. I wasn't so sure I could change that much, that fast.

At least with Joey, I'd never have to worry about that. He was more interested in filling my head than knowing what was in it. But, was that what I really wanted either? And maybe I didn't want to go back to California. After spending time here, I realized that I belonged here in a way, with the slow pace and the laid-back people.

And then there were my parents. And Beth and TJ. I hated the thought of leaving them all when I'd just gotten them back into my life. It felt good, and I felt—whole. For the first time ever, I was surrounded by people who loved me.

"Was I wrong?" Dan asked again.

I looked at him, and there was no denying I still loved this man, strangely even more than ever. Maybe that love was strong enough that I could learn to forgive him - and open up like he had always wanted.

And who knew, maybe I could get what I wanted too, and he'd be willing to move here. He could find plenty of work here. I knew he was that good.

And maybe I could act again. There was that new studio in Atlanta that everyone in LA was talking about. I could work there, couldn't I?

And it wasn't like we'd have to live here in Easley. We could live in Anderson or some other nearby town where we'd still be close enough to see everyone but far enough that we wouldn't have to bump into Joey all the time.

Maybe we could even get our vows renewed by Pastor Phil, and this time in a church like Dan always wanted. I'd be willing to do that. As I looked at Dan, my head spun with all kinds of wild thoughts.

"Well, do you want me to stay or go?" he asked. "For the love of God, Karen. For once in your life, talk to me and tell me what you want."

I smiled as the image of the fork at Finley Road popped into my head, and for the first time, I knew exactly what I wanted. I picked up his suitcase and took a step up the stairs.

"Come on. Let's go inside. There's a lot we have to talk about."

THE END

Made in the USA
San Bernardino, CA
19 April 2019